Damaged

Book 1 of The Marvelous 3 Saga:
Sons of the Elite Series

Smauggy

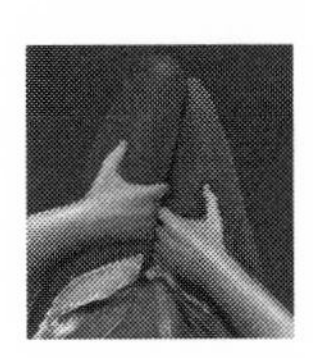

Contents

Preface

Unapologetically black. It's a motto that I've learned to live by ever since I began on my journey of self love back in 2009, when I graduated high school and started college. There had been so few examples of black women being loved. How do you learn to love yourself when you don't know what that looks like?

This is the very first book I've ever written, where I found that the joy in my writing comes from being able to create stories where black women are underrepresented. My stories are reverse-harem because black women deserve vast amounts of love. This book is the beginning of the Marvelous 3 Saga and the first of The Sons of the Elite Series. Although I am happy to share this world that I've created with you, the Marvelous 3 Saga has truly been the foundational support of my mental health journey.

Introduction

This story and all those that follow it are meant to center people who are vastly flawed. It was written with the intent to highlight certain sensitive topics within the black community, specifically concerning black women and their sexuality.

This book touches on themes of sexual assault, violence, and racism. Many of the situations have been personally experienced. I hope that readers will allow black female protagonists the space to be vulnerable, human, and imperfect through their journey of self love and being loved by others.

For a full cinematic experience, including casting and soundtrack, check out my website **www.smauggy.com**.

1

Needed Back Home

~*~

"Ryan, can you shift the light 45 degrees to the right? Emma, I need a 10-blade scalpel. I need a reading on those vitals!"

Emma rushed to Gabrielle's side presenting her with a sharp scalpel.

"Blood pressure is slightly elevated, but breathing is steady," Eric responded.

"Thanks, Emma. Ryan, could you angle the camera another 15 degrees towards the left? I need to get in this crevice."

"Yes, Doctor."

Ryan shifted the camera slightly to the left.

"Aaaaand stop! Right there! Hold it..." Gabrielle said as her hands moved firmly with keen precision. She pulled one of the bullet fragments from the first layer of flesh of the patient's lung.

"You got it!" Emma squealed.

"Don't celebrate just yet. I have to get the other half," Gabrielle said with her eyes still focused on the task at hand. She placed the first half of the bullet fragment on the plate Emma was holding and turned back to the patient.

"This will be a little tricky. Ryan, come on this side and angle upward by 45 degrees."

Ryan moved to Gabrielle's left, angling the camera light.

"I just need... One. More. Push..."

She cut slightly deeper into the lung, reaching the other half of the bullet. Blood began to gush as she scooped it out. .

BEEP! BEEP! BEEP!

"Vitals are dropping!" Eric shouted.

"Quick! Pass me the sealant!" Gabrielle said with urgency.. Emma quickly passed the liquid which Gabrielle took, squirting it onto the wound.

She then called out for a needle, for which Emma passed over. Gabrielle then began to sew up the wound before dabbing it with a clean cloth.

"Vitals are stabilizing," Eric sighed heavily.

Relieved, Gabrielle wiped her sweaty forehead with the back of her gloved hand. "Alright, let's patch him up," Gabrielle smiled as she backed away from the patient.

"I can't believe you got that out. The bullet was so deep- it looked impossible," Emma Emma looked on in astonishment.

"Well... that's what we're here for, Ems. To make the impossible... **possible**," Gabrielle smiled. She headed towards the door, pulling down her mask and taking off her gloves. With a hop in her step, she exited the operating room. Walking through the hallway, she headed towards the private waiting room.

"Hey! Gabby!" Ryan called out, jogging after her.

Gabrielle turned around. "Great work in there Ryan!" she grinned with pride..

"I was going to say the same to you! I don't know how you do it!" he chuckled.

"Just gotta have a little faith, Ry. Now for my favorite part. Wanna join?" Gabrielle smiled from ear to ear, turning to face the waiting room. Her eyes searched the waiting room, before landing on a family. An elderly woman with two small children, waited anxiously in the corner of the room. She motioned for Ryan to follow her as she walked over to the family.

"Ms. Ellison?" Gabrielle called, walking up to them.

"Oh! Dr. Johansson! Please! Please, God, tell me he is okay! Please!" the elderly woman pleaded.

"Ms. Ellison, your son is going to be perfectly fine. We were able to remove both bullet fragments. He's going into recovery now. You should be able to see him soon," Gabrielle beamed at the family.

"Oh, thank God!! Thank you, Dr. Johansson! Children, did you hear? Your father is going to be okay!" the elderly woman cried out as she embraced her grandchildren.

Gabrielle smiled fondly, watching the small family shower each other with comforting affection.

"Thank you so much, Dr. Johansson!" the woman said suddenly embracing Gabrielle. "And you! Thank you too!" she said turning to Ryan and hugging him as well.

"Come on. I'll take you to his room now where you can wait for him," Gabrielle said almost as happy as the elderly woman. One of the children eagerly ran to grab Gabrielle's hand. She looked down at the small child and smiled, picking her up into her arms as the little girl squealed with glee. As they walked down the hall together, Gabrielle heard her name being called.

"Dr. Johansson! There's a call for you on line 4!" called the nurse.

"Can it wait? I'm tending to a family," Gabrielle said tickling the laughing child she held in her arms.

"It's your mother... she said it's important," the nurse called out.

Gabrielle furrowed her brow and frowned as she turned to Ryan.

"Go talk to your mom. I'll take them," Ryan said, plucking the child from her arms.

"Are you sure?" she asked with concern, giving the child up to him reluctantly.

"Yea, go!"

"Ok... Ms. Ellison, Dr. Goldsberg will take care of you and see that you get to see your son. I have to go, but I'll see you soon to check up on you all, okay?" she said, turning to the elderly woman.

"Yes, yes. Thank you," the elderly woman said grasping Gabrielle's hands tightly and smiling gratefully.

Gabrielle could feel the cold wrinkle of her skin against hers and smiled somberly at the elderly woman. She said her last farewell and headed towards the reception desk to pick up the phone.

"Hey Mom, is everything okay?"

"Gabby? Baby? Oh, I'm so glad to hear your voice," came her mother's voice from the other end.

"It's good to hear from you too, Mom. Are you alright?"

"I-I know you're working, baby girl, but... but..." Gabrielle heard her mother begin to choke up before a sob escaped her lips.

"Mom? Mom! What's wrong? What happened?" Gabrielle asked anxiously.

"It's Steve. Steve Richardson. He... he passed away in the hospital earlier this afternoon from a heart attack. Can you come home, baby? The fam-"

Gabrielle immediately zoned out from her mother's words. Tears brimmed in her eyes, widened from shock as Papa Steve's face popped into her mind. The thin lines on his weary, kind face perfectly sculpted the image of a man who had been nothing but a father to her, especially since her own father had passed away when she was just a toddler.

She could still see his warm smile and feel his heavy hand on her shoulder as he told her how proud he was of her for graduating college and getting accepted into medical school. The tears rapidly gushed down her face as the phone faltered in her hands.

"Papa Steve..." she breathed out, choking on her own shock.

"Gabby? Gabrielle!" came her mother's voice again.

"Yes! Mom... I'm sorry I just... I-... I can't believe it," Gabrielle sobbed, heavily fighting back her tears as she leaned on the edge of the nurse's desk to hold herself up.

The nurse looked at her worriedly, craning her neck to see if the doctor was okay. Gabrielle merely nodded as she lowered her head.

"I know, baby, I'm sorry. Can you come home? We really need your help here. His family is an emotional wreck... They need all the help they can get."

Gabrielle thought back to Charlie and Chris, Papa Steve's two sons and her childhood best friends. She couldn't imagine what they were going through. They were both so close to their father. And Mrs. Sally... her heart must be so broken.

"Yea, Mom. I'll um... I'll book a flight tonight," Gabrielle said making eye contact with the worried nurse who picked up another phone to make a call.

"Thank you, baby. I'll see you soon. I love you."

"I love you too, Mom."

Gabrielle hung up the phone and headed to her office to pack her things to leave.

~*~

Back at her apartment, Gabrielle began to pack her clothes when her fiancé, Damian, strolled into the room and leaned against the doorpost, watching her.

"Going somewhere?" He eyed her suspiciously from the corner of the room with his arms folded across his chest.

Gabrielle jumped slightly startled and looked back to see her fiancé. Wearing a thin white shirt that contrasted nicely with his caramel-toned skin, Damian's ever-chill demeanor paired well with his typically classy appearance.

"Damian! Hey, baby. I tried to reach you earlier. I know this is really sudden, but I have to fly back home to Pennsylvania. You won't believe it, but Mr. Steve Richardson just passed away," she said, stuffing her clothes into her bag. She could feel the tears starting to well up again but quickly wiped her eyes to keep them at bay.

"Damn... I'm sorry to hear that, my love. You okay?" he asked her, stuffing his hands into his pockets.

"Yea... I don't know... It's hard for me to process everything. This was so sudden and unexpected. I haven't been home in years..." she sighed heavily and turned to him clutching a sweater in her hands.

"Well, you don't have to go... Stay here until your mom provides more details on the funeral arrangements," he said walking up to her and gently removing the sweater from her clutches. He swiftly grabbed her by the waist, pulling her body against his and looked into her deep brown eyes with his charming hazel ones.

"... I can't, babe... She actually needs my help with the funeral arrangements. I'm guessing Mrs. Sally is a little too broken up to take care of it right now," Gabrielle furrowed her brow. She looked up at him as an idea clicked.

"Why don't you come with me?" she perked up.

"You know that's not possible... I have the art gala I have to prepare for next week," he said softly nuzzling her neck.

"Shoot... I almost forgot," she said smacking her forehead.

"It's okay... You'll be back by then," he said placing small light kisses on her neck.

"Um... yea, for sure I'll try to be back by then," she said, closing her eyes against his tender, fleeting pecks.

"You'll **try**?" he asked abruptly as he stopped kissing her to look her in the eye.

"Uh... y-yea. I mean I just don't know what to expect: when the funeral will be or how long things will take-"

"Well, you'll have a week to figure it out. I **expect** to see you at the art gala," he said, gripping her a bit more firmly by her waist and tightening his grasp around her wrist. He looked at her with such intensity, a very stern look on his face as his eyes went dark. "I've been preparing for this art gala for months. I **expect** my fiancée to be there."

"R-right... of course, Damian," Gabrielle said anxiously.

He eyed her for a tense moment before he softened his gaze.

"Good girl," he said, going back to his kind demeanor. He loosened his death grip from her wrist and gently placed a light kiss on her forehead.

"Make sure you wear the red dress I bought you. You look best in red," he said walking towards the door. "Let me know when you're leaving."

Gabrielle swallowed thickly as she watched him walk out of the bedroom.

"...Okay..."

~*~

"You sure you'll be okay? I can come with you!"

"No, no... Thank you, Ems. I'll let you know when I land," Gabrielle said to her friend and fellow colleague over the phone.

"Immediately! I know which flight you're on!" Emma threatened.

"I know, I know. I promise," Gabrielle chuckled. "I'll talk to you later."

Gabrielle hung up the phone and sunk into her seat as she waited for the plane to take off. She glanced down at her wrists and rubbed them softly, still sore from when Damian grabbed her.

She thought about Chris and Charlie and how much fun they had together growing up as kids... going to middle school together... then conquering high school together. Charlie and Chris were like her brothers. And despite their very different backgrounds, they knew her well and she knew them well. But not as well as they knew each other. They were only 2 years apart and always so in sync.

Oftentimes, it seemed as if they knew what the other was feeling. They were constantly connected. And simply... *inseparable.*

For a while, people thought they were twins, until Chris's hair darkened and Charlie's eyes became greener.

She closed her eyes and saw her brother Eli, Papa Steve, Charlie, and Chris. She remembered when Steve took the 4 of them to see Spider-man when it first premiered in theaters. She partially blamed Steve for her love of comic books and superheroes and had always been regarded as a bit of a tomboy growing up in PA. But ever since she started attending med school and became engaged to Damian DuPont, she trained herself to shed her traditional ways and conduct herself like a modern professional woman.

They had become LA's newest power couple, after all... and she had to keep up their image.

She looked down at the beautiful, large 3-carat diamond ring that Damian had proposed to her with at the most expensive and well-known restaurant in LA less than 4 months ago. She remembered being taken completely by surprise. She and Damian had never discussed getting married. But how could she possibly say no to that ring... *to him*?

She and Damian had been through so much together. There were things about her that only he knew and through that trust their relationship grew.

But to Gabrielle it always felt... *binding.*

The Future Mrs. Damian DuPont: Most highly esteemed surgeon and wife of Mr. Damian DuPont, the most talented and well-known artist in LA.

This is what she always wanted.

Right?

She took off her engagement ring and tucked it into her jean pocket. She hadn't told her family and friends yet.

She would when the time was right...

When her flight landed, Gabrielle breathed in the fresh crisp air of good ol' Pennsylvania. It had been 4 years since she last stepped foot in her hometown and 8 since she had last seen her friends after graduating from college. Medical school and residency had taken up so much of her life. She eagerly searched the crowd until she landed on a familiar face.

"Eli!" she squealed running towards her brother. With a grin, Eli opened his arms wide and braced himself as he caught her in his arms and spun her around. His bright white smile contrasted beautifully with his rich dark mocha skin ever so similar to his sister.

They chuckled in each other's arms savoring the warmth of their embrace and letting their sibling love rekindle. Gabrielle gawked at Eli as he set her back down on the ground.

"Damn, Eli! You been working out, boy?" Gabrielle teased as she pinched his arm.

"Ay, shaddup!" Eli laughed, playfully pushing her. "It's been 4 years, baby sis. That's no bueno."

Gabrielle twisted her mouth awkwardly. "Yea, I know... I've been so caught up with school and work... I mean I visited for Christmas..."

"You came and left the same day, Gabby. You didn't even get to see the Richardsons," he crossed his arms looking at her judgmentally.

"I know. I'm sorry... Work has just been so demanding... but...there's no excuse to not see family. I hope you can forgive me," she frowned, looking up at him with her big brown eyes giving him puppy eyes.

He smirked at her as he leaned off of his car and pulled her in for a long embrace.

"Man, I can't be mad at you, sis. You're doing big things. I'm proud of you," he said resting his cheek on the top of her head.

She smiled up at him and noticed the sudden change in his expression.

"I just wish you were here on better terms," he said sadly. He looked down at her and saw the tears start to brim.

"Aww, damn... c'mere, sis."

He pulled her in for another long embrace.

"I just... I can't believe he's gone," she said softly as her tears dripped onto his shirt and she buried her face into his chest.

"I know... Me neither... Come on let's get you home. Ma has been talking about you all day," he motioned for her to get in the car.

They pulled out of the parking lot and headed to their mother's house.

~*~

Gabrielle glanced out of the window as they drove into the more rural parts of Pennsylvania. She felt a warmness blanket her, as she took in the multi-color leaves of the trees.

She loved PA in the fall.

They pulled up to their mother's house, and before Eli had finished parking, their mother came running out of the house and down the stairs of the patio. Gabrielle rushed out of the car and met her mother halfway as they lovingly collided into a warm embrace.

"Mama," Gabrielle said contentedly as she took in her mother's familiar perfume. She hadn't realized just how much she missed her mother until she felt her in her arms.

Clara pulled back to look at her daughter, her cheeks puffing up into a smile as she took in her daughter's matured appearance.

"My baby girl. It's been too long," Clara said heartily, holding her daughter by the shoulders and taking a minute to look her over. "Have you been eating enough?"

"I missed you too, Mama," Gabrielle said, rolling her eyes and hugging her mother again.

"Come in the house. I just got through making dinner," Clara said grabbing her daughter by the hand and leading her inside.

Gabrielle walked into her old home and was immediately hit with a wave of nostalgia as she breathed in the familiar smell of her childhood mixed with her mother's delicious cooking.

Fried chicken. Mac and cheese. Cornbread. Collard greens. Sweet potato pie.

"Did you do all this for me?" Gabrielle asked with a huge smile on her face as she walked into the kitchen to see her mother pulling out containers.

"Of course! Who knows when the last time was you had a decent meal!" Clara said as she started piling some of the food into containers.

"Uh... Mom... You know I'm not leaving for a while," Gabrielle informed her.

"Well good, but this ain't for you. I've been cooking some meals for the Richardsons as they go through this hard time. I know dear Sally can barely keep it together, let alone make food for her family, the poor woman," Clara said sadly.

"The boys are still living with her?" Gabrielle asked, surprised.

"Child, please. Them boys moved out as soon as they got the money for it. No, Sally being the loving soul she is has taken in a few kids temporarily from the church who lost their parents until the end of the week before they move on to their adopting families. Lord knows their house is large enough to house the entire town."

"Oh, that's sweet of her," Gabrielle said thoughtfully. "I haven't seen the boys in a while. How are they?"

"Charles and Christopher? Oh... those poor boys... you know how much they loved their father. They're holding up as best they could. You'll find out for yourself. I need you to take this food over to Sally. She'll be delighted to see you," Clara said, closing the last container.

"Sure, okay," Gabrielle said nervously. It had been a while since she had seen any of the Richardsons.

"Hey Gabby, come check this out," called Eli from the living room. Gabrielle walked into the living room to find Eli going through a large box in the middle of the floor. "Moms has been cleaning out the attic and found this old treasure," he grinned, looking through the box.

"Oh wow!" she breathed excited. In the box was an old X-men action figure of Storm. She picked it up. "I forgot about my X-Men collection. You used to pop the heads off of all of my female X-Men figures. Papa Steve tried to put them back on, but the heads were square-shaped," she shook her head.

Eli laughed loudly as he reminisced. "You would get so pissed, you wouldn't talk to me for a week. Good times."

She rolled her eyes as she continued to rummage through the box. Her eyes widened in surprise as she spotted something else. It was a Dragonball-Z themed football. She picked it up.

"Oh my goodness! Remember this?" she turned to Eli, tossing the ball to him.

He held out his hand, catching the ball. He gently squeezed the ball. "Oh yea, we used to play all the time with this. Can't believe it's not flat," Eli replied with a smile.

"Gabrielle, come eat this food! You need to head out to Mrs. Sally's before it gets too late!" Clara called out.

"Okay mama!" she shouted as she tucked the football under her arm, heading to the kitchen.

~*~

2

The Boys Are Back in Town

~*~

Gabrielle changed into a pair of jeans and a comfy L.A. Rams sweatshirt before leaving for the Richardson Estate. Borrowing Eli's car, she pulled into one of the Richardsons' many driveways.

The Richardsons were among the wealthiest families in Pennsylvania and all of the Northeast region. Their estate was definitely a reflection of that wealth.

Catching a glimpse of Sally through the kitchen window, Gabrielle walked towards the door carrying food in her arms and knocked. But the door was already open.

"Hello? Mrs. Sally?" she called out, stepping into the large estate. When she didn't receive a response, she headed towards the kitchen.

"Mrs. Sally?" Gabrielle softly called again to the blonde-haired woman leaning over the counter. Sally jumped startled and turned with big, teary blue eyes towards Gabrielle.

"Gabrielle?! Gabrielle Johansson?! Oh, my darling! It is so good to see you again!" Sally smiled brightly as she rushed towards her. Gabrielle quickly placed the food on the table before pulling Sally into a loving embrace.

"You've truly grown into such a beautiful woman," Sally said, pulling away to look at her.

"Thank you, Mrs. Sally. I've missed you so much. I'm... I'm so sorry about Papa Steve," Gabrielle said, remorsefully.

"Oh, my dear... thank you," Sally cooed, her eyes brimming with tears.

She glanced over the containers of food on the table and chuckled. "Did your mother make me dinner again?"

"She sure did," Gabrielle grinned.

"That woman. I don't know what my life would be without her. You have to catch me up on your life in L.A.! But first, you must go see the boys. It'll be a lovely surprise for them to see you after so long. Christopher is in the back, I believe, talking to some of the construction workers. And Charles is... probably breaking and rebuilding something... somewhere... He's been even more distant lately, but that's normal, all things considering..."

"Construction workers?" Gabrielle asked.

"Yes. Steve was leading the construction project that built homes for some of the homeless children in the local Philly area. Christopher decided to help finish his commitment."

"That's so sweet of him to do that," Gabrielle said fondly.

"Yes... He gets that trait from his father..." Sally trailed off. She zoned out for a moment, lost in her thoughts, until she looked up at Gabrielle.

"Why are you still here? Go!" she shooed Gabrielle towards the back.

"Okay! Okay!" Gabrielle chuckled as she walked out through the back of the house. She turned the corner and was immediately tackled by a huge, fluffy golden retriever.

"Thor!" she laughed, falling to the ground as the dog licked happily at her face. His tail wagged ferociously from pure excitement.

"I missed you too, boy!" She ruffled his fur and nuzzled his face with her nose.

She stood up to pet him before continuing around the corner of the house. She found a group of men in construction gear circling a taller, more animated gentleman at the center.

Gabrielle almost didn't recognize Chris.

He was wearing a dark pair of jeans and a black, long-sleeved sweater that clung deliciously to his finely-sculpted physique. His sophisticated, business-like demeanor complemented by his well-groomed, dark, brown hair made him stand out from the group of haggardly-looking construction workers in safety gear.

Gabrielle bit her lip and awkwardly shifted her weight from one leg to the other. Her pupils dilated at the way his muscles flexed as he crossed his arms over his broad chest. He pensively rubbed the short beard on his chin that looked as if it were conditioned by angels.

Thor nudged her, trying to get her attention. But when she didn't respond, he barked loudly, causing all of the men to turn in her direction.

"Shh! Thor!" she whispered frantically.

But it was too late. Gabrielle felt embarrassed when she saw Chris's bright, blue eyes widen in shock. She tried to wave, but Thor tugged at her sleeve, restricting her movements.

She immediately regretted her presence.

The men turned to face Chris again who spoke rather anxiously. He talked with his hands and obsessively looked back at her, as if to make sure his eyes weren't deceiving him.

Gabrielle anxiously bit her nails, waiting for him to finish. Her heart began to race the moment he started walking in her direction. She didn't understand why she felt so nervous, suddenly. This was her childhood best friend. Yet, she felt like she was meeting him for the first time.

“Well, look who’s back all the way from the West Coast! Gabrielle Marie Johansson!” Chris gasped in fake bewilderment. He walked up to her with open arms and pulled her in for a hug. His deep, baritone voice took her by surprise. It was crisp and commanded attention.

“Nice to see you too, Richardson,” Gabrielle smirked. His arms completely enveloped her body. His chest felt hard and firm against her, but his touch was gentle, warm… and secure.

“I can’t believe you’re actually here!” he said, effortlessly lifting her off of the ground. He excitedly swung her around. “It’s been like what... 10 years? A whole decade?!”

“Excuse you! You saw me at my college graduation. It’s only been 8!” she corrected him.

“Only? Gabs, come on,” he said putting her down. “It was clearly long enough for you to switch teams on us. I mean L.A. Rams? Really? How could you ditch the Steelers? I’m hurt,” he smirked, feigning offense. His hands still held her by the waist.

“You know damn well I always preferred the Eagles,” she teased. “But yea... I guess that’s still a really long time, isn’t it?” she said rather embarrassed.

“Just a bit,” he teased with a wink. He gently pinched her waist like he used to do when they were kids.

Gabrielle chuckled and looked up to see Chris’s soft blue eyes staring deeply into hers. His thumb tenderly rubbed her waist as he took in her beautiful dark brown eyes, her soft plump lips, and her smooth dark brown skin.

A warm smile crept on his face.

“What?” Gabrielle smiled back.

“I… I’m just really glad you’re here,” he said, pulling her into another soft embrace. He inhaled deeply, taking in her scent. Cocoa butter and vanilla. Exactly as he remembered.

Gabrielle felt Chris's arms tighten around her waist. The smell of his pine-scented cologne overwhelmed her senses. She nervously bit her lip.

"I'm really sorry about Papa Steve, Chris... I'm so... heartbroken..."

She tightened her embrace before releasing. Chris removed his arms from her waist and looked down at her. The same warm smile painted his face, but it hadn't quite reached his eyes.

"Thanks, Gabs..."

Gabrielle habitually licked her bottom lip and stuffed her sweaty palms into her jean pockets. "Where's Charlie?" she asked.

"Uh... think he's by the shed. He's been trying to fix one of dad's old motorcycles."

"Whaaaaat? Papa Steve used to ride?!"

"I know, right? Came as a shock to us too. We found it when we were going through some of his storage. His employer gave us the key to empty it after he..." Chris trailed off, looking down as he stuffed his hands into his pockets.

Gabrielle put her hand on Chris's arm in comfort. He looked up at her longingly, not at all indifferent to her touch. He smirked at her and straightened his posture.

"Anyway, Mom told us he got that bike for his 30th birthday. Charlie mainly rides bikes, so he's trying to fix it up. Come on. He should be over there still."

Chris led Gabrielle to a shed where loud rock music was playing. Charlie was found lying back on an old skateboard, working a ratchet into the underside of a motorcycle. Only his torso and legs were visible.

"Charlie," Chris called. But Charlie neither heard him nor responded. Chris walked over to Charlie and kicked him lightly in the leg to get his attention. Still no response.

"Charlie!" Chris shouted, this time yanking the skateboard from under the motorcycle.

"What?!" Charlie exclaimed irritably. His annoyance quickly diffused when he noticed Gabrielle. He stood to his feet and looked at her rather perplexed.

He turned the radio down and faced Gabrielle and his brother.

"...Gabs?" His voice was deep like his brother's, but significantly hoarse.

"Hey, Charlie," Gabrielle smiled, stepping forward to hug him. He wore a soft green shirt that clung to his muscular build. A bit of dried oil stained his arms and hands. Gabrielle noticed that his green shirt accentuated the green of eyes that she had become so accustomed to as a teen. His blonde locs that he had inherited from his mother had grown longer and thicker than she remembered. And he sported a short unkempt beard that matched his rugged appearance.

Charlie hesitantly took her into his arms. He embraced her with such caution, she could feel the tension in his hug.

"Huh... it's been what... 12 years?" Charlie said.

"10 years," Chris snickered. He folded his arms across his chest, casually leaning back against the shed's main post.

"8- Chris!" Gabrielle scowled at Chris who stuck his tongue out at her in return. "8. 8 years," she said to Charlie.

"8, huh? Feels longer," Charlie said, leaning back against the table. With his arms folded across his chest, Charlie gave her the same intense look that Chris was giving her. Only his glare was significantly less friendly. It seemed that the brothers' ability to be completely in sync with each other still hadn't changed after all these years.

“Yea...ugh...I’m sorry about that. I didn’t expect work to... control my life so much,” Gabrielle said embarrassed. She looked down at her hands, away from Charlie’s intense gaze. “But, I’m here now! And I’m honestly just... really happy I got to see you guys,” she perked up, trying to dissipate the awkward tension in the room.

“Sure...” Charlie scoffed, rolling his eyes.

Gabrielle looked between Charlie and Chris sizing them up. “Jeez... When did you guys get so big? You’re towering over me.”

“We’ve always towered over you,” Chris smirked.

“Mm. I *distinctly* remember being like 3 inches taller than Charlie back in 4th grade,” Gabrielle teased.

Charlie sucked his teeth. “We were 9, Gabs.”

“Still! It happened!” she retorted. The fact that they both laughed brought her relief.

“Besides... now it’s just intimidating. And why are y’all so damn buff?” Gabrielle said pinching Charlie’s bicep. “Are you training for the NFL?” she teased.

Charlie rolled his eyes with a shake of his head. “That’s what happens when you ditch us for 12 years. You miss out on important life changes... **like puberty**,” he said coldly.

“10,” Chris reminded him.

“8! Oh my gosh! I can’t with y’all,” Gabrielle said, throwing her hands in the air with exasperation.

“Well, she says 8,” Chris grinned mischievously. His playful smirk made her cheeks flush.

“Feels an awful lot like 12...” Charlie said coldly. He glared at Gabrielle, lacking his brother’s playful smirk.

Gabrielle shifted uncomfortably. *I deserve this...* she thought as she wrapped her arms around herself.

“Charlie. Chris. I'm- I'm really sorry about your dad. I can't believe he's really gone. I wish... I'm sorry I wish there was something I could have done to help,” she said apologetically.

Chris put a comforting hand on her shoulder. “Hey. It's okay, Gabs. There's nothing anyone could have really done,” he said encouragingly.

“Yea, shit happens,” Charlie mumbled, turning back to the motorcycle.

Gabrielle looked at Charlie with worry, completely put off by his attitude. She looked up at Chris who merely shook his head, as if to tell her not to push Charlie further.

“So... how's the bike coming along?” Gabrielle inquired, looking over Charlie's shoulder.

“It's fine,” Charlie said curtly, trying to ignore her.

“Oh, shit! You found that engine cover you were looking for!” Chris exclaimed.

“Fuck, yea! I couldn't believe it myself! Pretty difficult to find for this model as old as it is. But I only found the front end. Need to find the back end which is gonna be difficult in this town,” Charlie said, wiping his dirty hands on a towel.

“You should try Benny's Thrift Shop. He's always got whacky mechanical stuff in there,” Gabrielle said, trying to enter the conversation.

“Benny's Thrift Shop has been shut down for 4 years,” Charlie said without looking at her.

“What?! Benny's is closed?!” Gabrielle said shocked.

“More like burned down. Bunch of idiots were smoking around

his shop and dropped their cigarette in a pile of leaves right outside his back door. He couldn't salvage anything," Chris said, shaking his head.

"Oh no! Poor Benny! That's awful! I remember going to his shop all the time to find parts for our robotics class back in high school. How is he getting through?" Gabrielle asked.

"Well, he moved back to Florida to be with his son and his son's family. Couldn't support himself anymore without that shop," Chris said, rubbing the back of his neck.

"Oh my goodness! He's not even here anymore?!" Gabrielle said, covering her mouth in shock.

"Yea. You'd know that if you visited more frequently than 12... s'cuse me... **8** years," Charlie said with an aggravated sigh. He turned around to face her and she could see pure frustration in his unfriendly glare.

The tension in the room grew thick. A wave of guilt washed over Gabrielle and she couldn't look him in the eye for long.

"Charlie... I-"

"Hey, Chris!" a man in a hard construction hat called from outside of the shed. "We're headin' out now. Yer mother is callin' fer both of ya."

"Thanks, Joe! Be there in a sec!" Chris called back. The men nodded and left the premises. Charlie followed immediately thereafter, without giving Gabrielle a second glance.

Gabrielle watched stunned as Charlie sauntered off like he wanted nothing to do with her.

"Come on," Chris gestured to her. She rushed to catch up with Chris and followed the boys into the house. Once they entered the house, Sally called them into the kitchen.

"There you boys are! I was wondering when you would actually come back inside. Did you see Gabrielle?" she asked, carrying food to the table.

"I'm right here, Mrs. Sally," Gabrielle said, walking into the kitchen.

"Oh good! Did you and the boys get to catch up?" she asked, placing the food on the table.

"A bit..." Gabrielle was still disturbed by how cold Charlie had been towards her.

"I'm glad to hear that! The boys don't live here anymore, but it's such a treat when they visit. Especially now that my Steve..." Sally faltered as emotion clogged her throat.

"Mom?" Chris said, alarmed. Both brothers came to their mother's side for support. Sally smiled at her two sons as tears cascaded down her cheeks.

"I'm okay," she smiled ruefully. They walked her to the table and sat her down between the two of them. Their eyes kept careful watch of their mother.

"As you can see, I'm being very well taken care of," Sally smiled up at Gabrielle.

Gabrielle stood at the entrance of the kitchen, watching the three of them fondly.

"You and Papa Steve raised a beautiful, supportive family. I know Charlie and Chris are taking good care of you," Gabrielle said solemnly.

She garnered a look from all three of them at once that made her anxiously step back. "I-..."

"Won't you join us, Gabrielle? You **are** part of this family. I want to hear more about your time in L.A.," Sally said. She squeezed Charlie's hand while he poured her a cup of water.

Gabrielle glanced at Chris. He winked at her, encouraging her to join them as he took a bite of mac and cheese. For just a moment, she considered joining them until she caught a glimpse of Charlie glaring at her. She could only see his intense green eyes over the rim of his cup, but it felt as if he were staring into the deepest parts of her soul.

"Umm... actually, I better be getting back to Mama and Eli," she said, reluctantly.

"Are you sure?" Sally asked. Chris couldn't hide his disappointment.

"I am. There are a few things I have to help them take care of. But thank you, Mrs. Sally. I'll make sure to give you some time later," she said, nervously glancing at Charlie.

"Oh wait! Give this to your mother for me!" Sally said, handing her an envelope. "Oh, Gabrielle! It's so good to have you home again." She pulled Gabrielle into a warm embrace.

Gabrielle wrapped her arms around Sally and met the brothers' gaze. Chris still looked disappointed, and Charlie looked even more agitated.

"Thanks, Mrs. Sally. Have a good night," Gabrielle said waving goodbye.

~*~

When Gabrielle arrived back home, she headed straight for her old room and relaxed on the bed. She glanced around at all of her old teenage decor.

"I really need to redecorate," she sighed. She sat back on her bed and pulled out her cell phone to see if she had any missed calls.

None from Damian.

She sent Emma a text, letting her know she safely arrived home. Then, she called Damian. 3 rings and no response. She called again, but only received his voicemail.

"Weird..."

She held the phone to her ear, waiting for the beep. "Hey, babe. It's me. Just wanted to let you know I got home okay. Um... call me back when you get this message. Love you."

She hung up the phone and frowned. A strange feeling settled in the pit of her stomach.

Grabbing her laptop, she opened a web browser to check her social media. She scrolled through her newsfeed and saw pictures of Damian tagged by another woman. The pictures revealed him at a dinner party. Gabrielle smiled at how dashing he looked in his suit, as he held a glass of champagne.

She continued scrolling until she noticed a common theme: there was a beautiful brunette in every picture with him. She scrolled down to another picture of him embracing the same woman. His hands were wrapped intimately around her waist. The woman looking up at him was clearly flustered by Damian. They looked as if they were about to kiss.

"What the hell?" Gabrielle said furiously. She called Damian again, but again, it went to voicemail.

"UGH!" she grunted before tossing her phone on the bed and closing the laptop shut.

~*~

Sally got up from the table with her plate and walked to the sink.

"Mom, don't worry about that. We'll clean up," Chris said, taking the plate from her.

She smiled at him as he turned to wash the dishes in the sink. She walked to the corner of the kitchen and grabbed a broom.

"Ma, come on. I'll take care of it," Charlie said, grabbing the broom from her. "Just let us handle it."

"You should go relax in the living room and watch TV. Or maybe get some sleep. You've been up a while," Chris said over his shoulder.

Sally sat down at the kitchen table and watched her sons clean. The still silence caused them both to look at her questioningly.

"I just… I miss him so much," she broke down. "You both remind me of him. I just want to be around the both of you. Then it feels like he's still here." Tears fell from her face as her hands began to shake.

"Mom…" Chris said remorsefully. He dried off the last plate and rushed to kneel beside her. Grabbing her frail hands between his, Chris looked up at his mother just as she tenderly caressed his cheek.

"You look just like him when he was your age," she said between sobs. "You look so much like your father."

Charlie leaned on the broom and silently watched his mother sob into his brother's chest. Anguish tightened his chest. Each sob from his mother's broken heart tore at him.

"I know you both have your own places to stay. But… it's been so long since you've been home. Please stay with your mother," she sobbed into Chris's shoulder.

Chris looked at his younger brother with sadness in his eyes. They read the intent in each other's gaze and exchanged looks of understanding.

"We'll stay, Ma. We're not going anywhere. We're here for you," Charlie said softly, taking a few steps towards them.

With red, puffy eyes, Sally looked up from Chris's shoulders and into the tender forest green gaze of her youngest son. She raised her hand, softly stroking Charlie's face. He gently grabbed her hand and held it to his face as they indulged in each other's touch.

After sharing an intimate moment, Charlie let her hand go, allowing Chris to walk her out of the kitchen and up to her room. A few moments later, Chris walked back downstairs to join Charlie.

"How is she?" Charlie asked.

"It's... gonna take her some time..." Chris sighed heavily, rubbing his forehead.

Charlie plopped down in the kitchen seat. "Losing dad was hard enough..."

"I know..." Chris said, pouring himself a glass of water. "We just gotta be strong for her right now."

Charlie nodded. He looked up at the ceiling, lost in his thoughts for a brief moment before speaking. "I really wasn't... expecting to see her..."

Chris arched an amused brow. "Is that why you were so cold to her?"

Charlie scowled. "I wasn't cold..."

"No, you're right. You're like that with everyone," Chris chuckled.

Charlie gave his brother a rueful smile. "She's different..."

"Of course, she is. And... she's off limits."

"I'm sure she won't be staying long enough for that to matter anyway."

Chris shrugged. "Probably not." He took a large gulp of water. "Still..." He swished the water in his mouth before swallowing. "She's even more beautiful than when we last saw her."

"Which was over 8 years ago. I still only remember her as the dorky teenage girl we grew up with, not this... gorgeous fucking woman, goddammit!"

Chris sunk into his seat and looked up thoughtfully. "You noticed that too, huh?"

Charlie dropped his head on the table, groaning in agony.

Chris chuckled, amused by his brother's theatrics. "Just grin and bear it for now. She'll be gone sooner than you know it. Then you won't feel tempted."

"As if that's any better," Charlie mumbled.

Chris looked at his brother with a frown. It was hard enough keeping his own feelings at bay, but safeguarding his brother's feelings? The task felt impossible. As the eldest, Chris was expected to be the more responsible and stable brother. Yet, seeing Gabrielle sent him into a spiral of emotions and it frustrated him that his first thought was to kiss her the moment he lay eyes on her.

He knew Charlie's coldness was his brother's own method of keeping his feelings in check. The more deeply he felt for her, the colder he came off.

The fact of the matter was... Chris and Charlie had been in love with the same woman for years. It was in high school that they had come to this troubling realization. Being in sync with each other allowed them to read how the other felt. The brothers only had each other to find solace when Gabrielle moved across the country for undergrad.

By society's standards, Gabrielle wasn't considered the prettiest girl in high school. But it wasn't her looks that made them fall for her. It was friendship that blossomed into something more.

Chris thought back to one of the many nights he and Gabrielle used to spend on his patio.

"I wanna go to med school to be a doctor," Gabrielle said, sipping her strawberry milkshake.

"Don't you have to be in school for like a million years for that?" Chris said, stirring his milkshake with his finger.

"Kinda yea... But it's worth it. I just wanna be able to help people. Help save them so they don't die... like my dad... I just... hope I'm smart enough to get in," Gabrielle said, feeling discouraged. "Med school is so hard..."

Chris watched her with a smile. "You're the smartest person I know, Gabs. I'm sure you'll get into the best school there is," Chris said, nudging her with his elbow.

Gabrielle looked up at him and grinned. "But...?"

"What? No 'but'?" Chris said innocently.

"There's always a 'but' with you, Richardson."

"Well... you have a nice butt, if that's what you mean," Chris laughed.

"You idiot," she said, rolling her eyes.

"But seriously... I have no doubt you'll be one of the best doctors there is," he said encouragingly.

Gabrielle looked into Chris's eyes and noticed that he was looking at her a little differently. At least different than she was used to. She blushed under his gaze and turned away from him.

"Thanks, Chris..."

"You still love her?" Charlie asked, interrupting Chris's thoughts.

Chris looked at his brother for a long moment and poured himself another glass of water.

"I never stopped..."

~*~

3

Goodbye Steve Richardson

~*~

It was Sunday morning, just a few days after Gabrielle had arrived back at home and requested a temporary leave from work. She had spent her time helping her mother and Sally with funeral preparations and the memorial in celebration of Steve Richardson's life.

Gabrielle stood in front of the mirror behind the door, smoothing out her black dress. She teased the kinky curls of her hair that framed her round, mocha-toned face.

"Gabby, you ready, baby sis? Time to go," Eli called from downstairs.

"Coming!" Gabrielle shouted back. She fixed her hair one last time and slowly exhaled "Okay, girl... You can do this..." she said to herself.

She descended the stairs to find her brother in a clean-cut, black suit. Leaning back against the wall, Eli was too preoccupied with his phone to notice his sister.

"Ooh! Baby boy! Don't you look fresh!" Gabrielle grinned.

Eli looked up at her and plastered a huge smile on his face. "Ay! You know them good genes run in this black ass family," he said, popping his color.

Gabrielle chuckled and gave her brother a small peck on his cheek.

"Where's Mama?" she asked, looking around.

"I'm here! Let's go! We ain't gon' be late! Not with all them white folks there!" Clara exclaimed. She rushed out of the kitchen with a pile of pans layered on top of each other.

Eli rushed to help her with the food.

"Really, Ma? Allllll this food? Did you cook for the whole town?" he said, taking the containers from her.

"Hush, child! The whole town is gon' be there. Gabby, help your brother," Clara ordered.

"Jeez, Mama. It's just the Richardsons and a few people from the neighborhood, right?" Gabrielle said, taking one of the containers from Eli's loaded arms.

"The entire Richardson family is coming. And you ain't met them none, have you? Didn't think so. So, hush. They don't call them the **RICH**-ardsons for nothin'," Clara said, motioning her children out the door.

"Wow, Ma, you a whole cornball," Eli snickered.

"She really is though," Gabrielle laughed. "She said RICH-ardsons. Help me."

"Y'all betta hush!" Clara snapped at them. Gabrielle and Eli laughed as they got in the car.

Despite the humor, Gabrielle considered her mother's words. She had only met the other Richardsons twice, when she was much younger. Chris, Charlie, Sally, and Papa Steve rarely had visitors. Their family was spread throughout the world. She wondered what they would be like.

"Now, don't get overwhelmed," Clara said as Eli pulled out of the driveway and onto the road. "This day is gonna be really hard for Sally and her boys. Make sure to be as supportive as possible," Clara advised.

Gabrielle nodded her head, remembering how cold and short Charlie had been with her. If he was that annoyed just seeing her, she couldn't imagine how he would be the day of his father's funeral.

They pulled up to the church where the wake was being held. Eli and Gabrielle followed their mother to the kitchen at the back of the church to store the food while the service went on. When they emerged, the choir had already started singing. The trio took their seats towards the back corner and looked on. Gabrielle could hear her mother humming as she swayed in time with the music. Soon, the music had ceased and people were directed to come to the pulpit to say their final goodbyes.

"Did they do an open casket?" Gabrielle whispered to Eli.

"No. They couldn't bring themselves to see him that way," Eli whispered back.

Groups of people walked up to the casket to say their goodbyes. They each placed memorable remnants of Steve in a small basket on top of the coffin that would be buried with him. The atmosphere in the church grew heavy with people's sobs.

Gabrielle scanned the congregation but saw no sign of Chris, Charlie, or Sally. As if reading her thoughts, Eli whispered that they were probably at the front.

The line finally started to dwindle. "Come on, baby," Clara said, patting Gabrielle's hand. Together, the Johansson family walked down the side of the aisle.

Sitting in the front row was Chris, Charlie, and Sally. Chris sat to the right of his mother, holding her hand while she wept quietly on his shoulder. Chris squeezed her hand tightly as he tried to keep his own tears at bay. Meanwhile, seated on his mother's left-hand side was Charlie. With his head in his hands, he anxiously rubbed his temples with his thumbs. Like his mother, Charlie's eyes were red and sore from crying.

Both brothers instinctively looked up when the Johansson family stepped up to the pulpit.

Clara said a quiet prayer before placing her late husband's watch, a gift from Steve, in the basket. She walked towards the other side of the pulpit to wait for her children. Eli followed suit, saying a small prayer. He placed a baseball card in the basket and walked to stand with his mother.

Gabrielle cautiously approached the coffin. She looked at the picture of Steve Richardson on the easel in front of her. He had his well-known, warm smile plastered on his face. His bright blue eyes seemed to light up the room. His white and grey-peppered hair added character to the fun and gentle father-figure everyone knew him to be.

"I'm... I'm so sorry, Papa Steve," Gabrielle whispered, tears brimming in her eyes. "I wish I could have been there. I wish I could have seen you... could have talked to you one last time." Though she whispered, she could still be heard by Charlie, Chris and Eli.

Gabrielle's vision blurred from her tears. Chris and Charlie watched attentively as she delicately brought her hands behind her neck to unlatch a necklace. She balled the necklace in her hand and started to tremble. Bringing the necklace to her lips, she kissed it, and tears fell onto her fingers.

Chris and Charlie exchanged concerned looks, unsure if they should do something. Then, Eli came to her side and held his sister steady. Gabrielle looked up at her brother, tears running furiously down her face. He smiled down at her with remorse lacing his eyes.

"It's okay, baby sis," he reassured her. Gabrielle gave him a slight nod and placed the necklace in the basket. Eli escorted her back to their mother.

Charlie felt a sense of guilt building like bile in his chest. Gabrielle and his father had always been close. He treated her as if she were his own daughter. Charlie should have known that his father's death would hit her fairly hard. He had been annoyed with her, but it was partially because he missed her so much. Seeing her in front him, after 8 long years without her, had been overwhelming for him. And now, all he wanted was to hold her.

Chris's somber, blue eyes followed Gabrielle as she walked to the back of the church. He had just witnessed a side of her he had never seen before, and it broke his heart. Chris always admired how close she and his father were. Losing him was like losing a father for her as well. He turned his head to face the front again, his brows furrowing in concern. He wished he could have rushed over to her and wrapped her in his arms while she cried. He wanted to kiss her tears away, her cheeks, her lips and tell her that... he loved her. Ever since the day she returned, his mind had been in a frenzy.

But Chris chased that urge away. He pulled his mother closer and kissed her forehead.

The priest walked up to them respectfully, announcing they were ready for the burial.

Charlie looked to Chris who nodded back at him. They both helped their mother up and waited as the ushers rolled the coffin outside. They walked outside with the congregation trailing after them.

Everyone gathered around the hole in the ground where Steve would be buried. Sally could barely keep it together as she leaned on her eldest son for support. She struggled just to hold her head up, breathing heavily from her relentless sobbing. With his head down, Chris tried not to reveal the tears he fought to keep from falling. Meanwhile, Charlie completely withdrew.

"Would anyone like to say any final words?" the priest asked the congregation.

Everyone seemed too heartbroken to speak up. But Gabrielle

cleared her throat and quietly walked to the front to face the crowd.

"Hi, everyone," she said. Chris and Charlie instinctively looked up at the sound of her voice.

"My name is Gabrielle Johansson, though most of you may know me as Gabby. I um... I'm not related to Mr. Richardson. Clearly," she chuckled nervously, wiping her sweaty palms on her dress. She was relieved when the crowd responded with a chuckle of their own.

"I lost my biological father to cancer when I was 4, and... never really got to know who he was. But that doesn't mean I grew up fatherless. Mr. Richardson embraced me and my brother Eli into his family. And he treated us as if we were his own children."

Gabrielle looked at Eli and her mother who were smiling back at her.

"He would take us to baseball games, walked us to school, gave us toys for Christmas, watched us when we were sick. Because of him, we never went without. He even tried doing my hair, which honestly, for a white dude is a pretty amazing feat." Her joke was met with warm bursts of laughter.

"Mr. Steve Richardson, or as I grew up calling him, Papa Steve, was the most patient, loving, kind hearted, selfless person I knew. There was something about him that attracted people to him. That just made you fall in love with him, as you all must know personally, because you're here... you're here for him."

She looked over at Sally, sporting a huge smile on her wet, flushed face. Tears ran down like rivers from her crystal clear blue eyes. Her hands were clasped in front of her with delight.

"Just as he's always been there for us," Gabrielle continued. "He was a true family man who loved his beautiful, kind wife and cared deeply for his incredible and loving sons."

Gabrielle looked towards Chris and Charlie.

"And when I see them, I know he's not truly gone, because I see him in them. His spirit, his kindness, his humor, his intelligence, his bravery, his love..."

Chris's face flushed pink as he looked lovingly at the dark-skin beauty before him. His gaze was broken when his mother grabbed his hand to look up at him with a smile.

Charlie started to sweat and couldn't look at Gabrielle for long. He quickly turned his head away and shifted his stance uncomfortably.

"So, let's not mourn his death, but rather celebrate his life, and the amazing legacy he left." Gabrielle finished and met an eruption of applause from the crowd. She smiled shyly and walked back over to her mother and brother for a family hug.

"Thank you, Miss Johansson, for that lovely speech. Is there anyone else?" the priest asked.

Suddenly, an older man stepped up to the center and stood facing the crowd.

"Afternoon," he said with a refined English accent. "Rather difficult to follow up such a heartwarming and well-spoken speech such as that one. Thank you, Miss. Johansson," he nodded to Gabrielle.

"My name is Eric Richardson. Steve was my second eldest brother. My siblings and I didn't quite grow up in the most decent of households. Our father was rather... **harsh** to say the least. That tends to be expected when you're part of a family as old as ours. We all had responsibilities. We all... **still** have responsibilities," he said looking at Chris and Charlie. The brothers shifted uncomfortably under his sharp gaze.

"And though my eldest brother and I were rather pessimistic about our childhood, Steve always had a more positive and optimistic outlook on life. And I can see here that he hasn't left anyone untouched from his kindness and generosity. I'm proud to call him my brother. I just wish I could have had an ale with him one last time."

Eric Richardson looked down momentarily, lost in his thoughts, before looking back up.

"We'll miss you, brother," he said finally. Everyone applauded as he walked back to stand next to his daughter.

The priest said a prayer for Steve and his family before giving the signal to begin the burial. Everyone watched as the coffin was lowered into the ground. A woman from the choir sang "Amazing Grace" while the dirt was thrown back into the hole.As the dirt was patted down neatly, people began to throw roses on Steve's grave.

Sally stood silently watching, when Clara walked up to her and hugged her comfortingly.

"We'll meet you back at the house and get everything prepared," Clara said hugging Charlie and Chris.

"Thank you, Ms. Clara," Chris nodded to her gratefully.

Clara gestured to her children and the family headed towards the car. Gabrielle looked back at the Richardsons to see Sally holding onto her sons for support. Charlie was looking down at his mother while Chris was looking back at Gabrielle.

~*~

4

The Family Reunion

~*~

"Gabrielle! Check on the mac and cheese for me. It should be ready to come out of the oven by now," Clara instructed her daughter while tasting the turkey neck broth.

"Yes, Mama." Gabrielle opened the oven and pulled out the large tray of mac and cheese layered with mixed cheeses. She hadn't had a feast like this since Christmas.

The Johanssons were in the Richardsons' kitchen preparing the food before everyone's arrival. Gabrielle wasn't at all surprised that her mother's tendency to serve had not wavered. It was in her nature to care for others.

"Start putting the food out on the living room table. We'll set it up buffet style," Clara said picking up a tray of collard greens. She carried them to the living room and her children followed.

They had just finished laying out the last bit of the food when Sally and her sons walked through the door.

"Wow! It smells amazing in here!" Chris said, walking towards the couch to take a seat.

"Clara, you are too much. You didn't have to do all this," Sally said with teary eyes. She looked over the vast arrangement of food with gratitude.

"Sally, hush. I wanted to. Now, I don't want you or your boys to lift a finger. We'll serve the food," Clara said comfortingly.

"I'm sorry, we'll do *what*?!" Eli blurted. He spun around abruptly holding a bowl of ice water, which splashed onto his sister's dress.

"Eli!" Gabrielle shrieked.

"Whoops! Sorry, sis," Eli chuckled. Gabrielle gave him a dirty glare and looked for a cloth.

"Here," Charlie said abruptly, handing her a small towel.

"Oh! Thanks, Charlie," she said grabbing the towel. She wiped the water from her chest and looked up to see Charlie's eyes lingering on her. He lifted his eyes to meet her gaze and immediately snapped out of it.

"I'll be outside," Charlie muttered. He glanced at Chris on the couch, eyeing him with a raised brow. Charlie rolled his eyes dismissively and walked outside to the patio.

Gabrielle stalked over to Chris and plopped down next to him on the couch.

"Is it me or does your brother all of a sudden hate me," she muttered.

Chris chuckled at the irony. "Far from it, Gabs."

He looked behind her and caught his brother lighting a cigarette on the patio.

"I really missed you, Chris," Gabrielle said suddenly. Catching him by surprise, she laid her head on his shoulder and rested her hand against his chest.

His heart sped up a bit faster as he grabbed her hand and held it close.

"I missed you too, Gabs," he said quickly.

"NUH UH! Girl, I know you are **not** getting comfortable. You. Are here. To **serve**," Clara said, knocking them out of their serenity.

"But, Mom!" Gabrielle whined.

"Child. The only 'but' I wanna hear is yours marching to the kitchen to start serving this here food," Clara ordered, waving a spoon in the air.

"Ugh. We'll catch up later," Gabrielle said, getting up. She turned to Chris and gave a quick smile before following her mother back into the kitchen.

Chris watched mesmerized as her hips switched all the way to the kitchen.

"Christopher. Some people have started to arrive. Be a dear and go greet them. And make sure your brother behaves. I can't handle an episode right now," Sally said, putting a glass of red wine to her lips.

"Of course, Mom." Chris got up from the couch and headed towards the patio.

"Hey," Chris walked onto the patio to greet his younger brother. Charlie turned slightly to face him and took a long drag of his cigarette.

"Hey..."

"You doin' alright?"

Charlie shrugged and looked down, taking another drag. "I miss him."

"I miss him too," Chris said. He leaned against the railing next to his brother, looking out over the front yard. They both watched as people pulled up to their estate.

"You might wanna ease up on Gabs," Chris said, turning to him.

Charlie raised an amused brow and snickered. "Ease up how? I haven't done anything."

"We've all been best friends since we were kids," Chris said. "Her last memory of us was when we went skinny dipping in the river by Rogers and threw eggs at Mr. Drear's house the night before graduation."

Charlie grinned mischievously. "Oh yea! Remember when Gabs threw one of the eggs through an open window she thought was closed. She smacked him right in the back of the head."

Chris threw his head back in laughter. "I have never seen her freak out that badly. She swore she was going to get arrested."

"Expelled at best," Charlie smirked.

"Right before graduation? That would have been pointless," Chris chuckled.

Charlie puckered his lips and rubbed his blonde beard thoughtfully. "That was an unforgettable night."

"Yea," Chris said fondly. "So, stop being a grouch."

Charlie rolled his eyes.

"Hey, I know it's your way of coping, but she doesn't know that," Chris added.

"Not that she'd ever get it. Oblivious as always," Charlie muttered.

They both nodded in agreement. Seconds later, their neighbors walked up to the patio to shake Chris's hand. Charlie couldn't be bothered to socialize.

"Thank you for coming. It means a lot to us," Chris waved off the last person walking into their family home.

"It's best that she stays oblivious. Especially considering our... family business," Chris said looking at his brother with tired eyes.

"Don't remind me," Charlie groaned. He closed his eyes and cocked his head up towards the sun.

"Heh. Anyway... she thinks you hate her," Chris said eyeing him.

Charlie's eyes abruptly popped open. He looked at his older brother in disbelief, then scoffed loudly.

"Yea, I know," Chris chuckled. "So maybe... tone it down a little. She cares about you."

Charlie dropped the cigarette to the ground and snuffed it out with the toe of his shoe.

"It's all I can do to stop myself from wanting her," Charlie said, looking at him with guilt. He tore his eyes away and dropped his head. "But... I'll try..."

Chris looked at Charlie with a warm smile. He appreciated that he and his brother had such a strong connection and felt comfortable enough to discuss their feelings, including being in love with the same woman. Being so in sync with each other had its positives and negatives. Always knowing when something was wrong with the other proved most useful. Falling in love with the same woman was not.

"Just... don't let it mess you up. There's not much we can do about it anyway. Losing dad is one thing. Mom can barely keep it together. I need my brother. Alright?" Chris said, placing a comforting hand on Charlie's shoulder.

Charlie nodded. Suddenly, the sound of an engine pierced the air. They both looked up to see a red Lamborghini and a blue Corvette pull up to the house.

Their uncle Eric stepped out of the red Lamborghini and walked to the other side to open the door for his daughter Natalie. Eric and Natalie were a perfect picture of British elegance, class, and wealth. With long, bone-straight blonde hair that accentuated her bright blue eyes, Natalie was practically a spitting image of her father. Natalie wore a sophisticated off-the-shoulder black pencil dress that stopped just above her knees. Her Christian Louboutin pumps accentuated the curve and strength of her legs as she walked. She linked her hand around her father's arm and together they walked down the pathway.

Eric Richardson was one of the most powerful men in England. He ran multiple large businesses in the United Kingdom, with thousands of subsidiaries in the United States. He was a force to be reckoned with and most people often feared him. Still, he was always a perfect gentleman. Being a witty quick talker made him the perfect businessman. It was what Chris admired most about him. When his uncle first approached him about his new role in the family business, Chris knew he had to mimic his uncle's calm, cool and collected demeanor.

Natalie oozed as much elegance as her father, with an air of grace that always made her stand out. However, as one of the few women in a male-dominated business, she had to be sterner just to be taken seriously. Thus, people usually regarded her as cold-hearted and nothing short of a bitch. Natalie was her father's Chief of Investments, one of the most important roles for the business. And lately, she had been raking in a lot of clients.

The brothers braced themselves as Eric and Natalie approached them.

"It's a pleasure to see you two again," Eric said, shaking Chris's hand.

"Nice to see you too, Uncle Eric. Thank you for speaking at the service," Chris said.

"Of course. Your father was a good man. And my favorite brother," Eric nodded.

"It's hardly difficult to see why," Natalie chimed. She glared at her uncle Gerald and cousin Arthur as they exited the blue Corvette.

Gerald had a rather rugged, Old English, look to him. Sporting a thick, short beard that barely hid the soft wrinkles of stress on his face, his light grey eyes was his most endearing attribute. Arthur, known to look like a younger version of his father, had a strong jawline. Its sharpness was magnified every time he made that dazzling smile that made women weak at the knees.

"Well, I'm going inside before I'm subjected to their idiocy. We'll catch up later," Natalie said, hugging her cousins.

Just as Natalie walked into the house, Gerald and Arthur stepped onto the patio.

"Well, if it isn't my little brother. And! My favorite nephews!" Gerald said in a thick British accent. A cigar hung casually from his mouth.

"We're your only nephews, Uncle," Chris said with a raised brow.

"Well… not if we count yer mother's side. And we all know what an awful lot they are," Gerald grinned. He plopped a large hand on Chris's shoulder, nearly making him stumble forward.

"Classy," Charlie said with disgust and a roll of his eyes.

"No. What's classy are these cigars I brought you from Glasgow. It's a gift to make you feel like a real man. Instead of that shit you keep using. Here," Gerald said, patting around his suit jacket.

"Er... perhaps after dinner," Eric said, gesturing to the door.

Gerald smirked amused. "But of course! Anything for the Queen's most loyal, royal pet. After you," he said smugly. Eric scoffed with a roll of his eyes and headed inside. Gerald trailed behind him.

"I would apologize for my father but, well… you already know how he is. So, I don't have to," Arthur snickered. He pulled Charlie in for a hug and shook Chris's hand.

"Yea… thanks for coming, Arthur," Chris smiled.

"I missed my cousins. But I'm sorry about your father. He was a good man," Arthur said in his thick English accent.

"Thanks, man," Charlie said with an awkward twist of his

mouth.

"Um... are you guys gonna come eat?" rang Gabrielle's voice from the doorway.

The three men looked up to see a smiling Gabrielle in a black apron flattering to her figure. She held a large wooden spoon dripping with tomato sauce.

"Well, hello. And who, pray tell, are you?" Arthur inquired. His eyes widened as he gazed upon her from head to toe.

"Hi! I'm Gabrielle. I think I met you before. Maybe when we were kids?" she said, tilting her head to the side.

"Ah yes! Gabrielle! Wow... you have **certainly** grown," Arthur grinned. He took her hand and kissed the back of it tenderly.

Gabrielle blushed, surprised by his comment and even more taken back by his welcome.

"Th-thanks?" she said retracting her hand. "And you're... Arthur? Charlie and Chris's cousin, right?"

Arthur looked back at his cousins with a Cheshire grin before he turned back to Gabrielle. "The one and only."

"It's nice to meet you again," she smiled politely. "You guys should really come inside to eat. These people were not playing. They must have emptied their stomachs before arriving. The food is nearly gone."

She noticed tomato sauce starting to drip from the spoon she was holding.

"Oh shoot," she said, catching the sauce with her finger. She quickly licked it from her digit, not realizing the effect she was having on the crowd before.

"Okay... now **that's** good sauce," she grinned. "And you know why? Because **I** made it. So, hurry up before you completely miss out-"

"Yes, yes, thanks, Gabs. We'll be inside in a second," Chris said impatiently waving her off. He knew if that performance she pulled was killing him, he could only imagine what it was doing to his brother. Arthur surely had no intention of hiding the effect it had on him.

"Fine, fine. Don't say I didn't warn you," she said, waltzing back into the house.

Chris heard a deep sigh from Charlie, who quickly turned around for another cigarette.

"Fuck me! Little Gabrielle ain't so little anymore, is she? If that's not perfection, I don't know what is. And that ass..." Arthur craned his head to follow Gabrielle's walk into the house, watching her hips switch side to side.

Charlie roughly shoved Arthur in the chest. He glaring at his cousin heavily annoyed.

"Oh, my apologies. Does she belong to one of you?" Arthur eyed Charlie suspiciously.

"She doesn't belong to anyone," Charlie said irritably. He tried not to give himself away. He took a long drag from his cigarette and his death glare never wavered from Arthur.

"So then… she's available," Arthur smirked mischievously.

Charlie clenched his fist when Chris quickly stood in front of him.

"Arthur, please. This isn't the time. Everyone's already a little on edge. Let's just go inside and have a nice family dinner, alright?" Chris said, motioning Arthur towards the door.

"Christopher, Christopher. So rational. Always the diplomat. I suppose that's why our fathers chose you to take the lead. You must be so proud," Arthur smirked mockingly. He winked patronizingly at Charlie before walking into the house.

Chris sighed with aggravation and turned to his brother.

"Don't say it," Charlie said abruptly. He flicked the cigarette and snuffed it out. "I just wanna get through this fucking dinner."

"I know... Charlie, I know you better than anyone. I'm not trying to parent you, I just... you gotta learn to control your emotions a little better. For Mom. I can't referee another brawl," Chris sighed.

"I actually thought you'd be on my team," Charlie smirked at him.

"I'm always on your team. But that's not fair to Arthur. You'd knock him out with one blow," Chris smirked back. "Let's go."

They both walked into the house populated with people eating, drinking and talking.

They noticed Gabrielle talking to Eric and Gerald as she served them their food. She was blushing so hard her cheeks took on a pinkish tint beneath her dark brown skin. She looked as if she were trying to hold back laughter.

"Oh God," Chris muttered as he started towards them.

"Hey, hey now. Leave them be," Natalie said, stopping Chris with a hand to the chest.

"Natalie," Chris said looking down at her. Her bright blue eyes sparkled, and a pert smirk crossed her perfect face. Luscious blonde locks fell delicately around her face.

She handed him a full glass of red wine and then grabbed her own.

"Let's talk, cousin," she smiled up at him. He looked at Gabrielle one more time, talking to his uncles. She seemed more relaxed and was genuinely laughing. His uncles seemed as enthralled by her presence as he and Charlie were. He couldn't help the smile on his face. Her smile filled with pearly whites accompanied by a soft laugh echoed throughout the house. Her laughter was infectious as he noticed both uncles laughing with her. And they didn't even like each other.

"Come on," Natalie persisted, leading him towards the balcony.

"So... how have you been?" she asked, turning to him. She took a sip of her wine.

"I'm... fine," he said stiffly. He leaned against the railing and looked into the house.

"Except that you're not," she said, looking him over curiously.

"Excuse me?" Chris said with a raised brow. "I mean... it's just a rough time right now..."

"It is. And you've spent so much time tending to your mother and Charles that you haven't taken a moment to grieve and tend to yourself," she said to him matter-of-factly.

Chris's words caught in his throat.

"I...I guess you're right." He frowned and looked into his wine glass before taking another sip. "I don't consider my own needs that often. I can't. I have to take the lead."

"I know you don't. You got that trait from your father, bless his soul. But it's not healthy, Christopher. I knew you would do this. That's why I'm here. To remind you." She smiled up at him and leaned her head on his shoulder.

"Thanks, Nat," Chris smiled and kissed the top of her head.

"Glass is empty. Care to join me for another," she grinned. She twirled the stem of her empty glass between her long, slender fingers.

"Sure," he smiled. She plucked the empty glass from his hand and sashayed inside. Chris shook his head with a chuckle. He looked up to see Charlie walking towards him.

They could never seem to stay too far away from each other for too long...

"Hey. How are you managing?" Chris asked as Charlie sat next to him on the balcony.

"Let's just say... thank God there's alcohol," Charlie said. He took a chug of the beer and sighed. "What were you and Nat talking about?"

Chris shrugged. "She's just checking up on me. Trying to take on some 'older sister' duties again. Says I'm not really taking care of myself apparently."

"Well, she's right," Charlie said. Chris looked at him curiously. "I know you're always looking after me, Chris. You have ever since we were kids. And I appreciate it but... you have to look after yourself too. I'm just... disappointed as shit in myself that I haven't returned the favor."

"That's not your fault, Charlie. We're all a little fragile right now. Hell, I envy your ability to feel so much. Sometimes, I feel this business has made me... cold," Chris said. He caught Natalie walking back towards them with Gabrielle trailing after her.

"It's a blessing and a curse, I guess. More of a curse these days," Charlie said, taking a gulp of his beer. His eyes were instinctively set on Gabrielle.

"Charles! I'm so glad you could join us," Natalie said, handing Chris his wine.

"Nat," Charlie nodded.

"Hey guys," Gabrielle greeted the boys cheerfully. "Are you doing okay? Did you eat enough? Silly question. Neither of you have eaten. I know because I would have served you. Here. I made you both plates before the savages ate everything up." She handed them both their plates.

“Gab-,” Charlie started.

“Don’t turn me down, okay? Just eat. Please,” she said sincerely.

They both smiled at her with gratitude as they took their plates. “Thanks, Gabs,” Chis said.

“Do you need anything, Natalie? There’s still some more of my mother’s peach cobbler left,” Gabrielle offered. “It’s so damn good and she doesn’t make it often. So, consider it a treat.”

“Oh no, thank you dear. I’m quite full. Though I may take you up on that peach cobbler later. Save me a piece?” Natalie smiled at Gabrielle.

“Of course! I gotta get back and help clean up, but I’ll hide it for you. Keep it secret. Keep it safe,” Gabrielle joked with a snort. The 3 Richardsons smirked at her fairly amused.

“Sorry... Lord of the Rings references... make me... snort...ugh... I’m gonna go before I embarrass myself further,” she said nervously. She waved them off and stumbled back into the house.

“Okay... she is the most adorable thing I have ever seen,” Natalie sighed fondly. She watched Gabrielle assist her mother in packing up the trays. “Almost a little too perfect...”

Charlie and Chris purposely ignored her comments and quietly ate their food.

“So, you’re both in love with her, then,” Natalie said, tapping the side of her cheek with her pointer finger. Chris nearly choked on his food and Charlie looked at Natalie with wide eyes. Natalie could only scoff in offense.

“Oh please. I’ve known you both since we were children. You don’t think I can tell by now when you’re in love? I changed your diapers for goodness’ sake. Give me some credit,” she scowled.

Charlie sighed in frustration and continued eating his food.

"I don't blame either of you. She's a very beautiful girl. Kind and endearing. Heck, she got my father and Uncle Gerald to like her. And it looks like Arthur might just try to bring her back to England with him by the way he keeps flirting with her," she chuckled slyly.

This time Charlie choked on his food. Natalie looked at him, half worried and half amused.

"It's just... not something we really talk about, Nat. Can we drop it?" Chris said, feeling uncomfortable.

"You two? Not talk about how you're both in love with the same woman? I hardly believe that, Christopher. But sure. Whatever. I won't push it," she shrugged nonchalantly.

"Anyway, I see Gabrielle and I becoming good friends. I've asked her to show me around town for a bit, and she is more than happy to accompany me," Natalie said, finishing her wine.

"There's not really much to see around here, Nat. Especially considering your fancy, diva lifestyle," Charlie said.

"Well, I can be... regular... for a change. See how the average commoner has fun." She pulled a mirror from her purse and checked her face in the mirror.

"Commoner? Jeez, Nat. You sound like the Queen herself," Charlie rolled his eyes.

"Charles, don't flatter me," she chuckled. She looked at her face one more time before returning the mirror to her bag.

"And I want you both to come with us," she added.

"I'm sorry, what?" Chris asked, surprised.

"I want you to accompany me. Arthur invited himself and I'd rather take a smelly taxi than be alone with him for too long," she scoffed.

“I don’t know, Nat. We’ve got a lot to take care of,” Chris said, looking at Charlie.

“Oh please, Christopher. For one night? You can’t take a break to hang out with your cousin all the way from across the pond for one night? If anything, you need this just as badly as I do. Maybe more.” She put her hands on her hips and impatiently tapped her foot.

“...Fine.” Chris gave in and put his empty plate down.

“Charles?” she persisted.

Charlie looked at Chris, who gave him a pleading “don’t you dare ditch me” look.

“Fine...” Charlie muttered annoyed.

“Perfect! Now, I’m going to go mingle some more. Too much testosterone over here,” she teased. She gave them both a kiss on the cheek and disappeared back inside the house.

“Well, this should be fun,” Charlie said sarcastically.

~*~

Eric and Gerald joined Chris and Charlie outside on the patio, just as they were kindling a fire in the fire pit.

“There you boys are. Haven’t seen you the whole night. You haven’t been avoiding us have you?” Eric joked with a pat on Chris’s shoulder.

“No, just... trying to catch our breaths,” Chris smiled wearily at him.

“Here,” Gerald said, handing each of them a cigar.

“Uncle-” Charlie started.

“No. For your father,” Gerald said. The men cut off the end of the cigars and lit them, taking a moment of silence for Steve Richardson.

"...I... know I can be a bit of an ass," Gerald started.

"A bit?" Eric smirked. Gerald playfully gave his brother the finger..

"But your father was a really good man. A pain in my arse and one of the most self-righteous people I knew. But a good man... I see a lot of him in you. In both of you," Gerald said, looking at his nephews.

"Well thanks, Uncle Gerald. Means a lot coming from you," Chris said.

Gerald nodded when he noticed something in the driveway. "Is that bike out front yours, Charles," he asked.

"It was Dad's. I'm just... fixing it up," Charlie said.

"I knew it looked familiar. I remember when your father first got that bike. He loved it like it was his child. Rode it everywhere... It suits you. He'd want you to have it," Gerald said.

Charlie gave him a small smile. "Thanks."

After a few moments puffing on cigars and looking over the horizon, Eric broke the silence.

"That Johansson girl is really quite lovely. Is she with one of you?" Eric asked.

Charlie and Chris exchanged looks. "Just a close friend of the family," Chris assured him.

"Aye, I'd like to make her more than a friend. If I were 10 years younger," Gerald muttered.

"Uncle, please," Chris laughed.

"Eh... sorry. Your uncle's right though. She made me tolerate him for at least half an hour. Must be a record," Gerald joked.

"She did have a lot to say about your father. And about you boys. Main reason I asked," Eric said, taking a puff. "But enough of that. As much as I like reminiscing with you all... we have to talk business at some point."

Chris and Charlie exchanged looks just as Arthur came waltzing through the door with Natalie and Gabrielle in tow.

"What are you boys talking about?" Natalie interrupted.

"We were just about to have an important meeting, dear," Eric said, trying to dismiss them.

"Meeting? Honestly, Father, have you no respect? There will be no talk of business on the night of Uncle Steve's memorial. We should be talking about him. Right, Gabrielle?" Natalie said latching herself onto Gabrielle's arm.

Gabrielle looked down, smiling nervously. "Yeah... though I kind of feel like I'm intruding."

"Intruding? What on earth are you talking about?" Natalie said. She took a seat in the circle that Chris, Charlie, Gerald, and Eric already sat in around the fire pit.

Gabrielle glanced at all of them. "This seems a little... personal?"

"Well according to C-squared, you're already family, sweetheart," Arthur grinned. He winked at her and sat next to Natalie who rolled her eyes irritably.

"C-squared?" Gabrielle asked.

"It's what he calls them when he's too much of a lazy buffoon to call them both by their names," Natalie said, crossing her arms over her chest.

"Oh!" Gabrielle chuckled. "C-squared. That's clever."

"Don't encourage him!" Natalie sucked her teeth.

"Well, since my daughter has laid down the law of the land, Gabrielle, you really should come join us," Eric offered.

Chris and Charlie exchanged glances again, trying to garner if her presence was a good idea.

Gabrielle frowned when she noticed how awkward Chris and Charlie had been acting. She looked behind her into the house."I don't know. I should probably check on Mrs. Sally-"

"Is the fire pit on?" Eli's voice thundered as he walked outside.

"Eli! Join us!" Natalie waved.

"Y'all having a party out here?" Eli smirked. He wrapped Gabrielle into a hug and kissed the top of her head. "Hey, sis. You okay?"

"Yea, I just... how is Mrs. Sally? Does she need anything?" Gabrielle said, a bit agitated.

"Moms is having tea with her in the kitchen. They both seemed like they wanted to be left alone after everyone else went home. That's why I came out here to see what all the commotion was about."

"Oh..." Gabrielle said looking down.

"We were just reminiscing about Uncle Steve," Natalie informed him.

"Aw man, I've got stories about Papa Steve for days," Eli chuckled. He plopped a seat next to Arthur. Gabrielle stayed standing.

"Sis, sit down," Eli said. Gabrielle pouted and sat between Eli and Gerald, completing their circle.

~*~

The group talked for hours about their favorite moments with Steve Richardson.

"Remember when Steve covered for your ass when you hot-wired father's car and drove all the way to London?" Eric laughed, holding an empty beer bottle.

"I still got in a shit ton of trouble," Gerald smirked, puffing on his cigar.

"You would have gotten in so much more if Steve hadn't defended you," Eric grinned.

"Yea, the little boy scout was always saving my ass from his wrath," Gerald said thoughtfully. "Unlike you, who always tried to do me in."

"I didn't have to do much. You were already a mess," Eric teased.

"Like father like son," Natalie scoffed, hovering her hands over the fire pit.

"Damn right," Arthur laughed, taking another swig of his beer.

"I remember when Dad took me on my first joy ride," Charlie smiled, looking into his glass.

"I'm sorry. Did you say FIRST joy ride? As in more than one?" Natalie said surprised.

Charlie gave a wicked grin. "Mom used to get so pissed at me for taking the car out. She got on Dad about punishing me for it. Instead, he took me on a couple joy rides. But I mean, he also taught me about the importance of driving safely."

"That story was going well until you added 'driving safely'," Gerald grunted.

"You know, Charles. Sometimes I think you're more like me than you are like Chris," Arthur grinned.

"Uh, I HIGHLY doubt that. Charles is a rebel. You're just a menace," Natalie said.

"That's hurtful, Nat," Arthur feigned offense.

"Remember when Papa Steve taught us to swim?" Eli said, nudging his sister.

"That was one of the most embarrassing days of my life," Gabrielle murmured.

"Embarrassing? Now I gotta hear this," Natalie said. Her eyes lit up with curiosity.

Gabrielle chuckled. "Papa Steve offered to take Eli and I for swimming lessons at the local YMCA when our mom was working extra shifts. Eli was already so good doing all these tricks and being a big-headed showboat as always."

"Hey!" Eli exclaimed.

"But I struggled... badly. I was terrified of the water. One day, I forgot to wear my swimming cap and I had just gotten my hair done..."

Everyone looked at her fairly confused.

"They're white, Gabs. You gotta explain the struggle of your naps," Eli laughed.

Gabrielle gave him a dirty look before continuing. "My hair is naturally kinky, er... curly? My mom used to straighten it for school. But when it touches water it shrinks and goes back to its natural state which is frustrating since the hot comb is terrifying. I still have nightmares."

She shuttered dramatically causing the others to laugh.

"Anyway, Papa Steve tried to comfort me by giving me tips. But they didn't really help." She covered her face in embarrassment. "So then he stripped down to just his jeans and hopped in the pool just to help me learn to swim."

"He did what?!" Natalie exclaimed with a huge shocking smile on her face. Arthur started laughing uncontrollably while Eric shook his head.

“How come I don’t remember this story?” Chris said suddenly.

“There are some things I didn’t tell you for a reason, Christopher!” Gabrielle exclaimed with embarrassment.

“Honestly... that *definitely* sounds like something Dad would do,” Charlie smirked.

“That wasn’t even the worse part. I mean I learned to swim thanks to him. But my hair got wet. He didn’t read my mom’s text about wearing a shower cap until the nightmare had already happened. The look on his face when he saw my hair shrink into an afro is still burned into my memory.” Gabrielle could barely contain her laughter.

“This is gold,” Arthur laughed.

“But it gets better!” Eli said in between laughing hysterically.

“Eli please... don’t do this to me...” Gabrielle pleaded, covering her face.

“How could it possibly get better than this?” Natalie asked.

“Papa Steve tried to **fix** Gabby’s hair!” Eli struggled to say between his laughter.

Gabrielle, Chris and Charlie loudly groaned, covering their faces simultaneously.

“First he tried combing it,” Eli said. They all looked at him expectantly. “The comb broke.”

They all burst into laughter.

“Then he decided to take her to a hair salon,” Eli continued.

“Well at least now he’s making better decisions,” Natalie noted.

“But he didn’t know how to describe what he wanted. So, Gabrielle went blonde for a few weeks,” Eli said before doubling over in laughter.

"Wait... THAT'S why you wore that stupid Cinderella hat for the first month of school? You told us it was for a play!" Charlie said surprised.

Gabrielle raised her hands not knowing what to say. She covered her face, wishing she had a hole to hide in.

"You could totally pull off blonde," Natalie said, after she gathered her bearings. Gabrielle smiled at her brightly.

"Other than pure comedy, that story tells you all you need to know about my brother," Eric said, clearing his throat.

Gabrielle nodded. "It's true. He was a kind, selfless man who was always willing to go above and beyond for others." The mood changed to a more somber feeling.

"Papa Steve... he was one of my biggest cheerleaders. Heck, he rivaled my mother at times. I loved him and he loved me despite how different we were. Because of him, I never felt... *fatherless*..." Gabrielle trailed off and quickly wiped at the tears brimming over her eyelids.

"Hey..." Eli grabbed her hand and squeezed gently. Chris watched her intently while Charlie fumbled with his hands, wanting to say something but unable to.

"Shoot. I'm sorry, guys. I didn't mean to dampen the mood," she said apologetically. She tried to wipe away any other tears before they could escape.

"You're fine, dear," Natalie said comfortingly.

"You guys must have been really close," Gerald said. Gabrielle responded with a small smile.

"We should probably get going," Eli said, getting up.

"Yea, we have a long day tomorrow, as I'm taking you shopping, I believe," Gabrielle said, getting up as well. She tried to collect herself by not looking at the two that hadn't taken their eyes off of her. She felt embarrassed about being so emotional over Steve when his own sons had been able to hold themselves together.

"Yes! I'm so excited! Show me what this quaint city has to offer," Natalie said getting up.

"Well it's nothing like London, so don't get your hopes up too much," Gabrielle chuckled. The two women linked arms with each other.

"Are you guys staying in the estate?" Eli asked.

"No. We are taking temporary residence elsewhere," Eric said.

As everyone headed back into the house to leave, Eric called out to Chris.

"We'll need to talk soon," Eric said to him seriously. Chris merely nodded and proceeded to follow everyone off of the balcony and into the house.

~*~

Back at home, Gabrielle searched for her ringing cell phone and found it in her purse.

"Hello?" she answered.

"Baby... hey, how are you?" came Damian's smooth voice from the other end.

"Damian! I tried calling you days ago!" she blurted.

"Yea, sorry, babe. Work has been really busy," he said sounding distant and distracted.

"It's okay," she said quietly. "What have you been up to?"

"Just work."

"Hey um... did you go to a get-together or... dinner party recently?" she asked.

"Huh? Yea, something like that. Why do you ask?"

"Oh... I just noticed some girl on your newsfeed and was just wondering if she was like... a friend or a co-worker or something," she inquired.

"She's a co-worker," he said abruptly.

"Oh... what's her name?" Gabrielle asked. But she was met with silence until another woman's voice could be heard in the background.

"Babe?" Gabrielle asked.

"Huh? Hey, I gotta go. I'll talk to you later," Damian finally said.

"Wait! Damian!" But he had already ended the call.

"UGH! Forget this!" she said, tossing her phone.

~*~

5

"Let's Show 'em a Good Time!"

~*~

The next day Gabrielle met up with Tanya, Eli's girlfriend, and introduced her to Natalie. The 3 women spent the day shopping in the local Philly area. Towards the evening, they all rendezvoused back at the Richardson estate.

Arthur, Eli, Charlie, and Chris waited in the living room, talking amongst themselves, while the women got ready in one of the guest rooms.

"Is this red too harsh? Maybe I should go for something lighter," Tanya said rubbing red lipstick over her thick lips.

"No, it's perfect," Natalie complimented her. "But use this highlighter. It'll make your cheekbones *pop*," she said, making her lips smack. She handed Tanya a stick from her large bag of makeup.

"Thanks! Dang girl, you have everything! Even something for my black ass," Tanya joked.

"I take this loyal bag with me everywhere I go," Natalie said, hugging her bag.

Gabrielle looked at herself in the mirror. She wore a pair of form-fitted jeans, red high-top sneakers, and a nostalgic old Optimus Prime t-shirt that was much bigger on her as a kid.

"What do you think?" she asked the other two women. They both looked at her.

"Cute. But," Tanya said coming up behind her. She pulled the hem of her shirt tightly in the back and tied a knot so the shirt fit like a crop top. "There. Now you look less like a big kid and more like a sexy video vixen."

"I don't wanna be a video vixen," Gabrielle pouted. She admired her physique in the mirror. She was always wearing her white medical lab coat over a pair of slacks and a simple blouse. She rarely took the time to actually make herself look... attractive. Unless, it was for one of Damian's promo events showcasing his art. The now-crop top made her curved physique so much more apparent that it surprised even her.

Gabrielle pulled her hair back with her hand. "Up or down?" she asked the girls.

"Definitely down," Natalie responded.

She let kinky hair fall around her face and turned to see their final look."You guys look **hot**!" she exclaimed.

Natalie wore a small, ruched, white skirt with a sexy black top that had a plunging neckline. Tanya wore dark blue cheeky jean shorts, and one of Eli's old basketball jerseys from their high school days that she had redesigned for fashionable use.

"I'm surprised you still have that," Gabrielle noted.

Tanya smiled at her sweetly. "Yea... Eli gave this to me after his final game in senior year of high school when he made the winning shot. I've kept it ever since."

"You guys are too cute. When are you giving me nieces and nephews?" Gabrielle teased.

"Girl, bye," Tanya rolled her eyes, causing Gabrielle to chuckle.

"How long have you two been together," Natalie asked.

"Uh jeez... 15...16 years?" Tanya said thoughtfully.

"Wow! And you guys aren't married yet?" Natalie asked, surprised.

"Well, Eli hasn't necessarily proposed. But I'm not really in a rush. I'd like to make partner at my firm before I start building a family," Tanya said.

"Career-driven. I like that," Natalie winked.

"Would you girls hurry up!" Eli shouted from downstairs.

"Boy, hush! We'll be down in a minute!" Tanya yelled back at him. "We better go."

The women did one more final check on each other before descending the stairs.

"Took you long enou- Aw hell naw, woman! Why ya booty all out?!" Eli said exasperated.

"I'm a grown ass woman, Eli. I can look how I want! Besides, I thought you'd like it," she shot back at him.

"Yea... but that's mine. I don't want anybody else to see," he whispered. But not low enough as everyone else burst into laughter.

"Shut up, Eli," Gabrielle teased him. "Look at her shirt!" Eli gave his sister a death stare then took another look at Tanya's outfit.

"My old jersey!" he said shocked.

"Yea... thought it'd be a nice surprise," Tanya blushed as he took her into his arms.

"It is. You look sexy as hell. I love you, baby," he said, kissing her.

"EW! Okay can you guys get a room," Gabrielle joked, shoving the two of them.

Chris had been perched on the arm of the couch, talking to Arthur; when suddenly, he felt the sudden tension from Charlie sitting across from him. He followed his brother's gaze to Gabrielle and his breathing immediately hitched. She looked even more voluptuous than ever in her form-fitting jeans and retro crop top that exposed her small inviting waist.

"Aw, let the happy couple be. If I were with my beau right now, I'd be snogging the life out of him," Natalie joked.

"You have a lover?" Gabrielle asked.

"***Lovers***," Natalie said, emphasizing the plural. "And not the type you take home to meet your parents," she chuckled. "And what about yourself? Do you have a lover we don't know about?"

Suddenly Gabrielle could feel all eyes on her.

"What? Oh... um... hmm... well see... that's actually a funny story," Gabrielle fumbled nervously. She thought about Damian and instantly remembered images of him with the mysterious woman. Soon her mind was swarming with thoughts of him cheating on her; about all the times he was controlling of her. She felt conflicted about breaking up with him or sticking it out... *again*.

"It's a 'yes' or 'no' question, Gabby," Eli persisted, interrupting her thoughts.

"Well... that's subjective..." she looked at her brother Eli who looked back at her questioningly. She then looked at Chris and Charlie and her palms started to sweat.

"Hey... didn't Papa Steve give you that shirt when you were like... 14?" Tanya said. She noticed Gabrielle's anxiety and tried to help by quickly changing the subject.

"Yes!" Gabrielle exclaimed, grateful for Tanya's intervention. "I remember when he first got me into the Transformers. I was so obsessed. He got me this shirt for my 15th birthday. I loved it so much, I couldn't throw it away. Now it's more of a... retro look," she said, looking down at it fondly.

"I'm sure it didn't fit the same way," Arthur grinned knowingly.

“You pig,” Natalie said, hitting him in the arm.

“We should go before it gets too dark.” Tanya tried to get them out before Gabrielle could be embarrassed any further. She hooked her arms around Natalie and Gabrielle’s and headed out the door with the guys close behind.

Eli took the women in his car while the guys rode in Chris’s car.

They drove to an old urban spot that had been there since they were in high school. As they pulled up, they could hear loud music coming from one of the buildings. People could barely be seen through the heavily tinted windows.

“I remember this place. We used to come here after your games,” Charlie said.

“Yea, it’s been a while,” Eli said fondly.

“Is it... uh... safe,” Natalie said nervously.

“Don’t be racist, Nat,” Arthur poked her.

“What?! I’m not-! That’s not what I-... shut up!” she said, turning red.

“Come on,” Tanya said leading the way as they headed towards the building.

They walked into the club to see a large dance floor at the center and multiple bar tables surrounding. People populated both the bar and the dance floor.

“Remember we used to come here for our dance battles,” Tanya said, turning to Gabrielle.

“Crap, that was so long ago,” Gabrielle said, biting her lip.

“I wonder if any of them still come here,” Tanya wondered.

“I’m guessing they do,” Chris pointed to a group of women on the dance floor going hard.

"Oh my gosh!" Tanya exclaimed, running up to them

"And there she goes. Let's go find a table," Eli said leading the group to a few stools by the bar. Arthur ordered drinks for everyone as they all took their seats. Chris, Charlie, and Eli sat on one side while Arthur, Natalie, and Gabrielle sat on the other.

"Charlie? Charlie Richardson?" A tall man with a thick brown beard, intense brown eyes, and a shaved head approached. He wore a sleeveless black t-shirt exposing tattoos all over his arm.

"Donnie! What's up, man?" Charlie said firmly, shaking his hand.

"Good! Good! It's been a while. What brings you to these parts?" Donnie asked, cleaning a glass.

"My cousins came to visit. Just showing them around," Charlie nonchalantly gestured to the rest of the table.

Donnie nodded in acknowledgement when his eyes landed on Gabrielle.

"You look familiar," Donnie said to her. "You from around here?"

"I grew up here as a kid but I'm currently living in LA. My name is Gabrielle. Nice to meet you," she smiled.

Donnie's eyes widened before a huge mischievous grin spread across his face. "Oh, **you're** Gabrielle!"

Gabrielle looked at him confused. Charlie coughed loudly, covering his mouth and gave Donnie a menacing look. Donnie faked a pout before grinning again.

"Must have seen your name or face somewhere," Donnie said, brushing off his public realization. "Nice to see you again, Chris."

"You too, Donnie," Chris nodded.

"How's business?"

"On hold. Trying to take care of things for my Dad at the moment," Chris said.

"Good ol' Steve! Man, I love that guy. How is he? Tell him I said 'hi'!"

Everyone averted their eyes with discomfort and sadness.

"He uh... he passed away recently," Charlie said, looking down.

Donnie's demeanor completely changed. He frowned, looking between Chris and Charlie. "Shit... I'm sorry, guys..."

Charlie nodded, unable to look anywhere but his glass.

Donnie disappeared for a moment and returned with a tray of shot glasses. He passed them all a glass.

"On the house... for your father," he said.

"Thanks, man." Charlie gave him a small smile. Donnie nodded and then disappeared to tend to other customers.

They each raised their glass. "To Steve Richardson." Cheers resounded around the table.

Charlie watched as Gabrielle hesitated to drink. Her eyes glazed over, lost in her thoughts for just a brief moment before she finally downed the shot.

"I see some beautiful ladies that need my company," Arthur grinned. He hungrily checked out two dark-skinned black women sitting at the other end of the bar.

"Bruh... those fine ass sistas will wipe the floor with you," Eli laughed.

"Eli's right. Those women are way out of your league. You'll just end up embarrassing yourself," Natalie mocked.

"Please. My charm breaks all barriers. Including racial ones," Arthur grinned.

"You are so full of shit," Natalie rolled her eyes.

"Let me tell you all the ways you are wrong before you set yourself up for failure," Eli teased. He turned in his chair, getting into debate mode.

Gabrielle and Chris chuckled, watching them argue. Charlie took a sip of his beer with a roll of his eyes.

When Gabrielle finished her strawberry daiquiri, Chris asked if she wanted another.

"Hmm," she pondered. "What are you drinking?" she asked, eyeing his glass.

"You won't like it," Chris said.

"Don't presume to know me, Christopher Richardson," she said, scrounging up her nose.

Charlie snickered. "You know damn well that Chris and I like the hard stuff. You like the fruity stuff."

"How sexist of you, Charles! Gimme that!" She snatched the drink out of Chris's grasp. With a snicker, Chris lifted his hands in defeat.

"Don't say we didn't warn you," Chris teased.

Gabrielle made a face before taking a large gulp of the drink. She immediately froze, keeping the liquid in her mouth. Chris and Charlie watched her, waiting for a reaction she was not willing to give.

She reluctantly swallowed hard before making a pained face. They both burst into laughter.

"Told you," Chris said, grabbing his drink. Charlie waved for the bartender to bring her another daiquiri.

"My throat is on fire," she coughed. "What is that? Transmission fluid?!"

"I'm surprised you even know what that is," Charlie teased, passing her the daiquiri.

“You can thank Papa Steve for that one,” she giggled. Suddenly her face fell and she looked down into her cup. “I really miss him...”

Charlie and Chris watched her in silence. She stirred the daiquiri with her finger and brought it to her lips for a taste. When she felt their gaze upon her, she quickly looked up.

“Wow, I’m the worst. I’m not even his real daughter and I feel like I’m taking this harder than either of you,” she sighed.

“You’re as close to a daughter that he ever had,” Chris said comfortingly. She looked up at him and smiled. She went to say something to both of them when Tanya came running back with 2 of the women.

“Look who I found!” Tanya said excitedly. Gabrielle moved over to make room for two of the women from the dance floor. One was a thick dark-skinned black woman with braids down to her waist. She wore a golden halter top and white fitted jeans. The other was a brown-skinned black woman with cornrows, wearing a blue fitted body-con dress.

Eli, Arthur and Natalie turned to greet Tanya.

“Whaaaaaaa?! Gabby girl! Is that you?” Angie said excitedly.

“Angie? Rhaven! Oh my gosh it’s so nice to see you girls! I haven’t seen you in years!” Gabrielle exclaimed. She eagerly hugged both of them.

“Yea, girl. I heard you became some big hot shot doctor over in Hollywood makin’ all these coins. That’s why you forgot all us lil people?” Rhaven joked.

“No! No, I could never forget you guys. And L.A. is totally overrated. You gotta sell your soul a little to get to that level of success,” Gabrielle said.

"Well... all I know is... I needs me a sugar daddy," Rhaven grinned.

"Speaking of sugar daddies, I see you brought the rich white kids club," Angie said. Chris and Charlie smirked, very amused by the conversation happening before them.

"Ladies, you remember Charlie and Chris," Eli said, reintroducing the guys.

"Good to see you again," Chris greeted the women.

"Hol' up... LIL ASS CHARLIE AND LIL ASS CHRIS?! Zammm zaddyyy! Y'all glowed up!" Rhaven said shamelessly.

"Oh my gosh, Rhaven. Why? Why are you like this?" Tanya groaned. She rolled her eyes and turned away in embarrassment as Chris and Charlie laughed.

"I'm just saying..." Rhaven said, reaching to touch Chris's bicep.

"Rhaven! Stop it!" Gabrielle said, slapping her hand away.

"Ow! Jeez... I need to get me a fine ass white boy is all I'm saying..." she muttered.

Tanya rolled her eyes. "And this is Natalie and Arthur. They're Steve Richardson's niece and nephew."

"Oh! Oh... wow... I'm really sorry, y'all. Steve was a really great guy. That dude really helped bring this city up when we was down in the shit," Angie said, giving her condolences.

"Yea, damn. My pops was really broken up about it when he heard. They worked on so many housing projects together. He used to rave about all the great ideas Steve came up with and how hard he went to make sure we got those housing projects done. He really left his imprint on this city. We saw y'all at the funeral but... we didn't wanna disturb, y'all," Rhaven added.

"It's okay, ladies... and thank you for the kind words," Chris smiled sadly.

"Well, enough with this depressing conversation. Would you ladies like a drink?" Arthur asked.

"Ooh, I like this one," Rhaven flirted.

"Rhaven! No!" Gabrielle warned.

"Actually, we was just talkin' about doing one of our old routines from back in the day when we ran the High. You wanna join?" Angie asked Tanya and Gabrielle.

"First of all, when did y'all **ever** run the High," Eli interjected.

"Shut up, Eli!" Tanya said, putting her hand in Eli's face. "Hell yes!" she said excitedly, looking at Gabrielle.

"Oh man... I don't know if I remember. I haven't danced in a while. I don't know if I'm ready to embarrass myself," Gabrielle chuckled nervously.

"Come on, baby sis. Go enjoy yourself," Eli encouraged her.

"Here. This should help. A little liquid courage." Natalie pushed a tall shot glass towards her. Gabrielle grinned and downed the shot as they cheered her on.

"Okay! Okay! ... Let's go!" she said. She followed Tanya, Angie and Rhaven back to the dance floor to greet the other women from her dance group.

The others talked among themselves, until the music got louder. When "Run Up" by Major Lazer started playing, the rest of the club immediately hyped up. They turned to watch the women on the dance floor.

Gabrielle caught the attention of two men in particular. She swayed her hips to the music and sensually moved her body to the lyrics of the song. She and Tanya giggled to each other as they pulled an unsuspecting guy from the crowd to dance on.

An old familiar side of Gabrielle that had been repressed for far too long had reared its head. She pushed the thought of Damian possibly cheating on her to the back of her mind. She gave way to the music and grind her ass on the lucky guy behind her. She twerked seductively, dropping to the floor on the beat. He placed his hands on her hips to follow her movements as she playfully wiggled her ass on his crotch. She was completely unaware of the spectacular show she was giving to two envious men, both madly in love with her.

When the Nicki Minaj lyrics came on, the women pushed the man to the side while laughing hysterically. They broke out into a coordinated West Indian dance step that set the crowd on fire. As Gabrielle moved her body, she looked up and caught Chris looking back at her. She smirked at him flirtatiously before spinning into a line step with the others.

When the song finished, the crowd erupted into cheers as the music changed to another Caribbean banger. Trying to catch her breath, Gabrielle ran back to the table.

"Damn, baby sis! Didn't know you still had it in you," Eli laughed.

"Me neither!" she blurted. She shook her hands and jumped up and down with pure excitement. "I've been such a med school obsessed goober that I forgot I had rhythm!" The rest of them laughed at her animated revelation.

"Time to show Posh Spice how to have a good time," Gabrielle said. She grabbed Charlie's half-finished beer straight from his hands and guzzled it down, making a pained face.

"Hey!" Charlie said in shock. She winked at him and grabbed Natalie's hand.

"Posh Spice? Do you mean me? I'll have you know I was Baby Spic-woah!" Natalie was cut off as Gabrielle dragged her onto the dance floor.

"Let's go, Barbie!" Gabrielle laughed, leading her into the crowd.

The guys watched in amusement as Natalie struggled to get past her awkward white girl dancing and into a soft rhythm. Gabrielle turned to face Natalie, grabbed her hips, and slowly started grinding to get her into an easy pace. Soon Natalie caught on and the women wind together to the beat.

Gabrielle once again got lost in the music and moved her body completely in sync with the melody. Chris felt anxious and inappropriate watching her. He turned away from her momentarily, until he could calm his raging hormones. However, Charlie never turned away. He watched Gabrielle close her eyes and feel up her body to the beat of the song. He was entranced by her fluid movements. He had never seen this open, carefree, and unapologetic side of her.

Suddenly, a random guy came up to Gabrielle and started dancing with her. She looked at him hesitantly but didn't stop dancing and decided to appease him. She danced with her back to him as he placed his hands on her hips matching her movements. His hands started to inch up her waist as he craned his head into her neck to kiss her. He gave her a light squeeze under her breast, and she forcefully pushed him away.

Eli stood up to see over the crowd when he saw his sister push the guy away. Chris looked to see what had happened and caught the guy reaching for Gabrielle's ass. He pushed his crotch into her and leaned in for a kiss. This time she shoved him more harshly and slapped him in the face. Angry and embarrassed, the man went to aggressively grab her but before he could do anything, Charlie jumped in front of Gabrielle and punched the guy in the face.

The guy grabbed his nose, gushing blood. He reached up to hit Charlie but Charlie dodged his fist. He ducked and punched the guy in the stomach before elbowing him at the back of his neck, sending him face first into the ground. The guy's friends came rushing to fight Charlie, but he managed to take two of them on, protectively keeping Gabrielle behind him. Arthur and Eli ran up to help Charlie fight off the men while Chris pulled both Tanya and Natalie away from the brawl.

"Charlie! Charlie!" Gabrielle shouted. Charlie had already knocked out the two guys that tried to jump him. He was kneeling on the ground, hunched over, and wailing on the first guy that had harassed Gabrielle.

"Charlie! Please, stop! Charlie!" she shouted again, trying to grab his wrist. She was nearly yanked forward by the sheer force of his punch as she tried to hold him back.

Charlie looked up at her and saw fear in her eyes. She clung to his wrist for dear life trying to keep him from hitting the guy again. He looked down at the guy whose face was nearly unrecognizable and released him.

"Come on," Charlie growled. He grabbed her hand and led her out of the club with Arthur close behind. Eli tried to apologize to Security.

They all met up outside, heavily panting. Tanya ran up to Eli and embraced him passionately with great relief.

"Are you okay?" Eli asked her.

"Yes, yes! I'm fine," Tanya said, kissing him relieved.

"Gabs!" Chris said as Gabrielle ran into his arms. He squeezed her tight and could feel her panting heavily against his chest.

"Are you alright?" Chris said. He stroked her hair comfortingly and looked down at her.

"I'm fine," she smiled at him. She then ran into the arms of her brother and walked with him, Tanya, and Natalie back to the car. Gabrielle glanced back to see Charlie staring at her. He had the same dark look in his eyes as she walked away.

~*~

They drove back in silence, perturbed by the night's ending events. Eli took Tanya home and Gabrielle insisted she stay with the Richardsons to make sure they were okay.

When they got to the house Natalie hugged Gabrielle.

"Well aside from how it ended... thanks for a great night," she said to her.

"Good night, Nat," Gabrielle responded. Natalie walked upstairs to one of the guest rooms to sleep.

Gabrielle could hear Arthur and Chris in the den talking. She looked everywhere for Charlie but could not find him. She finally looked outside to the patio and saw him standing alone, smoking a cigarette.

"Charlie?" she called out. He glanced at her briefly and then quickly averted his gaze.

She walked up to him. "Are you okay?" she asked.

"I'm fine," he said, taking another puff of the cigarette. She looked down at his hand. It was bloody and wrapped with a cloth through which the blood had already soaked through.

"Your hand!" she exclaimed.

"It's nothing. I've dealt with worse," he insisted.

"Charles Richardson. I'm a surgeon, for crying out loud. At least let me bandage you up properly," she demanded.

He looked at her with deep, forest green eyes and sighed begrudgingly. He put the cigarette out and allowed her to guide him back into the house. Leading him to one of the bathrooms, she turned on the faucet and let the water run over his hand. Most of the blood belonged to the other guy, but she could see the cuts on his knuckles clearer now, along with some other old scars.

"You have so many... scars..." she said, running her fingers over them gently.

"Like I said... I've dealt with worse..." Charlie muttered.

She gently dabbed the cuts on his hand, pressing the towel to his wounds to stop the bleeding. He watched her intently as she focused on his injuries.

"Thank you," she said, breaking the silence. "For protecting me."

At first, he said nothing before finally responding. "You're welcome."

She put small bandages on his cuts and finally wrapped his hand with a fresh, new cloth.

"There," she said finally. "Much better."

She smiled at her handiwork and then looked up at him to see his green eyes staring deeply into hers. They had softened. For the first time since she had returned to PA, he wasn't looking at her like he hated her.

They locked eyes for a few seconds. Her breathing shortened. Her body closed the gap between them. She barely noticed her hand had crept up from his hand to his forearm, but he did. He couldn't look away from her. His eyes went from her beautiful brown ones to her full, plump lips. He wanted to kiss them so badly. To nibble on them. Suck on them.

Their lips were inches apart from each other. Gabrielle felt herself being pulled in. The intensity of his gaze had her lost in a different consciousness. She moved closer to him and slowly tilted her head up. Charlie watched her curiously, debating his next move. She slowly closed her eyes as if waiting for him, when a knock came at the door.

"Are you guys alright?" came Chris's voice from the other side of the door. Gabrielle opened her eyes startled and immediately stepped back.

She opened the door to see Chris. He looked at her, then at Charlie, curious and confused.

"I was just fixing his hand. He injured it pretty badly when he was defending my honor and all that," she teased. She looked back at Charlie whose gaze was still upon her. He lifted his eyes to Chris and raised his hand to show his brother her handiwork.

"She did a decent job," he assured Chris. Gabrielle scoffed, feigning offense. She smiled at Charlie but all that he returned was that same intense gaze.

Gabrielle turned to Chris. "I'm... gonna go to bed. Can I crash here tonight?" she asked.

"Of course," Chris said, letting her pass by him.

"Thanks... night, guys." She quickly rushed upstairs to one of the guest rooms. "What the hell was that..." she whispered to herself.

~*~

Charlie laid in his bed, back at his own apartment, going over the day's events. He had been more drawn to Gabrielle than ever. He wasn't sure how he could stay away from her. He tried being as cold and distant from her as possible, but she wouldn't stop being so kind and loving to him, as she'd always been.

He closed his eyes shut and held his breath. He tried to remember her soft touch as she tended to his injuries. He ran a finger over his knuckles, tracing her prior movements.

"She doesn't belong to me." He remembered Chris's words from earlier. Would it be so bad for him to make a move? No... he couldn't. It wouldn't be right.

He was grateful that Chris hadn't asked why they were in the bathroom so long. He couldn't wrap his mind around this strange thing he had going on with his brother. They were both in love with the same woman, but both agreed not to pursue her. Charlie was beginning to regret this agreement. He loved his brother. But he desperately loved Gabrielle. He wanted her so badly and each day that desire intensified. He didn't know what to do.

"She'll be gone soon. Back in L.A. and out of our lives again," he reminded himself.

He rolled over in his bed and closed his eyes. Falling asleep to the images of Gabrielle dancing, but with him.

~*~

6

The Businessman and the Doctor

~*~

It had been a few days since the funeral. Gabrielle was ready to head back to L.A. Her mother came into the room to see her putting her clothes into her bag.

"What are you doing?" Clara asked.

"I'm packing to go back to L.A.," Gabrielle responded.

"You can't leave yet. We still have so much to do!" Clara exclaimed.

"Huh? What do you mean? We've already had the wake and the funeral," Gabrielle said confused.

"We promised that we would help the Richardsons get Steve's building finished so those kids have a home. Sally is going to need all the help she can get. She's got so much on her plate," Clara said, sitting on the bed.

"Do you guys really need me for that?" Gabrielle asked exasperated.

"We need all hands on deck. You're part of this community, Gabrielle," Clara said sternly.

"I know, Mom. It's just... I have this thing in L.A.-" Gabrielle started.

"Family comes first." Clara stood up, kissed her daughter on the forehead, and headed towards the door. "You don't come home often. This is an important and sensitive time. You can stay a little while longer," Clara stated, rather than asked.

"Yes, Mama..." Gabrielle sighed. She put her shirt on the bed instead of in the bag. She waited for her mother to leave and then paced around the room. What was she going to do? She told Damian she'd be back in time for the art gala.

Overwhelmed with anxiety, she walked outside of the house and dialed Damian's number.

But again, she received no answer.

"What the hell?!" she said out loud. She dialed once more, and this time a woman picked up.

"Hello?" came the woman's voice.

"Hello? Who's this? Where's Damian?" Gabrielle said impatiently, her blood starting to boil. She could hear the woman giggling and Damian's voice in the background.

"Daaaaamian! Stoooop it!" the girl giggled on the phone. *"Sorry, hello?"* the girl said again.

"WHO **IS** THIS?!" Gabrielle shouted this time. No answer, whispering, and then a click.

"Okay. **Fuck** this!" Gabrielle said angrily. She stormed back into the house to unpack.

~*~

After calling the hospital to ask for an extended leave, Gabrielle threw on her favorite hip hugging jeans and a soft white t-shirt. She headed over to the Richardson estate where she spotted Sally in the garden.

"Hi, Mrs. Sally," Gabrielle greeted her.

"Oh! Gabrielle! So glad you came over," Sally said struggling to her feet. She warmly embraced Gabrielle.

"My mom told me you needed some help getting things together?" Gabrielle inquired.

"Oh, yes. I've been packing up as much stuff as possible for the building. There's still quite a lot. I have a few things in the living room. Could you wrap them in paper and put them in the boxes on the floor?" Sally asked.

"Certainly," Gabrielle responded. She walked into the house and spotted the items to be packed. She took off her sweater and sneakers to get comfortable and got started.

While wrapping, she came across a Teenage Mutant Ninja Turtle lunch box.

"I remember this! This used to be Chris's," she said out loud.

"Actually, it was Charlie's, but he made me swap it for the Power Rangers lunch box," Chris said. The tall oldest Richardson son stepped into the living room, startling her.

"Chris!" she smiled brightly. "I'm just packing up some stuff for the building for your mom."

"Wow... I haven't seen some of this stuff in over a decade," Chris said. He picked up one of his old action figures to inspect.

"Oh, that reminds me," she said. She revealed the old Dragonball Z-themed football from her bag. "Remember this?"

"Oh shit! Look at that!" he said, taking the ball from her. "This thing is still inflated?"

"Actually, Eli inflated it because he's a dork," she chuckled. "But he knew you would appreciate it. Remember we used to pretend it was a fireball?"

"We had some good times with this thing," he said. He squeezed it a little and pretended to throw it.

"Yea, I remember how many times Charlie and I crushed you and

Eli at football," she teased.

Chris scoffed. "Yea right..."

"Oh? Are we suffering from amnesia, Christopher?"

"Gabs... you've **never** beaten me at football. I mean... look at me," he said, showing off his muscular biceps. Gabrielle immediately got hot, taking in his very alluring physique but then quickly scoffed at him.

"That sounds like a challenge, Richardson," she said, snatching the ball out of his hands. She quickly put back on her sneakers and sweater in such a comical way it made Chris laugh.

"Oh please," he said laughing, as he watched her walk towards the door.

"What? Scared?" she mocked. She winked at him, beckoning him with her finger.

Chris hesitated for a moment. He tried to remind himself that her beckoning was an innocent playful one and not a seductive one. It's just a game after all. Like when they were kids.

"Alright, you're on," he grinned. He ran past her, through the door and snatched the ball from out of her grasp. Chris ran down the yard, giving him quite a bit of distance from Gabrielle.

"You ready?" he asked her.

"Are you?" she teased.

He smirked at her. "Okay...1, 2, 3, 4 hut, hut, hike!" He faked a throw and ran in her direction with the ball tucked under his arm. Gabrielle immediately charged after him. He tried to throw her off, but she was too fast. She leaped forward, head first, with both arms stretched out, aiming for his abdomen. She tackled him hard to the ground.

They wrestled around on the grass laughing. When they finally came to a stop, Gabrielle had landed on top of Chris with her hands on his chest. The football had escaped them and lay off to the side, while his hands held her steady by the hips.

"Damn. You pack a harder hit than I remember, Johansson," he laughed.

"I've always packed a hard hit, you goof," she snickered.

Gabrielle looked down at Chris and was taken back by the loving look in his eyes. He gazed at her fondly. The warm smile that crept across his pink lips was almost too inviting. The firm grip he had on her hips and the little bit of skin his fingers touched on her waist titillated her. Their lips were inches apart and Gabrielle couldn't tear her eyes away from him. She was completely enraptured.

In that moment, Chris found Gabrielle utterly breathtaking. She felt so good and perfect in his arms. Even though they were laying on the ground, he wished they could lay there like that forever.

He looked into her beautiful, deep brown eyes and saw it. She wanted him. As much as he wanted her. He felt her lean down a little and he moved his head up slightly to meet her.

"Chris..." she whispered nervously. He could feel her trembling with want.

Suddenly, his phone buzzed, startling them both. Gabrielle immediately crawled off of him and sat on the ground blinking. Her cheeks flushed and a rosy red tinted her mocha skin.

Chris sat up and blushed back at her before looking down at his phone. It was the office.

"Sorry. One sec," he said to her. "Hello?"

"Mr. Richardson, we have an issue at the West Hudson office. We really need your final say," came a voice from the other end.

"You guys can't figure it out without me? I'm still on bereavement," Chris responded.

"I know, sir. I apologize for that. But, we wouldn't have called you if it wasn't an emergency. We're not sure we'll even be able to make the deadline at this rate," the voice pleaded.

"Alright. Send the car and forward me the files. I'll be there in 20," he said.

Gabrielle furrowed her brows with a frown as he hung up the phone.

"Do you have to go?" she asked, trying to hide her disappointment.

His heart melted a little. He didn't want to leave her. Something felt off about her and he felt like she needed him. She seemed a bit more vulnerable than usual.

"Yea, I have to head to the office for an emergency meeting," he said apologetically.

She looked down with a slightly forlorn expression on her face. "Oh," she muttered, picking at the grass stems beneath her.

He slumped his shoulders in response. He couldn't just leave her. It didn't feel right. "Well, this isn't the norm but, would you like to come with me?" he asked her.

"To your office? Are you sure?" she perked up, somewhat relieved that he offered.

"Yea, of course. It shouldn't take too long. Plus, I'll take you to this really nice frozen yogurt shop that recently opened up on one of my properties."

"You had me at frozen yogurt," she grinned. He helped her to her feet as a black Mercedes pulled up to the side of the house.

"Looks like the car is here. Ready?" he said, holding out his hand to her.

"Oh wow! You got it like that, Chris?" she teased. Chris rolled his eyes with a smirk. She looked down at her attire. "Uh... should I change... or... something?"

"No, you're perfect the way you are," he said smoothly. He tried to ignore the butterfly feelings in his stomach and the reaction he elicited from her. She bit her lip and took his hand as they walked to the car together.

As they rode in the back of the car, Chris reviewed the files on his phone while Gabrielle gazed out of the window.

"This place looks so different now," she said in awe.

"Yea, a lot has changed since you left," Chris said absent-mindedly.

"And yet… it still feels like home," she said more to herself.

Chris looked up to see her staring intently out of the window. He could tell something was wrong. But he wasn't sure if he should prod her about it.

"Hey," he said, touching her leg. She turned to him to see the concern in his crystal, clear blue eyes. "You okay?"

"Yea, I'm fine." She shook off her bad vibes and smiled at him. "I'm just glad I get to spend some time with my best friend."

"Me too," he smiled back at her. The car pulled up to a tall, modern glass building shaped like a triangle. Its regality reflected in the scenic pond next to it.

"Woah! This is your office building? It's beautiful!" she said, taking his hand as he helped her out of the car. They walked up to the door where two doormen let them in. Walking into the mirrored lobby, Gabrielle admired the fancy chandeliers on a very high ceiling. Crowds of men and women in business suits moved like rush hour traffic.

"Chris?" she said nervously, looking around.

"Hmm?" he mumbled. Completely engrossed in his phone, Chris walked to the elevator, while she trailed closely behind.

"I feel *severely* under-dressed right now. Are you sure I'm allowed in here?" she asked, taking his hand to get his attention.

He looked down at her worried face and then looked around at the other people. "Gabs, you're fine," he chuckled. "I do own the business after all."

"You **own** it?!" she said shocked. She shuffled into the elevator after him.

"Yea, I'm the CEO," he shrugged, as if it should have been obvious.

"I'm mad you're saying that like it's no big deal," Gabrielle laughed. "You're like 'Oh yea, by the way, I'm the CEO. I also know Bill Gates and Elon Musk'," she said mockingly.

"I actually **did** meet Bill at a few conferences. I also worked with Elon on a-" Chris started.

"You're on a FIRST-NAME BASIS?!" Gabrielle blurted. "Damn, Chris! Well excuse the hell out of me, Mr. Big Shot!" She playfully poked him in the side. "Anyway… I still feel under-dressed."

"It's okay, Gabs, really," he reassured her. "I mean look at me." He opened his arms to show off his plain white t-shirt under his casual blue cardigan.

"That's not fair. You always look good," she said before she could stop herself. When she realized what she said, it was too late. Chris was already grinning at her.

"I mean... professional-like. You're always so well put-together. Businessman... CEO... type," she said nervously. She closed her eyes and mouthed "stupid", wishing the elevator would hurry up and get to their floor.

When the door finally opened, they stepped out into a sleek glass lobby that was carpeted and decorated with plush couches. A pretty blonde woman sat at a corner desk as reception.

"Mr. Richardson, sir!" she greeted, immediately standing up. "Mr. Hartfield is waiting for you in conference room B."

"Thank you, Cecilia," Chris nodded. He waved at her and headed in the opposite direction. Gabrielle smiled at the woman who only saw fit to respond with a cold stare of her own.

Gabrielle followed Chris down the hall, still unaware that she was holding his hand. He led her into the conference room where there were two men in suits.

"Christopher!" the older man called out greeting him at the door. "I'm so glad you could make it. My apologies. I know you're still grieving. It means a lot that you came down."

"Of course, Bill. This is my good friend Dr. Gabrielle Johansson. She came all the way down from Los Angeles to spend time with my family and honor my father," Chris said, introducing them.

"Dr. Johansson. It's a pleasure to meet you," Bill said, taking her hand.

"Pleasure to meet you, as well," Gabrielle responded.

Bill instructed the men to set up the presentation, addressing their concerns about one of the construction projects.

"You can have a seat in my office across the hall in the corner on the right. Don't want to bore you with this stuff," Chris whispered to her.

"Okay." She walked to his office while he spoke with the men. He had an incredible corner office view of the city and the pond surrounded by all the beautiful foliage. She sat in his leather chair and looked over his desk. He had papers everywhere but surprisingly was still very organized.

On his desk were several pictures of his family. Some pictures from college sports. Some pictures of his first business venture. She sat back in his chair and noticed a smaller picture near the corner of his desk. It was a picture of him, Eli, herself and Charlie from high school. They looked so young and happy. She held the picture in her hand and ran her thumb over each face, smiling to herself.

A few minutes later, Chris walked in to check on her. "Hey. You okay in here?"

"Yea. Your office is incredible! I'm officially jealous. Can we swap? Operating room for your corner office," she teased.

"Ah, if only I were as skilled and special as you," he grinned. He walked over to her and sat on the edge of the desk. She couldn't help but blush at his compliment.

"So, is everything going okay? You guys finished already?" she asked him.

"Well, no. We've got an issue at one of the properties. There's been complaints of tenants getting sick. We're trying to get to the root of the problem," Chris sighed deeply, with a shake of his head.

"Oh. Do you know, sick from what?" she asked.

"Unfortunately not. We might have to call in a specialist to get an expert opinion."

Gabrielle pondered. "Well, I may specialize in neurology but I did a lot of research on illnesses for my senior year thesis. Do you mind if I sit in and listen?" she asked.

"Oh! Of course. I didn't want to bother you with it though," he said to her.

"Nonsense, Chris! I'd love to help," she said eagerly. "Give me something to do!"

Chris chuckled amused. He got up and led her back to the conference room.

"Bill, Dr. Johansson is going to sit in with us. She's one of L.A.'s top surgeons so I'm hoping to get her opinion on this," Chris announced. He took his seat at the head of the table.

"That would be fantastic. Thank you, Dr. Johansson. Well, as we were just discussing: The tenants are all showing symptoms of muscle cramps, sinus issues, blurred vision, diarrhea and the like. Here's a list of other symptoms," Bill said, handing her a sheet.

"At first, we thought it had to do with rodents, but we've had the entire place inspected and even hired a league of exterminators. But nothing has changed," Bill continued.

Gabrielle looked over the paper listing all the symptoms reported.

"Do you have a description or picture of the surrounding area?" she asked. Bill handed her a sheet showing a beautiful tall building surrounded by a pond and garden near the woods.

"I'm not 100% positive, but it sounds to me like your tenants are experiencing Chronic Inflammatory Response Syndrome," she said finally. She looked up at all blank stares.

"Sinus issues, muscle cramps, diarrhea... These are all common symptoms of CIRS. Also, the majority of your tenants with this issue are at the lower levels of the building. You guys have a beautiful outdoors, but you're located pretty close to the woods. I believe you guys might have a mold issue," she said, handing them back the papers.

Chris cocked his head to the side sizing her up and looking very impressed.

Gabrielle turned to speak to Chris. "You guys should get someone to check out the corners and dampest parts of the building. You might have a mold problem. Don't forget to check behind walls. It can be pretty hard to find if you don't look hard enough," she said.

"That's very helpful! Thank you, Dr. Johansson. We'll look right into it," Bill said.

"Thank you for all of your help, Bill," Chris nodded. He stood to his feet, shaking Bill's hand.

"Thank you, Mr. Richardson. And I'm sorry again about your father. Give your mother my condolences." Bill respectfully nodded to Chris and then to Gabrielle.

"I like her. You should put her on our staff," Bill joked.

"No, can't put a price on her," Chris smirked. He glanced at Gabrielle who was furiously blushing from his compliment.

Chris walked the men out and turned to see Gabrielle staring out of the large window.

"You are pretty impressive, Dr. Johansson," he said, walking up behind her.

"Me?! Chris, you're a freaking rockstar!" she exclaimed, turning around. He chuckled and leaned against the edge of the conference table.

"What are you talking about?" he asked.

"You do all of this incredible work. And you do so much for those who don't have. I didn't know you were making apartment buildings for the homeless. Who even *does* that?! What are you? Captain America?" she teased.

Chris laughed amused. "I try to be."

"I'm so proud of you," she sighed. She sat next to him and leaned her head on his shoulder. "I think it's telling that we both decided to do something that involved helping people. Your dad is what inspired that in us. His goodness is infectious."

Chris smiled at her inspirational words. But his face immediately fell when realization set in. He hated having to hide so much from her. Suddenly, there was a knock at the door.

"Come in," Chris said. Cecilia the receptionist opened the door.

"Mr. Richardson, sir? Someone is here to see you from Gullatt & Sons," she said.

"I'll be there momentarily," he sighed. They walked out of the conference room and into the hallway where two men in suits were waiting.

"Give me a minute, Gabs. I'll be quick," he said to her. She nodded and watched him stroll towards the men. Gabrielle smiled, looking at him in awe. So proud of the man he had become. She felt warm and comfortable with him. She strangely missed being in his arms.

Her phone went off, knocking her out of her thoughts. She garnered the attention of many, including Chris. She mouthed "sorry" and walked further down the hall to take the call.

"Hello?" she said without looking at the caller ID.

"Gabrielle?" It was Damian. Her breath caught in her throat. *"Gabrielle!"* his voice came again.

"H-hey Damian," she responded hesitantly.

"I thought you were coming back home today," he said agitated.

"I tried calling you to tell you that my mother needed me a little while longer. You haven't answered any of my calls," she said exasperated.

"What the hell does she still need you for?" he demanded.

"The Richardsons are going through a really tough time, Damian," she whispered irritably.

"Bull fucking shit," he snorted. *"You're* ***my*** *fiancée. I expect to take priority over random people you've barely spoken to in years."*

"The Richardsons are family!" she whispered loudly, causing Chris to glance up at her. "And **now**? **Now** I'm your fiancée? When you've had strange women answering your phone and touching all over you?"

"What did you just say?" Damian snarled. She could hear the seething anger in his voice. Normally she would never talk to him like this in person and she questioned if she had lost her mind. Truth was, she was terrified of Damian. For what he's done to her, and what he could still do to her...

"I just...I keep seeing these pictures online of you with another woman. And every time I call, a woman answers your phone. What am I supposed to think?" she said, trying to tone down her anger.

Damian snickered condescendingly. *"You're imagining things again because of your insecurities."*

Gabrielle felt her anger flare up. "Are you kidding me?! I am **not** imagining things! And I'm not insecure! What the fuck, Damian?!"

"See... you're ***really*** *unattractive when you get all bitchy like this,"* he said between his laughs.

"Excuse me?!" she squealed. This time she was loud enough to be heard from down the hall.

Chris narrowed his eyes as he looked at Gabrielle. Something was wrong. Something was **very** wrong. She was pacing. When she squealed, he felt the need to intervene.

"You heard me. Now, stop being such a fucking insecure drama queen and bring your ungrateful ass home," Damian threatened. Gabrielle had hot tears streaming down her face. Her heart was gushing with anguish.

"I can't believe what I'm hearing! First you cheat on me and now you're talking to me like I'm nothing but shit! If you wanted someone else, all you had to do was end this. Stop putting me through this, Damian!" she cried, tears fully pouring.

"You're being a real pain in my ass, Gabrielle. And you're making me really angry. I don't know who the fuck you think you're talking to." She could hear the cynicism in his voice. *" I'm not ending this relationship. You're mine. You'll always* **be** *mine. It's not up for discussion."*

Gabrielle felt the air leave her lungs. His threats rang in her ears as the room started to spin. She gathered as much courage as she could to speak her peace.

"I am not yours, Damian! This is over! Leave me the fuck alone!" she seethed into the phone and ended the call. She closed her eyes shut, letting the tears fall. A part of her felt relieved. The other part felt utterly terrified. She clutched her chest trying to breathe. The room was spinning faster now, and she felt like she was going to pass out.

~*~

7

A Tale of Two Cities

~*~

With arms folded and eyes narrowed in concentration, Chris was in an intense conversation with his clients. But then he saw Gabrielle down the corridor abruptly slide down the wall to the floor. He heard her sobbing… and he felt his stomach lurch…

"Gentlemen, I'm sorry. But something important has come up and I really must be going. I want to make sure we get this situation resolved, so let's continue this later. I'll have my secretary schedule a meeting," he said, ending the conversation abruptly. He shook their hands and immediately took off in Gabrielle's direction.

"Hey! Gabs! What's wrong?!" he asked anxiously. He kneeled down in front of her. With eyes closed, her head leaned back in anguish. He could see tears still streaming down her face.

"Gabrielle!" he said again. He gently grabbed her by the shoulders and shook her to attention. Her eyes popped open and the look on her face was that of confusion.

Gabrielle caught Chris staring at her with the most anxiety-ridden look she'd ever seen from him. His beautiful bright blue eyes peeled into hers. She snapped out of her anguish and quickly shook her head.

"Chris. I'm sorry. I… I think I was out of it for a minute," she laughed nervously.

"What's going on?" he asked, helping her to her feet.

"I think... I'm just not feeling too well... maybe a bit hungry," she said, wiping her face.

"That's not hunger. What's going on, Gabs. Why were you crying? You can tell me," he insisted.

"It's nothing, Chris. Really. I didn't mean to freak you out," she said, trying to calm him down.

"Gab-" he started again.

"And if I'm not mistaken, you owe me frozen yogurt." She playfully pinched him in the waist.

Chris looked down at her bright smiling face. Her pearly whites were showing, but her face was still tear-stained. Sadness bled through her eyes. But out of respect for her feelings, he didn't want to push her. Not if she wasn't ready to talk about it.

He sighed with frustration as she latched onto his arm. "Alright," he said reluctantly.

They left the building and took a short walk to the frozen yogurt shop down the block. After they got their frozen treat, they walked to the nearby park by the pond.

Gabrielle hooked her arm around Chris's. "This place is so beautiful," she said, taking in the breathtaking view as the sun set over the horizon. "Did you design all of this?"

Chris nodded. "I had the vision in my head for years before I had the honor of making it a reality."

"It's a Christopher Richardson masterpiece," she grinned. "I'm so jealous of your talents."

"You have no reason to be jealous of me, Gabs," Chris chuckled.

"Are you kidding? I've always been jealous of you. Since we were kids," she laughed.

Chris raised his brows in surprise. "Really? For what?"

"Oh, you know. The fact that you guys just had everything and got whatever you wanted," she shook her head. "But I mean...you guys never acted like snobby rich kids like so many other people we knew. That's what I loved about you guys. You were always so humble, kind and giving. And you were like that to everyone, regardless of who they were or where they came from. Even willing to share your own father." She smiled to herself and clutched his arm a little tighter.

"Hmm, I never thought about it that way," Chris pondered. "You and Eli have always been so close to our family. It was never a second thought to us. What was ours was yours."

"You boy scout," Gabrielle grinned, teasing him.

"Now you sound like Uncle Gerald," Chris laughed.

"Drink this whiskey like a real man, Christopher. Put some hair on that chest!" Gabrielle guttered. She put on her best Gerald impression, sending Chris into a fit of laughter.

"I have never heard anyone do an impression of him. But this is already the best one," Chris laughed.

"Eli's the best with impressions. Remember all the impressions he made of Mr. Simmons?"

"Oh man, yes! That guy hated us. Especially after that prank."

"You mean the one when we put all the players' dirty gym socks in the vents of his classroom?" Gabrielle grinned mischievously.

Chris nodded. "That room smelled awful for like a month. He ended class 20 minutes early every day cause he couldn't take it."

"Whatever. He deserved it. He was the worst. Especially to you. I still can't believe he got you suspended from football for a whole season!"

"You really gotta get over that, Gabs."

"Never! I'm your ride or die, Chris! Anyone who dares come after you gon' catch these hands!" she said, clapping her hands.

Chris laughed heartily. He clutched her hand a bit tighter. A brief silence fell as they walked and Chris dared to ask.

"When are you going to tell me what's going on with you, Gabs?" He spoke up, looking straight ahead at the path ahead of them.

Gabrielle sighed heavily. "There's nothing going on with me, Chris..."

He stopped walking and turned to face her, grabbing her hand. "I've known you for over 20 years, Gabs… We're best friends... I can tell when something's wrong."

She couldn't handle the look of conviction in his eyes and looked down away from him.

"Hey…" He put a finger beneath her chin and lifted her head ever so gently for her eyes to meet his. "You can talk to me, Gabs. You know that, right?"

She looked into his eyes and saw the deep concern that made her feel safe. Her heart fluttered knowing he cared so deeply for her. But being this close to him made her feel other emotions. She looked from his eyes to his lips and swallowed hard. She pulled his hand away from her face and looked down.

"Yea, I know, Chris…"

Chris furrowed his brows. He felt a cold chill wash over him the moment she turned away.

"It doesn't seem like it…" he persisted. His gaze unwavering from her. It made her nervous.

"Stop doing that," she said abruptly.

"Doing what?"

"Looking at me like... *that*..."

"Like what, Gabs?"

Gabrielle pouted. She crossed her arms, annoyed that he wasn't making this easy for her.

"Like... like you want to kiss me..." she muttered.

Chris hesitated for a moment not sure what to say. He put his hands in his pockets and looked at her with a tilt of his head.

He knew what he wanted to say.

He said what he *had* to say.

"Now why would I go and do something like that?"

Gabrielle's stomach felt hollow even though she had just eaten. She didn't know why Chris's response bothered her so much. He was her best friend after all. Why would he have feelings like that for her?

"Well... th-that's what I said," she stammered. "So just stop it. You're sending mixed signals."

Chris saw how flustered she was and immediately felt bad about the situation he put her in. "Hmm... I guess that explains why I pissed off so many adoring fans back in high school."

"You're such a doofus," Gabrielle chuckled. Chris's shoulders relaxed when he heard her laugh. Crisis averted.

Chris checked his phone. "Your mom prepared dinner again. She wants both of our families to eat together tonight."

"Oh, that's sweet," Gabrielle said fondly. "We haven't done something like that since..."

Chris smiled at her sadly. "Yea... come on."

~*~

That night the Johansson family and the Richardson family dined together. Chris started a fire in the fireplace as they all settled into the living room. Arthur, Eric, Chris, Gerald, and Natalie played poker while Sally and Clara chatted over wine.

"This is nice," Tanya said sitting in Eli's lap. She leaned her head back against his chest.

"Yea, it is," Eli said, kissing the top of her head.

"Okay! okay! No more card games! We're playing charades!" Gabrielle said, walking into the living room with a board game.

"Since when do you need a board game to play charades?" Gerald inquired.

"Since forever. Get with the times, Uncle" Natalie teased.

"Let's pick teams," Gabrielle said.

"How about men vs. women?" Natalie suggested.

"Good idea! Wait... where's Charlie?" Gabrielle said, looking around.

Chris immediately looked out the window and saw his brother. "He might not want to play."

"That's not an option! This is a **historical** family event!" Gabrielle exclaimed.

Chris chuckled at her seriousness. "I'll get him. For history's sake," he teased. He strolled outside and saw Charlie sitting on the stairs of the patio, petting Thor.

"Not in the mood for family fun and games?" Chris said, taking a seat next to him.

"Never in the mood for shit like that," Charlie muttered, rubbing Thor's belly. Chris sighed with a smile. He knew very well why his brother would rather stay outside.

"It's nice to be around family... for them all to be here. It's not common for us, so... we should try to enjoy the moment while it lasts," Chris said encouragingly.

"They should have been here when it mattered most. When Dad was still alive. Now they're sticking around for moral support? It's bullshit," Charlie groaned.

Chris frowned as he ran his fingers through Thor's fur. The golden retriever looked back at the brothers happily with his tongue hanging out.

"I get it, Charlie..." Chris said finally.

Suddenly Gabrielle stomped out of the house and onto the patio. "What is taking so long?!"

They both looked back at her. "I tried to recruit him, Gabs, but he won't budge. Best we leave him be," Chris shrugged, trying to throw her off.

Gabrielle frowned and folded her arms. "No. No. No. This is family time, Charlie."

Charlie shrugged, emphasizing that he simply did not care. She walked in front of them and jumped off the steps to face them. She glared at Charlie who looked back at her unbothered.

"Come here, boy! Come here!" she said, patting her thighs. They both looked at her strangely until Thor quickly got up and trotted over towards her. Thor pranced around her legs as she ruffled his fur and nuzzled him with her face.

"That's a good boy! You're such a good boy, Thor! You wanna treat?"

Thor started jumping up and down playfully.

"Yea, you wanna treat? I wish I could, but Charlie has all the treats! He won't give me the treats!" She pointed to Charlie who was still looking at her bewildered until he realized what she was trying to do. He instinctively rolled his eyes.

"That's not gonna work, Ga-" Charlie started. But he was interrupted by Thor's whimpering. Thor looked at Charlie with big puppy dog eyes and Chris burst into laughter.

"What the hell, Thor!" Charlie said frustrated.

"I know, Thor! Charlie is such a meanie, isn't he? Keeping all those treats from you. Why you gotta be so mean to poor Thor, Charlie?" Gabrielle said. She looked at Charlie with the same puppy dog eyes that Thor was giving him.

"For crying out loud!" Charlie sucked his teeth and got up to walk towards the house. He whistled, calling for Thor to follow him. "Come on, you big baby."

Gabrielle smiled contentedly as she watched Charlie enter the house with Thor happily wagging his tail behind him.

"You never cease to amaze me," Chris chuckled. He got up just as Gabrielle was passing him and they both collided into each other.

"Ouch!" Gabrielle stumbled backwards. She lost her balance and nearly fell if not for Chris who grabbed her by her waist.

"You alright?" he asked, rubbing his own head.

"I think so," she chuckled. She tried to steady herself by grasping his forearms. "Are you?"

"Yea... you got a hard head, Johansson," he laughed.

"Hey!" she said poking him. "I'm the one who's injured here!"

"Hmm, let me see," he said, pretending to inspect her forehead. He playfully brushed her puffy hair into her face.

"Chris!" she laughed, trying to move her curls out of her face. She could hear him chuckling as he helped her move her hair out of her eyes. When she finally peeked through, she saw his blue eyes gazing at her again. That same look from earlier.

His grip on her waist tightened as he pulled her closer. His eyes leaving hers only to look at her lips. His expression was unreadable, and yet still she felt herself being drawn in... *again.*

She bit her lip nervously, and in response his eyes instantly darkened with desire in a way that lit her whole body on fire. He leaned towards her and she responded in kind.

"Are you guys coming in or what?" Natalie said from the door.

They quickly let go of each other and looked up at Natalie. She looked between them with a knowing smirk.

"Yea, we're coming now," Chris said sheepishly, rubbing the back of his neck.

Gabrielle bee-lined for the door. She walked right past Chris without saying a word. She entered the living room to see Charlie seated in the same armchair Chris perched a seat on the side of.

"Okay! Now that we have everyone here! Let's get started! Ladies first!" Gabrielle said. Natalie pretended to type on a computer and write something down.

"Uh... Writer!" Tanya guessed. But Natalie shook her head.

"Analyst!"

She shook her head again. She pretended to sit down in an imaginary seat and adjusted her imaginary glasses.

"Librarian! Secretary!"

She finally nodded. Natalie got up to step in a different direction when she retracted her foot in pain. "Ow!" she exclaimed.

"Hey! There's no talking in charades!" Arthur said.

"No, I mean... I just stepped on something." Natalie looked down at the carpet and picked up something silver.

Gabrielle's eyes grew wide and she instinctively patted her front and back pockets. Charlie eyed her curiously as she frantically searched her body.

"Is this... THIS IS A RING!" Natalie screamed with excitement.

"A ring?!" Tanya squealed looking at Eli, along with everyone else. "Eli! Are you-?!"

Eli's eyes widened and he put his hands up. "What? No, baby. I-"

"This diamond is huge! It has to be at least 3 carats. Are you sure you aren't proposing, Eli?" Natalie grinned at him.

"No! No-I..." Eli fumbled for his words, feeling very embarrassed.

Tanya huffed, folding her arms. "Well if it isn't Eli's... then whose is it?"

"Um..."

Everyone turned to Gabrielle who slowly raised her hand.

"It's... it's mine," she said. She crawled forward and plucked the ring from Natalie's hand before stuffing it into her pocket. "Must have fallen out of my pocket..."

Everyone looked at her in shock.

"I guess... I failed to mention that I was... engaged?" she said cringing.

"ENGAGED?!" Eli, Tanya and Clara exclaimed simultaneously.

"TO WHO?"

"SINCE WHEN?"

The questions came at her like rapid fire from a machine gun.

"Okay, okay... Let's give her a minute," Tanya said, settling next to Gabrielle.

Gabrielle sighed deeply knowing she couldn't talk her way out of this one. She had to be honest or it would spiral. She briefly glanced at Chris whose face was unreadable to the point it seemed emotionless. Meanwhile, Charlie looked extremely troubled.

"His name is Damian... Damian DuPont. We've been engaged for about... 4 months now but dated for 3 years. He's a professional artist. Very sought after," Gabrielle explained.

"Why didn't you tell us about him before?" Clara asked.

"There was just so much going on. There wasn't really a right time," Gabrielle frowned.

"You don't seem very happy for someone newly engaged..." Eric eyed her.

Gabrielle looked up and tried to stifle her raging emotions. "That's because I broke up with him earlier today on the phone."

Chris suddenly looked up at her with new revelation as he started to put the pieces together of why she acted the way that she did.

"Woah... why did you break up?" Eli asked with concern.

"Y'all all up in my business..." Gabrielle muttered.

"Gabrielle," her mother said sternly.

Gabrielle pouted and averted her gaze. "Because I'm pretty sure he's cheating on me."

Everyone visibly pulled back and there was a collective groan of frustration.

"Who the fuck is stupid enough to cheat on my baby sister," Eli said angrily.

"Eli Johansson, you watch your mouth!" Clara snapped at Eli. He recoiled under her glare. Clara walked up to her daughter and sat down next to her.

"I'm sorry he broke your heart, baby," her mom said, patting her hand. Gabrielle smiled with a shrug.

"I'm fine, Mom. Really," she said feigning a smile.

"Maybe we should head home," Tanya spoke up. "I think we should give Gabby her space."

Everyone agreed and prepared to leave. With an exhausted sigh, Gabrielle walked to the foyer to put on her jacket. She felt embarrassed for having her business out like that. But she took comfort in the fact that it was with family.

Chris approached her and leaned against the beam. He looked at her with his arms folded across his chest. "Why didn't you tell me?" he asked her.

"I wasn't going to tell anyone," she muttered. "Just my luck that Nat would find my secret during a family game of charades."

"But why..." he persisted, holding her gaze.

She hesitated and searched his eyes. "...Why does it matter, Chris...?"

Tanya came next to her and grabbed her hand comfortingly. Gabrielle followed Tanya out of the estate, but not before giving Chris one last look.

~*~

"Right now, we've got multiple operations in these 4 areas," Chris advised. He pointed to the northeast region of the United States map laid out on a large wooden table in his living room. "We've been most successful in the Northeastern region and we're gaining a lot of progress in the Midwest and Southeast."

Chris hunched over the large table with Eric, Gerald, and Natalie. Charlie leaned against the wall, across the room from his brother with his arms folded, watching them work.

"That's good. But we need to expand even further in the Southwest and Northwest. We should be claiming the entirety of the West Coast," Eric said, stroking his beard.

"The West, in general, is pretty tricky. The mid-tier gang activity there is pretty intense and most of those head dogs are very territorial. It won't be easy..." Chris frowned.

"We must. That's where the traffic is the heaviest aside from the Northeast. Once we get the West Coast, all operations will be dominated by the Richardsons," Eric said.

Chris twisted his mouth in concern. "Yea, but-"

"I have faith that you can do it, Christopher. That's why you're next in line to take all of this on. With the passing of your father, as unfortunate as that has been, the hindrance keeping you from the seat where you belong is no longer there. It's only a matter of time when the entire organization will look to you," Eric said proudly.

Chris tried to smile as best he could without letting anxiety and frustration overwhelm him.

"Thanks... Uncle," Chris said reluctantly.

Eric's phone went off. "Let's take a break," he said.

Chris sighed, wiping the sweat from his forehead when Charlie walked up to him. He grabbed his brother's bicep and pulled him backward.

"Walk with me," Charlie ordered.

Chris followed his brother to the kitchen. Charlie walked to the far end and leaned against the wall, arms still folded, his eyes staring intensely into Chris's.

Chris faced him and stuffed his hands into his pockets. He already knew what his brother's issue was. "What's u-"

"I thought we agreed we weren't going to do this anymore," Charlie said, cutting him off before he could start.

Chris sighed heavily. "The time isn't right yet. I need to see some of these assignments through."

"Bullshit! We agreed we would let Nat and Arthur take over. You can't do this anymore."

Chris gave him a frustrated look. "You know this isn't just something we can run away from, Charlie. This whole thing is ingrained in our very blood-"

"I fucking know that!" Charlie shouted angrily. He immediately looked down apologetically for blowing up. "I know that, Chris... I just... you don't need to be at the forefront anymore. You don't need to risk your life... *anymore...*"

Chris smiled gratefully at his younger brother. There was no one else that cared, protected, and loved him as much as Charlie. Chris put his hand on Charlie's shoulder encouragingly. "Just a few more months, Charlie. I promise. And then I'll let Uncle Eric know I'm done for good."

Charlie looked up at his brother, not necessarily believing him. He thought for a moment before speaking. "They don't deserve you."

"They don't deserve *us*," Chris clarified.

"I'm only doing this for you, Chris. I've only ever done this *for you.*"

"I know. And I appreciate that. There's no one else I trust more with my life."

Charlie gave a small smile. "Are you gonna tell them? About..."

"No. They don't need to know about that. Besides, we're taking care of it. Your men handled 2 of those gangs last week, right?"

"Yea, small petty activity. But still, their numbers seem to be increasing at a rapid rate and that worries me."

"The last thing we want to do is give our uncles the impression we don't have things under control. We do. And we will continue to, even if we have to make our tactics a bit harsher."

Charlie quickly looked at him. "Shit, Chris, how much harsher can we get?"

"Whatever is necessary to get the job done," Chris said with little to no emotion in his tone.

Charlie paused before cautiously nodding his understanding.

Chris broke from his serious face back into his signature warm smile. He checked his watch. "Come on. Let's go finish up with them so we can get them the hell out of my apartment."

~*~

Gabrielle sat at Tanya's table absentmindedly stirring her tea with a spoon. She looked into the cup and watched the ripples jump. She thought about her conversation with Damian. She wondered if she overreacted. Then she remembered the pictures and the way he spoke to her. It had been so much to think about that it overwhelmed her. She was lost in her thoughts and dived deeper when she remembered the looks on her mom and brother's face. Charlie... she had never seen him look so concerned. And Chris... not the expression she expected. Maybe he didn't care? But then why did he keep asking her?

"And I just think it's really important that we get that message across. Don't you agree, Gabby?" Tanya said putting the milk back into the fridge. When she didn't get a response, Tanya turned around to see Gabrielle staring into her cup. Complete silence from her.

"Gabby?"

Gabrielle sat up quickly startled. "Huh? Yes?"

Tanya frowned. "You okay, babe? You haven't said anything all day. And you haven't even touched your tea. It's probably cold by now."

"Oh..." Gabrielle said staring back into her cup. "I just... have a lot on my mind."

"Damian?"

"That's part of it..."

"I don't even know who he is, so I don't know how to help. I wish I knew more about him."

"There's no point, T. He's just not the guy I thought he was... the guy I fell in love with. I guess I'm just trying to cope right now."

Tanya thought for a second, leaning on the table next to Gabrielle. "I've got it. Let's have a purge!"

"What?! I saw that movie, Tanya, and I may hate Damian but I don't want to *kill* him!"

Tanya chuckled. "No, silly. Purge like... purge Damian out of your system. We'll go shopping, buy tons of desserts to eat, AND cap it off with a night at one of the hottest lounge spots in Philly."

Gabrielle looked up as if thinking. "Actually, that does sound like a lot of fun. It's been a while since I went shopping for myself and dancing really does make me feel better."

"Exactly! You go get ready and I'll call up Nat, Rhaven, and Angie so we can be a sexy ass entourage turnin' up in these here streets!"

"Alright, alright calm down. I ain't trying to get **that** turnt," Gabrielle laughed.

"We'll see," Tanya smirked, taking out her phone.

~*~

Chris and Charlie pulled up to a slightly dilapidated building on the far side of Philly. Chris wore a long black trench coat while Charlie wore a short black leather jacket.

"You sure you wanna do this now?" Chris asked as they headed for the small door.

"Better to set the record straight now rather than later," Charlie said. He took a few last few puffs from his cigarette before flicking it.

Charlie led Chris into the building and nodded at an elderly man sitting at a small security desk in the corner. He punched in a few numbers on the elevator control panel before 3 different doors slid open for them to step inside.

"That little old man is security? Really?" Chris mocked.

"It's mainly just for show," Charlie grinned, as the doors closed. The elevator started to descend.

"So... she's engaged," Charlie said suddenly.

"*Was*..." Chris emphasized. He watched the numbers change in the elevator.

"Why would she keep something like that a secret?"

Chris shrugged. "She's an enigma. But... I guess that closes that chapter for good."

Charlie raised his eyebrows at him curiously.

"I mean... we weren't going to pursue her anyway, but still..." Chris said quickly.

Charlie grinned. "You're worse than me, brother."

Chris rolled his eyes and raised his hands in surrender. "I submit."

"Oh really? That's a first!" Charlie mocked with laughter.

"Shut up, Charlie..."

The elevator finally stopped, and the doors opened to a large area. The floors were carpeted and glass cases from the ceiling to the floor encased all types of weapons and machinery.

"I see you made some renovations," Chris said, eyeing the area. Charlie gave him a knowing look before leading him out of the elevator.

They walked down a short narrow hallway before coming to a room clouded in smoke that smelled of cigarettes and beer. A group of men relaxing around a table played poker with money and poker chips spread out all over the tabletop.

"You're bullshitting me," one of the men said.

"When have I ever-"

"All the fucking time, Eddie!" the man said getting loud as everyone else in the room chuckled.

"You should know by now, just from working with him, that Tony is as much of a trickster as he is a mobster," Charlie said, interrupting them.

When they heard his voice they all scrambled to their feet to acknowledge him. "Sir!"

Charlie waved his hand casually causing them all to relax and sit back down.

"What brings you round these parts. You weren't s'posed to be due back for another week," Eddie said in his thick New York accent. "I told you I'd hold it down till you were ready."

"I know, Eddie. I appreciate you taking some time away from your HQ in New York to cover for me here. But I have something important I need to make you all aware of first," Charlie said. They all leaned in to listen.

"You all know about the increase of territorial markings around here," Charlie started. They all nodded. "We need to kill it. Now. Send a message that this won't be tolerated, or consequences will be deadly."

They looked at each other on full alert.

"What kind of message were you expecting to send," Tony asked.

"I'll leave it up to you guys to figure out. Just make sure it sticks," Charlie said.

"And is this coming from you. Or... *him*," a younger man said. He motioned to Chris standing idly behind Charlie. Charlie squinted as if trying to figure out who the man was.

"You wanna run that by me again?" Charlie threatened, taking a step forward.

"I'm just wondering who's calling the shots since this guy is al-" the young man continued.

"Quit while you're ahead, kid," Eddie said raising his hand. The young guy looked at Eddie and then back at Charlie now a bit anxiously.

Charlie leaned his head back and folded his arms across his chest. He looked more intently, still trying to figure him out. "Who the fuck is this?" he said flippantly.

The young man's eyes widened with anxiety.

"Charlie..." Chris started. He tried to calm his brother but Charlie raised his hand to quiet him.

"Uh... he's the new guy you picked up from Richie, 'member?" Eddie said.

Charlie locked eyes with the kid steadily shrinking under his gaze. He gave him a hard stare while thinking. Then he broke into a smile. "Oh yea... you are one of Richie's boys."

The young guy sighed relieved.

"I don't know how Richie gets down, but that shit don't fly here. Talk to me like that again and you'll be staring down the barrel of a 45," Charlie said quickly, sternly, and without blinking.

The young man immediately straightened up, looking terrified as Eddie and Tony tried to stifle a laugh.

"You got that?" Charlie snapped.

"Y-yes, Sir," he stammered.

Charlie looked at Tony. "I expect to see something by the end of the week."

"You got it, boss," Tony nodded with a tip of his hat.

Charlie turned and motioned Chris back out of the room. "Poor kid," Chris chuckled as they headed back to the elevator.

"The mouth on these smart asses are gonna get them killed one day," Charlie murmured as they headed back up.

"Oh, I don't know... Arthur is still alive," Chris said. They both laughed out loud.

Suddenly, both of their phones went off at once.

Chris looked down. "Text from Tanya?"

"And Nat..." Charlie said reading the text.

~*~

Charlie and Chris stepped into the loud lounge with multi-color lights flashing in the dimly lit room. People swarmed every bar table, and the floor was crowded with men and women dressed in trendy sparse clothing.

"You sure this is the place?" Charlie said, looking around apprehensively.

"Yea. 27th on 27th. That's what Tanya told me," Chris said, checking the lounge out.

"Hey sexy." The brothers turned around to see a woman in a sheer dress walk up to Charlie.

"You look lonely. Need some company?" she said seductively. She traced her finger down his chest. Charlie grinned at her and was about to say something when Chris interrupted.

"Sorry, but we're just looking for our friends."

"I can be your friend. I can be *both* of your friends. I love me a good threesome," she smirked, eyeing them both.

"Oh jeez..." Chris said, covering his face annoyed. He spotted Natalie's golden blonde hair and bright red dress from across the room.

"There they are," he said, pointing them out to Charlie.

"I promise you'll have *way* more fun with me," the woman said, tugging on Charlie's arm.

"Uh... tempting, but we really have to go. Thanks," Charlie said. He plucked her hand off of his arm and followed Chris towards the ladies in the back. They found the women in a small area of the lounge with soft plush couches.

"You guys are here! Thank God!" Tanya said desperately, running over to Chris.

"What's wrong? Is Gabs okay?" Charlie asked.

"Uh..." Natalie made a face and pointed them in the direction of Gabrielle.

Gabrielle was standing on one of the couches with no shoes on. She wore hip-hugging, low-rider jeans and a white sleeveless crop top with an elastic band just beneath her breast that emphasized her hourglass figure. Her curly hair wildly flung about as she belted to Beyonce's "*Don't Hurt Yourself*."

Chris turned to Tanya and Natalie. "What the hell happened?!"

Tanya and Natalie looked at each other. "Well see... what had happened was..." Tanya started.

"She was feeling really depressed and we tried to cheer her up," Natalie responded.

"How is *this* cheering her up?" Charlie asked, watching Gabrielle do air guitar on the couch.

"Ok, well, first we went shopping and then we went out to the bakery which was all good but she was still just... not with it. So, I called in my favors and got us into this bougie ass lounge," Tanya explained.

"Bougie?" Natalie said, offended. "I love this lounge!"

"And we got on this Beyonce kick. Asked the DJ to play all of her badass songs," Tanya continued. "And I think we forgot to watch how much she was drinking. Which was a lot."

Chris and Charlie looked at both of them. "How much is a lot?" Chris asked worriedly.

"Well, she doesn't need to be rushed to the hospital or anything..." Tanya trailed off.

"Girl please! She is 100% white girl-wasted," Angie said. She walked up to them with a glass of water and Rhaven trailing behind.

"Why did that water take so long?!" Natalie shrieked.

"Girl! We had to fight our way to the damn bartender for this water!" Angie said, annoyed.

"All these thirsty ass hoes tryna get some dick and I'm just trying to make sure my girl doesn't die from alcohol poisoning," Rhaven rolled her eyes.

"I thought you said it wasn't that bad?!" Charlie said angrily, turning to Tanya.

"It's not! They're exaggerating!" Tanya squealed, trying to calm Charlie.

"Nah, forreal though... Baby girl is straight up shit faced," Rhaven said, shaking her head. She watched Angie attempt to pull Gabrielle off the couch to drink the water.

"Nooo! I'm *hic* not thirsty! Dance with meee!" Gabrielle laughed pulling Angie by the arm. Angie looked back at all of them and shrugged in defeat before dancing with Gabrielle to Beyonce's "*Partition*."

Chris sighed and Charlie shook his head as they watched Gabrielle whip her hair wildly while winding and grinding her body on one of the poles.

"What's with the poles?" Chris asked.

"For strippers... duh," Rhaven mocked.

"Yea... uh... Gabby might have explored some *other* career options tonight," Tanya said, hiding her face.

"That's not funny, Tanya," Chris said aggravated.

"She's not lying. She's gotten the attention of many men. And some women. I'm actually really impressed. She'll need to teach me some of those moves once she sobers up," Natalie said pensively. Chris shot Natalie a dirty look when just at that moment a man approached Gabrielle and tried to grab her by her waist.

"Back the fuck up!" Charlie said angrily. He violently shoved the man away.

"Okay. We gotta get her out of here," Chris said.

"Yes! That's why we called you!" Tanya exclaimed, even more exasperated than before.

"Why didn't you guys just take her home yourselves?" Chris asked curiously.

"She wouldn't budge. She just won't leave. And..." Tanya trailed off looking away from Chris.

"What?" Chris asked.

"She kept asking for you and you only," Tanya said looking up at him. Chris looked slightly taken back.

"Alright," Chris said. He headed for Gabrielle who was dancing on the table while Charlie was still threatening interested men.

"Gabs." Chris looked up at her and saw her eyes close. She felt up her body and moved in sync with the music.

"Gabrielle," he said again, reaching for her hand. Her eyes popped open and she looked down to see Chris staring back at her. She felt as fuzzy and light as everything else looked, but there was no mistaking those familiar blue eyes.

"Chris!" she beamed at him. "Did *hic* you come to dance *hic* with me?"

"No, Gabs. I've come to take you home," he said, trying to motion her off the table.

"Noo! I don't *hic* want to," she pouted at him.

"Gabs, come on," he persisted, tugging at her.

"No!" she said defiantly, folding her arms. Then she smirked at him and gave him a teasing look that made him stop breathing for a second. "Make me..."

"Alright, enough of this shit," Charlie approached. He grabbed Gabrielle by the waist and lifted her off of the table.

"Oh!" she said surprised. She tried to find her balance as he set her down on the floor.

"Are you gonna come quietly or is this gonna be a fight?" Charlie warned her.

"Hell no! I'm *hic* staying right- woah!" she yelped. Charlie threw her over his shoulder, using one arm to secure her legs to his chest.

"Jeez, Charlie..." Chris mumbled.

"You got any better ideas?" Charlie glared at him. When Chris shrugged, they headed for the exit.

"Wait!" Tanya called after them. They turned around to face her. "Here are her shoes and her bag. Please make sure she drinks lots of water!"

"We got it, we got it!" Charlie said impatiently. He turned back around, annoyed with Gabrielle toying with the back of his jacket.

"Thanks, Tanya," Chris said, taking Gabrielle's belongings from her.

"You'll have to take her to one of your apartments. Her mom can't see her like this," Tanya added.

"Right... we'll take care of her," he said. He went to turn around and follow Charlie when Tanya grabbed his arm.

"Chris?" she said abruptly and he turned to face her.

"Gabby is... not herself. She went through a range of emotions today. She's still grieving over Steve and she's both heartbroken and hateful of her ex-fiance. She's got a lot of regrets. She may say things she doesn't mean. Please remember that," Tanya warned.

He paused to take in the gravity of what she was saying before he gave her a nod and followed after Charlie.

Charlie opened the car door and laid Gabrielle down on the seat.

But she quickly scrambled to face him. "I really *hic* like it when you manhandle me like that," she teased him. She kneeled on the seat of the car and scooted towards him, wrapping her hands around his neck.

Playfully nibbling his ear, she whispered. "You should do it more often, Charlie..."

Charlie froze for a second trying to figure out what exactly was happening. Then he shook his head and carefully removed her hands from around him.

"You're drunk, Gabs. We'll get you home and into bed," he said, pushing her into the car.

"Will you be *hic* coming with me?" She gave him a sexy pout and bit her bottom lip as she gazed into his now darkened green eyes.

"Gabs, stop," Charlie said half to her, half to himself. He closed the car door before she could say anything else. Leaning on the door, he sighed deeply and touched his ear where she had nibbled. He tried to keep his emotions under control when he saw Chris approaching.

"What's wrong?" Chris asked, noting the look on Charlie's face.

"She's a flirtatious drunk," Charlie muttered.

"How convenient," Chris said sarcastically, opening the front car door. "She's gotta stay with one of us. Tanya advised against taking her home."

"Great," Charlie muttered, rubbing his forehead. He ran his fingers through his blonde hair and breathed deeply. "She can crash at my place. I'll take the couch."

"You sure?"

"No."

Chris grinned at Charlie's reluctance and obvious annoyance.

The drive to Charlie's apartment was agonizing for both men.

"So, why are you both *hic* single, honestly, *hic* truly, I'm dying to know," Gabrielle said dryly. She leaned through the open middle section of the car between the brothers.

"Gabs, sit back and put your damn seat belt on," Chris ordered her.

Gabrielle frowned. "Why you gotta be so *hic* grumpy, Christopher? You're supposed to be the *hic* fun brother," she said, playfully running her hands through the back of his hair.

Chris cringed and tried to move his head out of the way. "You're gonna get us all killed distracting me like that. Go annoy Charlie," he grumbled.

"I dunno," she said slyly, moving over to Charlie. "Charlie doesn't seem *hic* very receptive to my advances." She wrapped her arms around Charlie's neck and drew circles on his chest with her finger.

She leaned in from behind, bringing her lips towards his ear again as she did before. "Come on *hic*, Charlie, don't you wanna have a little fun?" she whispered sensually. She started to gently nibble on his ear again.

Completely surprised, Charlie held his breath for a moment. He closed his eyes for a brief second, relishing the sensation of her warm, wet tongue licking his ear. He nearly came undone as she tugged on his lobe with her lips.

"Gabrielle! Put your seatbelt on. Now!" Charlie demanded. He reluctantly removed her arms from around him.

"Ugh... you're no fun. Both of you are *hic* so unbelievably boring," she said. Plopping herself against the backseat, she folded her arms and kicked her feet up on the door.

"What the fuck? Is she just really horny or some shit," Charlie muttered. He rubbed his ear and opened the window to get some air, hoping it would cool him down.

"Considering this is my first time seeing her *this* drunk, I'm gonna assume yes," Chris said, pulling up to Charlie's apartment.

"Hey! I hear you *hic* talking about me!" she huffed from the back.

Chris and Charlie gave each other a quick glance, talking with their eyes. Charlie raised his brow at Chris before Chris sighed in submission. "Fine... I'll bring her in."

Charlie grinned. "I have to move the car anyway. I don't like anyone knowing who my visitors are," he said. They both stepped out of the car. Chris tossed him the keys and opened the door to find her laying down with her feet up. With one hand playing with her hair and the other teasing the hem of her shirt, Gabrielle looked up at Chris and smirked.

"Come to have your way with me," she winked at him. She sensually bit her lip, making him feel hot all over.

Chris sighed in frustration. "Gabs. Please behave," he groaned. He placed his arms on either side of her and pulled her out of the car. Instead of hoisting her over his shoulder like Charlie, he gently wrapped her arms around his neck and lifted her underneath her knees, holding her bridal style.

"And if I don't," she said softly. She buried her face in the crook of his neck and nuzzled him. "Are you gonna punish me, baby?" she whispered in his ear. She pecked his neck with small kisses.

Chris struggled to hold Gabrielle in his arms as her fleeting kisses made him weak at the knees. He tried his best to ignore her and bumped the car door shut with his hip.

Charlie started the engine and looked over at Chris carrying Gabrielle. He grinned mischievously at his brother's predicament.

"You sure you can handle her?" Charlie teased, grinning widely.

"Shut up," Chris muttered. He turned around and headed for the door as Charlie sped off to park Chris's car.

Chris carried an intoxicated Gabrielle to the door and fumbled with the keys. Gabrielle teased his neck with her tongue while running her hands down the length of his chest.

"Oh Chris..." she moaned into his shoulder.

"Okay, you know what," he said exasperated as he carefully put her down. "Just... stay still until I get the door open."

Finally opening the door, he helped her inside and closed the door behind them. He walked her over to the quaint couch and sat her down.

"Wait here, I'll get you some water," he said, turning to leave.

"No wait!" she said, grabbing his hand. Just as Chris turned to her, she pulled him down onto the couch. She swung her leg over his lap and straddled him between her legs.

She laid her arms on each of his shoulders grasping onto the back of the couch. Her lips inches away from his. Chris froze as she ran a hand down his chest. She teased the bottom hem of his shirt before lifting it to feel his skin. Flushing her body against his, she pushed her face into his neck, kissing the same spot she did before.

"Oh Chris, I want you so badly," she moaned into his neck.

He closed his eyes for a moment and sighed in ecstasy. The way she moved her body against his felt so good. He affectionately ran his fingers along her arms, feeling goosebumps on her soft skin. Upon feeling his touch, Gabrielle pulled back and peered deeply into his now darkened blue eyes. She bit her lip and leaned down to kiss him.

Chris's heart skipped a beat when he realized Gabrielle was going to kiss him. *What am I doing,* he thought to himself.

"Gab-" he said quickly moving out from under her. Consequently, she fell face forward into the couch. "Sorry..." he muttered standing. He felt awful watching her writhe on the couch.

"Really, Chris?!" she said frustrated.

"You need water," he muttered. He quickly turned and headed towards Charlie's kitchen.

"Ugh!" Gabrielle groaned. She plopped her entire body onto the couch in frustration.

Chris grabbed a cup from the cabinet and poured water from a pitcher. He wiped his forehead as his thoughts overwhelmed him. *We almost...no not like this,* he thought.

The door slammed shut and Charlie walked into the hallway, setting Gabrielle's things down. He saw her lying on the couch, whimpering to herself, her face in one of his pillows.

"Is she-" Charlie started.

"She just needs some water... and some sleep," Chris said, walking towards his brother. Charlie looked Chris over and noticed how haphazard his normally neat shirt was.

"Don't ask," Chris said to Charlie when he caught him staring. Chris walked over to Gabrielle and perched himself on the table in front of her.

"... Gabs, come on. Drink some water," he said, patting her head.

"No!" she cried into the pillow.

"Gabrielle..." Chris insisted. She looked up at him and it was then that both brothers realized she was actually full-blown crying.

"Hey! What's wrong?" Chris said worried. She paused for a moment and sat up on the couch with her legs folded beneath her. Her hands fell in her lap and she looked down forlorn. Even with her large curls, they could see tears falling down her face. Chris glanced at Charlie who had moved in closer to lean against the wall. Neither of them knew what to do.

"I don't know what's wrong with me," she said finally. "Did I just *hic* become extremely unattractive all of a sudden? Am I *hic* unbearable to look at or *hic* be around?"

"Gabs, just because we don't want to sleep with you while you're drunk, might I add, doesn't mean there's something wrong with you or that you're unattractive," Charlie said.

Gabrielle wiped her face. "It's not that... I don't understand why he cheated on me. Did I bore him? Did he just get tired of me?"

Chris took on a somber expression as Charlie scowled in irritation. "Him cheating on you is not your fault. He's the idiot, Gabs," Chris said comfortingly.

"I just... I don't *hic* understand. I gave him everything. Even *hic* when I didn't want to. I tried to be good for him," she said softly. "And even when he threatened me, I *hic* stayed to support him."

Chris's eyes widened suddenly upon hearing this and looked at her more intently. "What do you mean threatened you?" Chris probed.

Gabrielle looked up and saw a concerned look on Chris's face and an angry expression forming on Charlie's.

"It's nothing. Damian *hic* just has a bit of a temper. It's just how he is," she said casually.

"A temper?" Chris asked, raising his voice slightly.

"Gabs," Charlie said in a low voice. Gabrielle looked up at him. "Has he ever hit you?"

She looked between both of them as they peered at her with a mind-numbing intensity, waiting for her reply.

"Wha... I... I don't want to *hic* talk about this anymore," she said holding her head.

"Gab-" Chris started.

"No! Please... I just want to sleep," she cried out, taking them both by surprise.

"Okay... let's get her to bed," Charlie grumbled as he moved towards her. Chris moved back to make room as Charlie swiftly picked her up and carried her to his bedroom.

Upon arriving in his bedroom, Gabrielle was already half asleep when Charlie lay her down on his bed. He pulled the sheets over her and brushed her hair out of her face as she snored lightly. He caressed her cheek and took one last concerned look at her before leaving.

"She's already knocked out," Charlie said, re-entering the living room. He saw his brother sitting on the couch, pouring himself a glass of whiskey.

Charlie sat down next to him and sighed heavily. Chris went to take a sip of the whiskey when he caught the heavy look on his brother's face. He nonchalantly passed the cup to Charlie before pouring himself another glass.

"What do you think?" Charlie said, sipping his whiskey.

"I don't know. Her hesitation to tell us the truth makes me weary," Chris said, staring into his glass.

Charlie grunted in affirmation. "If it's true, I'll kill him."

Chris sighed. "Charlie..."

In seconds, Chris's phone went off. He pulled his phone out of his pocket and checked his alert. Charlie watched as Chris's face distorted with anger.

"Wha-" Charlie started.

"I gotta go," Chris said, abruptly getting up. He quickly downed the rest of the whiskey and rushed to put on his jacket.

"Let me know when she wakes up," Chris said. Charlie barely spoke before Chris was out the door.

"He doesn't even know where I parked his car," Charlie chuckled.

He took a minute to finish his whiskey and placed the empty glass on the table. He got up and stretched, yawning loudly before he walked quietly back to his room.

Peeking inside, he saw Gabrielle lightly snoring. She twitched slightly before falling deeper into her slumber. He closed the door and walked back to the living room to sleep himself.

~*~

8

Gotta Get You Into My Double Life

~*~

Chris walked across the warehouse floor, observing the scattered broken boxes. The contents were either missing or completely ruined, mixed with blood, gunpowder, and debris. He shook his head in disappointment as he wiped frustratingly at his forehead.

He walked over to an open crate and found a child's dirty teddy bear. Dread clutched his heart. Picking it up, he looked it over with his leather-gloved hands.

10 of his men stood behind him armed with ak-47s pointed at 5 other men kneeling on the ground with their hands behind their heads. The men watched their boss scour the remnants of the warehouse in his long black trench coat. He resembled a displeased shadow among distorted chaos.

"Who led this patrol," Chris grumbled. His trembling anger was so palpable that it made the men sweat with panic. But Chris was met with silence.

"Do **not** make me repeat myself," he said an octave lower, with more intensity.

"I-I did, sir," stammered one of the men kneeling on the ground. Chris turned around to face him, an irate flicker in his gaze.

"And your name is?" Chris asked, stepping in front of him.

"P-p-parker, sir," the man stuttered nervously.

"Parker. How long have you been with us, Parker?" Chris bore his eyes into the man's head.

"Th-three years, sir."

"Three. So, then you're aware of the policy I so *meticulously* put in place concerning the involvement of children." Chris tilted his head to the side. He stood tall, showing his height and looked down at the man with an authority that thickened the air in the room.

"Y-yes, sir. B-b-but-"

Chris held up his hand to silence him. He crouched down in front of the man with a menacing look on his face. A sneer plastered across his mouth, twisting his conventionally attractive features.

"Were there children here, Parker?"

"S-sir, I-"

"It's a 'yes' or 'no' question, Parker. Were. There. Children?" Chris looked into his eyes without blinking. His pupils constricted to the point Parker only saw blue and white. His dead emotionless gaze sent Parker on edge.

"Y-yes, sir."

"Interesting," Chris said, standing up. Parker dropped his head from Chris's gaze and his body trembled with fear.

"How much?" Chris asked.

"Excuse me?"

"How much were you offered to include a child in this shipment?"

"S-sir! I-"

"How! Much?!" Chris shouted this time. His voice boomed as it reverberated off the walls.

"E-eight hundred..."

Chris paused. An eerie silence fell until his boisterous laughter pierced the air.

"800?! 800 fucking dollars to sell a *child*?! Parker! Parker, Parker, Parker," Chris said, shaking his head in frustration. "I'm beyond disappointed. I'm fucking outraged!" Chris snarled. He walked towards one of his armed men. "800 for that child's life...and 800 for yours..."

Parker looked up at him wide-eyed. "Sir!"

"I don't like this part of the job, Parker. We're not exactly saints, I get that. But I have standards. I lay down a couple of basic rules. And I'm assuming they're not that hard to follow. Do I not pay well enough? Have things gotten so boring, so tedious, so unsatisfactory for you all that you actively go out of your way to defy my most **basic** requirements?" Chris said. By the time Chris finished speaking, Parker was sobbing.

Chris scoffed in disgust and wiped his mouth with a sneer. .

"If this is your last attempt to appeal to my humanity, I'm afraid you have failed. You lost that privilege when you involved a *fucking child*. I'm not swayed by your pathetic tears. Just as you weren't by the kid you stole freedom from," Chris said tightly.

"But, sir-" Parker sobbed.

"You better shut the fuck up cause I'm not done," Chris snapped. Parker immediately shut his mouth, swallowing his sobs.

Chris shook his head. "I don't like taking the lives of others, Parker. But you sealed your fate when you went against my policy. And I can't have that. Not now. Not ever." Chris signaled to one of his men and turned away.

"Please! Sir-!" the man cried out before a bullet went seamlessly through the front of his head and out the back. His body fell with a thud to the ground. Blood gushed out from the open wound. Chris turned with a sigh to face the rest of the kneeling men.

"Do I look like I fucking enjoy this?!" he shouted angrily at them. They all looked at him apologetically, as fear danced in their eyes.

"You all know the nature of the business. We know what we signed up for. I take what I'm dealt. I work with what I've got. And I make a damn masterpiece. I don't feel like I ask for much from you. All you have to do is your fucking job. *No. Fucking. Kids*! Is that **so** damn difficult?!" Chris shouted with rage.

The men furiously shook their heads. Chris rubbed his face, sighing with deep frustration.

He felt his phone buzz in his pocket. He checked a message from Charlie letting him know that Gabrielle was awake. His jaw tensed with anxiety. She could never find out about the kind of work he was actually involved in.

"Clean this shit up. I want the remaining men debriefed by tomorrow morning," Chris said. He walked out of the warehouse with the teddy bear clutched under his arm.

"Yes, sir!" the men said. A few of the armed men pulled the others up and walked them to a van while the rest started to clean out the warehouse.

~*~

Gabrielle moved her legs, desperately trying to find the coolness of the bed. She felt the soft cotton sheets beneath her and eased her body further into its comfort, relishing in its rugged scent.

She hummed in bliss when she popped her eyes open suddenly and quickly sat up.

"Where the hell am I?! Ow!" she said, grabbing her head. "Shit..."

She glanced around the room and saw posters of AC/DC and Metallica on the walls. A red bass hung in the corner. The dresser was scattered with tools and empty liquor bottles.

"What in the world..." She threw the sheets off of her and realized she was still in her clothes from last night. Suddenly, it all came rushing back to her.

"Oh... no... Oh God no! No, no, no!" She jumped out of the bed and started pacing.

"The bar! The girls! I danced on a table! Or was it a couch? How much did I drink?!" she asked frantically. An intense pounding reverberated in her head that made her cringe.

"Ugh! My head," she groaned. "She grabbed her head and sat down. "I need to stop moving so fast... Okay, think, Gabrielle, think. Tanya and Nat brought me to- and then Angie and Rhaven took me near- and then Chris and Char-"

Her eyes widened and she abruptly shot up from the bed when the realization hit her. "CHRIS AND CHARLIE! OH MY GOD! No, no, no, no!"

She jumped up and down on her toes, wringing her hands with anxiety. In seconds, the pain returned and she grasped her head in agony. Slowing her breathing, she counted backwards, using the dresser to steady herself. "4...3...2...1... Okay... Whose house am I in?"

She looked around the room, taking in the decor again. "Cigarette butts. Power tools.... And my old Pikachu watch?" She stood up, walked to his dresser and picked it up. "How in the world... I knew Charlie stole it."

She set the watch down and scratched her head. Peeking out of the bedroom, she looked down the dark hall. She could hear the shower running but didn't know where it was coming from. For she had never been to his place before. Tip-toeing quietly, she tried not to make a sound.

But then the shower stopped.

Thinking the sound was coming from in front of her, she quickly turned around to walk in the other direction and bumped into something hard and wet.

"Woah!" Charlie quickly grabbed her arm and waist to keep her from falling flat on her butt.

"S-sorry," she said. Trying to regain her balance, she instinctively placed her hands on the hard, wet form she bumped into. After shaking her hair out of her face, she saw a wet, shirtless Charlie wearing black sweatpants. A damp towel hung around his neck. His wet, darkened blonde hair clung to his face. She noticed her hands flat against his firm chest.

"Ah! Sorry!" she said quickly, removing her hands. "I- I didn't mean. I didn't see you there." She tried not to look at him. Charlie looked down at her rather confused when he noticed her blush. An amused smirk crossed his face.

"You're up," he said to her. "You feelin' alright?"

She looked up at him through the dark brown kinky curls cascading over her eyes. "I've got a monster hangover, Charlie..."

Charlie smirked knowingly. He took a few steps back into the humid bathroom he just walked out of. "Not surprised after last night. Lucky for you, I have something for that."

She leaned forward to watch him. Her eyes lingered on his muscular chest and abdomen gleaming from the water. Her brows furrowed when she counted how many unsightly scars decorated his torso. He looked as if he survived a woodchipper. It disturbed her.

Charlie shuffled through the cabinet before he finally found a small bottle of ibuprofen. "This should do the trick," he said. He opened the bottle for her and handed her two pills. He grabbed a small cup and ran it under the faucet of the bathroom sink.

"Tap? Really?" she scoffed.

"What? You too 'bougie' for tap, Johansson?" he smirked at her.

"Just give me that," she said, plucking the cup from him. She popped the pills into her mouth and quickly swallowed them down with water. Sighing deeply, she leaned against the wall frame to relax. She lowered her eyes for a moment, until she felt his gaze. Glancing up, she caught Charlie staring her down with a highly amused look on his face.

"Why are you looking at me like that?" she said half annoyed, half nervous.

"Oh, you don't remember?" he mocked. He dried the top of his head with the towel.

"Remember what?" she said, playing dumb.

"About last night." She could see his smug smirk even beneath the towel that danced in his hands as he continued to dry his hair. She bit her lip nervously and quickly pulled his hand down from his head.

"You're white! It doesn't take you that long to dry your hair!" she snapped annoyed.

He looked at her curiously and chuckled. "Is that your way of trying to avoid the question?"

"No, I-..." she bit her lip again, trying to think. "I barely remember last night."

Charlie peered down at her, trying to gauge whether she was being honest. He broke into a wide grin and walked past her out of the bathroom. "Sure, you don't," he chuckled.

"Charlie!" She turned around to follow him. He lay the towel down on the door handle and walked into the kitchen.

"Well if you need a reminder, it was basically sexual harassment," he teased. He opened the cabinet searching for a box of cereal.

"What?! I... Did I..."

"You tried to," Charlie grinned. He poured cereal into a bowl and looked up at her waving the box.

"No. I can't even think of eating right now knowing I came onto you like that..." she said, dropping her shoulders in horror.

"You need to eat something, Gabs," he said. He retrieved another bowl for her and poured her some cereal. "Besides, it wasn't a big deal."

She watched him pour milk into both bowls before setting hers in front of her at the table.

"I just didn't know you wanted me that badly," he grinned, sitting down in front of her.

Gabrielle felt her whole body heat up in response to his teasing. "That's not! I didn't... I mean..."

He chuckled at her flustered demeanor. "Chill out, Gabs. I'm teasing you."

She looked at him for a cautious moment and then sat down to eat with him.

"Thanks for taking care of me," she said finally, after a few moments of silence. "I... honestly didn't mean to violate you like that. I don't know what came over me. I'm so sorry."

After a few bites, Charlie dropped his spoon into the empty bowl and stretched. Gabrielle watched mesmerized as every muscle in the scarred body before her flexed. Her curiosity was pushing her to inquire about his appearance.

"Don't worry. I won't press charges *this time*. But next time you might not be so lucky," he joked. Gabrielle gave him a quick nervous smile and looked back down into her bowl.

"Where did all that come from anyway," he persisted. The question caught her off guard. She looked up at him to see his questioning light green eyes peering intensely into hers.

"I- I honestly have no idea. I had no idea I even felt that way about y-" She abruptly stopped herself. Her eyes widened in shock at what she was about to admit.

Charlie eyed her, noticing her quick change in tone. "Felt about what?"

"Nothing!" she said quickly.

He gazed at her as if waiting for her to cave. But her lips stayed sealed. He grinned, far too entertained by her demeanor, and hopped off of the seat. He walked to her side of the table and spun her around in the chair. Leaning both hands on the table on either side of her, his eyes leveled with hers as he held her attention.

"Felt about... *what*," he asked again, an octave lower than before.

Gabrielle felt her heart beating so hard and fast in her chest she thought it would pop out of her rib cage. She only had to lift her eyes slightly to see how close Charlie's face was to hers. The intensity of his gaze raised her anxiety with each second. His emerald green eyes took on a life of their own, sweeping over her face as if looking into her soul. She glanced down at his pink lips and felt herself drawn to him. It was a feeling that seriously confused her.

"Honestly," she swallowed. "I-I don't even remember what we were talking about," she admitted. She tried desperately to slow her breathing.

Charlie watched as that familiar red flush rushed to her dark brown cheeks. He didn't know what came over him to make him so bold as to be this close to her. He knew damn well that resisting her was a feat on its own. Watching her bite her bottom lip turned him on so much that he instinctively leaned in closer. He could see a flash of excitement in her big brown eyes, peeking its way through her luscious brown curls.

Charlie broke his intense gaze with a smirk. He leveraged the table to push himself backwards away from her. Gabrielle sighed as she felt the sexual tension between them alleviate. She was glad he moved first as she wasn't sure what her next move would be.

"It's okay to be attracted to people, Gabs," he said rubbing the back of his neck. "It's harmless."

Gabrielle nodded quietly just happy he was ending the intense moment. "...right."

"Did the pills kick in?" he asked. He walked towards the sink to put the dishes away.

"Just about," she said watching him. She squinted her eyes, taking a closer look at him. She couldn't believe he had even *more* scars on his back. They looked even more painful.

"Ch-Charlie?" she stammered.

"Hmm?" He could barely hear her over the sound of the water rushing from the faucet as he washed the bowls. She got up from her seat and approached him. Her eyes unwavering from his skin. She could feel her stomach falling as she started to count them. Some that ran from his back and over his broad shoulders. Emotion clogged her throat that her best friend has suffered this much. She reached up and gently touched his back.

Charlie immediately jerked at her touch. He dropped a spoon he was washing into the sink.

"Gabrielle!" he growled, abruptly turning on her.

"I-I'm sorry!" she said, shrinking back from him.

"You can't just sneak up on me like that! What are you doing?" he asked surprised.

"I-... your scars," she said softly. Her eyes roamed over his arms and chest. Although she could see he was clearly agitated, she couldn't stop herself from reaching out to touch him.

Charlie flinched at her touch when her fingers lightly grazed his fairly aged scars. He fought to keep himself from shivering. His whole body ached from how badly he wanted her.

"It's fine. These are old," he shrugged. He tried to temper his body's response to her physical contact that ignited something in him. He couldn't pull his gaze from her. She seemed to be fascinated yet terrified by the look of him.

"Charlie these... these look like they just healed haphazardly on their own," she said worriedly, still investigating him.

"So? That's what the human body does."

"But you couldn't have possibly gone to a doctor to help heal these wounds. You left them alone. You have so much scar tissue," she said. She ran her fingers over a long scar on his bicep.

He abruptly grabbed her hand to stop her from touching him. "It's not a big deal, Gabs," he said defiantly.

She furrowed her brows and looked at him disconcertingly. "What have you been doing, Charlie? Why do you have so many? Is something wrong? Did someone hurt you?"

Now she was really aggravating him. There was no way he could tell her about the kind of work he was involved in. Why did she always have to poke her nose where it didn't belong?

"It's none of your fucking business, Gabrielle. Just drop it!" he growled at her. She looked at him horrified before her face was overwhelmed with anger. His heart sank and he immediately regretted his reaction.

"You're such an asshole!" she said. She hit him hard in the chest with both hands. "Don't you know I just care about you!" She huffed loudly and turned to walk away from him.

"Gabs... wait," he said, grabbing her wrist to keep her from walking away.

"Let go of me, Charles!" she said angrily. She tried to yank her arm out of his grasp, but to no avail.

"Gabrielle," he said, pulling her to him. She stumbled into his arms, nearly losing her balance. But he held her steady with his hand gently against the small of her back. Gabrielle felt dangerously close to Charlie. She was so close she could see the small tints of grey in his bright green eyes. For a moment, she couldn't remember how to breathe.

Charlie looked down at her apologetically, when he started to feel her heat radiating off of her. He caught her eyes flickering between his eyes to his lips, despite trying to keep her angry expression. Her plump lips tempted him. It took everything in him not to bite them.

He struggled to find his words. "I didn't mean to take my frustration out on you, Gabs. It's... a sensitive topic for me. That's all."

Gabrielle's face softened as she felt her heart aching again. She couldn't imagine Charlie being injured or harmed. Being in pain. And by what? How? By whom?

Charlie felt himself being lured in again and willed himself to take her lips with his. He shook his head slightly and let go of her waist, putting some distance between them.

"I care about you too," he said finally.

Gabrielle smiled sadly at him. "You never told me what it is that you do, Charlie."

He thought for a minute, not really sure how to answer that question. "I run a gym."

"You run a gym?" she asked rather surprised. "Like... for people to work out? Or-?"

"A gym for fighters to train."

"You train fighters?" she asked. He nodded.

"What kind of fig-"

"If you don't mind. I don't really like when people prod into my life," he said cutting her off.

Gabrielle sighed at how cold and distant he made himself. "Okay, Charlie… I understand."

He took a deep, heavy breath and rolled his shoulders back to crack the tension in his neck.

"We should get you home. I'm sure Eli and Tanya are worried about you," he said.

"Yea... I don't even know how to get home from here though."

"You wouldn't. But I'll drop you off."

"You sure?"

"Of course."

Gabrielle returned to his room to pack her things and noted her old Pikachu watch on Charlie's dresser. She looked at it admiringly before latching it on to her wrist. Charlie walked into the bedroom, fully dressed in a black shirt and boots. He eyed her admiring the watch on her wrist and smirked. "You found it."

"Yea, I can't believe you still have this, you thief. You told me you bought your own," she glared at him.

"I did," he shrugged.

She scoffed. "Clearly not! This one is missing the blue button that Thor bit off. See?"

Charlie took a few steps towards her and gently grabbed her wrist. He turned her hand over in his, caressing the back of her hand. Gabrielle held her breath as the calluses on his hand scraped against her skin. She glanced at him and saw his eyes peering intently at the watch as if he were trying to find the missing blue button she spoke of.

Charlie relished the softness of Gabrielle's skin against his. He longed to feel more of her, but her hand would have to do. He admired the contrast of her dark skin tone against his.

"Heh... I guess you're right," he smirked. He caressed the top of her hand with his finger. "Would you like it back?" he said, looking up from her hand to her eyes.

Gabrielle was speechless for a moment, unsure of what to say. The feeling of his skin against hers made her mind go blank. When those intense green eyes landed on her, she panicked unsure of what he said.

"Huh?"

Charlie smirked. "I asked if you wanted it back."

"Oh... no. I mean you can hold onto it for now. Save childhood memories and all," she said with a nervous laugh. She pulled her hand back from him and removed the watch from her wrist. He took it from her, placed it in his pocket and turned to exit the bedroom.

When they stepped outside of his apartment, Gabrielle looked around for a car but did not see one.

"Um.. where's your ride?" she said.

"Right here," Charlie said, pulling up his bike.

"Woah! Is that Papa Steve's?" she said, admiring the bike.

"Yea, finished it up a few days ago," he said proudly. He ran his fingers over the surface.

Gabrielle approached the bike and touched the finishing on the handle bars.

"Get on," Charlie encouraged her.

"Huh?"

"Mount the beast," he urged, grinning. Gabrielle stepped closer to the bike and swung a leg over. Her legs spread wider and her back stretched over more than she expected.

"It's a lot bigger than I expected," she said, settling on it.

Charlie grinned at her suggestive remark. "Is it now?"

Gabrielle shot her head up and looked at him embarrassed. "I just meant..."

"I know what you meant, Gabs," he teased her. "Let's hope the performance doesn't disappoint either."

Gabrielle felt her face flush hot and desperately tried to change the subject. "I never took you for a sports bike, kinda guy. Thought you were more of a Harley Davidson."

"I'm an all-types-of-bikes kinda guy. I've got a Harley in my garage," he grinned. "It feels different, and I'm a speed demon. I can appreciate them both."

"Should have known," she grinned. She looked over the hardware and ran her hands over the dashboard. "All of this looks so different from a Harley though... how do you..."

"I'll show you," he said, mounting the bike from behind her. He placed a hand on her hip and leaned forward, pressing his chest against her back. Gabrielle nearly stopped breathing when she felt the heat of his body against hers. She instinctively arched into him, desperate to feel more. Her body craved to be closer to him.

Charlie felt Gabrielle's body mesh against his. He wavered between teasing her enough to torture her and succumbing to his own temptation. Leaning over her, he guided her hand over the dashboard.

"I changed the entire interface, including the speedometer. That way when I go on long rides in the middle of night, it's not that difficult to see how fast I'm going," he explained.

"Do these midnight rides happen often?" she said. She nestled her head beneath his chin.

"Maybe..."

"Are you going to see someone or... do something...?" she asked. Gabrielle was prodding. He shook his head, grinning, and pulled back to rest both of his hands on her hips. She could feel the reverberation of his deep chuckle against her back.

His voice was low, deep, and husky against her ear. "You keepin' tabs on me, Johansson?"

Her body temperature skyrocketed as the air from his lips when he spoke tickled her neck and behind her ear.

"I'm just... trying to get to know you a little better, Charlie." She sank further into him.

Charlie frowned and immediately put distance between them by dismounting his bike.

"There's not much to know. Nor do you need to know," he said coldly. Gabrielle was startled by his drastic change in mood *again*! From flirting to shutting down in 5 seconds flat. She didn't understand why he always reverted back to treating her so coldly.

"I just meant that... that I was trying to catch up on lost time," she said apologetically. Charlie furrowed his brow, both annoyed at her prodding questions and his rudeness towards her. He promised himself he wouldn't let her get too close, but he also didn't want her to think he hated her.

"Sure..." he said, getting back on the bike, in front of her. "I've held you here for too long. Let's go." He held out a helmet to her. She hesitated, unnerved by his behavior and the fact that she would be riding this death trap.

"I... motorcycles go way too fast for me, Charlie," she said nervously.

"Then you better make sure you hold on tight," he smirked. He revved up the loud engine. She sighed and took the helmet, putting it over her huge fluffy hair. She hesitated before leaning forward to wrap her arms around his stomach. She held on tight and could feel the firmness of his abs.

Charlie's words faltered briefly as he tried to focus. "Here we go," he said. They pulled into the street with a loud roar.

~*~

Gabrielle spent the rest of the day apologizing to her friends for her behavior at the lounge.

"But do you feel better?" Tanya asked on the other end of the line.

"I do actually. I don't know why I allowed myself to plunge that far. I should be happy. I'm free! I can now go back out in the dating field and meet someone better," Gabrielle said, taking her brownies out of the oven.

"That's my girl. You're too good to be wasted on that guy. Do you, boo. You gotta live your best life."

"You're right. And I wouldn't have been able to do it without my friends. So, I'm thinking of having a little dinner party for y'all," Gabrielle said.

"Oh really? And whose house will you be hosting this at Ms. Homeless," Tanya chuckled.

"Excuse me! I am not homeless! I'm still trying to figure out when I'm going back to Cali. My leave is almost up anyway. But

I'll throw it at Eli's house. He's already told me he's okay with it."

"Mhm... and who's coming?"

"The usual. You, Eli, Rhaven, and Angie. I'll invite Arthur and Nat. Charlie and Chris..." she trailed off. There was a moment of silence.

"Speaking of Chris..." Tanya started.

"I haven't apologized to him yet. But I made brownies and I'm heading over to talk to him," Gabrielle said quickly.

"Alright, alright... good luck with that," Tanya chuckled.

"Whatever. I'll talk to you later, T," Gabrielle said. She hung up and packed some of the brownies in a container before heading out the door.

~*~

Chris sat at his desk holding his head up with one hand while he looked over the teddy bear held in the other. It was dirty and ruffled and missing one eye. He sighed as he tried to think of how old the missing child was. If it was a boy or a girl. What their name was. If they were still alive...

The thoughts haunted him.

He reached into his pocket and pulled out his cellphone to find no text messages.

"Fuck." Still no update on the missing child.

He opened up his laptop and furiously typed away. His eyes flashed wildly as he scrolled relentlessly down the screen. His frown deepened the more he looked and the more he realized he wouldn't find what he was looking for.

"Shit!" He angrily pushed himself away from the desk. He held his head in his hands as if he were trying to cradle all the thoughts in his mind from spilling over onto the floor.

A loud ring disturbed his thoughts. He blinked for a second, not sure if he had imagined the ringing or if there was actually someone at his door. He rarely had visitors.

"Hey, Chris!" He opened the door and looked down at the bright-eyed, kinky-haired, beautiful dark-skinned woman that held his heart in her hands.

"Hey, Gabs," he smiled warmly. He moved aside to let her in.

Gabrielle walked inside and her mouth dropped as she gazed around his high-rise, luxury apartment. "Holy moly, this place is gorgeous!"

"Thanks," he said. He took her jacket and hung it on the hook. His eyes lingered on her body, taking in her loose white blouse and pink shorts that nicely complemented her thick mocha brown thighs. "No offense but how the hell did you find out where I lived?" he asked.

"Oh... I'm sorry, your mom told me..."

"...Of course..." he sighed, stuffing his hands into his pockets. Gabrielle frowned at his unusual unhappy demeanor.

"I-I just... wanted to apologize," she said nervously. She rocked on her feet, trying to decipher his expression.

"Apologize? Apologize for what?" he asked, surprised.

"For the other night at the lounge. For taking care of me. Well... thank you for that actually. But I'm sorry that I basically violated you," she said, shaking her head from embarrassment. "I don't know what possessed me to act that way and I feel awful about it. I hope you can forgive me."

Still thinking about the missing child, he looked at her slightly confused. He tried to figure out what she was talking about, when he remembered her advances on him that night.

"Oh! Gabs, that's alright. It's no big deal. Really," he said comfortingly.

Gabrielle looked up at him, searching his eyes to see how he felt. "I just want you to know that that's not the kind of person I am. I would never do anything on purpose to make you feel uncomfortable like that."

Chris chuckled. "You're acting like you held me down to a bed and forced yourself on me. Don't worry about it."

Gabrielle immediately blushed at the mental image now in her head.

"Are you feeling better?" he asked her. The buzzing of his phone caught his attention. He checked a message from one of his men. Third debrief and still nothing about the child. Chris narrowed his eyes in frustration as a slight growl escaped his lips.

"I'm much better," she said. She noticed his drastic change in expression. "And... you? Are you alright?"

He looked up at her, startled by her question. "Yea, of course, I'm fine. Why do you ask?"

"You just... seem a little bit... *tense*," she said eyeing him suspiciously.

"Oh. I've just had a bit of a rough day at work," he assured her.

"I thought you were still on bereavement. Taking some time for yourself to get things sorted?"

"When you own your own company, you never truly have time for yourself," he chuckled, rubbing the tension from his neck. Gabrielle frowned though she understood his predicament.

"Well... maybe I could help you relax? I give a mean massage. And, I did bring you apology brownies." She lifted the container, grinning from ear to ear.

"Hmm. I did just have dinner but that'd make a great dessert," he chuckled at her goofy face. “I thought you were a surgeon not a masseuse.” He led her into the living room.

“C’est vrai, mon ami. But as a surgeon I know all the pressure points to alleviate tension,” she smiled. She placed the container of brownies on the table and sat on the couch, immediately sinking into its plush comfort.

“Oh my gosh... why does this couch feel like heaven? Can I live here? Can I take residence on your couch?” She blissfully rubbed her face against the pillow.

“Might be a little too small for you, Gabs,” he laughed, as she comically wafted her face into the pillow.

“I still can’t get over how amazing your apartment is. I can’t believe you live here,” she said sitting up. She jumped to her feet and ran towards the large ceiling-to-floor windows, pressing her face against the glass.

“Perks of running a REIT. This building is one of my company’s most profitable properties,” Chris said. He leaned against the wall with his arms folded across his chest, watching her quite amused.

“You *own* this building?!” She looked back at him completely flabbergasted.

He nodded with a fond smile. “It was one of my first developments.”

“You’re amazing, Chris,” she said walking towards his desk. “Seriously, I had no clue you were such an inspirational mogul. I’m sure there’s a lot of people looking up to you.”

Chris gave a small smile. But his face fell into a frown the moment she picked up the teddy bear on his desk.

“This is a strange item for a grown ass man to own,” she teased. She inspected the bear precariously. “Is it yours?”

He rushed over to her and quickly yanked the bear out of her hand, startling her enough to make her step back.

"Sorry, ah... it's a... old gift for a dear friend," he said. He stuffed the bear into the desk drawer behind him.

"Is... is this an adult friend?" Gabrielle asked, confused.

"Can you just drop it?" he snapped. His raised voice took her by surprise. Chris saw a fleeting look of fear in her eyes that made him want to punch himself in the face.

"I-I'm sorry, Gabs. I didn't mean to raise my voice at you like that," he apologized. Her expression quickly turned to that of concern.

"You really are tense." She reached up to touch his arm and his muscles instantly relaxed.

"Okay, massage time. Come sit," she said. She walked towards the couch and plopped herself down. Chris hesitated briefly before taking a seat on the floor in front of her. She slowly started to knead her knuckles into the dense part of his muscles. She worked her way from the base of his neck, across his shoulder blades, and along his spine. Chris felt himself sinking with bliss into the base of the couch as Gabrielle's hands worked away at his back.

"Jeez, you've got a lot of meat here, Chris," she chuckled. She struggled to knead deeper into his shoulders.

"Nice phrasing there, Gabs," Chris grinned at the double meaning in her words..

Gabrielle's eyes widened in embarrassment. "I just meant-!"

"I'm playing with you, Gabs...," he grinned. "Be careful. I don't want you to hurt your hands." With his head down, he savored the firmness of her fingers pressing into his muscles.

"It's alright. I can at least feel some of the tension melting away.

Here. Let me try something else," she said softly. She relaxed her hands and ran her fingers gently down his back. She carefully massaged his neck and ran her fingers over his shoulders and down the front of his chest when she heard a low moan escape from his mouth.

It made her stomach flip. "Does that feel good? Is this helping?" she asked, trying to stay calm. Chris was so caught up in the feeling, he merely grunted in acknowledgement.

"Sometimes this method is more effective than a tough massage. Tense muscles are just as sensitive to light touches as they are to rough ones. I learned that from a friend in medical school," she told him.

"That's interesting," he said. "Think you can try that method on my chest? I'm especially sore there."

Gabrielle paused briefly to consider his request. Was that a good idea? Could she handle seeing him shirtless? Touching him like that? Of course she could! She was a professional.

She stood from the couch and sat down in front of him, crossing her legs. Scooting closer towards him, she sat in between his bent legs as his forearms rested on his raised knees. She stared at him, assessing the best approach, when he lifted his head to look at her. She hesitated for just a moment before finally lifting her hands to his chest.

"Wait," he said quickly. "This will probably make it easier." Chris lifted the end of his shirt and pulled it over his head casually tossing it to the side.

"Better?" he asked, eyeing her.

This felt too familiar. Gabrielle was utterly entranced. She couldn't help her eyes roaming his finely-sculpted chest and torso. She immediately noticed his scars ever so similar to Charlie's, though they were slightly more faded.

Why on earth did they both have so many scars? What did she miss all these years she spent away from them? And who did this to them? She scrunched up her nose in concern, eager to question him. But she feared dealing with the same reaction she received from Charlie.

"Gabs?"

"Huh?" she said, looking up at him.

"Are you okay?"

"Yes!" she said, snapping out of it. "Sorry, I was just... thinking of the best technique for... this type of... physiology. Don't worry. I'm a professional. I'll have you feeling de-stressed in no time," she beamed at him.

He nodded, giving her a small smile, but his eyes never left her face. He watched her expression change from assurance to apprehension. Chris knew exactly what he was doing. He knew it wasn't fair for him to do this to her... or to himself, for that matter. But he needed to know.

Gabrielle tried to focus all of her attention and energy to her technique. She carefully placed both of her hands flatly against Chris's chest. She prayed that her palms weren't sweaty, but already felt herself unraveling from the sensual feeling of his firm muscles beneath her hands. Her fingers brushed over his faded scars, feeling the hardened scar tissue that didn't detract from his delicious form.

Focus Gabby! she thought to herself. She gently kneaded into his pectoral muscles, careful to avoid his nipples. Her fingers pushed firmly into the tense muscle underneath. Working her fingers downward towards his abdomen, she felt around the ridges of his dense abs.

"Shit..." she murmured. "I mean- you're in great shape! Er, no I'm trying to say that- that your abdominal muscles are a bit more hardened down here, probably from stress or... or working out," she stammered.

Chris could barely contain the grin threatening to give him away.

"I'll just stay up here," she murmured. She worked her fingers back upward. She could feel Chris's gaze upon her and tried desperately to avoid his eyes as if that would be the end of her. She focused entirely on her movements and got into a rhythm, firmly massaging up towards his collarbone.

When her fingers reached his neck, she couldn't avoid his gaze any longer. Not once had he looked away, and the intensity of that steel blue stare nearly made her stop breathing.

"Wow, I just... I just did this spot," she swallowed. "Work must really have you tense, Chris," she said, rhythmically drumming her fingers against his neck. Chris grabbed one of her hands and playfully rubbed his thumb against her palm. Finally breaking eye contact, he glanced at her hand and lightly ran a finger up and down her forearm.

"This tension isn't from work, Gabs..." he said, diverting his baby blue's back to her.

Gabrielle felt herself being lured in. Or was she leaning in? Definitely the latter. This felt like torture. Was he torturing her or was she torturing herself? Feeling his body like putty in her hands, she wanted to do more than just touch him. But how would he react? This was her best friend. One wrong move could ruin what they had forever.

She bit down on her lip, almost hard enough to draw blood and quickly withdrew both of her hands from his body.

"Do you feel better?" she asked him. He frowned at her sudden movement away from him.

"Much. Thanks, Gabs," he said, rolling out his neck. She wanted to curse her hands simply for not being on his chest.

"Please put your shirt back on," she blurted, thrusting his shirt at him. “I mean... here’s your shirt,” she said more politely.

Chris chuckled as he casually put his shirt back on. “Did I do something wrong?”

“No. I mean yes!... Stop it!”

“Stop what?”

“Stop doing whatever the hell it is you’re doing!” she said exasperated.

“But what am I doing?” Chris asked her this question with such innocence she almost believed him, if it weren’t for the smirk on his face that betrayed him. He placed both hands on her thighs as if to calm her, when it was doing something entirely different to her.

“Christopher Richardson! You know *exactly* what you’re doing!” she growled at him. She got up on her knees and reached for the pillow behind him.

“Gabs!” he laughed, before she stuffed the pillow in his face. “Why are you covering my face?!” His voice was muffled behind the pillow, sounding so comical it made her chuckle.

“So, you can stop looking at me like that,” she said.

When he muffled something she couldn’t hear, she removed the pillow from his face. “What did you say?” she asked.

“I said I’m not looking at you any differently than I normally do,” he smiled at her. His hair was a ruffled mess from her pillow assault and his hands were again resting teasingly on her thighs.

“You’re playing with me,” she accused him. She rose slightly above him, still threatening to cover his face with the pillow again. He looked up at her with his light blue eyes and an innocent smile, covering a peaking grin.

“I assure you there are *other* games I’d much rather play with you, Gabs..." he said sweetly, despite how naughty and suggestive the comment was. His gaze shifted from her eyes to her lips and he gave her thighs a playful squeeze.

"Oh, fuck it." Gabrielle threw the pillow over her shoulders and immediately descended upon Chris. She desperately wrapped her hands around his neck and slammed her lips into his. She scooted closer to him when she felt his hands stray from her thighs towards her waist. He held her up with a firm grasp. She coerced his mouth open with her tongue before both tongues clashed against each other. A moan escaped her lips as she combed her fingers through his hair. She felt on fire. Her body took on a mind of its own.

She kissed him passionately and hungrily as if she couldn't get enough of him. Running her hands down his chest, she licked at his lips and bit down gently, eliciting a moan from him.

Suddenly, a buzzing sensation startled them. Gabrielle immediately jumped off of Chris, who struggled to get his phone from his now tightened pants to silence it.

"Sorry..." he said smiling at her sheepishly. He tucked his phone back into his pocket.

Gabrielle blinked at him in distress at what she had just done. "What are we doing? What am *I* doing? Shit. Shit! I'm- I'm so sorry, Chris. I'm so sorry!"

She quickly got up and stumbled to the other side of the living room, putting some distance between them. Chris looked at her questioningly. With a sigh, he stood to his feet. "Why are you apologizing, Gabs?"

"Because! Because I kissed you! And I- I almost- I mean I wanted to and I- I can't do this! We shouldn't be doing this!"

"Why not?" he said, walking towards her.

"Because you're my best friend, Chris! I came over here to apologize to you and I nearly sucked your face off!" she blurted. "I mean what the hell? You're- you're like a brother to me!" she said flustered as she backed away from him.

"Well, you just kissed your brother, so..." he chuckled, as he took another step towards her.

"EW! Christopher!" she growled at him. "This isn't funny! I- what have I done? I need to control myself better. I don't know what's wrong with me. I don't-"

"The only thing wrong, Gabs, is how quickly you stopped," he teased her, enjoying this game more than he expected.

"Would you stop it! I thought you'd be just as appalled as I am. I'm not even your type," she frowned, folding her arms.

This time it was his turn to frown. "My type? And what exactly do you think my type is?" he asked curiously. He took a few more steps until he had backed her against the wall.

She blinked furiously, a bit surprised by his question. "Uh, maybe tall skinny blondes with big breasts and flowing silky hair," she blurted.

Chris gave her a funny face, not shy about showing his disappointment. "You think that's my type?" he asked.

"It's who I've seen you with, Chris," she said matter-of-factly.

He sighed as he couldn't necessarily refute the claim, since she was right. What he wanted to tell her was that all other women paled in comparison to who he really wanted.

"I like all kinds of women, Gabs," he said. He placed his hands on the wall on either side of her. Looking down at her with an inquisitive gaze, his eyes roamed her face as if he were inspecting her.

Gabrielle trembled from his closeness when he tenderly grabbed her shoulder. His fingers glided down her arm, before he brought his pointer finger beneath her chin, and tilted her head upwards.

He stared deeply into her eyes and softly stroked the side of her face. "Especially women with soft brown eyes..."

He playfully tapped the bridge of her nose with his fingertip. "A cute button nose..."

His thumb gently pulled at her bottom lip as hunger invaded his gaze. "And the most perfect... full... lips..."

Gabrielle swallowed hard. "Chris..." she whimpered. She couldn't tell if she was going to pass out or attack him right there. She had never been so turned on in her whole life, and yet here Chris was, with one look, making her want to throw her panties at him.

He smirked at the way she nervously bit her bottom lip. "Besides... soft kinky hair is better for pulling, don't you think?" he said with a mischievous grin.

Gabrielle's eyes bugged. "Christopher!" she said in shock. She pushed him away. "I cannot believe you just said that!" She grabbed the container of brownies from the table and marched towards the kitchen.

"What???" he said innocently, following her.

"You've never even slept with a black woman, Chris, so how would you know?" she said, walking to the counter.

"We could always test my hypothesis, babe," he teased.

She tried to ignore the dampness between her thighs. "Shut up, Chris. My god. You're just as annoying as an adult as you were as a kid, only your jokes are dirtier," she rolled her eyes.

"You can pretend you don't like it," he grinned, leaning against the counter next to her.

She gave him a dirty look. "Changing the subject: I'm having a little get-together. A dinner party if you will... And I was hoping you would come. It's really just a way of me thanking you guys for supporting me and being there for me when I was acting bat-shit crazy."

"Hmm. Sure, I'd love to come," he smiled. He watched her put a ridiculous amount of time and attention into removing the brownies from the container. He noticed her body was still trembling slightly, almost as if she were aching to be touched again.

"And you weren't acting crazy. You were grieving. The death of a father… and the death of a relationship. Not easy things to deal with. I know it's been hard for you, Gabs," he said, chasing away his tempting thoughts.

Gabrielle turned to face him with a smile. "It was. But ending that relationship was for the best. There's better people out there for me…" she trailed off.

Suddenly, his face turned serious. "Gabs, you mentioned before that… he threatened you."

She looked up at him surprised. "I did? Wow. I really *was* acting crazy," she chuckled nervously.

Chris frowned at her. "Are you saying it's not true?"

"What I'm saying is that this conversation is far too heavy when there's a delicious set of brownies waiting for us." She turned to face the counter.

Chris twisted his mouth in annoyance. Shut off again. "Gabs…"

"And they're the best brownies because I made them. With love," she smirked, looking back at him. But he impatiently grabbed her by the waist and turned her around to face him.

"Don't shut me out, Gabs. You know you can talk to me," he said holding her waist and searching her eyes.

She was completely caught off guard by the way he grabbed her, and it made her heart skip a beat. She could have melted into his arms with the way those beautiful blue eyes stared at her with such concern. If only the question that accompanied his gestures wasn't such a turn off.

She furrowed her brows as she tried to find her words. "I told you I'm fine, Chris."

He stared at her intently, waiting for her to give him more. But her lack of response informed him that was all she'd give him. He went to speak but she stuffed a brownie in his mouth before he could utter a word. "Gabs!" he muffled.

"Tell me that's not good," she giggled. She laughed watching him try to chew the brownie whole.

"Okay... okay it is good," he said, wiping his mouth. 'But-"

"Exactly! Oh, we should add whip cream. Like when we were kids," she said, searching his cupboards.

"Are you *trying* to put us both into cardiac arrest?" he laughed.

She found the whip cream and shook it. "Come on, Chris! Live a little!" she laughed. She sprayed whip cream on the brownie before taking a bite. A moan fell from her lips, enjoying the moisture of the brownie mixed with the fluff of the cream.

The provocative sound she made caught his attention. Leaning back against the counter, Chris watched with hooded eyes, as she savored the piece.

"That good, huh?" He swallowed thickly, getting more turned on by the second. His eyes followed her movements as she licked the cream from her fingers.

"Wanna try some?" she asked him. He merely shook his head and continued watching her.

"Come on! You loved this so much when we were kids. Are you too good for some tasty nostalgia?" she teased. She took another bite and moaned again in such a way it made Chris twitch. He shifted uncomfortably and cleared his throat.

He wasn't sure if she was aware what she was doing to him or if she was just that oblivious to the effect she had on him. He tried to chase away the image that popped into his head of him bending her over the counter, taking her from behind and making her moan himself.

"You really gotta stop doing that," he warned her, crossing his arms over his chest.

"Doing what?" she asked. She got even more whip cream on herself. "Wow, I guess I'm still a messy eater. Seriously, Chris. I'm going to feel so bad if I eat this whole thing without you. I made these for you, you know."

"You're a bad influence, Gabs," he said, feeling hotter.

"Me? A bad influence? I'm trying to bring you joy and happiness. But you won't eat these brownies. Why don't you love yourself, Chris," she joked. She smacked some whip cream on his cheek.

"Gabrielle!" he growled, lunging for her.

She shrieked with laughter as he overtook her, squeezing her tightly around the waist. "Okay! Okay! I'm sorry! I'm sorry!" she said with her hands up. Upon her surrender, he loosened his grip and moved to the counter to grab a towel for his face off.

"Still just as annoying as you were 8 years ago," he smirked, wiping his face.

"I think you mean 'still just as *lovable*'," she grinned. She laughed at his failed attempt to clean his face. "Let me do it." She snatched the towel out of his hand.

"None of this would have happened if you just ate the brownies like I said," she teased him, carefully wiping his face.

"Why do you want me to eat your brownies so badly, Gabs...?" he smirked suggestively. He interrupted her cleaning by taking a tentative step towards her.

Gabrielle immediately felt both intimidated and turned on. His eyes had darkened, and his demeanor had changed. "Because..." she hesitated. "I... put a lot of effort into those brownies and I wanted you to enjoy them, you weirdo."

"*I'm* the weirdo...?" he said mockingly. He took another step closer.

"Yes, you're the weirdo. 8 years later and you're *still* the weirdo, Chis," she teased him. Though she was still feeling anxious about his closeness, she tried to remind herself that this was just typical banter between the two of them. Same as it's always been. She was not giving into her temptation again.

Chris grabbed her hand and removed the towel from her grasp.

"I'm the weirdo that you kissed..." he stared into her eyes, with a grin. "And it kinda seems like you wanna do it again..."

She visibly gulped, unsure of what he was trying to do. His gaze was even more intense, and it sparked such a strong fire in her that she wasn't sure whether to pounce on him or run the other direction.

"Chris... don't do this... you're making this so hard for me," she pleaded weakly.

"You've already made this hard for me, Gabs. *Literally*," he smirked suggestively. He took another step closing the space between them. He wrapped an arm around her waist, flushing her body against his. He could feel her trembling in his embrace as she looked up at him with desire written all over her face.

He lowered his head to her ear and whispered heatedly. "My type... I only have one type, Gabs...Can you guess what that is...?"

He tightened his grasp on her waist and felt her short breaths on his neck. The way the smooth dark brown skin on her neck shimmered was all too much for him. He gave in, placing his lips tenderly against her neck. He felt her body sink into his arms as she wrapped her arms around his neck.

Chris's hands strayed from her waist to her wide hips and down her thick thighs. He picked her up and lifted her onto the countertop. He loved the way her large thighs spread on the table and gently caressed them, savoring her soft skin beneath his hands. His mouth moved from her neck to her collarbone, kissing lightly and leaving a tingling sensation. Gabrielle moaned from his contact as he gripped her thighs tighter. He pulled her closer to him and gently nibbled on her neck.

She ran her fingers over Chris's biceps, around his shoulders, and down his strong back. She traced over every detail of his muscles, her fingers outlining his scars. She felt herself melting into him. She wanted to get lost in him... with him, forever.

"Chris..." she panted in between breaths. "What about... dessert?"

Chris chuckled and gently kissed her shoulder. His fingers playfully ran along the inside of her thighs, provoking goosebumps to form on her skin that heated up against his touch.

He leaned in towards her, resting his forearm on the counter. Using his other hand, he teased the fabric of her damp shorts covering her dripping wet core. She gasped when she felt his fingers rub against her. He whispered calmly in her ear. "Oh, baby... *this is dessert.*"

He pulled away from her and tugged at the hem of her shirt, lifting it over her head. He revealed her black bra, cupping two beautiful brown mounds, her dark nipples just slightly peeking over the top. Gabrielle desperately grasped at his shirt, prompting him to quickly lift it over his head and toss it on the floor. As if seeing it for the first time, she stared in awe at the definition of his chest tracing her fingers from his collarbone, down his pectorals, and over his abs. Her fingers lightly grazed over the scars she became so acquainted with before.

"I think we're gonna need a little more room," Chris smirked at her. He wrapped her legs around his waist and held her tightly, showering her neck and chest with kisses.

He carried her to his bedroom and gently laid her down on the bed. Straddling her between his legs, he lifted her arms above her head and caressed down her arms. He kissed her forehead, her cheeks, her nose, and her chin before sucking on her bottom lip. Sneaking a hand behind her back, he unhooked her bra, freeing his prize from their satin prison. He sat back for a moment to admire what he had been craving to see, to touch, to kiss, to taste for years.

Gabrielle could see the dark desire in Chris's gaze as his eyes raked hungrily over her body. She squirmed beneath him, anxiously biting her lip. Her body no longer obeyed her. Chris grinned mischievously and lowered his head to take one of her taut, dark nipples into his mouth. She gasped in ecstasy as his tongue swirled around her areola, sucking and tugging with his lips.

He grabbed her other breast, massaging it tenderly and twirling her nipple between his fingers. Her body responded to him so strongly that she steadily became wetter. Gabrielle gasped loudly, so overwhelmed with pleasure that he looked up at her with concern to make sure she was alright.

"I'm fine," she panted. "I'm just- you're driving me crazy, Chris!" He grinned and leaned down, moving further down her body. He left feather-light kisses on her stomach that tickled enough to make her squirm. Reaching for the waistband of her shorts, he toyed with the clasps until it came undone and he quickly slipped it off of her.

Moving back up to her panties, he kissed the lining along her waist. His fingers caressed her hips as he moved further down. He had reached his goal when he saw how wet she was through her panties. Dragging his nose over the fabric, he inhaled her scent, feeling her wetness coat his nose. He sighed deeply, wanting so badly to taste her.

“Chris,” she said, her body tensing up. “What are you doing?”

He looked up at her and saw apprehension in her eyes. “Have you ever had anyone go down on you, Gabs?” he asked.

Her eyes widened and she quickly shook her head in embarrassment. “No...”

He looked at her surprised and then grinned. “Then, baby, you’re really gonna enjoy this,” he said, looking down at her hungrily.

“But, Chris-” she hesitated again.

“You trust me, don’t you, Gabs?” he asked meaningfully. She nodded.

“Then relax, baby. I’ll take care of you,” he smiled reassuringly. She hesitated before finally nodding. She laid her head back down and felt him pull her panties down her legs. She anxiously waited, her heat rising.

Chris ran his fingers up her leg and down her thighs, soaking in each detail. His eyes frequently darted to his target. Settling himself between her legs, he stroked her thighs ever so gently.

He stared at her pussy. Her round clit poked prettily through her wet lips. It looked so beautiful to him, so delicious. He softly kissed the inside of her thighs, sending shivers up her spine. As he kissed her thighs, he looked to see her pussy glistening from her juices as she got wetter from anticipation.

He pushed his face closer and licked her clit quickly and tenderly. He immediately felt her tremble and jerk beneath him. He rubbed circles on her hip bone with his thumbs to soothe her. He licked her again, this time slower, dragging his tongue from the bottom of her pussy to the top, stopping only to gently suck her clit into his mouth. Her juices trickled into his mouth with each lick. He pushed both of her thighs over his shoulders, elevating her and spreading her wider. He nearly came undone watching her brown and pink lips unfold before him as she continued to drip relentlessly.

"Goddamn, Gabs," he moaned before latching his mouth onto her clit again. He sucked it gently, slowly tracing the outside and inner crevices with his tongue. He made sure to reach every corner and crease. She bucked involuntarily towards him and arched her back, letting out loud breathless moans. He slowed down to make sure she enjoyed every minute of this as much as he did.

He used two of his fingers to spread her lips and dipped one of them inside her.

"Oh god!" she breathed out in ecstasy. "Chris!"

Her body writhed beneath him as he pushed his finger in again. He placed his mouth on her clit and sucked gently, then progressed more roughly as he continued to finger her.

He felt her getting wetter and removed his finger to feel the consistency between his finger and his thumb. He looked up at her to see her beautiful face contorted in ecstasy. With her eyes shut tight, she bit down hard on her bottom lip. The sight was all too much for him and he wanted nothing more than to mount her and fill her up, blowing her back out.

But for now...

He lowered his mouth again, flattening his tongue to lick her from bottom to top, stopping only to suck and flick her clit with the tip of his tongue.

Gabrielle was losing her mind. She was beyond overwhelmed. The feeling of Chris's cool tongue on her hot core was more than she could handle. This was all so new to her, but it felt so good. She felt him grip her hips and pull her down further onto his mouth. Then she felt his tongue dip into her.

"Fuck, Chris!" she panted. She firmly gripped his hair with both hands and squirmed beneath him. Squeezing her tighter, Chris continued sucking, licking and fucking her with his tongue. She felt an intense sensation rise within her and her legs began to tremble.

"Chris! I-"

"Just let it happen, baby," he said, lifting his head for a moment before he went back to eating her out.

"Oh fuck! Fuck, baby, fuck!" She desperately clutched the sheets and moaned loudly, reaching her climax. The feeling seemed to last forever, and she felt like she was floating. Her legs went weak and her whole body went tense before going limp. Chris didn't stop licking her the whole time she came. His eyes never left her face as he watched her reach her peak and scream his name in ecstasy.

~*~

Charlie arrived at the meat-packing building wearing boots, a compression sweater, leather gloves, a black beanie, and a switchblade tucked away in his back pocket.

He scouted the area to see no one was there. Proceeding around the back, he saw empty cars and flipped motorcycles. He peaked through the window and noticed several bodies lying around with a few more hovering over them.

Without a second to think, Charlie kicked down the door and immediately dodged a bullet that came flying his way. He slid across the ground, knocking the shooter out from under his feet. Grabbing the knife from his belt, Charlie sliced the shooter across the throat.

He noticed someone running up to him from behind and dodged him. He grabbed the guy by his forearm and twisted it behind his back, breaking his arm in two places. He used the guy as a shield from two other men shooting at him. After dropping the man riddled with bullets to the ground, Charlie flung his knife into one of the shooter's heads before pouncing on the other assailant. He knocked him to the floor and snapped his neck. Stealing the gun from the guy's hand, Charlie instantly shot three more men approaching him from behind.

He stood up to look at the rest of the carnage. Some of his enemies were lying on the ground dead along with many of his own men. Of the four of his men still alive, Charlie rushed over to the leader of the squad.

"Jim, what happened?" Charlie asked in anguish. He held Jim up to keep him from choking on his own blood. A huge metal rod stuck out of his abdomen.

"W-we were a-ambushed," Jim choked out.

"Ambushed? How? You guys were planning this raid for weeks!" Charlie exclaimed.

"W-we d-don't know. W-we got here a-and th-they were already w-waiting for us."

"Who? Who met you?" Charlie asked.

"B-B-beau-" Jim tried to finish but he soon succumbed to his wounds.

"Shit!" Charlie shouted. He gently lay Jim down and tended to the others. He walked over to two men struggling to get up.

"Come on," he said, helping them. "Let's get you guys out of here."

He took the remaining surviving men back to his van and drove off.

~*~

Chris sat at his desk in his bedroom, holding a tablet. He screened the files sent to him by his men after their final debriefing. He quickly read the summary, going back and forth between the debrief and the attached images. Noticing something off in one of the pictures, he narrowed his eyes and used his fingers to zoom in on the image on the tablet.

"Couldn't be..." he whispered to himself.

He quickly glanced behind him to see Gabrielle sleeping soundly in his bed. She looked ethereal. A smooth, dark angelic temptress in a sea of white sheets. Her curly hair framed her peaceful, relaxed face. She had a particular glow about her that made Chris smile to himself. A sudden grin crossed his face as he attributed her serenity to how intensely he tongued her down hours ago. She was so overwhelmed by the way he ate her out that she knocked out before they could do anything else. He was both disappointed and pleased with himself.

He turned back around and eyed the image again. Unable to figure it out, he took a screenshot of the item and texted it to Charlie.

Chris: *One of yours?*

It hadn't been but a few seconds before Chris received an immediate text back from his brother.

Charlie: *Shit. We need to talk.*

Chris furrowed his brows in confusion and agitation. This couldn't be good. He heard Gabrielle stir in his bed and looked back to see her stretching. Her half-open eyes blinked lazily. He got up from the chair and calmly sat on the bed beside her, watching her come to.

"Sleep well?" he asked. He looked down at her with a smile on his face.

"Hmm?" she moaned sleepily. "Chris?"

He chuckled at the adorable way she struggled to get out of her sleepy daze.

"I'm here..." he said.

A pleased smile crept on her face as her eyes opened wider to see him. "Did I fall asleep?"

He nodded with an amused smirk on his face. "Think I wore you out, Gabs..."

Her eyes widened and her cheeks flushed. "I'm sorry... that's so embarrassing..."

"I'd like to think it means you enjoyed yourself," he smiled. He stroked the palm of her hand with his thumb.

"I did," she said quickly. "I've just... never experienced that before. I guess I wasn't sure what to expect. I thought... that it might gross you out."

Chris chuckled and leaned down to kiss her forehead. "Babe... there's nothing gross about you."

He stood up from the bed and held out a hand to help her up.

"You really seemed like you knew what you were doing," she said suspiciously. She used his bed sheet to cover her naked body.

Chris gave her a mocking grin and rolled his eyes. "You trying to imply something, Gabs?"

Gabrielle hesitated trying to find her words. "You're a bit of a womanizer, Chris. Since high school, you've always had women falling at your feet. Can you blame me for being a little... wary? I don't wanna be another tally on your list of quick fucks..." she frowned.

Chris watched her for a moment, disturbed by her pout. He wanted to tell her she was wrong, but he'd be lying if he said his looks and charm didn't often get him what he wanted. Willing women were always in high supply, but it also made him picky. He didn't want Gabrielle to think so negatively of him.

He crouched down in front of her so that they were eye to eye. Resting his forearms on his thighs, he tilted his head to the side, looking at her inquisitively. His clear blue orbs stared so deeply into her eyes that Gabrielle tried but failed to avoid his unnerving gaze.

"Well first of all, I haven't fucked you... *yet*..." He spoke to her with such seriousness. His eyes searched hers, gauging for the reaction she involuntarily gave him. Gabrielle was completely taken back by the low and authoritative way he emphasized "yet." Mainly because she knew she would willingly give it up to him. Just as she did last night.

"Secondly...when I do make love to you, it won't be quick," he said heatedly. She looked at him like a deer caught in headlights.

She could feel herself getting hot again, despite wearing nothing but a sheet. She bit her lip nervously and immediately went to protest. "Chris, that's not what I-"

"And you would never be just some tally," he said, cutting her off. "You're not some random girl, Gabs. You mean so much to me."

He stood up, leaving her blinking in a daze as she tried to digest his words. He ran his hand through his hair and sighed. "And frankly… I don't deserve you..." he admitted.

Gabrielle frowned at his last sentence. She watched Chris grab her clothes from his dresser and hand them to her. "You should get dressed. I've kept you here for far too long," he said regretfully.

She took her clothes from him and made quick work of putting them back on.

"Let me take you home," he said, watching her get ready. His eyes lingered on her body, before he glanced up to meet her gaze and give her a longing look.

"You don't have to do that. I drove Eli's car here," she said standing up.

"You deprived that man of his car for half a day?" Chris laughed.

"He'll live," Gabrielle chuckled. "Speaking of Eli..."

Chris glanced up at her for a moment and then nodded knowingly.

"We should probably keep what happened here... under wraps," Gabrielle said, looking down. "I'm not really sure how the others would take it."

"That's probably for the best," Chris agreed. He thought about one person in particular who would be infuriated with what he had done. He couldn't even imagine how that conversation with Charlie would go.

"I don't know if we should do this again, Chris," she looked at him hesitantly. He frowned, not really sure how to respond. Now that he knew what she felt like, what she tasted like, he wasn't sure he could stay away. He was hooked.

"You and I are best friends and have known each other ever since we were kids. I can't- I don't want to ruin our friendship," she said. Chris didn't think their friendship would be affected. He was more concerned about protecting her from his dangerous lifestyle.

"I doubt our friendship will be affected, Gabs," he said matter-of-factly. He walked up to her and placed his hands on her hips, pulling her towards him. "And we shouldn't deprive ourselves of the things we want... and what I want is you," he said huskily into her ear, before nibbling gently on her earlobe.

"Spoken like a man who always gets whatever he wants," she mocked, pushing him away.

"Clearly not everything," he said, his eyes darkening. His grip on her hips tightened, and she felt his bulge grow.

Gabrielle chewed her bottom lip, not sure how to respond. "Chris... I-"

"Ignore me, Gabs. I'm just teasing," he said with a fake smile. "I just need to… learn to control myself around you."

"You mean like how you did earlier?" she teased.

"I'll try harder next time," he shrugged. "Though you didn't seem to protest too much."

She looked at him flustered. "Well, I didn't expect you to be so good at it!"

Chris chuckled heartily. He looked down at her, a mischievous glimmer in his eyes. "It wasn't so much my skill that made it good, but rather that you tasted so fucking delicious. I couldn't get enough of you..."

Chris hungrily licked his lips and Gabrielle barely had time to react before he quickly pushed her up against the door, kissing her fervently. He ran his hands along the curves of her body, sliding both hands behind her. He grabbed two handfuls of her ass and lifted her till she was hovering above the ground. Gabrielle gasped and wrapped her arms around his neck, running her fingers through his hair.

He sucked on her neck, running his tongue along her soft skin, and pecking at her chin. Giving her one long last kiss on her lips, his tongue wrestled eagerly with hers before he finally pulled away. Shoving his hands into his pockets, he quickly put on a calm and reserved demeanor in comparison to Gabrielle's disheveled appearance. She leaned against the door, still trying to catch her breath.

"Wh-... what was-" she panted.

"Just something to hold onto." He gave her a charming, innocent smile. Gabrielle grumbled to herself. She shook her head and fixed her shirt.

"I'm leaving now," she said both annoyed and extremely turned on. "Don't forget the party. Though now I'm questioning if you should still come."

Chris laughed as he opened the door for her. "I'll be there."

She rolled her eyes and waved him off before exiting his apartment for good.

~*~

Charlie arrived at Chris's high-rise luxury apartment. He nodded to the familiar face at the front desk.

"Good Evening, Mr. Richardson," the bellman said, holding the elevator door for him.

"Thanks," Charlie quipped, stepping into the elevator. He folded his hands behind his back and whistled softly to distract his mind from the events of the day. The elevator stopped midway and 3 gentlemen clad in all black stepped on, giving him a familiar nod.

"Mr. Richardson," one of the men acknowledged him.

"Mr. Richardson?" the younger man said, looking at Charlie confused.

"Ugh..." the other man said frustratingly. "This is... Mr. *Charles* Richardson, Johnny."

"Oh! The other brother! Nice to finally meet you, Mr. Charles Richardson. I'm such a huge fan. You're an inspiration!" Johnny said eagerly, extending his hand for a shake. Charlie looked at his hand and scoffed with an agitated look on his face.

"Fresh meat?" Charlie asked the older man.

"Yes, sir. Please excuse him. He's just... excited. He's still in training," the man said pushing Johnny's hand away. Johnny looked down, his cheeks flushed from embarrassment. He clasped his hands in front of him and waited until they arrived at their floor before he rushed outside.

"Take it easy, kid," Charlie said encouragingly, as the men walked out. Johnny looked back with a huge smile on his face just as the doors were closing. Charlie chuckled, shaking his head. "He won't last a week..."

When he arrived at Chris's penthouse suite, he went to knock on the door but it immediately swung open. A distracted Chris was clicking away at this tablet. Charlie stepped into the suite and locked the door behind him. He eyed his brother suspiciously, as Chris paced the living room, looking at his tablet.

"I see you've got new recruits," Charlie said. He referenced the kid he met earlier in the elevator.

"Huh?" Chris said, looking up at him. "Oh yea... let's hope they're any good," he murmured.

"That Johnny kid looks pretty young. I thought you had an age limit," Charlie said. He plopped down on the couch, stretching his arms over the back.

"I do," Chris said, not looking at him. He was fully engrossed in his tablet.

"He looked about 18..." Charlie persisted. Chris ignored his comment and continued analyzing the file on his tablet.

"Chris!" Charlie called out to him.

Chris looked up at him confused and then frowned. "I'll have Reynolds verify him."

"What's happening with you?" Charlie asked. He leaned over the table to pour himself a glass of whiskey.

Chris stopped pacing and leaned back against the wall. He locked eyes with his brother. "The image I sent you."

Charlie sighed heavily and downed the drink in one gulp. "Yea... I know it..."

Chris set the tablet down and folded his arms, waiting for Charlie to continue.

Charlie bit down on his knuckle, trying to think. "That logo you sent me is from one of my partners. The Snakes. They're a small-town gang on the come up. Led by one of the originals that I used to work with back before your Mafia monopolized all of the Northeast region."

Chris gave him a hard glare. "I run a business, not the Mafia."

Charlie raised his hands in defense. "Call it what you want, brother..."

Chris tensed up. "Well these 'Snakes' were at one of my warehouses. Ransacked it and bribed my men."

Charlie shrugged. "Sounds like your men need retraining. Were any of them 18-year old's?" he mocked.

"No, but there was a child involved," Chris said seriously.

Charlie looked at him startled and his jaw tensed. "What?"

Chris sighed and rubbed his face in frustration. "I'm still trying to look into it... find her... or him... I just..."

"I'll look into it. I'll ask around about a kid," Charlie said.

"Thanks..."

A loud buzz came from his pocket before Charlie checked a text message on his phone. It was from Gabrielle.

Gabs: *Hey, Big Head! Come to my party!*

"Party?" Charlie frowned at his phone. "Are we back in high school?"

Chris smiled softly. "Let her have this one. Who knows how much longer she'll be around..."

"Eh... I guess..." Charlie muttered, texting her back.

Charlie: *Do I have a choice?*

Gabs: *Nope.* ☺

Charlie rolled his eyes and put his phone back in his pocket. "It gets more and more difficult to ignore this woman. I assume she talked to you already," Charlie said.

"Um, yea..." Chris said a bit anxiously. He nervously rubbed the back of his neck. He remembered the night that he spent with her and couldn't even figure out how to bring it up to his brother. He knew he would have to sooner or later.

"By the way, Arthur has this new tech he came up with that you should check out. As much of a pain in the ass as he is sometimes, it's been pretty useful. He's helping me look into an ambush that happened recently," Charlie added.

Chris looked up at Charlie surprised. "Ambush?"

Charlie grumbled. "Yea... a group of my guys got ambushed during a raid that they had been planning for weeks. Still don't have the full details yet, but... when I find out..."

"Keep me updated..." Chris said.

"Course."

~*~

9

Back in the Day

~*~

"Alright, just a couple more minutes."

Gabrielle pushed the tray of pie back into the oven before closing it.

"Oh damn! Baby sis! That smells good! You makin' mama's famous peach cobbler?" Eli said. He walked into the kitchen sniffing the air like a hungry puppy.

"Yup! I been working on this cobbler since last night. Had to get it *just right*. I also finished the rice, plantains, chicken, and collard greens. I even put together some salad," she said, wiping her hands to take off her apron.

"Wow, you really went all out," he said, opening the fridge to pull out a Gatorade.

"Yea... I just wanted to show everyone how much I love and appreciate y'all," she said fondly. "Did you find the music?"

"Yup! Tanya has a couple others, but I have all the classic hits from the 90s. TLC, Mc Hammer, Blackstreet, Tupac, Boyz 2 Men... I even threw in some mixtapes," he grinned.

"Eli... what did I say about your mixtapes? Why you always tryin' to push those damn mix tapes?" Gabrielle shook her head. She started fixing up the living room.

"See? That's why I don't know how we related. You just don't get the magic of a mix tape," Eli said dismissively.

Gabrielle rolled her eyes and glared at him. "At least you're dressed appropriately."

"Please... my wardrobe still looks like the 90s now," Eli smirked.

"I don't know if that's something to be proud of, bro," she teased him. When the doorbell rang, she headed towards the door and opened it to greet Angie and Rhaven.

"HEYYY!" Angie and Rhaven sang simultaneously.

"Yay! I'm so glad you guys could make it," Gabrielle said, hugging them.

"What? Girl, you know I wasn't missing out on a 90s party," Angie said, walking inside.

"Forreal! I finally got an excuse to bust out my MC Hammer pants," Rhaven said. She showed off her bright blue and green pants and did the running man.

"Oh my gosh, Rhaven, what the hell?" Gabrielle laughed. "I'm mad you still have those."

"I'm mad she acting like she ever stopped wearing them..." Angie muttered.

"Did you bring any drinks?" Gabrielle said. She looked outside and noticed Tanya walking down the pathway.

"Plenty," Angie said, holding up two bottles of vodka.

"Uh... any normal drinks? I'm trying to lay off the alcohol for now," Gabrielle muttered.

"I MADE KOOL-AID! Gotta keep it 90s authentic, right?" Rhaven laughed.

"Kool-aid? Wow, I haven't had that since I was a kid," Gabrielle said holding the door open for Tanya. "Hey, boo."

"Hey," Tanya said, walking in. She sported a cute jean shorts jumpsuit with suspenders and a hot pink crop top underneath, complete with a jean jacket.

"You look so cute! Makin' the 90s look good," Gabrielle smirked. She gave her friend a hug.

"Girl, I know," Tanya said, flipping her hair teasingly. She looked Gabrielle up and down. "But where's your outfit?" she asked.

"I wanted to finish up cooking first. I'll go change now. Can you take the peach cobbler out of the oven in like 5 minutes?"

"Sure," Tanya said. She walked into the kitchen to greet Eli.

Gabrielle ran up the stairs to Eli's spare bedroom where she was staying for the time being. She sent a group text to Charlie, Chris, Nat, and Arthur.

Gabrielle: *You Richardsons still coming?* �� ��

Chris: *Of course we're coming.* ����

Natalie: *I have no idea what constitutes 90s clothing in America!* ����

Arthur: *Bell bottoms and platform shoes probably.* ����♂

Natalie: *You idiot.* ����♀ *That's the 80s... or was it the 70s.* ��

Charlie: *Group texting? Really? You guys are spamming my phone.*��

Gabrielle: *Don't be such a sourpuss, Charlie.* �� *Are you coming?* ����

Charlie: *Not if Arthur is going to be there.* ��

Arthur: �� *Aww shit... You're not still mad about that call-girl incident are you, mate?* ��

Gabrielle: ��

Natalie: *Call girl??? What call girl incident??? Arthur! What did you* *do?!* ��

Arthur: *Uh...*��

Charlie: *Yes. Yes, I am...* ��

Gabrielle: *Guys...*��

Chris: ▯�� *We'll all be there. See you in a few minutes. Maybe... next time group chat isn't the best way to go...* ��

Natalie: *Seriously.* �� *How do I block all of you?* ��

Gabrielle chuckled to herself and put the phone down. She threw on a pair of baggy shorts that sat on her hips and a loose long sleeve crop top that hung off one bare shoulder. It stopped just below her breast revealing her cinched waist. She tied the top part of her hair up into a bun and let the rest of it fray out in a large curly afro. After putting on some lip gloss, she ran back downstairs to find Angie and Rhaven doing the Harlem Shake.

"Dang, y'all. Already?" Gabrielle laughed.

"Might have had one shot," Angie winked.

"More like 3. We tryin' to get this party started," Rhaven said waving her hands in the air.

"Y'all are so stupid," Gabrielle laughed and immediately jumped in to join them.

"Y'all betta not break nothing," Eli said from the kitchen. He held Tanya closely by her waist.

"Boy, you ain't got nothing worthwhile to break," Angie said slyly. "This ain't Tanya's house."

"Dayum!" Rhaven laughed.

"That's cold-blooded Angie..." Eli shook his head.

"Your peach cobbler came out really good, Gabby," Tanya said. "You got any vanilla ice cream."

"There should be some in the freezer. I bought two containers last night," Gabrielle said.

Tanya looked in the freezer. "There's only one in here."

"What? I bought two!" Gabrielle said, confused.

"Oops…" Eli said looking away.

"ELI! Negro, you ate the whole container in one night!" Gabrielle said annoyed.

"I had just come back from practice and I was mad hungry. I didn't even know it was yours," he said apologetically.

"Goodness, Eli!" she groaned. "Let me see if I can run out and get some more before the others arrive."

She headed to the door and went to open it just as Chris had rung the bell.

"Oh!" she said surprised. "You guys are here!"

"Why is that so surprising? You just texted us," Charlie scoffed, stepping inside.

"Alright, smart ass." she rolled her eyes at him. Charlie pulled her in for a hug and looked her up and down, his eyes lingering on the bare skin of her stomach.

"I don't remember you wearing *this* in the 90s," Charlie smirked at her.

"That's because mama would have whooped my ass if I did. Adulthood is a beautiful thing," she teased him. Charlie chuckled and pinched her gently in the waist before walking inside. Natalie walked in wearing a short school uniform skirt and a white button-down shirt tied up into a knot, while her hair sat in two pig-tails.

"This is like a hot mash up of Spice Girls and 'Hit Me Baby One More Time'," Gabrielle mused, eyeing her outfit.

"Ah! I'm glad *somebody* got it! None of these boys could get it. So ridiculous," Natalie scoffed.

"I like it!" Gabrielle hugged her. Her eyes widened when she saw Arthur. He wore baggy sweats with a long shirt wrapped around his waist and an oversized shirt that clung to his physique. A pair of shades sat on his face.

"Wow! Arthur... this is really spot on," she said impressed.

"Don't look so surprised, sweetheart. The 90s were good to me," he winked at her.

"So, you were just messing with Nat on the phone, I'm assuming?" Gabrielle smirked.

"Annoying my cousin is my favorite hobby," he teased. Natalie rolled her eyes.

Gabrielle finally got to Chris. He wore a pair of dark, baggy sweats and a fitted black shirt with a flannel wrapped around him. "I don't think I've ever seen you wear sweats before," she said, eyeing his lower half.

"Hey, eyes up here, Missy," Chris said to her.

"Wha-! I didn't mean it like tha-," she said flustered.

"I'm just teasing you, Gabs," he chuckled. "Though... if you keep looking at me like that, we might end up continuing what we started last time." Chris was teasing but there was a hint of seriousness in his voice that made Gabrielle shiver from excitement. She bit her lip nervously, noticing a mischievous glimmer in his eyes. He smirked at her nervousness and continued the torture, raking his eyes over her body.

"The 90s looks good on you, Johansson," he said in a low voice, grinning at her.

"Th-thanks, Chris," she said, blushing furiously. "Would you stop that?"

"Stop what?"

"You know what!" she blurted and he immediately burst out laughing.

"Gabrielle!" Angie called from the living room. She knew she was being called but Gabrielle didn't want to move. Still grinning amused, Chris nodded at her.

"Go on, babe. We'll catch up later." He stepped down to give her a quick peck on the cheek. This man had already had his way with her and yet she still shivered at his slightest touch. She closed the door behind him and quickly shuffled into the living room.

"You so busy, you can't jam with us?" Angie said, twerking on her.

"There's only like 8 people here. You can't be that busy," Rhaven said, twerking as well.

"Y'all!" Gabrielle laughed. She knocked around between them before she managed to escape and took a seat on the couch between Chris and Charlie.

"I still can't believe you guys managed to find time in your busy schedules for lil ol' me," she chuckled.

"Give us a little more credit, Gabs," Chris teased.

"Yea, besides you kinda threatened us to come," Charlie grinned.

"I did what I had to do!" she said, sticking her tongue out at Charlie "Oh! I should get you guys drinks." She got up and walked towards the kitchen when they both gave her a hard look that made her wince.

"I'm not drinking today, alright? I'm laying off for now. Jeez. I can feel your judgement from all the way over here," she said, rolling her eyes. Chris laughed and Charlie shook his head.

"Actually, we have something so blackity black black, you might not be ready," she teased. The brothers looked at her curiously.

"Arthur, have you ever had kool-aid?" Gabrielle said, grabbing a couple of cups.

"Erm... is that some sort of drug?" Arthur asked. Angie and Rhaven burst into laughter.

"Actually, it might as well be, considering the way some black people drink it," Eli snickered.

"I think you'll like it," Gabrielle said, pouring three cups.

"Um, you might want to lay off the kool-aid actually. No pun intended," Tanya warned.

"Why?" Gabrielle asked, taking a sip. "I'm sure it's- OH MY GOD!" she sputtered. "Rhaven, what the hell?!"

"What? So, I spiked it a little," Rhaven shrugged.

"Not only that. This is diabetes in a cup! Girl, you tryin' to kill all of us?" Gabrielle blurted.

"I'm sure you're exaggerating," Eli said, taking a sip as well. "Oh shit... damn, Rhaven..."

"Dassit! Give me y'alls black cards back! Card Revoked!" Rhaven snapped.

"You can't revoke our black cards just because your kool-aid is OD," Eli said.

"Actually, this is quite delicious," Arthur said while downing the drink.

"And what?! At least *somebody* got some damn taste!" Rhaven said, snapping her fingers.

"Oh lord..." Tanya rolled her eyes.

Gabrielle handed Charlie and Chris each a beer. They both thanked her before Angie grabbed her by the waist, pulling her back.

“Okay, okay! This is a 90s party! That means 90s dance moves. Gabby?” Tanya said. She walked into the living room with Natalie, holding a drink in her hand.

“Remember Kid n Play?” Angie said, bumping her hip against Gabrielle.

“We used to do that dance every time we beat those girls from Hankton at every dance competition,” Gabrielle laughed.

“Which was all the time. We needed better competition,” Angie huffed.

“Yea, but we couldn’t afford to compete with other schools outside of Philly,” Tanya said.

“Emerston High?” Chris asked curiously.

“Nah. This was before Gabs and I started attending Emerston. We couldn’t afford it at first, so we went to one of the other public schools out of town,” Eli said.

“So then... how did you...” Charlie started.

“Your dad,” Angie answered. The Richardson brothers looked at them confused.

“Oh damn, y’all don’t know?” Rhaven asked.

“Steve Richardson advocated for Emerston to change their policy to allow attendance for children from lower-income households. In other words, all the black and Latino kids,” Tanya said. Chris and Charlie looked rather surprised by this revelation.

“Yea, your pops went hard for us black kids. Why do you think we loved him so much? He was one of the few white people that seemed to give a damn about us,” Rhaven said.

“He got a lot of hell for it too...” Gabrielle frowned. Chris looked at her trying to think of what she meant.

"The cement brick through the window incident?" Charlie asked suddenly. They all nodded.

"He told us that was a construction accident," Chris said annoyed.

"I think he was just trying to protect you guys," Eli said. Chris and Charlie exchanged looks of wonder. Their minds raced as they thought about their father.

"Hey! Let's liven it up a little. Weren't you about to show us a dance?" Natalie said suddenly.

"Oh yes! The Kid n Play. Angie, turn up the music so we can show these Richardsons a thing or two," Tanya said. Angie turned up the music and the atmosphere in the room immediately got lighter as they all danced. Tanya pulled Natalie from the recliner to dance, while Eli chatted with Charlie and Arthur flirted with Rhaven.

Gabrielle walked to the pantry in the kitchen to start setting up the food. She opened the cabinet door and placed a set of plates down. When she closed the cabinet door, she saw Chris standing next to her.

Startled, she dropped one of the plates that Chris quickly caught with one hand.

"Wow! Great reflexes!" she said.

"Sorry... didn't mean to startle you," he smiled charmingly, handing her back the plate.

"It's okay." She set the plate down and turned to him. "Did you need something?"

"I just wanted to check in on you and see how you were doing," he said nonchalantly. He gave her his signature charming smile and took a step towards her.

"Oh..." she smiled. She paused and looked up into his eyes. "...Is that all you came to do?"

His smile subtly transitioned to a mischievous grin. "Well... that's not the only thing I had on my mind..." He took another step towards her and he couldn't help his eyes roaming over her body, lingering on her most intimate parts.

"You're doing it again," she said nervously.

"Doing what?" he asked innocently. He took another step that brought him so close to her they were almost touching.

"Chris," she said hesitantly. He tenderly runs his hands down her arms, brushing his fingers across her skin.

"I can't stop thinking about you, Gabs..." he said softly. He grazed over the goosebumps forming on her skin. She froze in place, her eyes slightly closed, refusing to move as she tried to feel every shock from his touch against her skin. His finger gently lifted her chin and she opened her eyes to see his bright blue eyes piercing into hers. It nearly gave her a fright to see him so close to her. He leaned in and softly brushed his lips against hers.

"I miss tasting you," he said in a low, raspy whisper. He looked into her eyes and saw her desire. Grabbing her firmly by the hips, he pushed her against the closet door and kissed her again, more passionately. He took her puffy bottom lip into his mouth and sucked on it.

Gabrielle felt herself melting into Chris's arms. He wrapped the whole length of his hands around her waist, pressing her firmly against him. She raised her hands to his neck, pulling him in for a deeper kiss. He wrapped a large hand around her thigh and lifted her leg up to his waist. Stroking her inner thigh, he teased the hem of her shorts and snuck his finger to the front of her thinly-covered core.

"Chris!" she breathed out excitedly.

"Don't you miss me tasting you..." he groaned into her ear. He planted numerous kisses on her neck. She struggled to stop herself knowing very well how bad the situation could go down if they were caught.

"We can't do this here," she said finally. She reluctantly pushed him away. He gently dropped her leg so she could stand on her own two feet and put some distance between them. He gave her a half smile, though there was disappointment in his eyes.

"You're right. I'm sorry. For some reason... I just can't help myself around you," he chuckled. He shoved his hands into his pants pockets and looked at her longingly.

"That makes two of us," she panted. "I mean I'm trying but... you're not really making this very easy for me, Chris."

"I didn't intend to, Gabs..." he smirked at her.

"Christopher..." she murmured, pushing him aside. He chuckled as she playfully punched him in the shoulder.

"Do you mind helping me bring some of this stuff out to the dining room?" she asked him.

"Not at all," he said, grabbing several items. Chris helped Gabrielle lay out the food on the dining room table.

"Do you guys mind coming in here?" she called out to everyone else in the living room. They shuffled in and each took a seat at the table while Gabrielle stood.

"So, I made you all dinner because food seems to be the best way for me to show my appreciation and gratitude," she started. They all chuckled knowingly.

"You really didn't have to do this for us, Gabs," Tanya smiled.

"I wanted to! I had to... For myself. You all mean so much to me. And the last few days have been such a struggle. I just... I know I haven't been very honest and frankly I'm still trying to sort things out," she said. She looked down, playing with her fingers.

"I don't know when I'll be going back to California yet. I guess I'm just... nervous of what awaits me there," she sighed. She briefly looked up at Chris. He tried to give her an encouraging smile but only managed a simple frown. Charlie noted the direction of their gaze upon each other and stifled his groan with a sip of his beer.

"You don't have to go back, baby sis. You can stay here with us," Eli said encouragingly.

"I can't stay in your apartment, Eli. I'd need to find a job and get my own. And not only that but I had a whole life in California. It's hard to give that all up," she said worriedly. The atmosphere in the room tensed up and she immediately felt bad for being the cause of it.

"Honestly, enough of that. The point of this is to show you guys how much I love and appreciate you. So, dig in!" She took a seat next to Natalie and Tanya across from Charlie and Chris. Everyone at the table started talking and eating.

"Man, I've been waiting for this peach cobbler since last night," Eli said eagerly.

"Yea, and you ate the ice cream which means you get none," Gabrielle said annoyed. She cut a slice of the pie for each person.

"Whatever. It's good as is," he said, taking his slice.

"Wow! You've really outdone yourself, girl. This tastes exactly like how your mom makes it," Angie said.

"Why, thank you!" Gabrielle said proudly. She smiled watching everyone enjoy the pie.

"Oh! Before I forget!" she blurted with excitement. They all looked at her bewildered. "I got you all gifts!" She bounded out of the dining room, leaving them all dazed.

"Is she... is she always this over the top?" Natalie asked..

"Always," Chris, Charlie, Eli and Tanya said in unison.

"But you gotta love her for it. The girl is a huge mushball with a heart of gold," Tanya said. Gabrielle waltzed back into the dining room, carrying a large bag of wrapped gifts. She distributed one to each of them and wore a huge grin, watching them open their gifts.

"Gabby girl! I can't believe you got me these sunglasses! I've been eyeing them for a while now," Rhaven said, trying on her shades.

"It seemed like your style," Gabrielle grinned.

"YAS! These earrings are too freakin' cute," Angie said, holding up a pair.

"You really didn't have to do this," Natalie smiled. She wrapped a soft cashmere scarf around her neck.

"You guys deserve it," Gabrielle beamed. She was swelling up with excitement.

"Where did you get these cuff-links from?" Chris inquired, admiring the detail.

"They were actually the ones your dad wore to my graduation. He forgot to take them back when he helped my roommate start her car back up after it died. I had them polished and thought they would look best on you since you're Mr. CEO and all," Gabrielle said with endearment. Chris had no words. She could see the sentiment in his eyes at how moved he was by her gift and could only give her a heart-warming smile.

"I thought he lost this watch," Charlie said softly. He latched a gold watch around his wrist.

"Nope. Just another of the many things Papa Steve left me of him," Gabrielle smiled fondly.

"You should keep it though," Charlie looked up at her. There was a softness in his eyes that she hadn't seen before.

"I think he'd want you to have it, Charlie," she insisted. He looked at her fondly for a brief moment and nodded in acceptance of the sentimental gift.

"Oh my gosh this dress!" Tanya squeaked.

"Powerhouse suit fitting for all the black girl magic you be spittin," Gabrielle smirked.

"You are the best!" Tanya stood up, hugging her dress.

"Looks too small..." Eli said suspiciously.

"Boy, is you serious!" Tanya scoffed in irritation and threw a bread roll at him.

"Hey!" Eli said.

"Keep your sexist comments to yourself," Gabrielle said, throwing another bread roll at him.

"Really, y'all!" Eli tried to take cover and threw a bread roll, aiming for Gabrielle but instead hitting Angie.

"ELI!" Angie shouted. She immediately picked food off of her plate and threw it at him.

"Oh my god! Nooo!" Eli said in fear. But it was too late. Food started flailing through the air. The doorbell rang and Rhaven sneaked out of the food war to answer it.

"Gabby!" Rhaven called from the door.

"What?" Gabrielle laughed. She escaped the food war and headed towards Rhaven.

"There's a fine ass tall glass of chocolate milk looking for you," Rhaven teased.

Gabrielle tilted her head in confusion when she glanced past Rhaven and froze like ice at who she saw standing in the doorway.

She felt her blood run cold and the hair at the back of her neck stand on end.

"D-Damian?"

~*~

10

Small World

~*~

"Gabby? Who is it?"

Tanya walked into the living room with Eli and Nat following close behind. Damian adjusted the collar of his jacket and cleared his throat.

"I apologize for intruding like this. I've been all over Philly looking for my fiancée. Thank goodness I've finally found her," he said relieved. He locked eyes with Gabrielle who was frozen in a stupor.

"Fi-**Fiancée!** Oh, hell no! I think you mean EX-fiancée. Gabby broke up with your ass for cheating on her. Or did you forget?" Tanya said angrily. She stormed toward the door.

"Wait! Tanya!" Gabrielle reached for her arm and tried holding her back. Charlie and Chris walked into the living room and stood next to Arthur who sat perched on the armchair. Each ready to make a move, but waiting to see how this unraveled.

"I'm afraid you've got it all wrong. It was simply a misunderstanding," Damian insisted.

"A misunderstanding!" Tanya said angrily. Gabrielle clutched her arm tighter.

"Yes. A misunderstanding. Isn't that right, babe?" Damian urged, still holding Gabrielle's petrified stare.

"D-Damian... I-it's over. Okay? We're not doing this anymore.

You-... you made your choice." Gabrielle stuttered with such meekness and fragility in her voice, it took everyone else by surprise. They all looked in her direction as if to make sure it was actually her speaking.

"The only choice I made was asking you to be my wife. And you've made me the happiest man alive the moment you said 'yes'. I would hate to ruin all of this over nothing. Come on, babe, at least let me talk things out with you. Give me a chance to explain," he said. His hazel eyes bored even more intensely into hers.

Gabrielle could feel herself starting to sweat. She never expected Damian to actually fly out all the way to the East Coast for her. She didn't think she mattered that much to him.

"I... I don't know if that's such a good idea," she said in almost a whisper.

"Obviously it's not a good idea! If you're the punk ass bitch that broke my baby sister's heart, you betta get the hell up out of here before we have a problem," Eli snarled.

"I don't think there's any need for violence," Damian frowned. He remained in his calm, stoic demeanor. "All I ask is to speak to my fiancée for a few minutes. I missed her terribly."

"She's **not** your fiancée! There's nothing left between y'all and you're not talking to her! Just get the hell out!" Tanya snapped.

Chris analyzed Damian's face trying to get a read on the type of person he was. He already knew he wasn't good news. Chris knew all types of psychopaths, and Damian fit the profile. He was just trying to figure out which kind. He noticed a subtle smirk on Damian's face when Tanya threatened him. He was even more perturbed that he never removed eye contact from Gabrielle who seemed to be trembling under the weight of his gaze.

"Do you agree with that, babe?" Damian said with a voice so smooth it made the girls question themselves. "Do you believe there's nothing left between us? After everything we've been through together. The way you were always there for me... and I was there for you." His tone towards the end was almost threatening as his eyes darkened. Gabrielle's eyes widened and her heart quickened. She immediately let go of Tanya's hand.

"Um... actually... you're right. Maybe we should talk," Gabrielle said suddenly.

"What?!" Tanya and Eli blurted simultaneously. Everyone looked at Gabrielle like she had lost her mind.

"I-I don't really know what I saw... or heard. I might have been hasty in my assumptions. I should hear him out," Gabrielle stuttered. She meekly walked towards the door.

"Gabrielle! You have **got** to be kidding me!" Tanya said astonished.

"Just... give me a minute okay, guys?" Gabrielle pleaded. She briefly glanced at Chris and hesitated before following Damian outside.

"What the hell just happened?!" Tanya shouted, making everyone jump.

"Maybe there really *was* a misunderstanding," Angie shrugged.

"Yea, it seemed like she wasn't exactly too sure," Rhaven agreed.

"You don't actually believe that, do you? This guy is clearly bad news!" Tanya freaked.

"I agree with you, babe. But it's ultimately her choice. Let's just see what happens. Maybe she did misunderstand. Either way, I trust her. She wouldn't just go off with some guy who would hurt her," Eli said.

Tanya frowned and watched Eli, Angie and Rhaven start cleaning off the dining room table. She bit her lip, looking around when she noticed Charlie and Chris murmuring to Arthur.

"You!" she blurted. They all looked up at her suddenly, stopping their conversation.

"You agree with me, right? This guy is not to be trusted! Please tell me I'm not the only one who sees through him," she pleaded.

"Arthur is already running a trace on his background," Charlie said. He looked over his cousin's shoulder to the small device in his hand.

"You're what? Wait how?" Tanya asked. Arthur looked up at her, smirking, and lightly tapped his shades.

"AIl in here. Created it myself," Arthur said smugly. Several numbers ran across the screen on the small device in his hand. "Still needs some improvement, but it gets the job done."

"How did you guys- Did you get the same bad feeling I did?" Tanya asked. Chris nodded.

"Why didn't you say anything?! Why didn't you stop her?!" Tanya said frantically.

"Tanya, we can't just jump the guy. We have to be calculated about this. And the way that Gabs acted... I feel like there's a little more to this that we're not seeing," Chris frowned.

Tanya slumped her shoulders in defeat. "Yea, you have a point. Do you think he has something on her?"

"It could be anything," Charlie said. "Let's see what Arthur pulls up."

"A'right the screening's done... bloke is pretty clean," Arthur said, showing Charlie his device. "Pretty high-esteemed on the West Coast. Famous painter. Tons of adoring fans. Prestigious art school. No record. Not even a blip. At least on the US Government database."

Charlie grunted. "That just means we need to dig deeper."

"Wait... did you just hack into the Pentagon?" Tanya asked, shocked.

Arthur chuckled. "Just the FBI."

"Arthur! That is **so** BEYOND ILLEGAL!"

"Tanya... really?" Charlie said gesturing.

"Right. Sorry. I'm an attorney! I can't help but condemn you for your illegal behavior!" Tanya scolded.

"I'll make sure not to do it in your presence," Arthur said, giving her an innocent smile. Tanya merely rolled her eyes.

"Hold on," Arthur said, scrolling on his device. "He does have an usually high number of connections with some high-profile people. Eddie Gingein, Ryan Catolo, Logan Lynerson."

"Am I supposed to know who those people are?" Tanya asked, confused.

"They're traders..." Chris said, glancing at Charlie.

"Traders? Like... goods and services?" Tanya asked. She tried to figure out the look Charlie and Chris were giving each other. She squinted her eyes when Charlie gave Chris a slight nod, almost as if they were communicating in their own language.

"Hello! Don't shut me out with your weird secret Richardson code!" she blurted. The three of them looked at her startled.

"Uh... yea. Something like that. Listen, Tanya. We'll handle this," Chris said to her.

"What? No! Let me help! I can drag his ass to court and sue the pants off of him if he's involved in some illegal activity," she pleaded.

Chris gave her a warm smile and grabbed her gently by the shoulders. "If we need an attorney, trust me, you'll be the first one we call. But for now, let us take the reins on this. We'll keep you updated. Promise," he assured her.

Tanya sighed. "Fine... take care of my girl, please." They gave her a reassuring nod when the door opened and Gabrielle entered the house. She looked up at them startled almost as if she had forgotten they were still there.

"Gabby!" Tanya ran towards her and grabbed her by the arms. "Are you okay? Did he-"

"I'm fine," Gabrielle said calmly. "Really. I um... I'm gonna go back with him to his hotel. Turns out everything really was a misunderstanding. I just blew things out of proportion."

Tanya looked at her friend wide-eyed. "Gabby, you're telling me this, but I'm not convinced!" Eli stepped into the living room with Angie, Rhaven, and Natalie following.

Gabrielle huffed and glanced at Charlie and Chris watching her. "Please, don't worry about me, T. You know I can be a drama queen sometimes. Damian is a really great guy and I was stupid for assuming he would ever cheat on me. He... he cares about me..." she trailed off.

"You don't seem happy about it, dear..." Natalie chimed in.

"I'm just... exhausted... emotionally, I guess. It's been a roller coaster. I was engaged and then I wasn't. And turns out it was my fault to begin with. All because I jumped to conclusions without figuring out the whole picture first. Honestly, it was all me. We are... going to go talk things out and then hopefully we can start off on the right foot again."

Everyone sat in silence for a moment, causing Gabrielle to shift uncomfortably. "Well... I trust you, baby sis. As long as you're sure this guy is right for you, then I'm happy for you," Eli said, stepping to her. Gabrielle smiled gratefully at her brother.

"Does this mean the engagement is back on?" Angie asked.

Gabrielle bit her lip nervously. "I... uh... we didn't get that far..."

Her phone buzzed and she looked down at it to read a text from Damian. She swallowed thickly and quickly fixed her face when she remembered she was being watched.

“I have to go, guys. He’s waiting for me. I um... I’ll catch up with you guys later,” she said.

When Gabrielle left the house, Tanya dropped her head, rubbing her temples. She turned to Chris and Charlie, concern etched all over her face. “Please, fix this,” she said desperately.

~*~

“You’re sure he’ll be here?” Charlie said, eyeing the large, Oval-shaped glass building.

“No. But I have a strong feeling he will,” Chris said, fixing his tie. “Either way, a couple of my clients that he works with will be here. I can chat them up and find out more information about what their business with him is.”

“And you’re bringing Arthur but not me?” Charlie grumbled. He looked in the rear-view mirror to see Arthur fixing his collar.

Arthur gave him a taunting grin. “I’ve got the equipment, cousin. We need technology not fists on this mission.”

“It’s not a fucking mission...” Charlie grumbled under his breath.

Chris gave Charlie a sympathetic look. “It will look suspicious if both Richardson brothers attend a random art showcase. Hardly anyone will recognize who Arthur is,” Chris explained. Charlie groaned, rubbing his temples.

Chris opened the car door. “Meet us back at my apartment at 10. Arthur and I will take one of the cars in the garage.” Charlie watched his brother and cousin walk towards the building. He tried to get a look at who was inside to no avail. Sighing heavily, he drove off.

~*~

Gabrielle splashed water on her face and patted her skin dry. Looking at herself in the mirror, she struggled to fight the tears brimming in her eyes. She closed her eyes shut, wincing at the pain permeating on the side of her face. Reaching into her bag, she reapplied another layer of makeup to cover up the black eye that Damian had given her moments prior.

She eyed herself in the mirror, looking over her white sleeveless dress, and fixed her hair. She readjusted her necklace and dabbed at the sweat on her exposed cleavage. "Come on, girl, you can do this," she encouraged herself.

She stepped out of the bathroom and into the large crowded open-floor lobby. She was immediately overwhelmed by the amount of people that walked about. She scanned the crowd looking for the man she hoped to avoid. To her dismay, he noticed her before she noticed him, and he beckoned her over. Reluctantly, she walked over to him and he roughly grabbed her by the hand.

"And this is my fiancée, Gabrielle Johansson! One of the best surgeons in Los Angeles," Damian said proudly. She winced at how painfully tight he grabbed her by the waist. This was the 9th person that Damian was showing her off to for the night. She plastered on a fake smile and robotically shook the person's hand, whose name she could not even try to remember.

Her eyes glazed over as she listened to Damian give his regular spiel. He was smooth in the way he spoke. Captivating his audience whomever they might be. But she could not be swayed by his sweet-for-nothings any longer. He had revealed who he truly was to her, against her body and her face.

Gabrielle found herself instinctively wandering out of Damian's grasp yet again, for the umpteenth time that night. She managed to convince him it was because she was in awe of all the artwork and wanted to admire them.

She walked over to a painting that she knew all too well. Looking over its harsh use of red and brown colors and the exaggerated use of circles to emphasize large proportions, she gazed at the big sad brown eyes in the painting staring back at her.

She was looking at herself. This was one of Damian's first attempts at painting her. He had said he wanted to captivate her essence rather than her physical appearance. Back then, such a gesture made her swoon with love. But now it felt like such a violent act as she gazed at the exposed depiction of herself with new bruised eyes.

She felt a presence next to her but was too tired to bother seeing who it was. Just another patron coming to gaze at her unsuspecting body without her permission. She continued to get lost in the eyes of the broken soul before her.

"This is an interesting piece," the person beside her said. The voice seemed familiar but she was far too deep into her thoughts to care.

"Is it?" she said lifelessly, without moving her eyes.

"I see... a distorted portrayal of a young woman... who looks sad," the voice said.

Gabrielle scoffed. "Sad?... She's broken..."

"Is that how you feel, Gabs? Broken?"

She jumped at the sound of her name and looked over to see Chris staring at her with tender eyes. He wore a fitted, navy-blue suit with a dark blue, button-down shirt and a brown-dotted tie.

"What are you doing here?" she asked with wide eyes.

"Well, this is one of my properties. I had to come scope out the performance," he explained.

"You've gotta be kidding me," she muttered. "You shouldn't be here, Chris."

"I'm sorry?"

"You didn't have to come!" she blurted. "Things like this are beneath you! You're not required or anything. You didn't have to come and yet you did! Why did you come here?"

Chris's jaw tensed with angst. "You know why..." he said, looking into her eyes.

Gabrielle swallowed hard. "Please, Chris. Don't do this," she pleaded. "I know- I know I didn't end things between us on the right terms but-.but this is so much bigger than you and I."

Chris looked at her curiously. "What do you mean?"

She looked down with a frown, unable to speak her truth. Chris took a step towards her and gently touched her arm.

"Gabs, talk to me," he said softly. She looked up at him, tears brimming in her eyes, a cry desperate to escape.

"There she is!" Damian said boisterously. He approached Gabrielle and Chris with two other men. "I swear if I keep losing you like this, I'm going to need a leash, honey!" Damian and the two men laughed but Gabrielle barely chuckled. Chris did not find the joke funny.

"Gentlemen, this is my lovely wife, Gabrielle. She's one of the best surgeons in Los Angeles and the love of my life," he said, grabbing her possessively by the waist.

Gabrielle flinched and braced herself against Damian's chest. "Dear... you said 'wife'..."

Damian gave her a hard, threatening glare before breaking out into a smile. "Jeez... silly me. I meant fiancée. I'm clearly getting ahead of myself. I'm just so eager to make her mine," he said, nuzzling her cheek.

"You certainly are very beautiful, Miss," one of the men said, eyeing her like a piece of meat.

"And she's so radiant in white, isn't she? I can't imagine what she'll look like in a wedding dress. Stunning, obviously," Damian beamed, giving her a cheeky grin. Gabrielle plastered on her best smile. She struggled to speak but her throat felt so dry. She looked over at Chris who noticed her struggling and stepped forward.

"Mr. Richardson!" one of the men exclaimed. "It's an honor to see you here! You never grace us with your presence."

"I like to pop in every once in a while to check in on the performance of my properties," Chris smiled charmingly.

"But of course! The showcase is a rare treat. And we're happy to have Mr. DuPont and his lovely wife... er, I'm sorry... *fiancé* with us," the man said.

"Yes, Ms. Johansson and I are actually very good friends," Chris said, staring at Gabrielle. She immediately froze up and stared at Chris with wide eyes.

"Really?" the man said surprised. Gabrielle willed herself to speak finally.

"Y-yes. I am a Pennsylvania native, actually. I... I was visiting to pay my respects to Pa-...Mr. Steve Richardson," she stammered, trying to gather her bearings.

"So... *you're* the famous Christopher Richardson," Damian said, raising a curious brow. "My fiancé has spoken so much about you. You must be very good friends..." Chris noticed Damian's grip on Gabrielle's waist had tightened. The man clearly felt threatened. His concern was how that reflected in his treatment of Gabrielle.

Chris glanced at her and was disturbed by the unusual look of fear distorting her beautiful features. It made his chest tighten.

"We grew up together," Chris said, eyeing her. "The Johanssons have been very good to my family."

"Your father was a great man," the man spoke up. "It was a pleasure to have known him." Chris nodded in gratitude.

"Yes, my condolences to you and your family. I only regret that I could not be there for the service," Damian said, trying to pull Chris's attention. "I understand my fiancé had some business to attend to that kept her away from me. Those Richardsons sure kept you busy, didn't they, babe..."

Gabrielle could feel the tension in his tone and knew what it meant for her later. She had been trying desperately not to look at Chris, but it was already obvious to Damian that she felt something for him.

She gently removed his hand from her waist. "I'm sorry, honey, I'm feeling a little bit thirsty. I'm just going to get some water. I'll be back. Excuse me." She gave everyone a quick nod and abruptly walked away trying to stave off a panic attack. Walking over to the far end of the room, she slumped against the corner of the wall.

"You alright there, sweetheart?" She nearly jumped out of her skin. She saw Arthur in a dashing blue suit and white button down shirt with a blue tie, wearing a pair of dark shades.

"Arthur?! You're here too?!" she blurted.

"Christopher saw fit to bring me along for the ride," he grinned at her. His grin quickly turned down into a frown when he saw how flustered she looked. "You don't look too good."

"I'm having a really bad night." She slumped down even further and grabbed her head.

"Well, whatever it is, Christopher will be able to fix it," Arthur tried to encourage her.

"Fix it? Fix what?! There's nothing to fix, Arthur! Why are you guys here?" she said wildly.

"Uh..."

"Arthur!"

Arthur looked at her nervously when he glanced behind her. "Is that your fiancé headed this way?" he asked, pointing to Damian who was chatting with Chris from across the room.

Gabrielle felt panic tighten her heart. "I can't do this," she groaned helplessly. She turned and exited the room.

~

"I have to say, I'd been hoping to meet you for quite some time," Damian said. He held a glass of wine and kept his gaze locked on Chris.

"Is that so?" Chris's was stoic as he stood straight, his hands casually sitting in his pockets.

"Gabrielle talks about you and your brother quite often. What's his name? Charlie? I have to admit, I'm a bit jealous. She loves herself the Richardson boys." Damian swirled his wine in his glass and gave Chris a taunting look.

Chris remained expressionless. "Well, we have been friends for quite some time now. She is very close to my family."

"Hmm." Damian looked down into his glass, before looking back up at Chris with a serious face. "Listen... Christopher. May I speak to you... man to man?" Damian asked. Chris barely moved.

"Gabrielle is... a very important and valuable asset to me," Damian started.

Chris narrowed his eyes. "You speak of her as if she's some sort of merchandise."

Damian chuckled at Chris's seriousness. "Don't take my words so literally." He took a final gulp, finishing his wine and set the glass on the table. He clasped his hands behind his back and looked up at Chris, locking his gaze.

"I am very particular about my things. They are important to me for many reasons. I need things to be a certain way, otherwise, they don't work out the way I want them to. I have invested far too much time and energy into Gabrielle for you to compromise all of my work," Damian said firmly.

Chris raised a brow in subtle surprise so as not to give away his shock at what Damian was saying. "Come again?"

Damian shook his head in frustration. "Have you fucked her?"

Chris tensed up as a thick anger ignited inside him. "Who the hell do you think you are?!"

Damian took a step back and raised his hands in defense. "I meant no offense."

"In that case, you failed on that front," Chris snapped.

"What I'm trying to say is that I know she has feelings for you. She wants you, and I can't allow that. So, I want you to stay away from my fiancée. I don't want you anywhere near Gabrielle," Damian said finitely.

Chris paused, disturbed not only by his revelation but by his request. Damian studied Chris's face that had finally broken with emotion and nodded knowingly.

"From the look on your face, I can only presume that you have feelings for her as well. In which case, I stand by my request. It was a pleasure speaking with you, Christopher. I hope we can do business in the future."

Damian turned on his heels and left Chris standing alone with his thoughts.

~

"I got a shit ton of data from all the clients you had on your list. They've all got one common denominator besides you: Damian." Arthur leaned against a table, munching on grapes and winking at attractive women passing by.

“Then I need you to get more on Damian,” Chris said, scanning the room. “I’ve spoken to the same clients and all of their business with him is menial and baseless. There’s gotta be something we’re missing.”

“Well, I’ve got one last trick up my sleeve,” Arthur said. He found Damian in the crowd and headed straight towards him. Arthur approached Damian who didn’t seem to recognize him from earlier and immediately got into a discussion. They started speaking as if they had known each other for years.

“That son of a gun,” Chris grinned, shaking his head. Chris suddenly felt his arm being pulled before he was jerked around the corner and into the hallway.

“You have to get out of here! Please!” Gabrielle pinned Chris to the wall, looking desperately into his eyes.

“What are you talking about, Gabs? What’s wrong?” Chris said, trying to get a hold of her.

“Don’t ask questions! Just leave! Please! The longer you stay here, the worse it becomes!”

“Gabs, baby, just talk to me. Tell me what’s going on. You know you can tell me anything. Let me help you.” Chris gently grabbed her arms, running his hands up and down, trying to soothe her.

Gabrielle closed her eyes to his touch. For just a moment, she allowed herself to feel him rather than block him out. Chris analyzed her face. Her eyes were closed shut and her face muscles were still tense, but her body had relaxed upon his touch. He raised a hand to her face and gently caressed her cheek. The softness of her skin stirred him as he ran his thumb gently over her lips. Everything seemed so out of control and out of his hands. He was desperate to save the woman he loved. But from what, he did not know. His heart ached with uncertainty, but at that moment he was certain that all he wanted was her.

Chris leaned down, holding her hand against his chest and gently lifted her chin with his finger. He brushed his lips against hers for just a moment, expecting her to retreat. Instead, she pressed her lips against his even harder, kissing him fervently. But this kiss seemed less passionate, more desperate. As if she were kissing him for the last time. He felt the taste of salt on his lips and opened his eyes to see a few tears running down her face.

"Gabs..." he said sadly, pulling back. She blinked at him like a deer in headlights.

They heard footsteps coming towards them and Gabrielle quickly pushed Chris away just as Damian rounded the corner. Damian stared at them both dumbfounded and angry to see them alone together. His eyes switched from Gabrielle to Chris as if trying to sort out what they had been doing.

"Damian," Gabrielle said quickly, wiping the tears from her face.

"I was looking for you... **again**." There was a low sullen tone in Damian's voice as his gaze on her darkened.

"Are-are you ready to go?" she asked, putting some distance between her and Chris.

"**We** are ready to go," Damian said, stepping towards her. He grabbed her forcefully by her arm, yanking her forward. Chris instinctively growled at the forceful way in which Damian grabbed her.

"Hey! Don't you fuckin-" Chris started, rushing towards Damian.

"Chris, please!" she said blocking Chris. She pushed her hands against his chest to stop him from moving forward. Chris had fury in his eyes when he looked at Damian. He forced himself to look down at Gabrielle and was immediately shaken out of his anger when he saw the fear in her eyes.

"You have no idea what you're doing. You'll only make it worse," she whispered helplessly. He looked at her with worry and confusion overtaking his entire face. He searched her eyes for something she would not give to him.

"Gabrielle... you know how much I hate it when you make me wait..." Damian's voice was malicious and scornful.

Gabrielle turned to him and gave him a weak smile. "Damian, baby. Can we just… forget all of this happened?"

Damian gave her a dark look for her audacity, before a grin painted his face. He looked up at Chris with a mocking glare. "I guess you'll have to make it up to me back at the hotel."

Damian possessively wrapped an arm around her waist and abruptly turned, leading her away from Chris. She gave Chris a sorrowful quick glance and followed Damian out.

Chris balled up his fist and growled, getting ready to punch something when Arthur turned the corner.

"There you are- woah!" Arthur just dodged his angry cousin's rage. "Catch you at a bad time?"

"Did you find anything?" Chris muttered in a low rumble as he fixed his collar and jacket.

"I just have to do some re-calibrating and we should be able to find what you're looking for," Arthur said cautiously.

"Good. Meet me back at my apartment in 1 hour. I need to blow off some steam." Chris briskly walked away without waiting for a response from Arthur.

~*~

Chris rolled down his sleeves and threw his suit jacket back on. He looked over the bruising on his knuckles from punching the bag in his private gym on the lower level of his high-rise luxury apartment. Stuffing his hands into his pockets, he strolled out of the gym and headed towards the lobby.

"Good Evening, Mr. Richardson, sir!" The front desk security greeted him. Chris acknowledged him with a nod and pressed for the elevator.

"Your brother, Mr. Charles Richardson, went up a few moments ago," security advised.

"Thank you." Chris stepped into the elevator. As it ascended to his penthouse suite, his mind raced with the events of the night. He had never seen Gabrielle so desperate and fearful. He wanted to whisk her away from the monster who seemed to be pulling all her strings, but she practically begged him to leave her alone. What could he do? He didn't know what her situation was. If this guy had something on her, he didn't want to risk putting her in more harm's way.

But he couldn't just do nothing... He refused.

Chris breathed heavily, running his fingers through his hair. He couldn't keep his mind from thinking back to the way she kissed him. The way her body leaned into his. It was like she wanted him to take her away. Yet, everything she said and did was the exact opposite. He flexed his hands, squeezing the tie he had balled up into his fists. His fingers drummed impatiently, aching to touch her again.

He stepped out of the elevator, and before he even got to the door he could hear barking. Chris opened the door to his apartment and was immediately attacked by Thor.

"Hey, boy! What the heck are you doing here?" Chris ruffled the excited dog's fur, before pushing him off.

"He was getting bored at Mom's. Needed some company," Charlie said, stretched out on the couch.

"So, you brought him here?" Chris said sharply and with heavy irritation.

“Naturally...” Charlie smirked. He watched his brother crouch down and pet their dog.

“You couldn’t just bring him back to your place? I’ve got shit to do,” Chris groaned. He stood up and walked over to the table in front of Charlie, grabbing a half-full glass of whiskey.

“Hey, I was drinking that,” Charlie whined. Chris merely responded with a dirty look.

“I take it the night didn’t go as you had planned?” Charlie said, with a raised brow.

“What gave me away,” Chris said sarcastically. He muffled his frustration with the drink.

“You mean other than your bad attitude and the bruising on your knuckles?” Charlie said. Chris glanced over the blue bruises on his hand and scoffed, before taking another sip.

“You’re awful at getting out your aggression in a healthy way. You need to start revisiting my gym so I can show you how to properly de-stress. Start you training again so you don’t end up like... *this*,” Charlie gestured to Chris’s hand again.

Chris rolled his eyes. “That’s not my style.”

“Oh right. The elite businessman is too good to get his hands a little dirty. He must always remain professional and reserved,” Charlie mocked.

“That’s not... that’s not what I meant,” Chris frowned. Charlie carefully analyzed his brother and leaned over, resting his elbows on his knees. He folded his hands underneath his chin and looked up at him inquisitively.

“What happened?” Charlie asked.

Chris sighed, setting the empty cup down. “It was a shit show.” He leaned back against the edge of the wall and stuffed his hands in his pockets. His head fell back with a sigh.

"This guy... Damian... He's too elusive. I know too much about him and not enough at the same time. He knows too many of my clients, but their business is standard. Just simple art trading. And he's a cocky, insufferable asshole with a face I'd like to punch," Chris muttered.

Charlie chuckled. "Then what's the problem? Just take him out."

Chris gave Charlie a tired look. "I can't just take him out, Charlie. You know that's not how I operate."

"And it's cost you dearly..." Charlie said, lighting a cigarette.

"That's not relevant. This guy... he's got some kind of leverage on her that's keeping her tied to him. She won't tell me what. But she was relentless in trying to keep me away. Something else is going on." Chris closed his eyes trying to remember. "She was terrified, Charlie..."

Charlie thought for a moment as he tapped the end of the cigarette into the ashtray. Thor trotted up to Chris and nudged at him to pet him, but Chris was too lost in his thoughts.

"Hey. Hey!" Charlie said, getting his attention. Thor looked at him quickly. "Go to the room! Hey! Go to the room, Thor!" Thor bowed his head and sulked his way back to Chris's room.

"If you won't take him out, then I will," Charlie said finally.

Chris's eyes popped open. "Charlie! Have you listened to a word I've said?"

"Yea. And it seems to me that your hesitation is out of sentiment and concern, whereas I have none."

Chris slouched his shoulders against the wall. "I just want to do this right, Charlie. Where Gabs is concerned..."

"There's only one right way, as far as **I'm** concerned," Charlie shrugged.

"Arthur said he got the rest of what we're looking for at the art gala. Let's just wait to see what he has before we make our next move," Chris insisted.

Charlie shook his head as he snuffed his cigarette out in the tray. "Where is that dickhead anyway?"

"I don't know... I told him to meet me back here 30 minutes ago."

"Probably got distracted by a pair of tits." They both laughed when the doorbell rang.

"It's about time," Chris said, opening the door. He was surprised to see Arthur standing at the door holding a rectangular item draped with a cloth. Gabrielle stood behind him wearing Arthur's suit jacket over her shoulders.

"I plead the fifth," Arthur said quickly. He walked into the apartment and set the item down.

"Why are you pleading the fifth? And what are *you* doing here?" Chris asked Gabrielle. She stepped into the apartment with her hands behind her back.

"She stole my tablet," Arthur said, crossing his arms.

"I didn't steal it. You willingly gave it to me," Gabrielle glared at him.

"How did she manage to get it from you?" Chris asked, looking at Arthur bewildered.

"She seduced me," Arthur accused. Chris and Charlie looked at Gabrielle surprised.

"You seduced... my cousin?" Chris asked curiously.

"Oh please! All I did was sway my hips, give a flirty pout and he practically threw it at me. It didn't take much," she scoffed.

Arthur raised his hands defensively. "I'm a red-blooded male with a major weakness for the female form in all its splendor."

"Yea, you need to work on that," Charlie said condescendingly.

"And Charlie, what are you doing here?" she blurted.

"Why is that a question? Am I not allowed to visit my own brother?" Charlie asked.

"I just mean... why do you have to be here *now*?" Gabrielle whined.

"I still don't understand why that's a question, Gabs... what's the problem?" Charlie said, leaning forward.

Chris turned to her. "Why did you come, Gabs?" Gabrielle shifted uncomfortably under the weight of their gaze.

"I came to ask you to stop looking," she said finally.

"Stop looking for what?" Chris asked.

"Looking for whatever it is you're looking for! Just stop!" she snapped. Charlie and Chris looked at her surprised.

"Well, now that you've asked him, can I have my baby back," Arthur gestured to his device in her hands.

"No!" Gabrielle said, hugging the device to her chest. "Not until he promises."

"Gabs, what are you talking about?" Chris asked, confused.

"Arthur told me you were looking for information on Damian," she said. Chris and Charlie looked at Arthur disappointingly.

"I plead the fifth!" Arthur said defensively.

Chris shook his head in annoyance. "It has nothing to do with you, Gabs. Damian is connected to a lot of my clients and I'm trying to find out why."

"Damian is connected to a lot of people. That's not unusual for him. He's not just an artist, he's also a businessman. He knows how to hustle. There's nothing more you need to know," Gabrielle said quickly.

"Why are you protecting him?" Charlie asked annoyed.

"I'm protecting myself!" she blurted. All 3 of them looked at her startled by her unsettled anger. "The more you look into him, the closer you are to...to finding things out about me. Things that I have worked so hard to bury and move past. I... I can't have that past resurrected again," she stammered. Chris and Charlie exchanged concerned glances.

"I have done things... that I am not proud of. And it took me a really long time to get over them. I still haven't forgiven myself. Just thinking about it now is sending me into a panic attack. Please... Chris. I'm begging you. Just stop," she desperately pleaded. She searched his eyes for some acknowledgement of her cry.

Chris saw the same desperation in her eyes that he saw at the showcase. "Gabs... I..."

"Why don't you tell us what happened so we can help you," Charlie spoke up.

"No. No one can help me. These are my burdens to carry. There's no way I'd ever let any of you get involved in any capacity," she said, shaking her head furiously.

"Now, now...this is not how our earlier conversation went, sweetheart," Arthur said, stepping towards her.

"Arthur, please. I just need him to promise," Gabrielle pleaded, taking a step back.

"Christopher doesn't make promises he can't keep," Arthur said, looking at his cousin.

"Then make him!" she shrieked. She took another step back and wrapped his jacket tighter around her. Arthur hesitated with a frown. He considered a more serious approach than his usual candor.

"You're freaking out, sweetheart. Let's take it easy. If you want, we can go back to the car and talk things out like before. What do you say?" Arthur negotiated.

"Wait a minute. Since when did Arthur become a trusted ally?" Charlie said, glancing between Gabrielle and his cousin.

Arthur grinned at Charlie. "You underestimate my charm."

Gabrielle rolled her eyes and turned to the brothers. "Arthur was just at the right place at the right time. He..." She glanced at Arthur whose charming smile quickly faded to something somber. "He saw me having an argument with Damian and helped me get out of an awkward situation by chatting Damian up. He went the extra mile by purchasing one of Damian's pieces, and bought me some time to... de-stress... He asked me to accompany him to pick up his purchase. Arthur convinced Damian that he would have me back in an hour."

"Well, that's *one* version of the story," Arthur muttered. Gabrielle gave him a threatening sideways glance.

"Why are you with him?" Chris asked softly. She was startled by the unexpected question.

She hesitated for a moment unsure how to answer. "He may be a little rough around the edges, but Damian has been there for me when no one else was. I owe it to him... to stick out this relationship," she explained.

"Marriage isn't about owing someone, Gabs," Charlie said.

Gabrielle gave him a hopeless look. "You couldn't begin to understand..."

"Try me," Charlie insisted.

Gabrielle groaned. "This is not what I came here for. Chris, please just promise you'll leave this alone so Arthur can bring me back."

"Well, see... now I'm going to lose my status as favorite Richardson," Arthur said. He crossed the room, moving behind her. "Because to be completely honest, I never intended on bringing you back there." He stuffed his hands into his pockets and leaned against the door.

"What?!" she shouted, turning on her heels. "Arthur!"

"You need to tell them."

"That's not what we agreed to!"

"Well, alright then. I'll just take my jacket back and-" He reached for his jacket that she was wearing, but she abruptly stepped away from him, pulling the jacket around her. He gave her a sad smile and shrugged his shoulders, before nudging in their direction with his chin.

Gabrielle dropped her head grumbling. "You're just as annoying as your cousins. Is it like a Richardson gene to be so obnoxious and stubborn?!"

"Pot meet kettle," Charlie smirked. "You're just as stubborn as we are, Gabs."

Gabrielle rolled her eyes in frustration, though she knew he was right.

"Gabs, just tell us what's going on. Let us help you," Chris urged her. She looked between Charlie and Chris with hopelessness overwhelming her.

"No. No! I can't- you...You wouldn't understand! You'll just judge me harshly just like everybody else!" she cried.

"Have we ever judged you before?" Charlie asked her. She went to speak but stopped to consider his words.

"You-You'll never look at me the same again. You'll never forgive me," she said weakly.

"We've been best friends since we were kids, Gabs. You really think that's going to stop now?" Charlie encouraged her. He patted the seat next to him, beckoning her. She sighed and took a long moment to contemplate. Turning to Arthur, she handed him the tablet. She walked over to the couch and sat down in defeat.

"I'm gonna need a drink," she muttered.

"You sure that's a-" Chris started.

"There's no way in hell I can talk about this completely sober," she said abruptly.

Charlie poured her a little whiskey in his glass and handed it to her. The men watched her cautiously as she downed the drink in one shot. Gabrielle kicked off her shoes, curling her feet beneath her and pulled Arthur's jacket tighter around her.

"You guys know how passionate I was about getting into Stanford School of Medicine," she started.

"We threw a huge party to celebrate your acceptance," Chris nodded.

Gabrielle smiled warmly. "That day was surreal. My mom was so proud, and your dad got me so many school supplies it made my head spin."

"Stanford lived up to its reputation. The coursework was heavy. Being on the pre-med track was difficult enough. Working in actual med school felt... impossible. But I was a workhorse. I worked so hard. I gave it my everything and even though it meant sacrificing having a social life, I was getting straight A's. I had to in order to get matched with a hospital for residency. But it was rough... I had few friends because I was always studying. And the few friends I did have were studying just as hard as I was. It was often pretty lonely..."

"I met Damian through a mutual pre-med friend at a party. He was... *dazzling*. A perfect gentleman. He really knew how to charm a girl. I never took him for the type of person I'd date because we were just so… different. But he was so sweet, caring, thoughtful, and compassionate. He said all the right things to make me feel special… loved."

Chris shifted uncomfortably and crossed his arms over his chest, trying not to give himself away.

"He was a fantastic artist. And he was just as passionate about his work as I was about my studies. So, we got along great. Anyway, things started to take a nose-dive towards the end of junior year. When Obama's educational bill was shot down, many scholarships were cut, including mine. I had already taken out as many loans as I was allowed, and I didn't want to burden my mother about it. So, I took on extra jobs on campus. But it wasn't enough."

"Why didn't you come to us for help?" Charlie asked.

Gabrielle gave him a defeated shrug. "You know me, Charlie. I hate asking for things. I'd rather exhaust all my options and then some before I ask for help."

"Guess you really do have that stubborn Richardson gene," Arthur smirked at her.

She smiled at him nervously and looked down at her fingers. "What good it did me." She quickly grabbed the large bottle of whiskey and poured herself another glass. She gulped it down before anyone could stop her.

"I'm still too sober," she said, pulling at her curls. Charlie and Chris exchanged concerned glances as she continued her story.

"While in school, I was practicing ballet. It was the one skill I carried with me from high school and the one stress reliever I had to keep me sane." She crouched down further. "I had a spontaneous and pretty eccentric friend who… was aware of my financial situation and offered me another alternative to make money… exotic dancing."

The men tried to minimize their reactions so as not to stir her.

"I know it sounds ridiculous. Me? Exotic dancing? Yeah, right. I'm barely comfortable in a bathing suit let alone on a pole. At least that's what I told her. But she said that I was already a skilled dancer, that that's all I really needed to do was dance. She said that some nights she brought home 5-10 grand. Those numbers dazed me. I told her I wasn't sure but she really insisted I tried it lest I continue to struggle. I was exhausted from my 3 jobs and my grades were starting to slip. I was running out of options. So... I decided to give it a try."

"I was terrified at first. I didn't really know what to expect. But it really wasn't that bad because I got to decide what I wore and what I did. So at least I had that freedom. Somewhere along the way, Shawn, the club manager, thought I had really high potential. He was always a bit too handsy with me and overdid it on the flattery, but overall pretty harmless. I appreciated him because he helped me make extra money by scheduling me when attendance was at its highest. He even gave me a stage name... 'Ebony."

The three of them collectively rolled their eyes.

"I know right?" she chuckled. "So cliché. It's weird though. Eventually I became one of their most highly-demanded dancers... but that's when things got really bad..."

She took a deep breath and closed her eyes. "I tried to think of that job as mainly performance. I tried to ignore the gross male objectification, the disgusting unwanted passes, the misogynistic insults, and just... focus on my passion for dance. It helped somewhat. But I always felt ashamed in the end. Like I was losing bits and pieces of myself."

She wrapped her arms around herself protectively. "Another part of the job was just chatting guys up. You know... inflating their egos. Making them feel like they were the sexiest men alive. It felt demeaning to me, but it put better food than ramen on the table. I had a few incidents where guys forcibly tried to take me home. Nothing overtly violent, but that's when I knew I had to stop. I just didn't feel safe. It's strange... as a woman when I get catcalled on the street or something I expect the assholery that comes with it. But at that club I felt like an entertainment attraction. It's like... I wasn't even human to them. Just an item to play with. I still had about a semester's worth of tuition to pay for, but I decided to figure out another way to pay for school. Try working my 3 jobs again."

"When I gave Shawn my resignation, he asked me to do one last show. He said there was a really special client that would be there and was coming especially for me. That sounded weird to me but I guess my name had really gotten out there. So I tried to take it for what it was... an opportunity to finish paying off my tuition."

"Shawn never described the client to me, but that night I did notice a man who wouldn't take his eyes off me. It left me really unsettled but I tried to ignore it. At the end of the performance, Shawn rushed up to me with my earnings and yet another offer from this same client for a private show. I should have just walked off with what I made but, damn it, Shawn made it sound like I was crazy if I were to pass this up. Maybe I just got too careless... too trusting."

Gabrielle grabbed a pillow from the side and hugged it tightly.

"You okay?" Chris asked.

"Do you need a minute?" Charlie added.

She said nothing for a moment before shaking her head. She took a deep breath and continued. "I was really nervous that night. Everything felt wrong. I should have listened to my gut. All the girls tried giving me advice on what to do. But I feel like my nerves got the best of me. I don't know. I've spent far too much time thinking about it."

The men watched quietly as Gabrielle racked her brain. "His

name was John Henderson. He was a 37-year-old steel ore trader from Oregon. He had a wife named Sarah and 3 children: 2 boys, Jack who was 7 and Reggie who was 4, and a daughter named Lily who was 3..." The men looked at her bewildered at how much she knew about the man.

"John... was a man of few words but what he lacked in dialogue he made up for in his actions... that night he raped me." The room was stunned into silence as the last few words to escape her mouth permeated the atmosphere.

"I'd like to think that I fought hard. And I think... in the beginning I did, but at some point I just gave up. It was brutal. Painful. And it wasn't quick. It lasted forever. At least it felt like it did. And I can't help but blame myself for letting it happen."

"You can't possibly blame yourself for that!" Charlie said angrily.

"I've thought about that night over a thousand times. And every time, I think about how I could have avoided it from happening. Don't feel sorry for me. I only have myself to blame," Gabrielle said quickly.

Chris could barely contain his bridling rage. "It's not your fault-"

"But it is!" she said, cutting him off. Tears streamed down her face. Chris hesitated to say anything more and watched helplessly as she tried to wipe the tears from her face.

"Either way it doesn't matter anymore. What happened happened. And there's nothing I can do about it." She put both hands in her hair and anxiously pulled at her curls. "That night when he fell asleep, I tried to escape. I looked through his things to find a phone since he had broken mine when he..." She paused for a moment trying to stifle back her anguish.

"As I looked through his things, I found tons of pictures of me. Not just from the club but at school. Pictures of me changing in my dorm. Pictures of me in class. Of me sleeping. He was stalking me. He had messages in his phone talking to an anonymous person about me. Even after being raped, I don't think I've ever freaked out so hard in my life." She dug her fingers into her hair and squeezed her eyes shut to stop the tears.

"Did you call the police?" Chris said, trying to fight back his fury.

"I couldn't," she gasped. She calmly removed her hands from her hair and readjusted herself on the couch. She went to reach for the bottle one last time.

Charlie gently grabbed her hand to stop her from grabbing the whiskey. "Why couldn't you call the police, Gabs?" he asked softly. She pulled her hand back and stared blankly at the floor. There was a long silence before she finally spoke.

"Because... that night... I killed him while he slept," she said blankly.

The silence in the room was so palpable that they could hear Thor moving restlessly in Chris's room. He soon patted out of the room to see why it had gotten so disturbingly quiet.

"Thor!" she said in quiet excitement. He leaped onto the couch and seemed to feel the heaviness of the room. He settled onto her lap and lay his head down.

"I looked for the sharpest object I could find. I didn't have many options, so, I used a pen... I took a pen from his suitcase and I rammed it into his jugular... I watched him choke on his own blood as the life drained from his body." Her voice cracked as she stroked Thor's head.

"It's a strange thing. I've dedicated my life to saving people's lives. It's my passion..." Tears commenced rolling down her cheeks, falling onto Thor's fur. "And yet nothing gave me more satisfaction than to take his." She looked up at Chris, her eyes puffy and bloodshot red. "And that terrifies me! That's not normal right? That's not what normal, sane people feel." Feeling the tension in her body, Thor lifted his head and licked her face to soothe her.

The guys let a long moment pass, allowing Gabrielle to collect herself. She wrapped her arms around Thor's neck and buried her face inh is fur attempting to dry her tears. She looked up at their somber faces, just barely hiding their inner anger.

"So, you're probably wondering how I got out of that," she said, playing with Thor's fur. "For a moment I did nothing. I sat with a dead body for a few hours not knowing what to do. I had just taken a man's life... I contemplated taking my own..."

Chris could feel Charlie tense up at this confession as his eyes never left her. His body seemed to struggle between wanting to fight for her and wanting to comfort her.

"I didn't know who to call. There was no one I trusted enough to help me. I felt like I had no one. And then... Damian found me."

"What do you mean he found you?" Chris asked suddenly.

"I don't know how. He went looking for me. He told me he asked around. Somehow got to Shawn, and eventually found me sitting half naked in the corner of a cold room with a dead man lying on the bed," she said. Charlie and Chris exchanged disconcerted glances.

"Don't doubt him," she said. She noted their hidden Richardson brother language she knew all too well. "He took care of me. He made sure I was safe. He cleaned me up and took me to the hospital to make sure I was not impregnated. He took care of the body. He-"

"He took care of the body?" Charlie asked, alarmed.

Gabrielle shook her head. "I didn't ask for details. I didn't want to know. I just wanted it all to end." Charlie nodded sympathetically, but still felt tense at the holes in her story. He looked knowingly at Chris and Arthur who seemed to share the same sentiment.

"Thanks to Damian, I survived the most horrible moment of my life. I wouldn't have gotten through that without him. And yet, it still eats away at me... that I killed someone..."

Chris moved away from the wall and walked closer to Gabrielle. "I understand that he helped you, Gabs, but something doesn't seem right about him. I don't trust him."

Gabrielle gave Chris a disapproving look. "That's not really up to you to decide, Chris."

Chris looked at her disgruntled. He felt that her comment was more in reference to their relationship than about his criticism of Damian. "It is when your safety is at risk," he said sternly.

"My safety is not at risk!" she said defensively. She looked at him with frustration aflame in her eyes.

"Then what exactly did Arthur save you from?" Charlie said impatiently.

Gabrielle took a deep breath. "It was just a stupid argument. A lover's quarrel, if you may. It wasn't a big deal. Arthur saved me from a minor migraine."

Chris and Charlie both looked at her, their faces filled with doubt. She knew they didn't believe her. She looked to Arthur who tried to give her a supportive smile, but even he couldn't mask his frustration.

Gabrielle pushed Thor off of her and sat up straight. "Look... I will admit that Damian has a bit of a temper. We all have our flaws and he's been working on his."

"Has he ever lay a hand on you?" Chris asked her curtly.

Gabrielle frowned, biting her lip. "I mean... it's not like... he usually doesn't-"

"It's a simple 'yes' or 'no' question, Gabs. You don't have to defend him," Charlie said angrily.

"He's my fiancé! Of course I have to defend him! He's always defended me. And I really don't appreciate you all interrogating me like this when you don't even know him!" she snapped. Chris felt himself getting more frustrated with her defensive attitude. He went to speak when Gabrielle's phone went off.

"Hey, Damian..." she said answering the phone. "No, he got the painting... He's dropping me back in a moment, we just... stopped to get something to eat." She gave Arthur a knowing look and stood up from the couch. She raised her finger to let them know she would be a moment. "Yea sure..." she said. She wrapped Arthur's jacket tight around her and walked away from the men, towards the kitchen.

Arthur leaned back against the wall with his arms folded across his chest. He stroked his chin and watched Gabrielle closely till she walked all the way into the kitchen. "Right... I'm afraid my new best friend isn't being completely honest about the circumstances in which I found her," he said, turning to Charlie and Chris.

They both looked at him curiously. "What do you mean?" Charlie asked. He leaned over to pet Thor who was nudging his leg for attention.

"They weren't just... arguing. He was manhandling her," Arthur clarified. Chris narrowed his eyes and folded his arms across his chest.

"I was going over the data I pulled, which is... you're not going to believe... anyway," Arthur said, shaking his head. "When I found them, he had her pinned against the car in the lot outside of a cafe. He was holding her forcefully with both hands, shaking her. She looked frightened and weak. A stark contrast to the confident Amazonian black woman I'm used to snapping at me. She noticed me first and reacted in surprise, which caused him to notice me as well... That was the only reason why he let her go. I'm sure of it."

Chris rubbed at his temple in frustration. His fingers tingled with the anger he felt coursing through his body. "How did you get her out of there? Assuming what she told us was untrue..." Charlie asked. He anxiously rubbed his hands together just to keep them busy.

"It wasn't entirely untrue. When I approached them, I would have beaten the shit out of him, if she wasn't begging me not to provoke him. She seemed desperate. I didn't want to overstep my boundaries. So, I tried to think on my feet and made an offer for the painting. I had to make an impressive offer which she's still trying to pay me back for, but it's all chump change anyway. And I'm certain he hit her before I discovered them."

Chris straightened up quickly. "How do you know?"

"She was powdering her face in the car ride over here. We're all well aware that woman doesn't need makeup. Especially since we were only coming here," Arthur explained.

Charlie sunk into the couch.

"And why do you think she's wearing my jacket?" Arthur continued. They both looked up at him inquisitively. "It's not because she's cold, which is the excuse she gave me when she thought I didn't see... She kept asking me to forget it and not take it seriously. But men beating on women isn't something I can overlook," Arthur said annoyed.

Chris could feel his anger boiling over the rim. And from the way Charlie was reaching for his cigarettes, he could tell he was just barely hanging on to his self-control.

"Arthur, I really need to go now," Gabrielle said, stepping back into the living room.

Arthur turned to her with a smile. "You know I can't do that, sweetheart."

Gabrielle looked at him angrily. "Even after everything, you still won't-"

"It's *because* of everything that I won't," Arthur said, cutting her off with an unusually serious tone.

"Fine. I'll just take a cab," she muttered.

"You're not leaving," Charlie said abruptly. He had a low rumble in his voice and made every effort to make sure his anger wasn't perceived to be directed at her.

"Excuse me?" she said, looking back at him.

"You can either stay here with Chris or come back to my place. Heck you can even stay with Arthur, if you so choose. But you're **not** going back to him," Charlie said approaching her. He stuffed his hands into his pockets and looked down at her with an unwavering, authoritarian glare.

"What... are you guys putting me on house arrest or something?" she scoffed.

"Something like that, yea," Charlie said gruffly. He walked behind her to lean against the door, blocking her only exit.

She looked at him incredulously. "You have **got** to be kidding me! First of all, I am not some child that you can just ground and send to her room! And I certainly don't need a damn babysitter!"

"Not a child, but you sure are acting like one," Charlie sneered at her.

"Charles Niles Richardson, I swear on all that is good in this world that I will hurt you so damn badly," she snapped.

"Damn... I have never heard anyone use your full name like that," Arthur chuckled. Charlie rolled his eyes before fixing them back on Gabrielle.

"You guys think this is funny? I can't stay here playing these silly little games with you! If you had any respect for me, you would move and let me leave," she demanded.

"Take it easy, Gabs. We're just trying to protect you. Let us check some stuff out first and then... if it's all clear we'll take you back," Chris said. He stepped into the hallway to join them.

Gabrielle frowned, not feeling happy with the arrangement. "You're really not going to let me leave, are you?"

Her question was met with silence. "Honestly, I feel I could probably take on at least one Richardson if I had like... a tranquilizer. But three?" She sighed deeply, letting out every gush of angst she felt in her chest. She leaned against the wall with her eyes closed.

"Fine," she said.

Arthur stepped up. "I'm going to get the remaining equipment from the car," he said, walking past Chris. Charlie stepped to the side to let him leave.

"You guys are so annoying," she said anxiously.

~*~

Gabrielle lay on Chris's couch. She kicked her legs up over the edge as she petted Thor, lying on the floor next to her.

"Did you guys abandon me?" she called out.

"We're right here, Gabs. We're just talking," Chris said from the hallway. The brothers stood at the entrance of the living room. Both leaned against the frame, speaking in hushed voices as they waited for Arthur to return.

"You Richardsons and your secrets." She flipped off of the couch, causing Thor to stand up quickly and bark. "Ai, chill out," she said, playfully tackling him. She wrestled him until he pinned her down, licking furiously at her face.

"Oh my gosh, Thor, no with your awful doggy breath," she giggled, trying to move him off of her. She sat up on the floor and pulled Thor close to her as he playfully trotted around in her lap. "I love this dog so much. So loyal. So trustworthy. If I had the choice I would just live in a world with only dogs," she said pushing her face into his fur.

"Can't argue with that," Charlie smirked. He watched her, arms folded across his chest.

"You know your dad came to visit me one night?" she said. They both looked at her startled.

"At the club?!" Chris almost shouted.

"No, crazy! On campus. He was the only person from home to come visit me. He claims it was for a business trip or something but... somehow it felt like he came for me..." She looked down smiling fondly. "He came during one of the darkest times of my life just to light it back up again... despite how temporary it was."

Charlie tried to think. "I don't even remember him leaving for California."

"He told me he was traveling to Texas and decided to pop in. I laughed at that. They're nowhere near each other," she chuckled. "He came to visit a week after I was raped... and... the murder..." She took a deep breath and closed her eyes. "I was so terrified when I saw him. I can still remember feeling cold all over when I saw his face. Not because I was scared of him but... because I was afraid he had known what had happened to me... what I did..."

They watched her carefully, trying to take in the gravity of her words. She gently ran her fingers through Thor's fur. "But he was so happy to see me. And normally I would be too, but... I was so aggravated... almost angry to see him. I got defensive. He knew something was wrong. He can always tell when something's wrong..."

Tears started to stream down her face again. "I just wanted him to leave. I didn't want him to see me... that way. So disgusting, dirty, and broken. And he was just his normal, cheery, loving self.

It made me feel even worse. I tried to talk to him. He updated me on how you guys were doing. About your business, Chris, and Charlie's startup. About Eli and his team. He made me want to come back home... but I couldn't..."

They helplessly watched her as her sobs started to overwhelm her. "That was the worst argument I had ever gotten into with him. He kept asking me what was wrong, and I wouldn't tell him. He just kept prodding. Think you Richardsons have that in common," she chuckled ironically.

She bit her lip and looked up at them before quickly averting her eyes to avoid their gaze. "I hurt him that day. I told him that my life wasn't any of his business. That he wasn't my father and he had no right to try to get involved. I wasn't trying to hurt him... just trying to get him to leave me alone..."

Chris frowned, hesitating to speak. "I'm sure he knew you were just upset and not serious about what you said."

Gabrielle looked at him hopelessly. "Maybe... but it doesn't change the fact that I still said it... and that I hurt him. And that those were the last words I said to him before he..."

She dropped her head into her hands, trying to control her sobbing. Thor hopped up from her lap and anxiously circled her. He nudged her and licked her face, trying to poke his head into her space. "Ugh... Thor..." She smiled through the tears and rubbed his golden fur. "I miss him too, boy..."

"I had no idea you saw him after you went away..." Charlie said. He didn't know what else to say but felt the need to reassure her that their family still loved her.

"I underestimated how much he cared about me," she said softly. "When I went to pay my tuition, the Financial Aid office told me it was already completely paid off. He never said anything to me. Even after all I said to him he still..." Gabrielle rubbed furiously at her face. "Ugh, you guys will be the death of me," she chuckled through her tears.

"That sounds like something Dad would do," Chris smiled.

"Of course, it is. I tried calling him. I didn't have his cell number. I left a voicemail on the house phone but I never got a call back," she said.

"Think mom had switched the numbers by that time. Telemarketers," Charlie frowned.

Gabrielle stayed silent for a moment. "I just hate that the last thing I said to him was that he wasn't my father. I couldn't have been more wrong." She looked up at them. "I wouldn't blame you guys if you wanted me to leave right now. I can barely tolerate myself..."

Chris gave her an encouraging smile. "I'm certain that dad knew you loved him with all your heart despite how you may have been feeling at the time."

Charlie walked over and crouched in front of her, playfully rubbing Thor's head. He looked up into her eyes. "You'll always be a part of this family, Gabs. There's no getting rid of us," he gave her a cheeky grin.

She smiled relieved and got lost in his green eyes. Their longing gaze was interrupted when Arthur walked through the door. "Got it!" Arthur grinned, carrying a bulky bag.

"Is all that really necessary?" Chris said, eyeing the bag disapprovingly.

"Hey. I don't tell you how to do your job, you don't tell me how to do mine," Arthur said.

"Do you guys need me to stay here for this?" Gabrielle asked.

"It's probably best that you don't," Charlie said, standing to his feet.

"In that case... Chris, can I use your shower and borrow a spare change of clothes because I'm exhausted. And for as long as I'll be on house arrest, I'd like to get comfy. So, I'm thinking a movie, maybe some cereal, and a long t-shirt at least," she said. Chris looked at her bewildered by her long list of demands.

"Don't look at me like that! You guys are the ones keeping me here against my will! Thor and I would like to be properly accommodated, isn't that right, Thor?" She looked down at her furry four-legged friend who barked and nudged her leg with his head.

"The ruler of Asgard has spoken," she said smiling up at Chris. Chris shook his head with a grin on his face.

"Fine, follow me," Chris said, motioning for her to follow him. "Arthur, set up in the study room. I'll be back."

"Oh wait! Here!" Gabrielle shrugged off Arthur's suit jacket and handed it back to him. He grabbed the jacket from her and gave her a nervous glance before looking behind her.

"What?" she asked. She then remembered why she kept the coat on in the first place. She turned around to see Chris and Charlie looking at her with mouths agape, tension twitching their jaws. Dark blue bruises blemished her chocolate skin around her forearms, wrists, and shoulders. A large bruise settled onto her lower back exposed by her white jumpsuit.

"What the **fuck**?!" Charlie blurted.

Gabrielle shyly wrapped her arms around herself, trying to cover up. "It's not that bad..." she said, averting her eyes away from them.

"Not that bad?! Are you fucking kidding me?!" Charlie said angrily. He took a step towards her and she instinctively winced. She took a step back, slightly bumping into Arthur behind her. He grabbed her gently by her shoulders to keep her from knocking them both over.

“S-sorry,” she murmured both to Charlie and Arthur. Charlie’s eyebrows stitched in confusion at her reaction towards him.

“Why did you-” His eyes narrowed in anger once he realized. “Do you *really* think I’d hurt you?!”

“No! No, I-... it’s just instinct. It’s a habit. I back away from angry people out of habit!” she said defensively.

“Are you sure that isn’t something you picked up because he’s been hitting you?” Charlie growled.

“Charlie, let’s calm down,” Chris said, trying to manage the situation.

“Stop making assumptions, Charlie! You don’t know what you’re talking about!” she shot back at him.

“So, you’re really going to stand there and tell us that he hasn’t been abusing you?!” Charlie snapped.

“That’s not-”

“Why the fuck do you keep defending him?!”

“Charlie!” Chris barked. He grabbed his brother roughly by the shoulder to turn him around. Charlie yanked his arm away from Chris with a snarl on his face, glaring angrily at him. Chris returned the intimidating hard glare before his eyes shifted and his face softened. He motioned behind him. Charlie turned around, still fuming, when he saw Gabrielle holding herself. She was sobbing as Arthur tried to comfort her.

Charlie could feel guilt running through him. He wanted to apologize to her for his reaction, but he was still too angry to say anything else. He stalked towards the door and threw on his coat. “I need a smoke,” he grumbled before exiting.

Chris sighed as he watched his brother storm out of the apartment.

"You okay, sweetheart?" Arthur asked. He turned her around to face him.

"Yea..." she said, biting her lip anxiously.

"He'll be alright. Just needs a minute to cool off," Arthur assured her. She smiled at him and turned to Chris. Chris's hands sat in his pockets and his head was lowered. He looked at her with anger, sadness, and uncertainty. Gabrielle hesitated to say anything. Chris was surely the more stable one, but she wasn't sure what he was thinking.

"Chris?" she said softly. Chris blinked himself back and rubbed his neck.

"Yea... Arthur, go set up. Gabs, come with me." He turned around and walked past them.

Gabrielle looked to Arthur who smiled and nudged towards Chris with his chin. He headed towards the study room and paused to look back at her. "I'm here if you need me," he said. Gabrielle smiled fondly. She was happy with this new friendship she had formed with Arthur. Even if it was under awful circumstances.

Thor followed closely at Gabrielle's heels as she followed Chris to his bedroom. From the doorway, she watched him pull out a t-shirt and a pair of sweats.

"These will be a little big on you, but they're comfortable," he said to her. She grabbed them between her hands, her fingers brushing against his.

"Thanks..." she looked up at him. His eyes seemed glazed over. "Chris... are you upset with me?" she asked him.

He seemed taken back by her question. "Why would I be upset with you?"

She looked to the side and exhaled. "I don't know... I just... feel like I'm disappointing a lot of people today."

Chris put a finger beneath her chin, lifting her head so she was eye-level with him. "We're just worried about you, Gabs. We want to make sure you're safe," Chris assured her.

Gabrielle nodded. "I understand..."

"And in order for us to make sure you're safe... we need you to cooperate with us and be honest with us."

She sighed knowing what he was saying was right. "I know, it's just... not something I feel comfortable talking about..." She grabbed his hand, pulling it away from her chin. "Yes... Damian does hit me. He never used to before. I thought I was just becoming an unbearable person to be around that made him so... violent with me. I didn't want to make a big deal out of it. Not after everything he's done for me..."

"Nothing is worth him abusing you," Chris told her. Gabrielle closed her eyes as he gently caressed her battered arms. He softly ran his fingers over her bruises. "Does it hurt?" he asked her.

She shook her head. "Not anymore..."

She shivered from his soft fleeting touch against her raw bruised skin. Her eyes remained closed, soaking in his touch, her lips slightly parted. Chris felt himself leaning in despite all the warning signs telling him not to. Before he could stop himself, his lips were already against hers. She immediately opened for him, allowing his tongue to quickly find hers. He wrapped an arm around her waist, pulling her closer to him.

"Ah!" She winced from the pain of the pressure on her bruised lower back.

"Shit. Sorry." He cursed himself for not being more careful. He lowered his hand to rest right above her ass. "Is that better?" She nodded before quickly kissing him again. She ran her hands up and down his arms before wrapping her arms around his neck. She kissed him harder and tried to climb him. Chris could feel himself getting more and more excited. He had to stop himself before they reached the point of no return.

"Babe," he said reluctantly. Holding her steady by the hips, Chris removed his lips from her and tried to catch his breath. She blinked a few times trying to come to.

"Why is it that... when you touch me, all of my senses come alive?" she asked.

Chris chuckled warmly. "I'll tell you that once you can explain why I have a hard time controlling myself around you." They both laughed when suddenly they heard the door open and close. Thor bounded down the hallway to greet whoever walked in.

"Hey, boy..." They heard Charlie's voice.

"Arthur is probably done setting up by now," Chris said, reluctantly stepping away from her. "Feel free to raid my fridge. The shower is pretty straightforward." He walked to the bedroom door. "Come find me if you need anything."

"And if I only need you?" she asked suggestively. He looked at her surprised. His blue eyes shimmered with desire and intrigue.

"Let's hope we're alone by then..." he smirked. Gabrielle felt a tingle in her lady parts as Chris exited the room.

~*~

"So, I've broken the file into 3 parts. One is the information Damian has on Gabrielle, the other is the information he has on himself, and the other is all of the video footage from the club... ever."

"**All** the video footage? How in the world did you get that? Actually, don't answer that," Charlie said. Chris, Charlie and Arthur circled a TV screen in Chris's study room that was linked to Arthur's tablet.

"I had already started scanning through the data. Most of it checks out with what Gabrielle told us. She was top of her class through all of her years at Stanford. She did have a massive amount of loans-", Arthur started.

"Can you check that payment of her last tuition bill?" Chris asked.

Arthur clicked and scanned the screen. "Richardson LLP. You guys paid for her tuition?"

Chris sat back smiling. "Dad did..."

Arthur smiled knowingly then turned back to the screen. "Gabrielle's public record is entirely clean... until you get to what Damian has on her. This is... *explicit.*"

"What do you mean?" Charlie asked.

"He's got a lot of explicit photos of her. Not ones that she posed for either..." Arthur warned.

Arthur pulled up a few candid shots of Gabrielle on campus. One picture showed her stretching in her room with just shorts and a sports bra on. Another picture showed her getting out of a shower in a gym, barely covered by a towel. Another revealed her changing her clothes in a dressing room wearing just her underwear.

"Someone clearly took these with intent," Chris said.

"You think these are the pictures she was referring to when she looked through Henderson's phone?" Charlie asked Chris. Chris slowly nodded as his mind went to work.

"There's only one picture of her here that it seems she was aware was being taken of her, and that's for the club." Arthur pulled up a picture of Gabrielle wearing shorts and a crop top. She was posing with her back arched against a pole and her hands wrapped around it from behind. She had a provocative look on her face. "That's the only one."

"And what about Damian?" Chris asked.

"Oh, this guy. He's an enigma," Arthur said. "His network of partners is more differentiated than the UN. They range from art traders, to basic product transfers, to the black market... I'm talking your territory, Christopher..."

Chris leaned forward, quickly scanning the words on the screen. "Why the hell does he know all these people?"

"My guess is that this is a man who loves to make money and will do whatever he can to get it. Whether it's through his art or... other means." Arthur pulled up a picture of Damian with two other men in a room full of naked women.

"Is he... at a brothel?" Charlie asked.

"Yup..." Arthur said.

"You don't think he's... with Gabrielle...?" Charlie said looking at Chris worriedly.

Chris shook his head. "No. When I spoke to him, he came off more as the possessive type. He wouldn't give her up so readily..." They stopped when they heard footsteps followed by the sound of the shower turning. Then they continued talking.

"Now, here's where it gets interesting," Arthur continued. "Damian likes to show off his prized possessions, his most prized being..." he pulled up a video of Gabrielle and Damian at a showcase 2 years back. "... Gabrielle."

Arthur played the video.

~

"Damian, this woman is absolutely stunning. Such precise medical skills and high intelligence all wrapped up in a pretty package." A man with red hair and gray eyes smoked on a pipe as his eyes wandered greedily over Gabrielle's body. She stood near a table looking around aimlessly not sure what to do with herself. A long, red fitted dress hugged her curves nicely.

Damian stood next to the man with a smug grin on his face. "Yes, I know... I'm very proud of my work.... I mean... her."

"Are you sure you don't want to offer her up? I'd be willing to give you 2 milli-"

Damian flashed an offended look at the man. "I've already told you before that she is not available and won't be for quite some time. And when she is, her value will far supersede 2 million."

The man raised his red brow at Damian. "I'm sure she will... keep an eye on her then..."

~

"So he's involved in human-trafficking," Charlie said annoyed.

"It would seem like it... though not that heavily. He's made quite a few transactions of women of various ages. It's not pleasant. But... compared to the rest of the competition, he would not be deemed a heavy player," Arthur said.

"But he talks about Gabrielle like he's grooming her..." Charlie said.

"That doesn't make sense if he plans on marrying her," Chris said, rubbing his temples.

"Well that brings me to my next point. I think we should go through the video footage from that night at the club when she... was attacked. Maybe something else was going on she wasn't aware of," Arthur said. Charlie and Chris nodded and he pulled up the club video footage files.

~

"Gentlemen! Now for tonight's main event, the moment you've all been waiting for... EBONY!"

The music blasted throughout the club, barely drowning out the roars as the lights flickered to a low red hue. A voluptuous shadow ap-

peared on stage wearing a golden mini skirt and cropped red bustier. She strutted onto the stage and swiftly grasped the pole, swinging onto it gracefully. Her legs parted in the air, spinning in hypnotic swirls around the pole. Her arms effortlessly held her weight up on the pole as she delicately swung her body. Her audience was captivated by her perfect form.

She teased the crowd with her movements and swayed her hips to the music. The feathers on her skirt jiggling in line with her ass as she shook her rump to the floor and into a perfect split. Her audience cooed as she swiftly swung her legs and worked her body back onto the pole doing flips in the air. She ended her performance with a bow and flirty kisses blown to any lucky man in the audience. The crowd roared and cheered chanting her name.

Hopping off stage, she panted breathlessly, rushing for water. "You 'kay, Ebs?" a girl in a tiny white bra and thong called out to her.

Ebony looked up after gobbling down a cup of water. "Just my nerves," she said, giving a weak smile.

"You're the best dancer out there, Ebs! You shouldn't worry 'bout no nerves. You got the goods, girl! Every man wants ya," the girl said.

Ebony tried to give a reassuring smile. "I don't really take that as a compliment... but thanks..." she murmured to herself, walking to her dressing room.

"Eboneezer Scrooge!" A raven-haired girl called out to her. "Shawn wants ya. Get back out there!"

Ebony raised her eyes to the heavens in frustration. She turned around to head back out into the main club. The moment she stepped out, several men devoured her with their eyes. She hesitated to walk further and debated going back.

"Ebony! Come here, princess!" Shawn called from a few feet away. Ebony walked shyly up to Shawn who was standing next to a tall, tanned white guy with jet black hair that swooped perfectly to the side. Not a strand out of place. He had piercing green eyes that fol-

lowed her every movement. A small smirk appeared on his face the moment she locked eyes with him.

"Y-yes?" she asked.

"Ebony, I have a client here that would like a private show from you," Shawn beamed at her. Ebony eyed the man from head to toe. His build was intimidating. She felt herself shrinking under his sharp gaze. He had a toothy grin indicating his hunger for her.

"Uh... Shawn I-I don't do private shows," she stammered out. The man's smirk quickly disappeared and was replaced with a frown as he looked at Shawn questioningly.

"Er... give me a moment, sir," Shawn said. He grabbed Ebony by the arm and pulled her aside.

"Shawn, what are you doing? You know that I don't do this kind of thing. This is my last night..." Ebony said.

"Ebony, princess. Apple of my eye, you're already breaking my heart by leaving me. This client is giving me a 40% additional cut of his offer for you." Ebony raised an eyebrow not sure why that was a big deal.

"He's offering 12 million for you, princess!" Shawn blurted.

Ebony looked at Shawn, mouth agape. "What?!"

"You heard me, princess! I couldn't believe it myself but well who can blame him? Just look at you!"

Ebony looked back at the man whose eyes still hadn't left her. He seemed to be getting more impatient and hungrier for her. His eyes constantly scanned over her body.

"I... I still don't know," she hesitated.

"Listen..." Shawn tried to reason. "This isn't a booty call. He's not trying to have sex with you. You're just giving him a little lap dance. That's it. He knows the rules. No touching, no kissing, no fucking. You

can handle that, can't you, princess? For 12 million dollars!"

Ebony felt herself sweat a little. She looked back at the man who was now smiling at her. She sighed in resignation. "O-okay. But after this I'm done."

"You got it, princess," Shawn said eagerly. He grabbed her by the hand and quickly walked her back over to the gentleman. "I apologize for the delay, sir. We just had to settle some things. Ebony would be more than happy to accompany you this evening," Shawn said to him.

A wide grin slowly spread across the man's face. He locked eyes with Ebony and reached for her hand, lowering his mouth to kiss it. "I look forward to seeing you..." He had a strange voice that made her shiver with apprehension.

When the man turned to walk away, Ebony looked at Shawn with annoyance. "I'll make sure to go over the rules with him again... I promise," Shawn said to her apologetically. She sighed and headed back towards her dressing room.

~

"That's the last bit of footage I have of Gabrielle." Arthur sat back in his seat, chewing on his bottom lip, thinking.

"She looked completely frightened the whole time.," Chris said. He analyzed her face paused on the screen.

"No surprise there. Did you see the way that creep kept staring at her?" Charlie grumbled.

Chris analyzed the stills. "Can I go back for a minute?"

"Sure," Arthur said, handing the tablet over to him. Chris used his fingers to scroll back to way before Gabrielle performed and the other women were on stage. He paused at a specific moment and squinted.

"How do you zoom?" Chris asked.

"Like this," Arthur said using his fingers. Chris pinpointed an area in the audience and zoomed in.

"Is that the guy?" Chris said, peering closer.

"Yea... that looks like him," Charlie said. "And who's that next to him."

"That... looks like... Damian? Hold on, give me that," Arthur said, grabbing the tablet. He zoomed in and enhanced the visuals. They could clearly see Damian and Henderson.

"What the hell?" Charlie said.

"Can we get sound?" Chris asked.

"Lemme see..." Arthur clicked a few buttons and typed in a few codes before clicking play.

~

"She can be very shy in the bedroom, so be patient and gentle. I don't want to see a single blemish or bruise on her skin," Damian said. He took a sip of his drink, watching the girls on stage.

"She's shy...? Well, I can help her with that..." Henderson grinned, puffing on his cigar.

"I mean it, Henderson," Damian gave him a sideways glance. "I've put a lot of work into her and I expect you to leave her as perfect as you found her."

Henderson frowned. "I don't understand how much you think I can get away with. I'm paying you a pretty penny. She won't be untouched."

"I know that. I'm just saying... treat her better than you treat your wife."

"Ahh..."

"If you run into trouble, call Shawn. I can't have any evidence of my-

self being traced back to you."

Henderson nodded. "I don't understand why you don't just give her to me... I'd triple my offer."

Damian chuckled. "It's because of your willingness to triple your offer that I won't give her to you. I don't mind the obsession enough to share her a bit for a price, but... I'm still selfish..."

"I guess I can't blame you..." Henderson said as the music died down.

"Gentlemen! Now for tonight's main event, the moment you've all been waiting for... EBONY!"

"That's my cue," Damian said getting up. "Remember what we discussed." But Henderson was already gone. He eagerly scanned the stage for the woman he was obsessed with and whose body he craved to touch.

~

"Son of a bitch!" Charlie said furiously. "The motherfucker set her up!"

Chris sat there stunned not sure what to say or do. He knew what he had seen and what he heard, but he still had a hard time processing it. He was jolted out of his thoughts when Charlie abruptly stood up from his chair.

"I'm gonna kill the son of a bitch!" Charlie growled.

"Wait, Charlie!" Chris said getting up. "We gotta talk about this. We have to figure out what we're going to do."

"I already said what I'm gonna do! I'm gonna beat the shit out of him!"

Chris groaned in frustration. "Arthur. What incriminating files does Damian have on Gabrielle that if released would be detrimental to her? We need to make sure we can protect her from him causing any further harm."

Arthur typed away at his computer. “It seems just the ones of her at the club and of course the cover-up of the murder.”

“Is there a way we can destroy those files so he can’t use them against her?” Chris asked.

Arthur grinned. “Of course. But it won’t happen overnight.. It’s gonna take me some time.”

“How much time?!” Charlie growled impatiently.

“About a day? Two days tops,” Arthur advised. Charlie huffed and grabbed his coat as he walked out of the study and into the hallway. Chris quickly followed after him.

“Charlie, please don’t make any hasty decisions. Just give Arthur a day and then we’ll make our move.”

“I don’t wanna fucking wait, Chris! You always want to be careful and diplomatic and that’s not how I operate! That’s not how I get shit done!” Charlie snapped.

“Guys?” They both turned around to see Gabrielle sitting on the couch with her feet up in the darkened living room. Thor was asleep next to her. She held a bowl of popcorn while a movie played on the dimly lit screen in front of her. She looked between them confused.

“What’s going on? Are you guys okay?” she asked. She put down the popcorn and got up.

“Yea… yea we’re fine,” Chris said. They both eyed her in Chris’s long shirt. Her curly hair was pulled up into a messy bun. She had no pants on which made their breathing quicken.

Gabrielle noticed them both ogling her. “Sorry! I swear I have shorts on, see!” she said. She lifted the shirt to show a pair of black boy shorts that showed more skin than she realized.

“That… was probably not the smartest idea,” she said sheepishly. She quickly rolled the shirt back down. “The sweats were too big to stay on my waist so... Okay, I don't know why I'm talking about this, ignore me," she said embarrassed.

Charlie looked at her for a moment longer before he put on his coat, sighing in frustration.

"Are you leaving, Charlie?" she asked.

"Yea..." he grunted. Gabrielle felt uncomfortable with how disgruntled he seemed to be with her.

"You seem upset..." she said, stepping closer to him.

"That's because I **am** upset," he said fumbling around his coat pockets for a cigarette.

"Did I... did I do something wrong?" Her voice was faint and laced with worry. He looked at her and saw the sadness and concern in her eyes. His heart dropped as he stopped what he was doing to approach her.

"You didn't do anything wrong, Gabs... I don't mean to take my anger out on you. I'm sorry," he said, looking into her eyes. She searched his light green eyes for a moment before wrapping her arms around him and pulling him into a tight embrace. He hugged her back, resting his forehead on the top of her head and inhaling her scent.

Chris watched them embrace and felt anguish building up in his chest. He couldn't tell if it was jealousy or guilt from not telling Charlie about his unofficial relationship with Gabrielle. He knew Charlie wouldn't take it well.

Charlie let Gabrielle go and smiled down at her. He caressed her arms comfortingly causing her to wince. He frowned in confusion at her wincing when he remembered the bruises on her arm. Anger quickly returned to his face and he tried to fight the urge to curse.

Gabrielle, noticing his change in demeanor, tried to assure him she was fine. "Charlie, it's okay. I just-"

"I'll see you later," he grumbled. He quickly let her go and headed for the door. Charlie looked back at Chris reading the expression in his eyes before shaking his head and leaving.

"I feel like I just keep upsetting him," Gabrielle sighed sadly. Chris turned to her and tried to give her a reassuring smile.

"He just needs time to process all this. He'll be better by tomorrow," Chris reassured her.

"Always the optimist," she smirked. When she yawned and stretched her arms, he watched as the shirt lifted slightly above her waist revealing her hips and pelvis. A slight camel-toe peeked out from her shorts. It set his loins on fire.

"You... should get some rest," Chris said to her.

"I suppose you're right," she said, rubbing her eyes. She patted Thor on the butt to get him up and the two of them walked down the hallway to Chris's bedroom. Chris waited, thinking to himself before following her to his room.

"I told Damian I was staying with my mother. You're okay with me sleeping here tonight, right? I don't mind taking the couch," she said. She stood in front of the mirror and wrapped a spare scarf from her purse around her hair.

"Not at all, Gabs... you're a guest," he said, watching her.

"Did you guys find what you needed?"

"Just about..."

She glanced over at him to see his blue eyes staring at her intently, despite his lax demeanor against the door frame.

"I don't like being the cause of so much trouble, Chris. I feel like such an inconvenience..." He said nothing as he continued to stare at her in that lax demeanor.

"Why are you looking at me like that?" she asked. He strutted over to her and wrapped his arms around her from behind. Hunching over, he nestled his chin between the crook of her neck and shoulder.

"You're not an inconvenience..." he said softly. Gabrielle sighed and fully accepted the warmth of his embrace. His lips peppered the skin on her neck with warm kisses.

"Chris... I'm supposed to be marrying Damian..." He visibly winced but it didn't stop his onslaught of kisses.

"I've been with him and only him for 3 years.... I thought this is what I would want..."

Chris stopped kissing her and raised his head to look at her in the mirror. "What are you saying, Gabs?"

Gabrielle twisted her mouth in confusion. "I don't know, Chris... you complicate things..."

He took a deep breath and shamefully removed himself from around her. He stuffed his hands into his pockets to keep them from grabbing at her. "I'm sorry. I know this is inappropriate. I don't understand why I have such a hard time keeping my hands off of you."

Gabrielle turned around to face him and bit her lip nervously. "It's not like I want you to..."

Chris looked at her for a moment. His gaze followed the sensual movements of her biting her lip. She was clearly getting excited.

"You shouldn't say things like that to me, babe... " he said in a low voice. "I can barely keep it together as is."

"But it's true," she insisted.

Chris removed his hands from his pockets. He leaned in closer, causing her to step back against the dresser behind her. She placed one hand behind her to steady herself as Chris placed both hands on the edge of the dresser on either side of her. Peering into her large brown eyes, he gave her a challenging look.

"Then what **do** you want, Gabs?" He spoke with such erotic domineering force it made her stomach flip.

"I-..." She froze.

He watched her nervously bite down on her bottom lip, almost hard enough to draw blood. Her puffy bottom lip teased him so much that he growled quietly before taking it between his teeth. He sucked on her bottom lip before snaking his tongue into her mouth, eagerly searching for its partner to dance that familiar dance. Gabrielle moaned into his mouth as he kissed her forcefully. His kisses left her feverish.

He finally pulled away from her, licking his lips as he stared down at her with a grin on his face. "I'll give you time to think about it." He walked out of the room without giving her a backwards glance.

Gabrielle touched her swollen lips already missing the feel of his mouth against hers.

~*~

11

Truth & Lies

~*~

Chris leaned against the brick building scrolling through his phone for any updates from Arthur. He sucked his teeth to find nothing in his inbox.

Charlie briskly opened his front door and walked out, pulling his jacket tighter around his body. He had a fresh cut on the side of his head with a small bandage just barely covering it.

"You alright?" Chris eyed him.

"Fine," Charlie muttered. He headed for the parking lot and pulled a cigarette out of his jacket pocket.

"So, what's your plan?" Chris asked. He stuffed his hands into his pockets and fell in line with his brother.

"Find him and kill him," Charlie muttered, walking towards the car.

Chris gave his brother a disappointed frown. "That's your great strategy?"

"That's *always* a great strategy," Charlie huffed, giving Chris a sideways glance.

"As much as I like that idea, we both know that this guy is not part of our world where we're immune to the ramifications that come with your *great strategy*. And I prefer my only brother not end up wanted for capital punishment," Chris said with a raised brow.

Charlie got to the car and opened the door, jumping into the front seat. But Chris rushed to stop him from closing the door. “Listen, Charlie. I’m just as pissed as you are. But we can’t resort to irrational jerk reactions,” Chris said.

“I’ve had all day to stew on how I wanna fuck this guy up, Chris,” Charlie said angrily.

“Yes, and I see that some poor soul probably paid dearly for it,” Chris frowned. He noticed the cut on his brothers’ face.

Charlie looked away in annoyance. “And what are **you** gonna do? Talk to him?” he mocked.

“Maybe. Maybe that’s not such a bad idea. Look... we know he set her up. It’s his fault that she suffered and why she’s traumatized. And for that, I want him dead just as much as you do. However, until Arthur can confirm getting rid of all those files, we risk jeopardizing her. We have no clue what other contingencies he has set up,” Chris said.

“If we got rid of him, we wouldn’t have to worry about any of that,” Charlie muttered.

“Charles,” Chris said, lowering his eyes at him. Charlie looked at his brother and took a long drag of the cigarette. He looked down and sighed deeply before looking back up at Chris.

“Fine. I’ll let you talk to him. But if he doesn’t cooperate, if he gives you any trouble at all, I’m handling it,” Charlie warned.

“Deal,” Chris said. He tapped the hood of the car and walked to the other side to get in.

~*~

Chris and Charlie arrived at a tall building in the city square. It was one of many famous art buildings in Philly, and another property that Chris owned. They hopped out of Charlie’s truck and walked up to the double doors. Charlie looked around the large common area decorated with art pieces on the walls, ceilings, and furniture.

Chris walked up to the concierge who immediately straightened up when he saw him.

"Mr. Richardson, sir! It's an honor to see you here. May I help you with something?" concierge asked, stammering a bit.

"Heard you guys were doing an auction around here," Chris said nonchalantly.

"Yes! It's kind of you to grace us with your presence! We're having a small auction in Room 309," the man beamed.

"Thank you, ah..." Chris said leading for a name.

"Reggie, sir," the man rushed to say.

"Reggie. Thank you, Reggie." Chris signaled with his finger for Charlie to follow him. He stopped to ask one more question. "Do you guys have any other open available rooms?"

"Room 310 across the hall is available, sir," Reggie informed him.

"Thank you, Reggie. Keep up the good work," Chris said, tapping his finger on the desk. The brothers walked into a crowded room with two columns of seats and art pieces circling them. They spotted Damian speaking to one of the lead coordinators near the front of the room. Chris left Charlie at the back and walked right up to plant a seat front row and center.

The lead coordinator immediately broke his conversation with Damian upon seeing Chris. "Mr. Richardson! I didn't expect to see you here!" the lead coordinator addressed him.

Damian's eyes widened in surprise at Chris's unexpected arrival.

"Yes, well, I do have an appreciation for the arts," Chris smirked. He leaned back in his chair, one arm draped over the head while glaring at Damian.

"Oh! Where are my manners? Mr. DuPont, this is Mr. Richardson, owner of this building, sponsor of its services and owner of more than 3/4 of Philadelphia's properties. Mr. Richardson, this is Damian DuPont. He's visiting from Los Angeles and we were discussing having more of his work auctioned at other potential venues," the man explained proudly.

"We've met," Chris said curtly. He kept his eyes on Damian, impatiently tapping his finger on the chair next to him.

"Oh..." the man said nervously. He noted Chris's perturbed tone.

"Pleasure to see you again, Chri-" Damian started. But Chris abruptly stood from the chair showing his height.

"If you don't mind, I'd like a word with Mr. DuPont," Chris said to the lead coordinator.

"Why of course, sir," the lead coordinator said surprised. "Excuse me." He nodded and left the two alone.

"How did you find me?" Damian asked with a raised brow.

"A narcissistic psychopath such as yourself is not very hard to find. And I own half the city. Follow me," Chris demanded, directing him to the door.

"I don't recall you ha-"

"This isn't up for negotiation. Don't make me repeat myself." Chris left no room for further discussion.

Damian searched Chris's eyes for the reason behind his change in demeanor since their last encounter but found nothing. He adjusted his tie and headed towards the door. He noticed the other Richardson brother leaning against the back wall with his arms folded across his chest. Charlie's eyes followed Damian as he headed out of the room.

Chris exchanged looks with his brother before Charlie followed him to room 310.

"Have a seat," Chris ordered. He pointed to an empty chair in front of a table. Damian sat down and Chris sat across from him while Charlie guarded the door. Damian leaned back, putting on his typical air of arrogance. He peculiarly eyed Chris who sat motionless, his tense shoulders hunched over.

"I'm guessing you want to discuss my fiancée," Damian smirked.

"No. There will be no discussion. I'm going to tell you what you're going to do. You're going to get your things and leave the entire Northeast region. Tonight. I don't care where you go, but I never wanna see your face around here again. You're to cut off all contact and communication with Gabrielle at once. As of today, she no longer exists to you," Chris said coldly with his hands folded calmly on the table.

Damian laughed. "You must take me for a fool. If I'm leaving, I'm not leaving without my most prized possession."

Chris winced. He hated when Damian spoke about her as if she were an object. Charlie nearly leaped off the wall but Chris quickly put his hand in front of him, signaling for him to sit down. Charlie grunted and sat in the corner seat right behind Damian staring daggers into the back of his head. He fiddled with his hands just to keep them nonviolent.

"She's not leaving with you. This is not up for debate. Leave Philly tonight. I'm not asking," Chris demanded again. Damian sat back in his chair, looking at Chris amused.

"You know... I'm not new to men wanting to fuck my fiancée. I get it. She's a skilled intellectual, with an extremely attractive air of naivety and the body of a goddess. And normally, I'd willingly offer something like that up to the highest bidder."

Chris could feel his rage building up inside of him like boiling water in a pot. He tightly clenched his fists to drain it of blood so as to keep himself from leaping at Damian and choking him to death.

"But the thing about Gabrielle... is that I put a lot of time and effort into her. I invested in her. I broke her and I molded her into what I needed her to be... *fearfully* ***loyal***," Damian continued. He leaned forward in his chair and locked eyes with Chris.

"I wanted to work with you. We could have gained a lot from each other. But see now, you're a threat to my most valuable asset. Because she wants... ***you***. Her body doesn't even respond to me anymore and that's a problem. You've compromised the most important thing I've worked so hard to maintain," Damian complained.

"She's not a fucking product, you piece of shit!" Charlie growled from behind.

Damian turned and smirked mockingly at Charlie. "What has she done to you? To both of you?" he said looking at Chris. "I've heard so much about the famous powerhouse that is the Richardsons and yet here you are succumbing like weak simps to her feminine wiles."

Damian turned to Chris, staring at him, challengingly. "Has she got you two wrapped around her little finger? Did you get a taste of that sweet chocolate nectar and now you're hooked? Have you been inside that tight heavenly black hole and you're just eager to go back?"

Damian's voice lowered menacingly as his eyes darkened. "You think you can fuck her better than I can? The bitch has you seriously pussy-whipped. Nobody can make her scream the way I can," Damian said with a devious sneer.

Before Chris could respond, Charlie shot up from the chair, knocking it over. He yanked Damian's arm, pulling it high behind him, and slammed his face on the table.

"Talk about her like that again, and I'll rip your fucking arm off!" Charlie growled through clenched teeth.

Damian groaned in pain. Chris gave Charlie a disapproving look but knew he couldn't have stopped his brother. He wanted to rip Damian's head off himself.

"Let him go," Chris ordered. Charlie cursed his brother and angrily released Damian.

Damian rubbed his aching wrist. "I thought we were talking diplomacy here," he tried to laugh. But he was clearly frustrated with the assault.

"Listen, you little piece of shit. I'm trying to give you a way out *alive*. We know what you did to her. What you've *been* doing to her," Chris snarled.

"So, she told you? Interesting... that would make you the first... all this time she was too terrified to say anything. I made sure of it..." Damian said looking up thoughtfully.

"We also know that you set her up," Chris said to him. Damian's eyes flickered up at him, widening in shock.

"Set her up? I don't know what you mean..." Damian said feigning confusion.

"Cut the bullshit. We saw the videos," Chris snapped.

"Oh... did you enjoy the show? Is that why you're threatening me? You want your own priv-"

"We saw you talking to Henderson just moments before he raped her," Chris said, cutting him off.

Damian's eyes widened with guilt before he looked down. He fiddled with his tie. "It wasn't supposed to happen like that...Henderson got greedy... I guess I should have expected him to behave like that."

Chris looked at him incredulously. "This man... **raped** a woman you love and yet you defend him?!"

"I never said I loved her," Damian said quickly.

Chris hesitated. He felt angry, disappointed, yet relieved all at once. He quickly glanced at Charlie whose expression had changed drastically. He seemed lost in thought when he looked at Chris and shook his head.

"I want your ass off this coast. As of today, Gabrielle no longer exists to you nor you to her," Chris warned.

"And the murder?" Damian asked inquisitively.

Chris glanced at Charlie. "As far as I'm concerned, it was self-defense. And for your sake... you better keep that shit under wraps. Especially considering your role in the whole situation," Chris threatened.

Damian sat up straight and eyed Chris before slowly exhaling.

"Gabrielle is a rare and valuable commodity. She's important to me," Damian argued.

"She's a human being, not one of your art projects. You don't own her, and she doesn't owe you shit," Chris responded. Damian took a long look at Chris then glanced back at Charlie.

"Fine" Damian said reluctantly. He got up and headed towards the door. "I'll leave... tonight."

Chris followed him towards the exit. Before Damian walked through the door, he glanced at Charlie who was giving him a cold hard stare.

"Have fun with her," Damian mocked. "I'm sure she's just as eager as you are to hop on your dick-"

Before he could finish, Chris roughly grabbed Damian by the throat and violently slammed him against the wall. Damian struggled to breathe as he clawed at Chris's hand, which had a cement grip on his trachea.

"If you so much as *breathe* her name...I will hunt you down, kill you myself, and make sure they never find the body," Chris threatened. "Got it?"

Damian looked at Chris startled as he struggled for air.

"Nod for 'yes'," Chris said tensely. Damian desperately nodded until Chris let him go.

He gasped for breath, rubbing his neck. "I… I didn't know….that … that was how the Richardsons operated," he said weakly.

"You don't know a damn thing about us," Chris said menacingly. "Now get the fuck out."

The color drained from Damian's face before he quickly left the building. Chris watched him until he walked to a rental car and drove off. He sighed heavily and turned to Charlie.

"You should have let me take him out," Charlie said angrily. He roughly pushed past Chris.

"Charlie," Chris started, walking after his brother. Charlie spun around irate.

"He hurt her, Chris! He did things to her that…I can't even imagine her actually having to deal with!" Charlie growled. "He had her raped! He abused her! And you just let the son of a bitch walk out the fucking door!"

"She would not have wanted us to take revenge on him," Chris said, trying to calm him.

"How do you know that?! You don't know what it feels like to have gone through what she did! What if she *did* want to hurt him?! What if she wanted revenge for what he did to her?!" Charlie snapped.

"That was not our decision to make," Chris defended.

"But you did, Chris! You did make that decision! Just now! She told you to leave it the fuck alone and you talked to his crazy ass anyway! Not only that but you allowed that piece of shit to leave and get away with what he did to her!"

"Charlie, I know that we both love her. We both want to protect her and keep her safe. But you would have killed him. Another death is not what she would have wanted on her conscience."

"And that's the difference between you and me, brother," Charlie said snidely. "You care too much about what she thinks and how she perceives us. But I don't give a damn because her safety comes first. And while you're talking fucking politics, I'll be the one who'll actually keep her safe. I don't care if she hates me for it."

Chris looked at his brother forlornly. "Charlie..."

"Aren't you ever the responsible older brother," Charlie mocked. He leaned in towards Chris's ear and whispered, "If she gets hurt again because of him... I'm holding you fucking responsible."

Charlie turned around and stormed off leaving Chris standing in the parking lot by himself.

~*~

Chris entered his dark, quiet apartment and placed his keys on the small table at the door. He rubbed at the tension built up at the back of his neck. He felt physically and emotionally sore.

Peering around the dimly lit apartment, he was surprised to hear neither Gabrielle nor Thor who were both taking temporary residence at his place. He shook off his coat and stepped further into the apartment.

"Gabs?" he called out softly.

"In here..." came a quiet voice. He walked down the hall past the living room to his study area. He found Gabrielle in a large white t-shirt, sitting on the floor with her legs folded beneath her. An open photo album on her lap. As Thor slept nestled next to her, she stroked his head while turning the pages of the photo album.

She looked up at him with a smile. "Hey."

"Hey..." he said. He stepped into the study room. "I thought you'd be asleep."

"I... couldn't sleep," she said, looking down.

Chris frowned, stuffing his hands into his pockets and leaned against the door frame. "Are you alright? Did you eat?"

"I did. I'm okay... I'm just... dealing," she assured him. He nodded and watched her as she went back to looking at the photo album.

"I can't believe you have some of these pictures. It really takes me back," she smiled, scanning the photo album.

"You should see Mom's stash," Chris chuckled.

"Oh, I can imagine she has a gold mine," Gabrielle smirked. She turned back a few pages.

"This one is my favorite," she pointed. Chris walked over and crouched down in front of her to look at the picture she was pointing to. It was a Christmas picture of their families. Chris and Eli were playing with toys by the tree while Charlie was drawing in a book. Gabrielle sat on Steve's lap while he read to her.

Chris grinned and his cheeks warmed over. "Yea, I love that one too."

Gabrielle looked up at Chris, analyzing the expression on his face. "Are you okay?"

He looked up from the album and into her eyes. "Yea, I'm fine," he said quickly. When he saw the unconvinced look in her gaze he quickly followed up. "I just... got into a little argument with Charlie."

"Oh..." she looked down for a moment and then stood to her feet. "I was wondering what was taking you so long."

Chris didn't hear what Gabrielle said. His eyes lingered on her body, loosely covered with one of his large white t-shirts stopping just barely above her thighs. He could see the outline of her body through the sheerness of the shirt. Her nipples were pert, poking through the shirt, giving way to her lack of undergarments.

Gabrielle noticed his gaze on her body and blushed. "I'm sorry. I hope you don't mind. I borrowed another shirt just to get more comfortable."

Chris looked up at her suddenly and stood to his feet. "Huh? Oh no, it's alright. It's only fair since I've had you on house arrest," he chuckled lightly.

"What was the argument about?" she asked him offhandedly.

"Hmm?"

"You just... seem so tense," she said, stepping towards him. She placed her hands on the back of his neck and softly kneaded it with the pad of her fingers. "Do you want me to give you another massage?"

"Don't you remember the last time you tried to give me a massage?" he smirked at her.

She tried to hold back a chuckle. "Well... it's not like it was awful." She moved one of her hands from around his neck and down his chest. She rested her fingers against his sternum and looked into his bright blue eyes.

She closed her eyes and leaned forward, lightly brushing her lips against his. "Gabs..." he said, leaning back slightly. He took on a more serious tone and her eyes opened in surprise.

"I need to talk to you... about Damian," Chris said. She groaned in irritation.

"Don't be a mood-killer, Chris. We can talk about it later," she said, leaning in again.

"It's really important, babe," he said. He tried to maintain the distance between them. Her dark brown eyes peered into his light blue orbs and she pursed her lips.

"More important than this?" she asked. She took his hand and placed it on her chest, above her left breast and over her heart. When he looked at her with confusion, she glanced down and nibbled her bottom lip, trying to find her words.

"I've done a lot of thinking and the one thing I can't get off of my mind... is you, Chris." She looked up at him with big, hopeful, chocolate eyes that lured him in. "It terrifies me how badly I want you because... I don't know if you feel the same..."

Chris looked at her for a moment, a smile creeping on his face. He raised a hand to her cheek and softly caressed her skin. "Of course, I want you, Gabs... I always have..."

Gabrielle breathed a sigh of relief and leaned in again to kiss him. "Wait, babe," he said, stopping her. "I really think we should talk about Damian first."

Gabrielle huffed. "Chris... I've been anxiously waiting to tell you this all night. I've been missing you, craving you. I don't care about Damian right now. What I want... what I *need* is you," she said searching his eyes.

Chris hesitated for a moment, unsure of what to do. He wanted to sit down and tell her about Damian. He also knew that he shouldn't be going any further with her and that Charlie would kill him if he knew. But the look in her eyes and the grasp she had on him was more powerful than any other emotion he had been feeling.

He wrapped a hand around her waist and cupped the back of her neck with the other, pulling her to him. With his lips planted against hers, he kissed her fervently. He could feel her body immediately melt against his as her weight pushed against him. His tongue coerced her lips open and eagerly explored her mouth. The vibrations of her moan against him sparked a greater excitement in him.

Carefully walking her backwards towards his desk, he gently lifted her onto the tabletop. His hands took their time exploring her body as he buried his face into her neck to plant several kisses. She eagerly pulled at the hem of his shirt before her skin came in contact with his abdomen, making his body feel on fire. Her fingers traced the ridges of his abs, until they traveled south and rubbed unapologetically at his manhood.

He groaned in her ear at the sensation of her touch against him. Slowly running his large hand up and down the length of her thighs, his fingers danced playfully on her hips. His eyes widened and he stopped kissing her, taking a step back to look at her.

"Are you completely naked underneath this shirt?" he asked. Though he already knew the answer.

Gabrielle bit her bottom lip as her cheeks got hot. "I wasn't sure how much coaxing I would need to do..."

Chris gave her a naughty grin. "Trust me, baby, not much... but with that being said..." He grabbed her by her hips, pulling her off the desk and turned her around with her back to him. Gently lifting her arms, he guided them to wrap around his neck. He pushed his face between her head and shoulders, suckling at her soft skin. He hungrily cupped her breasts with both hands, through the shirt, and massaged her tenderly as she moaned her praises.

"Chris..." she breathed out.

"What do you want, baby?" he asked huskily in her ear. His voice was dark with desire.

"Touch me," she begged. He sneaked his hand underneath the large white shirt. His fingers teased her with feather light touches across her body. The shirt slowly lifted with his movements, exposing her naked bottom half and stomach. She could feel his fingers run lightly over the small mound of hair between her legs. Her body slightly tensed as his fingers glided downward, touching her lips. His mouth watered when he felt the puffiness of her lips and spread them with two fingers, using one finger to tenderly stroke her clit.

Gabrielle's breathing became ragged as her knees buckled and she almost collapsed in his arms.

"Woah!" he said, quickly catching her. "I guess standing isn't the best option for this," he chuckled.

"Sorry!" she squealed, covering her face in embarrassment. He gave her a quick kiss on the side of her cheek before bending down to pick her up bridal style. He carefully maneuvered around a sleeping Thor and carried her to his bedroom.

As he placed her down on his bed, Gabrielle watched him with hungry eyes. He lifted his sweater over his head, exposing his tight chest and finely sculpted abdomen and arms decorated with his scars. Chris watched her carefully, his eyes never leaving her face, as he unbuckled his pants and casually discarded them on the floor. He took great amusement in seeing her eyes widen with hunger when he lowered his boxers, exposing himself to her.

"Shit..." she murmured, biting her lip. Her eyes devoured every bit of him. She tried not to give herself away, but she could not remove her eyes from his thick manhood.

Chris kept watching her, trying to gauge her reaction. "You sure you want this, babe?"

She struggled to peel her eyes away from his manhood before she looked him in the eyes and nodded. "More than anything," she breathed out.

With a satisfied smirk, he knelt on the bed, causing it to sink beneath his weight. He grabbed both of her legs and swiftly pulled her down to him, making her squeal with surprise and excitement.

Leaning over her, he pushed the shirt up from her waist and peppered her thighs, waist, and hips with light teasing kisses. Running his nose along her mound, he gently nudged her thighs apart and lightly ran his tongue over her emphatically wet slit. He could feel her shivering beneath him. He ran his tongue over her slit again, sucking her clit into his mouth like a lollipop. He swirled his tongue along her inner folds and felt her shake more aggressively. Her moaning pierced the silence in the air.

"Damn, I missed tasting you..." he groaned.

Chris wrapped two strong hands under her thighs and pushed them up to angle her core directly across from his mouth. Positioning her in a more ideal spot, he admired the pink and brown folds that splayed out before him and plunged his tongue into her center. Gabrielle gasped and involuntarily bucked her hips forward. Her hands immediately grasped at his hair. Her breathing became heavier as she squirmed beneath him.

Chris worked his tongue like he was on a mission, making sure not to leave any crevice untouched. He curved his tongue, sliding it up from the bottom to the top.

"Shit, baby, you taste so good..." he moaned. He plunged his tongue further into her core. Chris held Gabrielle's hips down as she squirmed tirelessly beneath him. He could taste her juices flowing freely out of her and into his mouth. She sang a sweet melody of his name while he made her come.

He tenderly kissed her core and waited for her to calm down, gently running his fingers on the inside of her thighs. As Gabrielle tried to slow her breathing, she felt Chris chuckling against her. She looked down at him to see that charming joker smile, though his blue eyes were darkened with mischief and desire.

"Don't you dare fall asleep on me again. I'm not done with you yet, Johansson," he grinned. Her stomach tightened with anticipation. He kissed his way up from her hips to her waist to her chest before landing back at his favorite spot just at the curve of her neck. He held himself up above her with both elbows resting on the bed. Looking into her eyes, he smiled warmly before kissing her fervently. She could taste the salt of her juices on his lips and bit playfully at his bottom lip. She vibrated feeling his manhood rub against her core.

He raised himself to gaze into her eyes once more, pausing for a moment just to stare at her. She saw desire and want but there was something else she couldn't read. Was he battling with himself? His light crystal, clear blue eyes were unwavering in such a way it nearly left her unsettled.

"Chr-ooohhh!" she blurted startled. He swiftly eased himself into her. His gaze broke momentarily as his body immediately reacted to the tightness of her walls around him.

"Shit..." he muttered. He lowered his head against her shoulder as they both took a second to adjust to each other.

"Are you okay?" he asked, against her shoulder.

"I feel like I should be asking you that question," she teased.

He looked up at her with a challenging stare and a naughty smirk on his face. "You got jokes, Johansson?" he asked.

She went to answer but her words quickly morphed into a desperate moan as Chris raised himself to plunge deeper into her. Though it was difficult, Chris made it a priority to keep his eyes on her with each thrust. There was nowhere else he wanted to look but into her beautiful brown eyes as he became one with her. Using one arm to hold himself up, he rested his elbow on the bed while the other hand gripped her firmly by her hips.

He plunged deeper into her as her walls clenched tighter around him, causing him to wince. Keeping his eyes on her was all he could do to keep them from rolling to the back of his head. He couldn't remember the last time he had sex this good. Though he knew it was because it was her. He could feel her milking him for all he had in him.

Though her eyes were closed shut as she eagerly chewed on her bottom lip, his eyes roamed her face, taking in every detail. Every few seconds his name would escape her lips.

Chris readjusted himself and set both arms on either side of her, continuing to pound into her. His thrusts became harder and faster, and she found herself desperately clawing at his back.

Her moans were music to his ears. He smirked as he felt her arms grasping around his wide back. She whimpered and bit down on his shoulder, which only excited him more causing his thrusts to pick up force and speed. Wrapping a large hand beneath her ass cheek, he pulled her deeper onto him causing her to gasp.

"Chris!" she cried out.

"You can take it, baby..." He groaned so huskily into her ear that his voice was almost unrecognizable. Gabrielle wrapped her legs tightly around his waist as Chris continued to pound into her. The sound of his hips slapping into hers made a steady rhythm. His movements were swift and seamless like a cat but rough and agonizingly good.

"Oh god... Chris! Chris, I'm gonna come!"

At these words, he picked up the speed and length of his strokes, dragging out the motion as his manhood pounded roughly at her core. He could feel her walls clenching tightly around him, and at that moment, keeping himself from coming seemed like the hardest task he had ever given himself.

Gabrielle bit firmly on his shoulder, nearly breaking skin as she came hard. Her body shook violently with the power of her orgasm. She let out a long and loud moan that resounded throughout the apartment. As Chris felt her tense around him, he immediately pulled out and released his load onto her stomach joining her in a high climax. Their bodies sweaty and panting, moving in motion together.

They stayed like that for a moment, just breathing hard and trying to catch their breaths as they came back down to earth.

"Are you okay, baby?" Chris asked first.

Gabrielle nodded before chuckling into his shoulder. "Shit, Chris..."

She could feel him chuckle against her as well before he gently rolled off of her. Chris laid there looking up at the ceiling trying to process the ferocious orgasm he just experienced. He reached over his bed and grabbed a towel from the dresser which he used to wipe his semen off of her stomach. After cleaning himself off, he felt Gabrielle cuddle up next to him and his arms instinctively wrapped around her. Pulling the sheets up to cover their naked sweaty bodies, he kissed her forehead and fell asleep with her safely in his arms.

~*~

Gabrielle woke up hoping to feel the warmth of the man she fell asleep with. But he was nowhere to be found. She shot up from the bed and looked around the room, but he was nowhere in sight. Swinging her legs over the bed, she threw on one of his t-shirts before tiptoeing out of his bedroom.

She looked to the left and the right. The kitchen was lit by the brightness of the sun, but there were no sounds coming from it. Tiptoeing down the hall, she looked into the sunlit living room to find Thor still sleeping on the couch.

She furrowed her brows trying to think where he might be, when she heard a faint voice coming from his study room. Quietly heading towards the study room, she saw him sitting shirtless at his desk wearing an earpiece.

"And you're sure that's all of it?... Alright, I want a debrief by midday..." Chris said.

Gabrielle quietly tiptoed up to him and lightly tapped him on the shoulder. "Ba-"

Chris immediately jumped, startled by her touch. Gabrielle jumped with him shrieking a little. "Sorry!" she squealed.

He swiveled around in his chair and looked at her with surprise. "Gabs! I didn't know you were up!"

"I just woke up... I'm sorry I didn't mean to startle you..." she said, apologetically.

"It's alright," he chuckled nervously. He rubbed the back of his neck. Suddenly, he looked at her seriously. "How long have you been standing there?"

"Not long. I just walked in as you were hanging up, I think."

"Oh," he said, a bit relieved.

"I missed you when I woke up and saw you weren't there," she said. She sat down on his lap with her leg on either side of him, straddling him on the chair.

"Oh, did you now?" he said, giving her a knowing grin. He wrapped his arms around her waist, and felt up her spine, playfully touching the dimples in her lower back.

"Mhm..." She wrapped her arms around his neck and kissed him. Relaxing her body against him, she pressed her breasts against his chest. They sat there for a moment in each other's arms, kissing and enjoying each other's warmth.

"I should shower," she said, finally pulling back.

"Can I join you?" he asked, kissing her collarbone.

"Will you behave?" she grinned, running her fingers through his hair.

"No," he chuckled. He sweetly nuzzled her breasts with his face.

"Christopher!" She laughed, getting off of him. He watched her with a smirk on his face as she headed for the exit.

"I'm going to go warm up the water. Don't keep me waiting..." she said. She looked back at him with a provocative look on her face. He gave her a quick nod with a knowing grin. Chris watched her sway her hips out of the room, when his phone went off again.

He checked to see a text from his brother.

Charlie: *How did she take it?*

Chris groaned, reading over the text. He was tasked with telling Gabrielle about Damian setting her up and how they forced him to leave the state. That was his goal last night... before things got a little carried away.

When he heard the water turn on, he put his phone on the desk and got up to head towards the bathroom. He had to tell her... before she found out in the worst way.

He opened the door of the large bathroom to be hit with a cloud of steam. He could see the silhouette of her body in the shower. He quickly discarded his pants and opened the screen door. Gabrielle's hair had shrunken and fell in tight curls around her face. With her head leaned back and her eyes closed, she let the hot water cascade down her dark brown body. Chris stepped into the shower behind her and delicately wrapped his arms around her, letting the water fall on him as well.

Gabrielle turned around in his arms to face him and gave him a content smile. She stood on her toes, arching her head back to kiss him. He wrapped his arms tightly around her, pulling her wet body flushed against his.

Their passionate kisses intermingled with the steam from the hot water made the temperature rise. Chris gently pushed Gabrielle against the shower wall and let his hands roam her body, as if they were exploring her for the first time. He pushed his face into her neck, nibbling softly. He massaged her breasts, teasing her nipple as it slipped through his wet fingers.

Gabrielle ran her hands up and down Chris's back, pulling him closer to her. She desperately needed to feel his body against hers. Chris's fingers ran down her chest and over her soft stomach before slipping between her thighs. She moaned, feeling his fingers playfully stroke her lips and part them. Biting down on her lip, she quickly inhaled as he pushed a finger inside her, his thumb stroking her clit. It's as if there was a magnetic pull between his hands and her core as they always seemed to gravitate there.

As the water cascaded down his dark brown hair and over his broad shoulders, Chris pulled back to watch her face while he fingered her. He loved watching her expressions while he pleased her. He knew he had come in with a mission but all that fell to the wayside when he saw her. It's like she scrambled the thoughts in his brain. His desire always overcame his logic. He was addicted to pleasing her, to feeling her body respond to him.

He worked his finger inside her and pushed in another finger, causing her to shudder against the shower wall.

"Fuck, Chris," she moaned out. He grinned and leaned in to take her lips with his mouth again. He fingered her harder and faster as her breathing got heavier.

"Oh, Chris...Chris..." she moaned, sinking further down. He leaned in towards her ear and whispered huskily.

"Come for me, baby..." he groaned. Almost as if directly obeying, Gabrielle moaned loudly as she climaxed all over his hand. Her chest heaved and she gripped his back tightly while her body released everything.

Her orgasm came in waves. She felt like she was riding out the high for a while and wasn't sure if she'd ever come back down.

After a few moments, she tried to catch her breath as Chris removed his fingers. She opened her eyes to see him smiling satisfactorily at her.

“Was it good?” he asked her with a smug grin.

Gabrielle rolled her eyes. “Come here, you.” She grabbed his face and pulled him into a passionate kiss. Chris used both hands to brace against the wall, his body covering hers.

She snaked her hand down his lean chest and abdomen until she found her prize. Chris groaned excitedly, feeling her hand wrap around him. She stroked him a few times, her thumb playing with the tip of his head before she directed him to her center. Chris allowed her to take the lead as she gripped his hips and pulled him inside of her.

She grunted while her hands held onto him. “Why do you feel bigger?” she groaned.

Chris chuckled against her ear and abruptly thrust inside her, making her squeal with pleasure. His strokes were soft and gentle as he let his fingers play in her kinky hair. He examined her face and playfully ran a thumb over her lips. She moaned with each thrust as he pounded into her. Her eyes fluttered open, looking at him lovingly and he smiled back down at her, ready to kiss her again.

“Chris... I love you...” she breathed out.

He looked at her for a long moment, his eyes not moving from hers as his heart began to sink. His smile quickly faded. Dropping his hand from her face, he reluctantly pulled out of her.

Gabrielle stared at him, blinking, with confusion etched all over her face. “Chri-”

“We should get out,” he said, cutting her off. He washed off the remainder of his body and turned off the water. Stepping out of the shower, he grabbed a towel from the rack, wrapping it across his waist.

Gabrielle watched him, stunned. He grabbed a small hand towel to dry his hair and beard before exiting the bathroom. Snapping out of it, she stepped out of the shower and grabbed a towel wrapping it tightly around her body. She quickly followed him out of the bathroom and into the bedroom.

"Chris, I thought… I thought we were on the same page…" she said, trying to hide the hurt.

Chris turned to her standing in the doorway with the towel wrapped around her. Her curly fro sat on her head like a wet crown. He sighed and pulled a t-shirt over his head.

"We need to talk, Gabs..." he said finally. Her face was a mix of hurt and confusion.

"Okay..." she said hesitantly.

"I picked up some clothes for you on the way home last night." He handed her a pair of pants and a blouse. She took it from him, still disturbed by his drastic change in attitude.

"If we're going to talk, then let's talk now, because I don't like this," she said to him.

"Don't like what?"

"How you can go from loving on me to distancing yourself from me so quickly."

Chris sighed. He leaned back against the dresser and motioned for her to sit on the bed in front of him. She took a seat and folded her hands between her legs nervously, as she looked up at him with anticipation.

Chris struggled to find the courage to speak. "Arthur let us on to some of the information he pulled on Damian..."

Gabrielle looked at him waiting for more.

"He... knew about John Henderson. Actually, he accepted an offer from him allowing Henderson to... have his way with you." Chris struggled to get the words out as delicately as he could.

Gabrielle blinked at him for a moment, not really understanding his words. "That doesn't make any sense," she said suddenly. "You're telling me the man that I've been with for 3 years... that proposed to me and asked me to be his wife and the mother of his children... was paid off by my rapist?"

Chris floundered a bit, trying to think of something better to say. "When we spoke to him, it seemed that it wasn't meant to go as far as him actually... raping you."

"Oh! So, the accepted offer didn't include actual penetration and that makes it okay?!" she yelled, abruptly standing.

"You know that's not what I'm saying. I'm on your side, Gabs," he said, trying to calm her.

"When did you talk to him?!" she growled angrily, rushing to put on her clothes.

"We spoke to him yesterday... we told him to leave the state," he said, watching her carefully.

"You what?!" she spun around. "Why would you do that?! He has way too much information on me! Why would you- do you have any idea what yo-" She started freaking out and moving frantically about the room.

"Gabs, Gabs!" He got up and held her steady by her shoulders. "We took care of it, okay? We got rid of all the files he had on you. And we made sure that he would never come near you again."

Gabrielle looked at him with tears streaming down her face. "I- you don't know him like I do! It's not enough! Damian, he's- he's quick and he's smart and he's always 3 steps ahead. He won't- he won't leave me alone. It's not that easy!" she cried slumping into Chris's arms.

Chris braced her against him and sat her on the bed as she cried into his arms. He held her within his embrace, allowing her to sob against his chest and could feel her heart beating furiously.

"Gabs, baby," he said, pulling back. He waited for her to slow her crying, when she peered up at him through two pained brown eyes overwhelmed with fear. He held her steady in his arms and gave her a firm look. "I promise you... I will never allow him to hurt you again."

The last bit of tears rolled down her cheeks as she looked into his eyes. She could see how serious and confident he was about what he just told her. She nodded at him and he soon enveloped her into his arms again.

"Where did he go?" she asked weakly.

"Back to L.A.," Chris said, stroking her hair. She was silent for a moment, trying to think.

"Then I can't go back..." she said, pulling away from Chris.

"Gabs, I've made sure that-"

"You may have scared him off but that doesn't mean there aren't other ways for him to make my life a living hell," Gabrielle said looking down. "I...I can't go back."

They sat there in silence, their rapid thoughts thickening the air.

"I need to go home," Gabrielle said suddenly, getting up from the bed.

"Let me take you," Chris said, getting up after her.

"To be honest, Chris... I'm not sure I want to be around you right now..."

It felt as though he had been kicked in the chest with a heavy boot when she uttered those words.

"I told you that I loved you, and you just... shut down on me. I get that you wanted to tell me about Damian, but I don't know what that has to do with me confessing how I feel about you," she said, searching his eyes.

His shoulders hunched as he stuffed his hands in his pockets. "...What do you want me to say, Gabs?"

"I want to know how you feel about me, Chris. I want to know what this is. What are we doing? You said that you wanted me. What does that mean?" she pleaded.

Chris shifted nervously, cursing himself for allowing their relationship to go so far. He hadn't anticipated her falling in love with him. That was dangerous territory. He and Charlie promised never to pursue Gabrielle for her own safety. And yet his actions had done just that. He wished he could tell her he felt the same. That he had been in love with her since before she left his life for the past 8-10 years. But he couldn't... he could never have her...

"What I feel for you... is purely lust, Gabs... I'm... sorry for leading you on," he lied. He averted his eyes to avoid what he knew to be pain in her gaze. Gabrielle's mouth dropped open and he knew he had put the last nail in the coffin.

"I-I'm leaving," she said, abruptly. She turned on her heels and stormed out of the bedroom. He followed her out and watched her gather her things. Thor, who was wide awake, jumped excitedly at her feet.

Chris followed her. He wanted to tell her the truth and tell her it was all a lie. He tried calling out to her, already knowing it wouldn't do any good. "Gabs-"

"Fuck you, Chris!" she yelled, slamming the door shut behind her.

~*~

"You did **what**?!" Charlie growled. He dealt another blow to the heavy bag that hung firmly from the concrete ceiling of his gym.

"I know... it was stupid of me... and I disregarded everything we said-"

"You were fucking reckless, Chris! What the fuck were you thinking?!"

Chris slumped against the brick wall behind Charlie and watched his brother relentlessly punch at the heavy bag.

"I wasn't thinking... I made a huge mistake that I'll probably regret for the rest of my life..." Chris choked out.

Charlie stopped punching the bag and took angry deep breaths. He turned to face his brother and his anger subsided when he noticed the remorseful look on Chris's face.

Charlie started to unravel the cloth around his hand. "Was it worth it?" he asked.

Chris looked up at him with dark, stormy blue eyes reflecting his mood. "No... and yes..."

Charlie raised an inquisitive brow. Chris exhaled, running his fingers through his hair.

"For just a moment, I got a taste of her. To feel her in my arms... To feel the warmth of her body against mine and her trust in me emboldened by the way she felt...To have her look at me like... nothing else mattered." Chris looked down shaking his head. "And now I may have jeopardized our entire relationship for good. She probably hates me."

Charlie strolled over to Chris and put a comforting hand on his shoulder. "Give her a couple of days and she'll be back to bugging you."

Chris gave his brother a sarcastic look. "This is Gabrielle Johansson we're talking about here. The same girl who ignored me for 2 months for stealing her Dragonball Z DVD back in 9th grade."

“A couple of weeks then,” Charlie chuckled. He felt his brother’s heart sink further.

“I didn’t think it was possible to love her any more than I already did,” Chris groaned regretfully. “Fuck.”

“Alright, seems like now is a good time to start helping you get out that anguish,” Charlie said.

“Ugh... Charlie-”

“Don’t argue with me. Just suit up,” Charlie said. He slapped his hands together while Chris took off his jacket and sweater, stripping down to his shirt.

“Just like old times?” Charlie smirked at him.

Chris put on a faint smile. “...just like old times...”

~*~

12

The Dinner Party

~*~

"Charlie's men took out 4 threats in the West and another 6 in the South in less than 2 weeks. We just need to shut down the other 2 in the East and we should be good to go." Chris pointed to a map projected onto the wall from his computer in his private basement.

"10 gangs in 2 weeks. That's impressive, Charles," Eric said. He stroked his chin while looking over the map.

"Somebody's gotta keep the motherfuckers in line," Charlie grinned.

"How soon can you get the remaining 2?" Eric asked.

"3-4 days at most," Charlie estimated.

"Sounds good. Then you'll have this entire section under your name, Christopher. It may not seem like much, but your ownership of this area is extremely important not only to our family name but for what's to come."

Chris gave him an inquisitive look. "What exactly is there to come, Uncle?"

Eric smirked. "Get this sorted first and you'll soon find out." He stood up, readjusted his suit jacket and glanced over at Charlie. "I know you're on a temporary leave with family affairs after making your final deliverable. So, I appreciate your hand in this."

"I'm only doing this for my brother..." Charlie said curtly.

"But, of course. Richardson brothers seem to come in packs of 2 these days..." Eric trailed off. "Nevertheless, update me once this has been resolved. The sooner we finish, the sooner I can return home. No offense, your town has its own unique *charm*. But it's certainly not London," he smirked. Chris walked him to the door and saw him out.

"What a pompous ass," Charlie murmured. Chris snickered when his intercom buzzed.

"Yes?" Chris asked, pressing down on the receiver.

"Sir, there's a woman here to see you," the man on the other end answered.

"Any idea who it is?"

"Says her name is Tanya Johnson."

"Tanya...?" Chris said, looking at Charlie confused. "How did she?"

"Probably Nat," Charlie finished.

"I'll be right up," Chris responded.

"Very good, sir."

Chris punched in the alarm for his basement and headed up with Charlie to the lobby.

"Where is she?" Chris asked the man at the front desk.

"Oh... I let her up... I thought you said..." the man started.

"I said 'I'll **be** right up', not '**let** her up'," Chris said annoyed.

"My apologies, sir! Should I go ge-" the man panicked.

"It's fine," Chris waved his hand dismissively. He headed for the elevator and heard Charlie chuckling next to him.

"Jeez, who's doing recruitment nowadays?" Charlie teased, as the elevator closed.

"Shut up, Charlie..." Chris mumbled. When they reached the penthouse suite, the doors opened and they met Tanya waiting at his door. She was wearing a delicate black pencil skirt and a dark blue blouse with a black suit jacket and a pair of black heels. She held a briefcase in one hand and a cell phone in the other.

"Chris!" she beamed. She turned to him with a huge smile and hugged him. "**And** Charlie? I didn't expect to get a two-for-one deal," she joked, hugging Charlie.

"Nice to see you, Tanya. I didn't know you knew where I lived," Chris said. He opened the door to his apartment and let everyone in.

"Natalie let me on to where your mancave resided," she said, walking inside. She quickly scanned his apartment, eyeing the details. "Hmm. Less Batman, more Bruce Wayne," she said. She set her briefcase down. "Not too shabby, Richardson."

"Thanks?" Chris said. He motioned for her to sit down on the couch. "So, to what do I owe this visit?" Charlie poured a glass of whiskey and offered her a glass to which she denied.

"Well, first, I just wanted to check in on you and see how you were doing... both of you really. I'm glad Charlie is here because finding out where you live is like trying to find the lost city of Atlantis," Tanya grinned.

"Thank you. I'd like to keep it that way," Charlie said, taking a sip of his whiskey.

"Okay, Mr. Mysterious. Anyway... how are you guys?" she asked. Chris and Charlie looked at each other not really sure how to answer, as it wasn't a typical question they often got.

"We're fine. I mean I'm fine. I think Charlie's fine. Are you fine, Charlie?" Chris asked.

"Just fine," Charlie said, snickering into his glass.

"Okay... if either of you say 'fine' one more time," Tanya huffed.

"Well, it's kind of an odd question, Tanya. Something you usually ask over text, not travel to someone's apartment for. Why don't you tell us the real reason why you're here?" Chris said. He took a seat on the table in front of her. Tanya folded her hands neatly in her lap.

"Well... I know you had some type of falling out with Gabby a few weeks ago," she started.

Chris immediately tensed up. "She told you about that?"

"Of course, she told me about that. Ever since that girl decided to stay in Philly, I've been her human diary. I mean... sometimes it's nice cause I'm an only child and it's like having a sister to talk to all the time. And then other times... it isn't so pleasant... such as when she's ranting about you..." Tanya sighed.

Chris winced and Charlie put a comforting hand on his shoulder. "Relax. It's probably not that bad..."

"Well, it was at first. She was pissed as hell. But I think it was more because she felt like you were using her. I had to talk her off the ledge multiple times and remind her that you're not that kind of person," Tanya explained.

"Thanks for having my back, Tanya," Chris said, giving her a weak smile.

"Of course, Chris. I know you. I know that's not who you are and that you care about her. I just... think you could have handled that... and *her* a little better..." Tanya advised.

"You're right about that one," Charlie said, folding his arms across his chest.

"So, did you just come here to tell me that she hates me?" Chris asked. He rubbed the tension at the back of his neck.

Tanya laughed. "She doesn't hate you, Chris. Don't think she ever could, even if she tried. No. She also told me about what you and Charlie did for her… regarding Damian. It… it really meant a lot to her. She may not have verbally thanked you both, but she really is truly grateful for your intervention."

Chris breathed a sigh of relief. "That's good to hear."

"But now that she's pretty much stuck here in Philly, she's had to restart her life. And that hasn't been really easy for her. Without a job, she couldn't get an apartment. So, she's been taking residence with either me or Eli… whichever one of us isn't annoying her," Tanya chuckled. "She's lucky he and I haven't moved in together already."

"I can get her an apartment," Chris volunteered.

"That's sweet of you, Chris, but I don't think she'll be accepting any favors from you anytime soon," Tanya said politely.

"That's fair…" Chris murmured.

"Anyway, she was recently hired at Pennsylvania Hospital which is probably one of the best things to happen to her in a while all things considered. So, I'm throwing her a surprise dinner party. Just with a few close friends so she knows that we're here for her and support her. And I really would like it if you both came," Tanya smiled.

"You sure that's a good idea?" Chris asked.

"Absolutely. You may not be her favorite person right now, but I know how she feels about you. About both of you. You're her best friends and she could really use some TLC," Tanya encouraged.

"Well… as long as you think it's a good idea…" Charlie said, glancing at his brother.

"So, you'll come?" she asked. They both nodded. "Perfect! Here's my address. She normally gets home around 8 so be there no later than 7:30," she said. She wrote her address down on a piece of paper and handed it to Charlie. "I'm so glad you guys are coming! She's been so depressed lately. I really think this will cheer her up." Tanya grabbed her things and headed for the door.

Chris closed the door behind her and looked at Charlie. "You sure this is a good idea?"

"What the hell do I know," Charlie shrugged. He looked over the piece of paper.

"You told her we were going!" Chris blurted.

"I don't know how to say 'no' to Tanya!" Charlie said defensively.

"Lawyers..." Chris said, rolling his eyes.

~*~

Charlie and Chris pulled up to Tanya's estate. The front section was walled with glass windows, decorated with a golden floral curtain.

"Color me impressed," Charlie said, getting out of the car.

"She's one of the most esteemed attorneys in Philadelphia. I'm not surprised," Chris said, heading down the pathway.

They rang the doorbell and Tanya quickly answered. "Well don't you two look absolutely dapper," she smiled as she let them in.

"Nice place," Chris said, giving her a quick peck on the cheek.

"Why thank you! And you brought roses?" She looked at Charlie holding a bouquet.

He gave her a nervous shrug. "We weren't really sure what we should bring," Charlie said.

"These are perfect," she said, taking them from him. "Come in! Make yourself at home!" She wore a spotted sheer red dress with black undertones.

"Hey man! What's good?" Eli said, approaching them in a light grey suit. He gave them both a hug. "I had gotten so used to seeing you guys before. I feel like it's been a while."

"Yea... just work. You know how it is," Charlie said.

"Yas! The zaddies have arrived," Rhaven said, turning the corner.

"Rhaven! Don't you start!" Tanya shouted from the kitchen.

"Angie, you're on Rhaven duty," Eli said.

"Excuse me?!" Rhaven blurted in offense.

"Why am I on Rhaven duty? Why can't **you** be on Rhaven duty?" Angie rolled her eyes.

"Y'all! I'm standing right here!" Rhaven said, folding her arms annoyed.

"Trick, if you knew how to behave yourself, nobody would need to watch your ass in the first place," Angie mocked.

"You know what-... okay yeah, you right," Rhaven grinned.

"Are Nat and Arthur coming?" Eli asked Tanya. He helped her carry the rest of the food to the table.

"They both said they were busy with some family issues," Tanya said, looking at Chris and Charlie.

"Don't look at us. We only speak to them on a need-to-know basis," Charlie said, raising his hands defensively.

"Y'all good being the only white folks here?" Angie teased.

"Please. These two are used to being the only white people as far as this family is concerned," Eli joked.

Tanya's ears perked up when she heard footsteps outside. "Okay! Everyone, she's coming! Hush!" Tanya said excitedly. Gabrielle struggled to unlock the door to the house, and they could hear her curse outside.

"Damn. Struggle life, Gabby," Angie chuckled. Tanya abruptly shushed her.

"Well *somebody's* gotta help the poor girl. Is she always like this?" Rhaven said impatiently.

"Ugh. I'll go," Tanya said. She moved from her hiding spot. "Hey boo!" she said excitedly, opening the door.

"Hey... Sorry. I don't know why I struggle with that door so much. And why are you greeting me like a damn 3-year old?" Gabrielle said, walking into the dark house.

"Because!" Tanya beamed.

"Because what, Tanya? You're an octave higher than my ears can handle right now." Gabrielle put her bags down and began taking off her heels. "Can you turn on the light? Why is it so damn dark in here?" she whined.

Suddenly the lights flickered on. "Surprise!" everyone shouted.

Gabrielle blinked in confusion and looked around. "What the-what is this?" she asked bewildered.

"It's a surprise dinner party! To congratulate you on your new job at the hospital!" Tanya exclaimed.

Gabrielle thought for a minute before a frown crossed her face. "Oh..."

"Oh?!" Tanya said in shock.

"I mean! Thank you! This- this was... really sweet of you, T. You didn't have to do this for me. I started that job weeks ago," Gabrielle gave a small smile.

"Still! It is a cause for celebration! And what's a better way to celebrate than with those who care about you!" Tanya said, gesturing to everyone else. Gabrielle glanced around the room taking everyone in when her eyes landed on Chris. She struggled to hide her pout.

"Thanks, guys..." Gabrielle said weakly.

"Come! Sit! Sit!" Tanya said, pulling her to the table.

"That dress is banging!" Rhaven said. She looked over her fitted blue dress. "What kinda doctor are you? The sexy naughty type?" Angie gave Rhaven a hard glare.

"No..." Gabrielle muttered. She sat at the head of the table. "I had to pitch a proposal today. So, I had to look my best..."

"2nd week on the job and they already got you pitching proposals?" Eli smirked.

"Mm..." she grunted. She looked down with a forlorn look. Everyone glanced at each other a little nervously from her lack of enthusiasm.

"So, now that we're eating, Gabby, tell us about your new job. How do you like it? A bit different from L.A., right?" Tanya said. She took a seat after serving everyone's food.

"That's for sure..." Gabrielle muttered. She stirred her food with her fork. Tanya frowned and Gabrielle could sense she was upsetting her. "I mean... yes... I like it. It's great. I'm having a blast."

"That sounds like sarcasm," Charlie said.

"What do you guys want me to say? That I love my job?" Gabrielle frowned.

"Well... don't you?" Eli asked.

Gabrielle sighed into her cup. "It will take some getting used to."

"Okay... what about your co-workers?" Angie asked.

"They're fine." Gabrielle put her cup down, slightly irritated with all the questions.

"Are we bothering you, Gabs?" Tanya asked her.

"What? No!" she said, quickly looking up. "This was great and

I'm glad you guys are all here."

"Then why do you seem so unhappy?" Chris asked apprehensively. She looked up at him with sad eyes.

"You guys don't need to know about my problems," she said. She started stuffing food into her mouth.

"Oh, come on, boo! That's what we're here for!" Tanya grabbed her hand comfortingly. Gabrielle looked at her with cheeks stuffed with food. She finished chewing and sighed.

"Fine. You guys want to know how I'm really doing?" Gabrielle got up and wiped her face. "I'm a black woman who spent over 5 years working my ass off in medical school to get chosen by one of the best hospitals in Los Angeles. I was told repeatedly that my grades and my experience were perfect, but I didn't have that 'L.A. Look.' What the fuck is an 'L.A. Look' you might ask? It's a blond, thin, white woman. Not a kinky-haired black woman such as myself. I had to drag their asses to court to fight their racist policies. And when I won that long and tedious case and got accepted into the hospital, I had to deal with racist, perverted, misogynistic men! I had to work my way to the top, working twice as hard as my mediocre white counterparts who didn't do shit for nothing! And now that I finally made it, I have to start my whole life all over again because niggas. Ain't. Shit!"

She huffed loudly. "And when I say niggas, I mean Damian Ain't Shit DuPont. Now, here I am trying to get a job that should be relatively easy for me to get because of my education, reputation and experience. But nah! Why? Cause I'm a fucking black woman in fucking racist ass America! Why the hell would I expect such grace? I was personally asked by the head of the hospital to join their team of neurosurgeons. I was even requested to apply for the role of head surgeon. But the punk ass bitch took one look at me and suddenly had a change of mind! It wasn't until his own fucking boss who knew me strictly for my reputation came in and gave me the position on the spot that I even got in! On my first day, I was confused for a fucking cleaner! I had on a suit! But this black woman can't possibly be a doctor, right?! So what the hell am I even doing this for?!"

She plopped down in her seat practically shaking. "It doesn't matter what I've done. They see my skin color and they think the worst of me. They barely give me a chance. I'm tired of this. I've put in my time and work all those years just to have to relive this trauma all over again. I'm angry all the time. All the fucking time!"

She pushed her plate forward and dropped her head into her arms. They all looked at her with shock and sadness.

"Baby girl..." Angie said, reaching to grab her. "I know how it is, boo, trust me. Black women always get the short end of the stick."

"We really do. You remember how much I went through just to get to where I am in my firm. I'm still trying to make partner, sis. All these others barely do the work and yet there they are sitting pretty. They're always moving the goal posts. It's a struggle," Tanya said. She walked over to Gabrielle and rubbed her back.

"Black women always get shit on. As far as I'm concerned, nobody deserves us," Rhaven said, sucking her teeth.

"Hey!" Eli said defensively.

"Not you neither, nigga! You just lucked out with Tanya. Somehow, she fell for your basic ass," Rhaven teased.

"That's cold-blooded, Rhaven. I'm hurt," Eli said, clutching his chest.

"I know you guys probably aren't used to this kind of conversation," Tanya directed her comment to the brothers.

"Not entirely, but it is frustrating to know that this still happens. This country was built on racism so I can't say I'm the least bit surprised, unfortunately," Charlie said. He rested his chin on his folded hands and leaned on the table, watching Gabrielle. "Chris and I are well aware of the privilege we hold as white men, but we often forget what that looks like on the other side of the spectrum. I'm sorry to see how it's hurt you, Gabs..."

Gabrielle looked up at him through teary, frustrated eyes that softened with gratitude.

"It's true," Chris started. "This country has a long way to go and I'm sad to say any real actual progress may not be in our lifetime, if we're being realistic. But you, Gabs," he said, daring to look her in the eyes. "Yes, you are strong and resilient as are most black women, especially in times when the world is unkind and undeserving of you. But that doesn't mean you have to be all the time. You're allowed to be vulnerable and fragile enough to ask for help. We're all here to help and support you."

Gabrielle looked at him shocked, with wide eyes as she digested everything he said. She could feel herself falling in love with him all over again and willed herself to push those thoughts away.

"Thank you... Chris," she said weakly.

"These are the most woke white boys I have ever seen. Can I take one home with me?" Rhaven murmured.

"Rhaven! Shut up!" Tanya glared at her.

Charlie laughed. "We grew up with Mama Clara. She didn't allow us to be ignorant."

"Not at all," Chris chuckled, as he held Gabrielle's gaze.

"At least she didn't beat your ass," Eli sulked.

"She beat your ass cause you were always gettin' into trouble. She didn't beat Gabby nearly as much as she beat you, Eli," Tanya lectured him.

"I feel so attacked tonight," Eli said, feigning hurt. Tanya chuckled and gave him a kiss.

"Let's clean up and relax in the living room," Tanya said. They all picked up their plates and headed to the kitchen. Gabrielle stopped Charlie by stepping in front of him.

"What's up..." Charlie asked.

"I want you to train me," she said to him seriously.

He raised his eyebrow and tilted his head to the side. "Train you?"

"Yes, you told me you run a gym," she said.

"For fighters."

"Then make me a fighter!"

"That's not... no... it's not the same thing," Charlie shook his head.

"Charlie, please," she begged. She looked into his eyes and desperately grabbed his shoulders. "I want to learn how to defend myself. I don't... I don't want to feel helpless like that again…" She looked away from him, trying to keep the tears from escaping.

He sighed heavily and shifted his weight to one side. "Alright... but just self-defense."

"Thank you!" she blurted. She threw her arms around his neck and planted a huge kiss on his cheek. "You don't know how much this means to me." She grabbed his plate and dashed away to the kitchen.

"What was that about?" Chris asked, approaching him.

"Just… Gabs being... Gabs.." Charlie said, watching her in the kitchen.

As everyone prepared to leave, Gabrielle strolled up to Chris and Charlie just as they were heading to the car.

"So, how soon can we meet?" she said eagerly. Chris looked between them with confusion, while Charlie checked his phone.

“We can start tomorrow if you want,” Charlie said.

“That’s perfect! I get off work at 6. But I need your address,” she said eagerly.

“What’s all this for?” Chris asked.

Charlie glanced up at Chris. “Gabs wants me to give her self-defense training.”

Chris looked at Gabrielle regretfully. “You do know that Charlie and I would never let any harm come to you.”

Gabrielle gave him a grateful smile. “I do... I also know that you’re both only human and I can’t expect either of you to be there for me at all times. I need to know how to defend myself…”

Chris wanted to protest just out of his protective instinct. But he decided against it. She was right. Charlie’s eyes lingered on Gabrielle, admiring her will to empower herself.

“I’m fine with 6:30. I’ll give you directions to the gym,” Charlie said.

~*~

13

New Places, New Faces

~*~

Gabrielle checked her text to go over Charlie's directions to his gym. She was excited not just to start her training but because this was the first actual step to learning more about him. He had been so closed off and distant from her the moment she arrived back in Philly. She hoped not only to learn self-defense but to finally get through that hard, tough exterior he kept putting up.

She hopped out of bed and threw on a pair of comfortable grey form-fitting sweats that hugged her hips, a black sports bra, and a loose red jersey that she tied in a knot at the back.

Jumping into Eli's car, she sped off to his gym. Upon arrival, she came to a large gate guarded by a man sitting in a tall booth. The man leaned out of the window and looked down at her. "Name?" he asked.

"Um... Gabrielle? Gabrielle Johansson. I'm here to see Charl-" she started, when the gates started to slide open.

"Oh! Thanks!" she said. But he had already gone back to whatever he was doing. She drove into the large lot and was immediately overwhelmed by how large the building was.

"This... is a gym?" she said, skeptically. She pulled into a parking spot next to a few black Maseratis lined up in a row. Walking down a long winding path, she approached a large door and knocked just as it was opening. A massive man in a black muscle shirt and black cargo pants met her at the door. He sported a shaved head and thick pepper-grey beard. He eyed her with steel grey eyes, suspiciously looking her up and down.

"Hi! I'm...um... Gabrielle... Johansson..." she said nervously. She was greatly intimidated by his enormous stature. He looked as if he had fought in all wars. His grey eyes held her gaze until he finally spoke.

"Ms. Johansson." He had a thick Russian accent. "Please, come in." He stepped to the side, allowing her to enter.

"Follow me," he said. Stepping in front of her, he led her down a dark hallway. Gabrielle glanced around, noticing all of the ancient weaponry on the walls, from mallets to swords, to large axes.

"I didn't know Charlie liked to collect these sorts of things," she said playfully, trying to spark conversation.

"He is a collector of sorts," the man said simply. He finally hooked a right to a brightly lit room with a fighting ring at the center. Soft red mats decorated the floor of the room and the light bounced off of the red walls and back to the red ring.

"Everything is so red!" she said, surprised.

"It is so that the blood is not too easy to notice," the man said. She looked up at him with wide eyes, waiting for the punch line or the laughter but none came. "He will be here shortly," the man said. He turned to leave.

"Wait. What's your name?" she asked. He turned to look at her as if considering if he should tell her or not.

"Vladimir," he said finally.

"Vladimir," she smiled. "Nice to meet you, Vladimir." He hesitated at her kindness and moved his mouth until he gave her a strange smile. He quickly turned and exited the room.

She put her things down on the floor and started stretching. Pulling her arms forward, she stretched out the muscles and hunched over to touch her toes without bending her knees.

A few minutes later, Charlie strolled in wearing the same black fitted tank as Vladimir and a pair of dark sweats. He was typing away on his phone with one hand and holding a bottle of water in the other. He looked up to see Gabrielle bent over, touching her toes giving him a wide shot of her ass. He grinned before coughing loudly to get her attention. She stood up abruptly, turning to him.

"Oh! Hey! Sorry! Was just doing some stretching. Trying to see how limber I am," she chuckled.

Charlie raised a questioning brow. "What exactly do you think we'll be doing here, Gabs?"

"Uh... I honestly don't know. But I'm not taking any chances at pulling a muscle."

Charlie laughed, shaking his head. "Let's get started." He placed his phone and water by her things and jumped into the ring. He jutted out an arm to help pull her up.

"For your first lesson, I'm going to show you some very basic moves. We'll run it a couple of times and build from there," he advised. She nodded and stood next to him getting ready to follow his movements.

Charlie showed Gabrielle a few moves that involved blocking and maneuvering from out of tight holds. For one move, Charlie stood behind her and grabbed one of her wrists. "Now, try to release my hold and block my 2nd attack like we practiced," he said.

Gabrielle twisted her hand and his with it, pulling his body forward. She tripped him with her foot to push him to the ground. Charlie stumbled backward and smirked at her. "You're a fast learner. Good," he said. "Now try this one." He maneuvered behind her and tightly grabbed her arms from behind.

Gabrielle tried to free her arms the way he instructed. But her mind flickered to a precise moment in her past, when John Henderson had raped her. She remembered when he slapped her hard across the face, knocking her to the floor. He had held her hands behind her back and tore off her clothes, ignoring her cries.

She began to panic. She tried writhing herself free, but Charlie's grasp did not budge.

"That's not what I taught you," Charlie said from behind. "Unlock my hold like we practiced." But her panic only intensified as she whimpered and writhed some more. Her eyes darted frantically around the room.

"Stop! Please! Let go of me!" she screamed. Charlie immediately released his hold on her. She fell to her hands and knees, sobbing. Charlie cautiously crouched down in front of her.

"Gabs...?" he asked worriedly. He went to console her, but she flinched at his movement. He quickly retracted his hand. He remained crouching in front of her, anxiously waiting for her crying to cease. After a few seconds, she finally sat back on the floor and wiped her face with her shirt.

"I'm sorry," she said, taking deep breaths. "I just... I just panicked."

"What happened? What did I trigger?" Charlie asked her. His brows stitched together in concern. Gabrielle could see anguish, anger, and deep concern on his face as if he already knew the answer to his own questions.

"Nothing. I just... I was having a moment, I think," she said. She wanted to avoid the topic of her abuse. Charlie gave her an unconvinced look. "Really! I'm fine!" she insisted. "I just maybe... got too anxious or something," she said dismissively.

"Gabs... I think you have PTSD," he said gently. He looked deep into her eyes and she felt like he was looking into her soul, trying to find the source of her problems. As if it didn't matter what lie she tried to conjure, he would know the truth regardless.

"I'm sorry," she said. She bit her lip nervously and looked down. "I thought I had gotten past this."

"Don't apologize, Gabs. It's not your fault and not that easy," he said, putting a comforting hand on her shoulder. "It's gonna take some time. You only recently confessed this dark truth in your life. It's going to take a minute for you to actually heal." She looked up at him and whimpered helplessly.

"I think we're done for today," he said standing up. He extended his hand to her and helped her up as well.

"But not for good, right?" she asked.

"Gabs..."

"Please, Charlie. You said... I need to heal. This is it! This will help me heal! Knowing that I can protect myself," she pleaded. She grasped his hand between hers.

"You need therapy, Gabs," Charlie said quickly. "Not training on how to become the next Rambo."

"God, you sound like Chris," she muttered, throwing her head back.

"Because he's right," Charlie said.

"I'm already looking into it... I just need this one thing from you," she persisted.

He looked at her hesitantly, seeing the desperation in her eyes.

"I promise, I'll be okay. I'll be more communicative," she tried to persuade him. "Please. I need this."

He looked at her and exhaled in resignation. "Alright. But if I see that this is becoming too much, I'm calling it quits. I don't want to re-traumatize you," he said sternly. She squealed, jumping into his arms and tightly wrapped her arms around his waist.

"Thank you so much, Charlie! I promise I won't let you down!" she said excitedly.

He was caught off guard by her sudden hug. At first, he kept his arms open in surprise, not sure if he should reciprocate. But then, he wrapped his arms around her. One moment, he smelled her intoxicating scent, and in a second it was gone when she released him.

"You da best, Charles!" she said. She hopped out of the ring and grabbed her bag. "I'll see you soon!"

He watched her jog out of the gym and shook his head in frustration. Suddenly, his phone went off. Charlie looked down to see a message from his brother.

Chris: *Get here, ASAP!*

~*~

When Charlie arrived at Chris's penthouse suite, he went to knock on the door but it immediately swung open to a frantic Chris. Charlie stepped into the suite and locked the door behind him. He eyed his pacing brother suspiciously.

"You alright?" Charlie asked him, taking a seat on the couch. Chris stopped pacing and looked at him. His hands were clasped behind his neck in frustration. He was clearly upset. Charlie hadn't seen his brother this frustrated since his father passed.

"No. No, I'm not," Chris growled. He started pacing again. He walked over to the bar table by the window and poured himself a shot of whiskey. After downing it quickly, he immediately poured himself another.

"Shit, take it easy," Charlie said. He rested his hands behind his head. "What's got you freaked out? And pass me a glass."

Chris downed another shot of whiskey and poured a glass for his brother. "I just got through talking to Nat," he said.

"Well that explains the shots. I know she's a handful, Chris, but our cousin isn't that bad," Charlie smirked, with a sip of his whiskey. Chris sat down in the armchair across the table from Charlie and swallowed thickly.

"Evidently… the Beaumonts are here… in Philly," Chris said, with his eyes down. Charlie sat up straight with his eyes narrowed and his fists tightly clenched.

"Who?!" Charlie exclaimed angrily. He accidentally shattered the glass of whiskey in his hand. Chris watched the whiskey mix with Charlie's blood and spill from the table onto the carpet.

"Dammit, Charlie…" Chris muttered. He rushed to grab a towel and wrapped it around Charlie's hand.

"Shit… sorry," Charlie cringed. He wrapped the towel around his hand and tried to rub out the whiskey on the carpet with the bottom of his shoe.

"I don't care about the damn carpet. Just keep the towel wrapped around your hand while I go get some bandages," Chris scolded him. He got up to head to the bathroom. Charlie squeezed the towel around his wounds to stop the bleeding. He glanced at his other scars from injuries prior. He didn't mean to be so reactionary. But he couldn't believe what his brother had said.

"Beaumont?" Charlie muttered, almost as if he were trying to see if he had heard his brother right.

"You heard me correctly," Chris said. He returned from the bathroom with a couple of bandages. Sitting on the floor in front of Charlie, he gently removed the towel to clean and dress Charlie's wound.

"Why are they here? What do they want?" Charlie glared at his brother angrily.

Chris looked at Charlie and sighed. "I met with Nat earlier…"

~

"Arthur, where the fuck are you?" Natalie said angrily into the phone. "You were supposed to be at the warehouse 10 minutes ago!"

"Easy, easy, Nat," came Arthur's cool voice from the other end. "You know how much I love testing out a new ride." Nat could hear the wind whipping from the speed of his car through the other end of the phone.

"I don't give a shit! Get to the bloody warehouse and do your fucking job!" she seethed. She hung up the phone and twirled around in Chris's office seat to look out the window.

"Bloody wankers. All of them," she muttered in her thick English accent.

Chris opened the door to his office to find Natalie sitting in his seat with her feet propped up on his desk. She wore a red pencil skirt, a button-down white blouse and white heels with red bottoms. Holding a glass of red wine with one hand, she typed away at her phone.

She looked up to finally acknowledge him. "Christopher..."

"I'm surprised they just let you in," Chris said annoyed. He leaned against the wall in his office and crossed his arms clearly agitated by her presence.

"You shouldn't be. I have access to everything, Christopher. You know that," she smirked at him. "Beautiful office by the way. Philly looks halfway decent from up here. Of course, it's not London, but... what can you do."

Chris rolled his eyes. "You said you needed to talk."

Her smirk faded and she moved her legs off of the desk to stand up. After smoothing out her skirt, she walked towards the window and took a sip of her wine.

"You've been doing a great job with the shipments. There's been an acceleration of growth in the past few years with several new high-profile clients thanks to your leadership," she said.

"Thanks?" he said with raised intonation in his voice. He was annoyed and confused that she was telling him what he already knew. "Is that the only reason why you asked me here?"

"What happened between you and Gabrielle? She seems all of a sudden very... angry with you," she asked abruptly.

Chris shifted uncomfortably and looked down. "We had a bit of miscommunication..."

"I recall you intervening in a falling out she had with her ex-husband," Natalie said.

*"**Ex-fiancé**." Chris corrected her sharply.*

*"My apologies.... ex...fiancé..." Natalie noted the tension in his voice and turned around to face him. "Does she know what you do, Christopher? I mean... what you **really** do?"*

Chris raised his brows before shaking his head frustratingly at his cousin. "No, of course not. What does she have to do with anything?"

Natalie picked up a folder from his desk and handed it to him. She turned back around to look out of the window, sipping her wine. Chris looked through the folder to find several files on Damian DuPont. He leafed through the files, reading basic information he already knew from Arthur.

"What is this?" he said impatiently.

*"It's a file on Damian DuPont, Gabrielle's **ex-fiancé**," she said, with mocking emphasis.*

"Why are you showing me this?"

"Keep looking..."

He continued to leaf through the papers until he came to a document that listed all of the clients Damian had been meeting with in Philly. There was a list of prices next to each client's name. The last line on the document had Damian's name and a large dollar amount crossed out in red. Attached to it was a note: ***"Don't interrupt again. Final warning."***

Chris narrowed his eyes, trying to understand. "Nat... what is this?"

"That, my dear cousin, is a check statement for Damian DuPont. It's the amount of money he was generating while in Philadelphia for his showcases. That last line is to signify the loss in profit since you and Charlie decided to threaten him within an inch of his life. Why did you have to get so involved, Christopher?" she said annoyed.

Chris narrowed his eyes. "That piece of shit was abusing Gabs. We got involved to save her!"

Natalie sighed, considering his words. " I see... but you're being far too careless, cousin." She took another sip of wine, put the glass down, and turned to Chris. "You love her... don't you...?"

Chris looked at her for a long second. He hated that his love for Gabrielle was so obvious. He looked back down at the document and didn't utter a word, not wanting to give himself away.

"That's just going to make this even more difficult, I'm afraid," she said, leaning back against the desk. "I received those documents in this envelope." She handed him an envelope with a white and blue embroidered B on the cover.

Chris looked up at her suddenly with eyes wide open. "The Beaumonts?! ***They*** *sent this file?!"*

Reluctantly, she nodded.

"Why?"

"Because, cousin... he's one of theirs..."

Chris felt as if all the air had been sucked out of his lungs. "Damian works for the Beaumonts?!"

"And for quite some time now, apparently. He was doing quite well too. That is until you, Charlie, and Arthur got involved..."

"We couldn't just continue to let him get away with hurting her!" Chris said angrily.

"I understand that. But I doubt your actions would have been so... severe and hostile if your feelings for her weren't so strong."

Chris clammed up, unable to dispute her assumption.

"You're in dangerous territory, Christopher..." Natalie warned.

"Then they're probably the ones who bribed my men and messed with my shipments!"

"Possibly. But that's not the point. You fucked with one of their most valuable assets, Christopher. This is a warning for you to back off."

Chris groaned angrily, rubbing his face in frustration. Natalie shook her head. She wanted to help him find reason.

"Christopher. You know the business that we're in... It's not pretty. It's not moral. And it's not safe. The Beaumonts are our sworn enemy and you, my dear cousin, are their biggest threat. Maybe they are trying to sabotage your business. But, if they find out you have any liabilities they could leverage, they will use it against you. Against us!" she exclaimed.

"We'll...we'll be more careful," he assured her.

"For all our sake, I sure hope so," she said to him. "And keep your distance from Gabrielle. Don't allow your feelings to cloud your judgement. You know we Richardsons aren't allowed much happiness for long..."

She looked at Chris with remorse. "My father wants to meet with you. Follow the directions in my text. I'll see you soon, cousin."

~

"Shit..." Charlie muttered after he listened to Chris relay what had happened. Chris finished his whiskey and let his head fall back against the couch, his hand covering his eyes. Charlie took the empty glass out of Chris's grasp and went to pour more.

"Punk ass motherfuckers," Charlie muttered. "Now I'm certain they're the ones who attacked my men."

Chris looked up at him surprised.

"Yea... I was gonna tell you about that..." Charlie trailed off.

Chris shook his head in frustration. "I wanted to warn you because I know that you're training her," Chris said.

Charlie frowned. "I am. But the sessions are short, and my gym is known to few. We should be fine."

"You're sure?"

"I'm positive," Charlie assured him.

"Good..."

"I'm coming with you. To this meeting with Uncle Eric," Charlie said, standing up.

Chris looked up at him sadly. "You don't have to do th-"

"I'm not letting you do this alone, Chris," Charlie said unwaveringly. Chris smiled gratefully at his brother and nodded.

~*~

"I'm sorry I didn't tell you sooner," Chris said. He kept his eyes on the road as they traveled to meet with their uncle. Holding a cigarette outside the car window, Charlie turned his head and looked at his brother with a raised brow.

"Tell me what?" Charlie asked.

"About... about us..." Chris muttered. Charlie sighed and looked straight ahead.

"You have nothing to apologize for." Charlie took a drag of his cigarette. "You love her."

"So, do you, Charlie," Chris said quietly. "I... I tried to keep my distance. But when I'm around her, I just- I lose all sense of reason. It's hard enough trying not to lose control altogether."

"That makes her a liability," Charlie muttered.

"And that's why I'm in the position I'm in. I should have been more careful. It's like... being with her almost makes me feel like a normal guy with a regular life. With her, I forget just how fucked up our lives are," Chris frowned.

"Which is why we gotta keep her safe and keep her out of it," Charlie said. Chris nodded in agreement.

They pulled up to a luxurious, gothic-style building that gleamed in the moonlight. The brothers strolled to the door and took the elevator 6 floors down to a finely, polished area heavily decorated with statues, paintings, and various dated weapons.

"I'll see you there in a few minutes," Charlie said, turning the corner. Chris nodded and walked down the long familiar hallway, glancing at each picture of the men who came before him. He stopped at the last picture of his grandfather. His grandfather looked regal in a navy blue officer's suit. His white mustache curled delicately upward. His face serious with the signature piercing blue eyes found in every great Richardson man.

"He was a lot meaner than he looks," Gerald's grizzly, deep voice with thickened Scottish undertones called from down the hall. "I hated the fucking bastard. But he was damn good at his job. He was powerful. Everyone feared him. And all who crossed him quickly saw death. He was not a man you wanted to fuck with."

Chris looked at the picture of his grandfather again. He often wondered what he was like and only heard terrible things. He looked at those piercing blue eyes again.

"I will never be like you," Chris whispered to himself.

"Are yer gonna stand there talking to yerself all day or are yer gonna join us?" Gerald called.

Chris walked down the rest of the hallway and followed his uncle into the main gallery. He spotted Natalie talking to her father. Arthur, with his signature smug look, chatted with Charlie. Natalie noticed Chris and her father turned around to acknowledge him.

"Christopher! I was wondering where you were," he said walking towards him. "Now we can begin. Everyone take a seat." Everyone took their places around the polished wooden table. Charlie sat down next to his brother.

"Charles," Eric smiled surprised. "I thought you refused to dabble in the family bus-"

"I'm just here for my brother," Charlie said curtly.

"Of course. If only my own brother were so loyal," Eric said, giving Gerald a sideways glance. Gerald stuck his middle finger up at Eric, while taking a sip from a beer mug.

"The business has been doing supremely well. In fact, we've surpassed all expectations. With Gerald's hold on Western Africa and Australia, Natalie on Western Europe and South America, Arthur on East Asia, myself with Europe, and Christopher in North America, this is the largest expansion we've ever seen. Job well done," Eric said to the group.

"Some better than others," Natalie said coldly, looking at Arthur. Arthur rolled his eyes, popping a grape into his mouth.

"Yes, well. Arthur has done well in East Asia. Though his methods can be a bit… unusual for our clients," Eric said.

"I learned from the best," Arthur smirked at his father.

"Twit," Natalie scowled at Arthur.

"Get on with it, brother. We haven't got all day," Gerald snapped, annoyed.

"One of our most important negotiations will be taking place in Japan, and this is something I would only entrust to Christopher," Eric said nodding in Chris's direction.

Chris sat up abruptly. "Me? Why not Nat?"

"Natalie has a prior engagement she needs to handle in Barcelona that she absolutely cannot miss. Furthermore, it's time you started visiting our other locations as you will be this business's next heir," Eric said sternly. Chris instinctively slouched in his chair.

"You've become a very important part of this business, Christopher. You are extremely well known not only for your wit and your skill but also your power of influence and persuasion. And as you all already know, the Beaumonts have us on their radar. I don't plan on fighting with them. Not while we're making so much progress. We need to cut all loose ends and liabilities. So... Christopher, I'm sure Natalie spoke to you about Ga-"

"It's been taken care of," Chris said, cutting him off irritably.

"Good," Eric said, straightening his jacket. "Arthur will be assisting you while you're in Japan, since he knows the area and clients well." Chris sank deeper into his chair. Charlie slid the rest of his beer to him which he desperately chugged.

"No worries, cousin. I'll show you a real good time in Japan," Arthur winked.

"Remember you're there for a job, not to play games and sleep with your clients, Arthur!" Natalie scowled.

Arthur rolled his eyes. Everyone got up from the table and packed their things to leave.

Chris was about to leave when Eric stopped him. "Christopher. Before you leave, I want you to know how proud I am of you. You've become one of the most powerful and highly ranked in all of our family's history. You do what needs to be done and you do it well. You should be proud of yourself," Eric said, with his hand on Chris's shoulder.

"With all due respect, Uncle, I don't really feel the same way. I only agreed to take on this extra responsibility so that my brother didn't have to be so deeply involved." Chris spoke with an agitated huff in his voice as he averted his eyes in angst.

"I admire the way you and your brother look out for each other. You work better together, rather than alone. And I'm not sure how much longer he can work with that rap tap vigilante business he's been running. He would be better taken care of under our belt. But I will not push," Eric said, rocking on his heels. Chris huffed loudly to show his impatience.

"I am. Sorry. About Gabrielle. She's a lovely woman. But we are all without spouses for a reason. You know what happened to my wife... and Arthur's mother... I'm sure you do not want the same fateful end for Gabrielle. Alas, no one would understand let alone accept what we do," Eric said, sympathetically. He turned to leave, his pristine, polished shoes spinning on their heels, when he stopped to look back at Chris.

"I would suggest looking into high-end escorts. Find another way to get out your... *aggression*. Might not be so bad to take Arthur up on his offer," Eric said before leaving.

Chris felt his body temperature rise as his anger boiled up inside of him. He clenched his fists, watching his uncle walk away. Charlie put his hand on Chris's shoulder and Chris jumped. He grabbed Charlie's hand forcefully, nearly yanking it off.

"Hey! It's just me," Charlie said, trying to calm him down.

"Sorry..." Chris muttered. "Let's get the fuck out of here." Chris rushed outside with Charlie in step behind him.

On the drive back they sat in silence. Chris had an excruciating headache that made him want to scream.

"You don't have to do this," Charlie said, breaking the silence.

"Yes, I do, Charlie" Chris said reluctantly. He pulled up to Charlie's apartment, allowing his brother to exit the car. Charlie leaned into the car window.

"You'll be alright?" Charlie asked. Chris glanced down, lost in his own thoughts. He looked up at his brother with apprehension in his eyes.

"Just... just promise me you'll look after her," Chris said. He spoke with such sadness and regret, as he anxiously rubbed his temples.

"I would have regardless of whether you asked me to," Charlie smirked. Chris grinned at him knowingly. Charlie tapped the hood of the car and watched Chris speed off. His smirk quickly disappeared, and a frown painted his face. He could feel his brother's anguish. He could feel his despair.

~*~

"Shoot! Shoot! Shoot!"

Gabrielle stumbled into the closet, trying to put on her black heels. She smoothed out her high-waist, midi black skirt and straightened her white blouse on her shoulders. She was getting ready to head to work for an important meeting with the visiting Healthcare Administration Board. Unfortunately, she had missed her 3rd alarm.

"That's the last time I binge-watch Insecure on HBO," she grumbled. She stomped down the stairs with her purse and threw on her jacket. "See you later!" she yelled to a sleeping Eli.

She hopped into the car and pulled up to a Dunkin Donuts with a line out the door. "Are you kidding me?" she said frustrated. She got out of the car and leaned over to see there was only one person at the counter.

“Great,” she grumbled. Turning the corner, she saw a Starbucks with a slightly shorter line. “Guess I’ll have to suffer paying $7 for a cup of coffee,” she rolled her eyes.

As she waited in line, she texted one of her colleagues to let them know she was running late. Still on the phone, she stepped forward and knocked into someone in front of her, dropping her purse.

“Oh shoot!” she said embarrassed. “I’m so sorry. I should have been paying attention.” The person she knocked into bent down to pick up her purse and handed it to her.

“That’s quite alright,” he said in a deep, thick Irish accent. She grabbed her purse and looked up at him. She was startled by his piercing blue-green eyes that were in stark contrast with his neat, bright red beard.

“Thank-... thank you,” she said. She put the strap of her purse on her shoulder. He nodded at her with a smile and stepped to the side. She looked away from him for a moment to order her coffee, but when she looked back for him, he had disappeared. Shrugging, she stepped to the side and took out a folder to review what she would discuss during the meeting.

A few minutes passed and Gabrielle grew impatient that her name still wasn’t called. She approached the barista, trying not to be rude. “Hi, I was just wondering how much longer I’d have to wait,” she asked, drumming her fingers on the counter.

“What did you order?” the barista asked.

“Caramel macchiato,” she said.

“Oh, we already called that... did you not grab it?” the barista said.

“Clearly not!” she said annoyed.

“I’m sorry. Did you say caramel macchiato?” The same deep voice called from behind her. She turned around to find the red-bearded man smiling at her and holding a cup with chicken scratch on it.

"Sorry. I believe I may have taken yours by accident," he said.

"How in the world?" she said confused.

"I thought it said 'Michael'," he chuckled. She tilted her head to the side to read the cup. "Oh yea. I guess I can see that," she laughed. "Jeez, someone needs to work on their penmanship."

"My apologies," he said, handing her the coffee.

"Thanks," she said, grabbing it from him. "Um... it was nice meeting you... Michael?"

He nodded with a smile. She contemplated telling him her name, but figured there was no use as she wouldn't be seeing him again. She hurried out of the Starbucks and sped off to the hospital.

~*~

"Are you ready for this?" her colleague Dr. Rachel Wynn asked.

"As ready as I'll ever be. I know this program worked really well in L.A. I'm just hoping they're receptive to it here," Gabrielle said. She straightened her white medical lab coat and stepped into the conference room, with her folder tucked under her arm.

Gabrielle listened to the director, who originally recruited her, speak to the group of people responsible for approving or rejecting her program. Ignoring the noise around her, she studied her notes.

"And now, I'll turn it over to one of our star surgeons and the founder of this program, Dr. Gabrielle Johansson," the director said.

"Gabby... that's you," Rachel whispered.

Gabrielle looked up startled. "Oh! Right!" She stood up, grabbed the clicker for the projector and turned to the crowd.

"Good morning, everyone. Thank you so much for taking the time to discuss a program that is so dear to me," she started. As she spoke about the program, she scanned the room making eye contact with each person to drive the passion she felt about her program into each individual. That is, until she landed on a familiar set of piercing blue-green eyes.

"I-I... um," she paused for a second and tried to refocus. "I'm sorry. Just trying to gather my thoughts for a moment."

Michael stroked his beard, watching Gabrielle very attentively. He was impressed with her work and the reputation she managed to develop for herself. Especially in such a short amount of time at such a large hospital. The fact that she was willing to drive an entirely new program was an even bolder move that truly intrigued him.

Gabrielle finally gathered her thoughts. "When I first started my journey to become the doctor I am today, I learned my best lessons by not only shadowing other high-esteemed surgeons, but also being given the responsibility to take on assignments that required me to really dive into the field. When I first created this program in Los Angeles, many were skeptical of its success. But from this program, L.A. has produced some of the most incredibly talented and trustworthy doctors America has to offer. It's not only beneficial to the hospital in the way that it offers fresh talent, but it is also a truly life-changing experience for doctors in training."

Gabrielle walked to the other side of the room and dimmed the lights. She threw up a few graphs on the screen. "With this program, the success rate of surgeries including post-ops in Los Angeles increased by 15%. This Rotational Surgery Program is so important to me. Not only because it helped shape my skills today, but also because it allowed me to provide such a rare opportunity to so many others. Now, I'd like to play this short clip for you of those who have been impacted by this program, both doctors and patients. And I really hope that these testimonies will be taken heavily into consideration when making your decision. Thank you."

Gabrielle took her seat next to Rachel as everyone applauded. "You did great!" Rachel said, giving her a thumbs up. Grabbing the water next to her, Gabrielle smiled relieved.

~

At the end of the meeting, Gabrielle pretended to busy herself. She made quick glances at the director speaking to the gentleman she ran into at Starbucks. She took a moment to appreciate his appearance, eyeing him from head to toe. She bit her lip nervously as she admired his physique.

He sure knows how to wear a suit, she thought to herself. She looked up to see him staring at her and immediately averted her gaze, again pretending to 'busy' herself with papers.

"Dr. Johansson, please come over. I'd like you to meet Mr. Michael Bo," the director called. Gabrielle quickly walked over. She reached for his hand and he gave her a firm handshake.

"I was very impressed with your presentation, Dr. Johansson." His deep voice rang out so smooth, catching her off guard again. She didn't think she'd ever get used to it. "You are clearly very passionate about this program."

"I am, sir," she assured him.

"Michael is one of the most esteemed members of the Healthcare Administration Board for the United States," the director added.

Gabrielle's eyes bulged. "I'm sorry. Did you say 'for the United States'?"

"That's right. We were very surprised to learn he would be sitting in on this meeting. We were certain we would only receive attendance at the state level."

"Well, I had heard so many good things about this program from the West Coast. I assumed it would be better if I heard about it from the founder herself," Michael said. His gaze lingered on Gabrielle.

"It's... wow... it's an honor, sir, thank you. I hope we did not disappoint," she said excitedly.

"Your presentation was impressive. Though, I do have a few questions that need answering," Michael said.

"Such as?" she asked.

"For one, I'm interested in if and how you've calculated the cost of the program, who exactly qualifies, and what kind of effect you expect it to have on the economy of the local community. Surely, all of these factors must be taken into account. Especially considering the variation in cost of living between Philadelphia and Los Angeles," Michael said.

Gabrielle looked stunned for a moment. She tried to dissect his questions in her head, figuring out how to answer him without looking foolish. She knew these answers. Why was she struggling to answer them?

"The cost of the program is relatively similar to that of Los Angeles, especially since the number of participants in the beginning stage would start at the same rate. That would mean the rotational surgeons training here would be paid the starting salary of a new surgeon in Philly just as a starting surgeon in L.A. would be paid that of one starting in L.A. The program starts off with 4 junior surgeons and-"

"But have you taken into account how much the salaries of an additional 4 surgeons would cost the local economy? Is Philly as equipped for that after the recent bridge collapse 15 miles from here?" Michael watched her, gauging for her reaction.

Gabrielle's mind raced, trying to think quickly on her feet. "I didn't... I mean I think that-" She floundered before she took a deep breath and stood up straight. She would not allow this guy to come in and downplay what she'd worked so hard to create.

"I may need to update my information for more real time specs. If you'd allow me the time, I can confirm those numbers to assure you that we are more than ready for a program of this calibre. I'd be more than willing to answer the remainder of your questions," she said calmly.

He grinned at her surge of confidence and professional reply under his barrage of questions. "I look forward to it, Dr. Johansson," Michael said, looking at her intrigued.

She mustered a fake smile before turning on her heels and walking away.

~*~

Gabrielle placed a neat and formally-printed document in front of Michael, who sat at the desk of the office he was temporarily residing in for his visit.

"The answer to all of your questions," she said proudly. "I even added charts."

He looked up at her with a bit of surprise on his rather regal and well-defined face. "You did all this in 2 hours?"

"1 hour. I had 6 patients I had to see," she said, straightening her white medical lab coat. He grabbed the piece of paper and sat back in his chair, quickly reading over her document.

"Well done," he said, glancing up at her. "But I still need to know the demographics of those this program is targeting."

Gabrielle slumped her shoulders exasperated. "I already mentioned that this is targeting young and budding surgeons with minimal fieldwork."

"That's experience. I need background, culture, language. This needs more depth to drive the point home of what a difference this program will make," he said, placing the paper down on the desk. Gabrielle frowned in frustration. This was starting to feel personal.

"I'm not trying to be difficult, Dr. Johansson." Michael folded his hands and leaned forward on his desk. "I just know the kind of people who work in Corporate. I know what they're looking for. I'm only trying to help you. I'm sure you don't want to put all this work into something you care about, just to see it get rejected."

She hesitated unsure if he was being sincere or just trying to get a rise out of her.

"I have a conference call with them in an hour. Get the rest of the information for me, and I'll see what I can do," he said. She hesitantly nodded before leaving, feeling a bit defeated.

~*~

"And then he just like... ran out of the emergency room butt-ass naked!" Gabrielle laughed. She sat on the edge of the ring with a towel hanging around her neck and a water bottle in her hand. Charlie stood on the ground with his elbows on the floor of the ring, his head at eye-level with her waist. She handed him her water bottle for a sip.

"Damn, seriously? Did you at least run after him?" Charlie laughed, taking a sip.

"Hell no! Not with his dick hanging out and swinging around like Tarzan. But one of the male nurses tackled him to the ground," Gabrielle chuckled. "And this is why we don't do drugs, kids."

"Didn't know hospitals could be so crazy," he laughed.

"Oh, you have no idea. There's a reason why there are so many soap operas and shows about it," she grinned.

It had been a few weeks since Chris and Charlie had found out about the Beaumonts' presence on their territory. They decided to keep a low profile. While Chris prepared for his trip to Japan,

Charlie trained his men 24/7 in case of another attack Meanwhile, Gabrielle was heavily involved in implementing her program.

"Alright, come on. Break time's over," Charlie said. Gabrielle pulled her legs up and rolled into the ring.

"You gonna let me tackle you this time," she smirked. She playfully jumped up and down on her feet.

"I thought you wanted to learn self-defense," Charlie mused. He swiftly jumped into the ring with one hand. "Besides, you couldn't take me even if you tried."

"Sometimes I gotta be on the offense," she said, doing fake punches in the air. "And are you challenging me, Richardson?"

"No, because you have to be a threat to pose a challenge," he taunted her.

"Excuse me!" she squealed. She slapped her hands together and charged at him, head-first, tackling him to the ground. Charlie laughed as Gabrielle struggled to pin him down. "Give up, Richardson! And maybe I'll have mercy," she said, pinching him incessantly in the sides.

"Okay! Okay! I give up!" Charlie laughed. He writhed from her tiny pinches and gripped her hips to hold her back.

Straddling his waist with her legs on either side of him, she raised her arms in the air in victory. "CHAMPION!" she shouted, followed by fake chanting. "Gabby! Gabby! Gabby!"

Charlie laughed at her. "You got lucky this time, Johansson. Pinching is a foul," he grinned.

"Hey! Hey! Hey, Mister! You gave up! Don't you go taking back your surrender," she said. She leaned down, wagging her finger in his face. Her curly hair fell from the bun and dropped down, covering her entire face and half of his.

"Gabs!" he laughed loudly, as her hair curtained his eyes.

"Oh shoot! Sorry!" she giggled. She tried to move her hair out of her face, but it had become so entangled she completely gave up with a frustrated groan.

"Here," he said. He pushed her hair out of her face and behind her ear. She giggled at her clumsiness and stopped suddenly when she felt his hand brush against her cheek. Looking down at him, she noticed him staring at her intently. His green eyes bored into hers. That familiar hot feeling started to well up inside her. Her lips parted slightly as she closed her eyes to his soft touch against her face.

Charlie watched as Gabrielle closed her eyes. His grip on her hips tempted him to pull her closer. Her skin felt soft against his calloused hands. Her breasts tucked into her sports bra and soaked shirt heaved heavily against him. He felt the sweat from her neck drip onto his chest. Suddenly her eyes shot open and she scrambled off of him.

"Um... I'm sorry," she said dazed. She quickly stood to her feet. "I should go."

"You don't want to finish training?" he asked. He internally cursed himself for letting her go.

"Let's just pick up again tomorrow," she said. She hopped out of the ring and grabbed her bags. Walking towards the door, she nearly smacked into Chris.

"Chris!" she shouted startled. She nearly fell back on her butt.

"Hey, Ga- woah!" Chris blurted. He quickly grabbed her by the elbow before she fell. He tried to help her steady herself, but she abruptly slapped his hand off of her.

"I'm fine," she said curtly. She straightened her bag over her shoulder. Chris's Adam's apple bobbed anxiously.

"Can I... can I talk to you for a minute," he asked, rubbing the back of his neck nervously.

"No," she said, trying to walk past him.

"Gabs, please. It's important," he said. He gently grabbed her arm, pulling her towards him.

"I really don't want to talk to you, Chris," she said. She turned around to walk out in the other direction, but Charlie blocked her. With both hands on her waist, he gently pushed her back. She looked up at him with deep frustration, as if he had just committed some grave betrayal.

"Charlie!" she said, annoyed.

"Just... talk to him, Gabs," Charlie said. He cocked his head to the side, looking at her with raised brows. She deeply exhaled and turned to face Chris. There was so much sadness, pain and regret in his gaze that her heart nearly broke.

"Okay..." she said softly. Chris grabbed her bags from her hands and walked out the door with her following. Charlie watched the two of them walk off to Chris's car and sighed heavily before leaving to shower.

~*~

"Where are we going?" Gabrielle asked, after they drove for a few minutes.

"Just a drive...then I'm taking you back to your brother's house. You're staying with him for the time being right?" Chris asked.

"Yea..." she said looking out the window. After a few moments of silence Gabrielle spoke up again. "You said you wanted to talk..."

"Yea..." Chris sighed. "I'm... going out of the country for a couple of weeks."

Gabrielle looked at him suddenly. "Where?"

"To Japan... it's for business," he said to her.

"It's always for business," she muttered, looking back out the window. "You could have just sent me a text."

"It's not really a normal trip, Gabs. I-… I don't know for certain when I'll be back…"

He pulled over to a secluded wooded area by her brother's home and turned off the engine to face her. "I didn't want to leave without saying goodbye," he said to her.

"Goodbye," she said abruptly. She opened the door and got out to walk towards the house. Chris groaned and quickly followed after her. She walked off without him, but left the door open for him. He stepped into the quaint small home and found no one there.

Gabrielle put her stuff on the floor by the stairs. "You can go now," she said, ignoring him.

"Gabs." He grabbed her by the waist and abruptly turned her around.

"Don't!" she snapped. She placed her hands on his chest, trying to push him away, but his grip on her waist was firm. His hands on her body sent shivers down her spine and her want for him grew heavy. With one finger, Chris lifted her chin to see tears falling down her face.

"Dammit, Chris. I'm trying to get over you," she said, through her tears. She tried to avoid his eyes. She could feel his gaze and wanted to fall into him so badly. For him to say it was all a joke. That he wasn't leaving the country and that he actually just wanted to stay here with her. That he really did love her the way she loved him.

"Baby…" he said softly, and it made her heart swell. She gave in and looked up at him to find those familiar blue eyes looking at her with love and sadness. But it couldn't be love, because he said he didn't love her.

Chris felt anguish tightening his chest as he watched tears fall from her face. Tears that he had caused. It was poetry in motion as they rolled down her round nose and over her plump lips.

Those soft lips that he had been aching to kiss again. When she finally looked up at him with those sad alluring brown eyes, he couldn't help himself any longer.

He placed his lips on hers, waiting a moment for her to retaliate. But when she didn't, he hungrily enveloped her lips with his and pulled her head closer. One hand wrapped behind her neck while the other tightly grabbed her waist.

He was surprised but grateful with how quickly she gave him entrance into her mouth. His tongue made love to hers. It seemed like she missed him just as badly as he missed her. He could feel her heat radiating off of her. He slowly walked her backwards, pushing her against the wall. His hand snaked up her shirt, rubbing the pad of his fingers over her bra. She ran her hands over his back and biceps as they passionately kissed. His fingers squeezed beneath her bra. Seeking out her nipple, he squeezed gently, causing her to moan into his mouth.

Gabrielle felt weak at the knees. She had missed these lips. She missed his touch and the way his hands made her body sing. Her body went limp as Chris teased her nipples, but he held her up. Wrapping his hand around her thigh, he lifted it to his waist. He moved from kissing her mouth to kissing her neck and grazed his fingers over her core through her sweats. Rubbing gently through her pants, he felt her wetness seeping through the material.

Gabrielle moaned loudly, surprising herself. Her eyes popped open and she immediately pushed Chris off of her. She readjusted her clothes, trying to compose herself as Chris looked at her longingly.

"I'm… I'm tired of you toying with me, Chris," she said wrapping her arms around her. "Please just leave."

"Gab-"

"Leave!" she blurted. Chris looked at her with anxiety, desire, and sorrow. He reluctantly left the house, closing the door behind him.

~*~

Charlie watched his brother hand his bags to the male flight attendant.

"Will that be all, Mr. Richardson?" a blonde female flight attendant asked.

"Yes, thank you. Actually... I might need this," Chris said, grabbing his laptop bag.

"No, you will not. We're drinking the whole way there," Arthur said from behind. He patted Chris hard on the back and grabbed his laptop bag to hand back to the woman. "Take care of that, will you, love?" he winked at her.

The flight attendant blushed and took the bag. "Yes, sir."

"I've never seen Christopher let loose before. Ever. I'm fucking excited," Arthur teased.

"We're there for business, Arthur," Chris said sternly.

"Doesn't mean you can't have a little fun, cousin," Arthur winked. "Get your kissing and crying out now so we can go." Arthur slapped Charlie on the back before strolling towards the boarding platform. Chris shook his head, watching Arthur walk away.

"When will you be back?" Charlie asked.

"I don't know... Gonna try to wrap it up in 3 weeks. Don't want to be there longer than I have to," Chris said.

Charlie nodded. "You will keep me updated, right? Let me know if something is wrong or you need me?" he asked.

"Of course. You'll get sick of me," Chris grinned. Charlie smirked amused but then immediately frowned as his face fell. He pulled his brother in for a rough hug.

"Be careful, brother," Charlie said into Chris's shoulder.

"You too, Charlie," Chris said, squeezing his brother tightly. Charlie watched his brother walk towards the plane. Chris turned around one last time and waved goodbye.

~

Chris sat on the private plane on the other side of the aisle from Arthur who was already drinking. He scrolled through his phone, looking at old pictures, and came across one of Gabrielle wearing Eli's football jersey. Her hair was beautifully curled around her face and she wore a bright smile. Leaning over a railing, she cheered her brother on from the stands.

"Ah, Christopher. Why do you do this to yourself?" Arthur asked, sitting next to his cousin.

Chris looked at his cousin confused. "What do you mean?"

"You're *pining*," Arthur said with emphasis.

Chris scoffed. "I'm not... pining."

"I get it. Gabrielle is beautiful. Intelligent. Kind. I can see why you love her. I mean bloody hell, if I could have my way with that as-" Arthur started.

Chris shot him an agitated, dirty look before he could finish his thought. "Sorry. Alls I'm sayin' is you've got to move on, bruv. She's gorgeous but she's clearly off limits. No sense in pining away for something you can't have," Arthur advised.

"What you need is a woman in the same world as you. You need a broad who knows what she's doin'. Who will absolutely blow your fuckin' mind," Arthur teased with a huge grin on his face.

"I'm not hooking up with a prostitute," Chris said coldly.

"What? No, I wouldn't proposition that, ya silly twat. I'm just sayin'... you'll be surprised what you can find in Japan. A tall, handsome bloke like you? Ladies will be fallin' all over ya," Arthur smirked, popping a grape into his mouth.

The blonde flight attendant walked over to them. “Can I get you any drinks?” she asked, her eyes lingering on Chris.

“No tha-” Chris started.

“I’ll have another beer. And my cousin here, will take a shot of whiskey,” Arthur said.

“Yes, sir,” she said. She handed Arthur a beer and then poured a glass for Chris.

“Thank you,” Chris smiled at her. Her finger grazed over his hand flirtatiously.

“Please let me know if you need *anything* else,” she said, placing emphasis on the word “anything” with flirtatious eyes. She walked away with an exaggerated twitch in her hips that made Chris roll his eyes.

“Fuckin’ A. Well, she clearly wants you. You could take her right now if you wanted to,” Arthur smirked, elbowing Chris in the side.

“She’s not my type,” Chris said curtly. He sipped his whiskey and looked out the window.

“Christopher. All I’ve ever seen you fuck is blonde and redheaded broads with huge tits. So don’t give me none of that bullshit. Besides, I’m not suggesting you propose to her or anything. Just... have a little fun,” Arthur insisted.

Chris turned his head to see the blonde flight attendant staring at him. She blushed at being caught and looked down before looking back up again to smile at him. He smiled back and took another sip of his whiskey without looking away.

~*~

14

Getting to Know Michael Bo

~*~

Gabrielle sat on a stool in the examination room, going over her patient's files. Her white medical lab coat curtained her black skirt and red blouse that matched her red flats for comfort.

She paused to look up at the woman sitting on the examination bed. "How have you felt since the surgery? Any pain in your abdomen? Are you able to eat and use the bathroom without complications?" Gabrielle asked.

"No pain, Doctor. I feel so much better thanks to you. It's been so long since I knew what it was like to eat without fear of another gallbladder attack," the patient said, gratefully.

"I'm glad to hear that, Mrs. Green. If you would please lie down for just a second. I just want to feel around your abdomen for any hardness or swelling," Gabrielle advised.

The woman lay down on the bed, allowing Gabrielle to gently feel around her stomach for any abnormalities.

A knock came at the door before a nurse opened it. "Dr. Johansson?"

"Yes?" Gabrielle asked.

"You're wanted on the 18th floor."

"I'm with a patient right now, Erica."

"I told them that but they insisted on your presence."

Gabrielle sighed. "I'll be done in a few minutes. They can wait."

"But Doctor-" the nurse started.

"How does that feel, Mrs. Green?" Gabrielle asked her patient.

"No pain!" Mrs. Green smiled.

"Good," Gabrielle said, jotting down notes in the file. Taking the hint, Erica closed the door, allowing them to finish.

Gabrielle finished up with her patient and sent her on her way. Feeling frustrated with the constant interruptions to her work, she changed into her heels and headed to the corporate offices on the 18th floor.

"Dr. Johansson," the receptionist acknowledged her, upon seeing her exit the elevator. "They're waiting for you in corner office 1806."

"Thanks..." Gabrielle mumbled. She reluctantly headed down the corridor.

She approached the office and heard two male voices inside. One was her boss, the director, and the other...

She knocked. "Come in!" her director said.

She walked in to see her director perched on the edge of his desk. Michael sat in the leather chair at the large wooden and finely furnished desk. His electric blue-green eyes immediately landed on her the moment she walked in.

"Sir..?" she asked.

"Dr. Johansson! You remember, Mr. Bo," her director said.

She nodded in acknowledgement. "How could I forget..." she muttered under her breath. Reading her lips, Michael grinned, far too amused by the irritation visible on her face.

"Mr. Bo has decided to stay in Philly and help us with our administrative issues. He'll be in charge of our division from now on until things have been sorted," her director advised.

"Oh... I'm assuming you mean that you're laying people off," she quipped.

"Dr. Johansson..." her director sighed.

"I'm just saying what everyone else is thinking..." she murmured. "The executives from the board only visit when it involves reduction in force."

Michael waved them both off and smiled at Gabrielle. "I am an advocate for full transparency and disclosure, so I won't deny that. But that's only one of my many responsibilities here, Dr. Johansson. I wouldn't dwell on it."

She gave him a cold look that she quickly masked with a stoic expression.

"I'd be kinder, Dr. Johansson. Mr. Bo has also agreed to help implement your rotational program," her director informed her. Her eyes widened as her mouth dropped.

"Pre-prepare? Does that mean the program was approved?" she asked, startled.

Her director smiled at her joyously while Michael's eyes never left her. He folded his hands beneath his chin, watching her intently.

"Oh m- Thank you so much! I can't even begin to tell you how grateful I am," she squealed.

"Yes, well... there's still quite a bit of work to be done. A couple of kinks that need to be ironed out before your program is launched. I was able to get the program approved by the Board, but only with the promise that a few changes were made." Michael's deep Irish accent reverberated throughout the room.

"Of course! Anything," Gabrielle said, nodding her head.

"I'm glad you agree with those conditions. Because starting today, you'll be reporting directly to Mr. Bo. I'm very happy for you, Dr. Johansson. I'm excited to see where this program takes us as a hospital and as a community," her director smiled.

Gabrielle didn't hear the rest of what her director said. She was still stuck on being told she was now reporting directly to Michael Bo.

"I'm sorry? I'm not reporting to you anymore? I don't understand," she said. Her eyes were almost pleading for her director to change his mind. A faint grin teased the corner of Michael's mouth.

"This is the best opportunity for you, Dr. Johansson. My boss is now your boss. It's best to work exactly with the source of approval rather than to go through a middleman. Look at it as a promotion," her director explained.

"Yes... yes, of course," Gabrielle frowned. Her phone went off, letting her know she was needed in the ER. "Well, thank you very much for the great news. It seems I'm needed back downstairs. May I?"

Her former boss nodded in approval.

"I look forward to working with you... *Dr. Johansson...*" Michael's blue-green eyes flickered mischievously as she caught his grin hiding behind his folded hands.

"L-likewise, Sir..." she said, trying not to reveal how she truly felt. She quickly left the room without a second glance.

~*~

It had been two weeks since Gabrielle started working for Michael Bo and the man had been running her ragged. Her patience for him was as thin as her tolerance of his presence. To no surprise, layoffs had come to the hospital at a lower level and tension was high for the entire hospital staff.

Gabrielle walked into Michael's office and plopped her latest report on his desk.

"I hope this satisfies you," she said, with a tinge of irritation in her voice.

Michael leaned on one hand as his blue-green eyes looked from the report she placed on his desk to her agitated stance. His eyes subtly raked over her curvaceous body, clothed in a fitted black dress and her standard white medical lab coat, draping over her shoulders.

"I get the feeling you don't like me very much, Dr. Johansson," he said with an amused smirk. She dropped her crossed arms to her sides and took a step back, a bit surprised by his comment.

"I'm not... particularly fond of you. No," she squeaked. She was surprised she would even admit that to the man responsible for both her job and her program.

He smirked at her with an amused air before standing from his chair. He adjusted his dark grey suit jacket and moved out from behind the desk, taking a few steps towards her. Gabrielle instinctively backed away from him.

"And why is that?" he asked, standing tall. His authoritative and self-assured demeanor greatly intimidated her. Something about him made her feel unsettled.

"I..." she tried to think. She didn't really know how to answer that question. Truthfully, she didn't like him from the beginning. Only at Starbucks did she find him remotely decent.

"You're not very kind," she said finally.

He smirked down at her, with a mocking glare. "It's not my job to be kind, Dr. Johansson. Being kind doesn't keep this hospital running. And it certainly doesn't keep it from being shut down."

Gabrielle's eyes widened. "You wouldn't-"

He scoffed, insulted, as he leaned back against his desk. "That's not why I'm here..."

She nervously bit her lip as he looked away from her. His eyes came back up to lock her in a gaze. "Perhaps we got off on the wrong foot. Why don't we go out for a drink?" he offered.

Gabrielle looked at him surprised. "Is it... appropriate for us to-"

"It's just a drink, Dr. Johansson. It will give us the opportunity to learn more about each other and strengthen our working relationship. I'd rather remove all contention so that the implementation of your program is flawless and without error," he assured her.

Gabrielle hesitated for a brief moment before nodding in agreement.

"Perfect. I'll meet you after work," he said. He turned around to sit back at his desk. She watched him for a split second, before exiting his office.

~*~

Gabrielle met Michael in the lobby of the hospital. He watched her hug a few nurses, saying goodbye, before she approached him. Her tan coat wrapped nicely around her body, and her curly hair fell prettily around her face.

He cleared his throat, trying to pull himself out of the rabbit hole his mind often went down whenever he looked at her. "Ready?" he asked her. She nodded and followed him out of the hospital.

An aged man in uniform, with a silver beard and light grey eyes waited for them near a car.

"Hi," she said, approaching him.

"Miss..." he said, opening the door for her. She stepped inside and scooted over for Michael to sit next to her. Michael heard her scoff and he looked up at her questioningly.

"Something on your mind?" he asked.

"No, nothing," she said quickly.

"If you have something to say, Dr. Johansson, I'd rather you be honest in our... attempt to build this working relationship," he said. She glanced at him with a small pout.

"I guess I shouldn't be surprised you have your own driver," she said, looking out the window.

"Why is that?" he asked.

She looked at him. "You seem like the type of man who comes from money..."

Michael grinned at her candor. Never had a woman been so straightforward and shameless with him. "His name is Drake. He's been with my family since I was a youngling," Michael said, going through his phone.

"This poor man has been serving you for that long?" she asked, mockingly. Gabrielle was surprised by her sudden change in attitude. She hadn't even had a drink yet, and she was already loose with her lips.

Michael chuckled with a shake of his head. "My, my. Feeling a bit bolder today, are we?"

"Bolder than usual," she teased. She felt herself loosening up in this non-work environment. "Where are we going?" she asked. She looked out of the window, unfamiliar with their current surroundings.

"To a rooftop lounge in New Jersey..." Michael said, still looking at his phone.

"New Jersey? Why New Jersey? There are so many nice places in Philly," she said surprised.

Michael looked up at her for a moment. "New Jersey isn't very far from Philadelphia. And besides... this lounge is rather nice..."

Gabrielle scrounged up her nose and looked outside again. They soon came to a beautiful, windowed building with sensual red lights that danced towards the sky. The door opened and Gabrielle stepped out.

"Thank you, Drake!" she said, making eye contact with the driver. He was a bit surprised that she knew his name let alone was thanking him. It was not common practice.

"You're welcome, Miss..." he said. He watched her walk towards the restaurant, as Michael followed closely behind her.

When they stepped into the building, Michael gave his ID to the host who directed them to a private elevator. Gabrielle nervously stood in the elevator not saying a word. Michael's presence felt so imposing that she didn't know what to do with herself.

"Are you alright?" she heard him say in his husky Irish accent.

"I'm fine," she said quickly, refusing to look at him.

The elevator finally opened when they reached the top. The rooftop was walled with strong glass to keep the winds at bay. A server approached them to walk them to a private area.

"It's a pleasure to see you here, Sir," the server said excitedly. Michael merely nodded as he took a seat on one of the lounge couches.

Who is this man...? Gabrielle asked herself. She didn't realize she was still standing and staring at him until his eyes landed on her. He gestured for her to take a seat. She blushed embarrassed and sat down on the couch on the other side of the table, across from him. The server took their orders and left.

"So... Gabrielle..." The way he said her name made her tingle from her head to her toes. "Tell me about yourself." His eyes locked onto her and they seemed even more emboldened in their colors. He had a relaxing yet confident air about him that seemed to magnify with each movement he made.

“Um... what do you want to know?” she asked nervously. She felt naked under his gaze.

“Everything...” he said coolly. She was caught off guard by his response and his tone. The way his eyes grazed over her did not leave her indifferent.

“Er... well. I have an older brother, Eli... My family all comes from Philly. We can’t really trace back our roots that much except to West Africa at best. Hmm... let’s see...I’m a bit of a nerd...huge fan of Lord of the Rings,” she listed.

“You like Tolkien?” he asked, raising a dark red eyebrow.

“Don’t look so surprised,” she smirked, faking offense. “I was a Tolkien fan girl for most of my childhood years. I could probably recite the movies by heart.” Gabrielle quickly cursed herself for admitting it, and Michael chuckled amused by this declaration.

“I uh... I also like cooking and dancing,” she continued.

“You’re a dancer?” he asked.

“Since I was a little girl.”

“Hmm... I guess that explains your build,” he quipped quickly.

“Excuse me?”

He gave her a sarcastic look. “It’s a factual statement. Dancing is a great way to stay healthy.”

She took a large gulp of her drink to stifle the emotions he was making her feel.

“So, what about you? I’m sure there’s a lot behind the great man that is Michael Bo, Head of the U.S. Health Administration Board,” she quipped.

He smiled fondly at her and sat back comfortably on the couch. “I come from rather old family traditions. My family is from an ancient part of Europe."

"Ireland?" she asked.

"That's... part of it."

"I'm just assuming because of the accent..." she said slightly embarrassed.

"I gathered..." he said, giving her a mocking grin.

"Any siblings?"

"I have a brother."

She glanced at him and couldn't help but wonder if his brother was as handsome as he was.

"So, why would such a great and powerful man like yourself go into Health Administration?" she asked, chasing away her inappropriate thoughts.

"Who says I'm great?" he challenged her.

"I googled you... you're pretty damn great," she said, before she could catch herself. Michael looked at her very intrigued. "I mean... you've done great things," she said quickly.

"You googled me?" he probed.

"I wanted to know more about who you are."

"You could have just spoken to me."

"Well, I'm talking to you now," she said curtly. He couldn't help but chuckle in amusement at her lack of tact.

He sat back and looked at her. "Probably the same reason you decided to become a doctor."

Gabrielle looked at him sarcastically. "I highly doubt that, Mr. Bo..."

“Is that so?” he said to her. “And just ‘Michael’ is fine...”

“Well... Michael. I decided to become a doctor because I wanted to help the marginalized. Those who are often overlooked because of their perceived place in society as insignificant and lesser than... People like me,” she said firmly.

“I am aware. I’m particularly fond of your work in Kenya 2 years ago. If you had stayed another year, you probably would have seen that hospital through to completion,” he smiled, coolly at her.

Gabrielle’s mouth dropped. “You know about my work in Kenya? But... how-”

“I always do my research before I invest my time and energy into something...” Michael’s eyes probed her for a reaction and he could see a slight flush come to her dark cheeks.

“What did... you think I could have established an entire hospital?” she asked softly.

“I think you still could...” he challenged her. Gabrielle blinked at him, both encouraged and surprised by his words. The server brought them another drink and a bowl of strawberries.

Gabrielle looked down at them. “Strawberries?”

“Healthy, sweet... they’re your favorite, right?” he asked.

“Yes, but... how did-”

“I took a guess...” he said. His eyes still locked onto her. “Besides, you’ve had quite a few drinks already. Figured you should probably eat something.”

“That was thoughtful... thank you...” she smiled, grabbing a strawberry. She took a bite, savoring the sweet taste and licking the trickling juice from her lips. She went to grab another when she glanced up to see Michael still watching her. His eyes had darkened, his pupils enlarged, and he had that same subtle grin on his face.

"Please," she gestured to the bowl. "I don't want to be selfish."

"It's for you," he insisted.

She smiled shyly and took a moment to look around the rooftop. She noticed their location was rather private, while everyone else seemed to be in a noisy and crowded area.

"This place is really elegant," she said. She got up from the couch to look around. He watched her walk towards one of the floor-to-ceiling windows. His eyes lingered on the curves of her body.

She looked out of the window at the cars and trucks passing below. The stars peppered the dark night sky. "I'll admit... It's beautiful. But, I still don't see why we couldn't stay in-"

She turned around to face him and jumped startled to see him standing right in front of her. "Philly..." she finished. She gulped hard and looked up into his blue-green eyes. His gaze held hers for a brief moment.

"I told you," he said, averting his eyes. He glanced up to look out of the window. "I like this place." She took a step back from him until she felt the coolness of the glass behind her.

He looked down at her with concern. "Is something wrong?"

"N-no," she said quickly. *Yes! You're way too close, buddy!* she thought to herself.

"You're breathing rather heavy," he said, taking another step towards her.

"I...I guess I just feel a little warm." She felt her throat dry up from her nerves.

"I'll fetch you some water," he said, turning around. Gabrielle sighed heavily.

"Come on, girl, get it together!" she said to herself. She looked up to see Michael smoothly walking towards her. He held a glass of cold water in one hand while his other hand casually sat in his pocket. He looked straight out of a James Bond movie and it made her feverish.

"Thanks," she said, taking the water from him. She quickly turned around to look outside again. She didn't trust herself to keep facing him.

"The report you gave me earlier was good, but it's missing a few things..." he said.

She sighed, trying not to get angry. "What was it missing?"

"There needs to be more detail on the type of operations the surgeons will be involved with."

"I already gave the type of operations," she said exasperated.

"You gave a broad generalization. We need to know which ones are gastrointestinal, meningeal..." He heard her groan in frustration. "You're angry with me," he said, nodding.

"You're picking on me!" she snapped.

He turned to her in surprise. "Picking on you? You think I'm picking on you? Is that why you challenge me so much?"

"I don't challenge you..."

He gave her a mocking grin. "You have quite a mouth on you, Dr. Johansson..."

"Well maybe if you stopped picking on me so much, you wouldn't have to worry about my mouth!" Gabrielle immediately regretted raising her voice. This was her boss she was speaking to after all. She expected him to get angry with her and fire her on the spot. But then she noticed his darkened blue-green eyes zero in on her lips.

"...I am not... *picking* on you, Dr. Johansson. I am merely trying to make sure your program is implemented flawlessly, without mistakes. If you risk mistakes, you risk rejection from the board," he said. He looked from her lips to her eyes. Gabrielle felt herself getting hot, as the proximity between her and Michael got smaller.

"I wish I could appreciate your... attention and concern, Sir. But sometimes, it feels a bit more personal than that," she said firmly. She tried to mask her nervousness.

"I assure you that when it comes to my work, I make sure to keep it professional." Michael stepped closer to her, his eyes glancing at her lips again.

"Are you sure about that?" she asked. Her breathing got heavier and more sporadic.

"Why do you doubt me?"

"Because of the way you're looking at me... right now..." she said breathlessly.

Michael stopped for a moment and finally looked into her eyes. A mix of confusion and desire played in his blue-green irises. "And how am I looking at you... Dr. Johansson..." His voice was low and challenging, intending to provoke her.

She swallowed hard and bit her lip nervously. This felt like a trap. A trap she was far too eager to jump right into. She went to take a step back when one of his hands quickly wrapped around her waist to stop her from moving away from him. He raised his other hand to her lips and ran his thumb teasingly over her bottom lip.

"Well?" he asked her again. His grip on her waist tightened as he pulled her closer to him.

She knew what he was about to do. She knew this was wrong. But she also didn't want to stop him. She was heavily attracted to this man and craving for him was slowly winning out over her conscience.

"Michael..." she breathed out, staring into his alluring eyes.

He leaned forward and roughly possessed her lips with his own. He kissed her hungrily, pushing her back against the cold window and felt her body relax against his. She ran her tongue over his lips before possessively sucking his bottom lip into her mouth. She placed a small hand over his chest and felt the firmness of his muscles underneath. Eager to have more of her, his hands strayed down from her waist to her hips, peppering her neck with impatient kisses. Each kiss left a hot tingle on her electrified skin.

Gabrielle felt her body betraying her at how eagerly it responded to his touch. It didn't make any sense to her how badly she wanted to give into him completely. She wanted him to take her right there. All of her alarm bells were going off.

"We can't," she said, struggling to push him away. He looked down at her, starving; his eyes still feasting on her. "Y-you're my superior," she said weakly, already missing the warmth of his lips against her neck.

"Hmm..." he hummed, as if trying to understand her comment. His eyes scrutinized her face, looking for any kind of leeway.

"We... we should probably go," she stammered.

"Is that what you want?" he asked her.

No, she thought to herself. "I think it's for the best," she assured him.

He reluctantly removed his arm from around her and put distance between them. She walked back to the table to gather her things and waited for him to take the lead.

The car ride home was eerily silent. There was nothing but music from the radio. She quickly glanced at Michael to see him looking down at nothing. His brow was furrowed in concentration. Just then, he looked up at her and she quickly looked away.

Gabrielle felt awkward. She couldn't stand the silence between them. They both felt the tug of wanting to pounce on each other or remain silent and pretend nothing had happened.

"Thank you for tonight," she said. "The strawberries were particularly good." She raised her eyes to the heavens and felt like cursing herself for her lack of conversational skills.

Michael glanced at her with a side grin. "The strawberries? Really?" he said sarcastically.

"Yes. They were very red... and sweet." She cringed at her inability to speak like a normal person.

He gave her an amused smirk. "Hmm... well... that wasn't the only thing that was sweet..."

She felt her face getting hot and quickly averted her eyes from his gaze. This man made her feel like a kid on the first day of school. She had no idea what to do with herself and foolishly played with her hands in her lap. She tried to think of something else to say to change the direction of the conversation when she felt his hand on her thigh. She looked up at him and saw a heated look in his gaze.

Remembering their situation, he quickly retracted his hand and looked away from her. "My apologies, I-"

She jumped into his arms before he could finish. Wrapping her arms around his neck, she planted her lips against his. His hands ran possessively up and down her waist before he effortlessly pulled her onto his lap. Her skin was hot against his fingers that ran along the inside of her thigh. He felt her heat radiating from her core, luring him in for a touch.

As his fingers crept up the side of her thigh towards its target, he felt her lips brush softly against his ear. "You're treading dangerous waters, Mr. Bo..." she groaned, nibbling sensually on his ear.

Her voice was low, raspy and laden with desire.

He smiled to himself as his fingers brushed against her softness, causing her to shiver against him. She kissed him hard as he touched her again, eliciting a moan from her.

"We're here, sir..." Drake said over the radio com.

"Thank you," Michael responded calmly over the com. He continued stroking Gabrielle who was purring on his lap.

"We can't do this again," she breathed heavily. Her actions betrayed her words as she kissed his lips again.

"No, of course not," he grinned against her neck. He sucked on her soft flesh, leaving a swollen mark. After a few moments, Gabrielle reluctantly moved herself off of him.

"Goodnight, sir..." she said, stepping out of the car.

"Goodnight, Dr. Johansson..."

~*~

"And the way he kisses... oh my gosh, T..."

"Girl... you betta calm your ass down," Tanya said over the phone.

"I know! But he just makes me feel so... I can't describe it. But I like it... **too much**. I don't know what to do with myself." Holding her cellphone between her ear and shoulder, Gabrielle washed the dishes in Eli's sink. She dried them off with a towel and carefully placed them in the rack.

"I get it, Gabby, but... this is dangerous. Men like him usually use women for their enjoyment," Tanya said hesitantly. She could hear Gabrielle sigh deeply on the other end. *"Are you sure you're not just rebounding from Chris?"*

"NO! Of course, I'm not!" Gabrielle said, offended.

"I'm just asking... You guys were... I mean you still love him, don't

you?" Tanya asked.

"I don't want to talk about him, T," Gabrielle huffed, putting away the last dish.

"Okay..." There was a long silence on the phone.

"Michael doesn't seem like the kind of guy who would just use me. I feel like he genuinely likes me. He makes me feel good and I just miss having someone treat me the way he does."

"But your boss, Gabby?" Another frustrated sigh came from Gabrielle's end. *"I'm just looking out for you, hun. It could get very ugly. If things went sour, you'd be the one to suffer. Not him. He's white. He's male. And he's powerful... And you...you're-"*

"Yea, yea I get it," Gabrielle said. She rubbed her forehead in exasperation. "Dammit!"

"I'm sorry, boo..."

~*~

Michael strutted into the waiting area and scanned the room for Gabrielle. His hunger for her drove him to possess her body yet again. He finally found her tending to a family and started towards her, when a young, petite blonde woman tugged at his arm.

"Well, hello there," the woman said in a deep, southern accent.

"May I help you?" he asked, looking down at her.

"I'm one of the new transfer doctors, starting in radiology," she drawled. "Does a handsome feller such as yourself know where I can get set up?"

Gabrielle turned around at the sound of Michael's voice to see him with a rather attractive young woman. He had a huge smile on his face and the woman seemed to be not only handsy but far too engaged for Gabrielle's liking. She furrowed her eyebrows in frustration as she watched them walk out of the waiting room together.

~*~

Gabrielle entered Michael's office and plopped a file down on his desk in front of him. "Per your request," she said, not looking at him. She turned on her heels to leave.

"Gabrielle." He called for her before she was able to exit. She sighed and slowly turned around to face him. He had picked up the file and was already leafing through it when his eyes looked up at her.

"Is something wrong?" he asked, concerned.

"Nothing," she shrugged.

"You seem angry with me. Is it because of last night?" he probed.

"No," she said irritably. He stood from his chair and walked to the front of his desk to lean back against it. Gabrielle huffed. She could see he wasn't going to let her leave until she confessed.

"I would rather you not toy with me. I'm not another notch on your rich leather belt to conquer," she said, folding her arms across her chest.

He looked at her quite confused. "I'm sorry? I don't follow..."

"Do you take all of your conquests to lounges? Have you always had a thing for black women or am I just an experiment for you?" she persisted.

Michael was taken back by her accusatory language. "I'm interested in all types of women, Gabrielle. My attraction to you is not because of your race," he said. He still did not understand where all this was coming from.

"But especially blonde ones," she huffed.

Michael pondered for a moment until he realized why she was

upset. A grin tugged at the corner of his perfect lips. At seeing the grin on his face, Gabrielle scoffed in disgust. She rolled her eyes and turned to leave. "I'm going back to work," she said.

He quickly grabbed her wrist and pulled her towards him, nearly knocking her off balance. He held her firmly by her waist and looked down at her with a stupid grin. "You're referring to the woman in the waiting room, I presume," he said.

She scoffed at the smug look on his face. She tried to push him away but he wouldn't budge.

"I thought you said you didn't want me…" He gently kissed his new favorite spot on the side of her neck. She went weak at the knees and her toes tingled with excitement.

"I didn't say that," she said weakly. "I said that… that we couldn't do this… because… it's not appropriate," she breathed out.

"Mm…" He softly kissed her neck and ran a hand gently down the sides of her arm. "But you're jealous of another woman you don't know…" he said, taunting her.

"I'm **not** jealous! I just… I don't like being played with," she said, pushing him off of her.

Michael grinned. "You didn't seem to protest when I played with you last night…"

"Michael!" she snapped at him. An embarrassed and heated flush came to her cheeks.

He looked into her eyes and noticed how serious she was. "I was not flirting with that woman. She's a new doctor. I was just showing her to her station," he explained.

Gabrielle's eyes softened as she took a minute to digest what he said. She tried to figure out how to keep herself from looking even more foolish. "Oh…" was all she could muster.

Michael chuckled as he let her go. "You're bloody sexy when

you're jealous, love."

"I am not... I was not jealous," she huffed, folding her arms.

"And for what?" he asked. He got up and moved behind her, turning her around to face him. "After last night... you should know by now that it's just you that I want."

He wrapped one hand around her waist while the other gently grabbed the back of her neck. He kissed her aggressively. Rather than protest, her body relaxed at his touch as she opened herself to him. He pushed her back against his desk and lifted her up so that she was sitting on the table top. His hands ran along the outside of her thighs to her hips before sneaking a hand between her legs and underneath her dress. Gabrielle sighed when his fingers grazed against her already wet core.

"Since the moment I first lay eyes on you, I couldn't get you out of my mind," he moaned into her ear. He teased a finger past the fabric of her panties and made contact with her clit. She hitched her breath and tightened her grip on his shoulders.

"All I can think about is making love to you. Making you mine..." His haggard breathing matched hers as he made himself hungrier and harder the more he touched her. He slid his finger between her wet lips, teasing the entrance.

"Michael. You know we can't... we shouldn't..." she said. She didn't know why she even bothered to attempt to dissuade him when she couldn't even dissuade herself.

"But you want to... I know you do... don't you...?" he said. His finger slipped inside her, causing her to gasp. She lowered her mouth to his shoulder and breathed heavily. She was far too turned and struggled to keep down a moan, when they heard a knock at the door.

"Mr. Bo? The auditor is here for your 11 o'clock appointment," someone said from the other side.

"Thank you. I'll be there momentarily," he said, firmly over his shoulder. He turned his eyes back to Gabrielle who was still falling apart from his finger, gently probing inside of her. He slid his finger out, feeling her body twitch under the agonizing slowness of his movements.

"I'll find you later..." he whispered into her ear, gently kissing the soft spot behind her lobe. He tortuously grazed his fingers over her core before removing his hand altogether. She looked up at him horny as hell. Straightening her dress, she quickly walked out of the office.

~*~

"I can't do this!"

"What do you mean?"

"I mean I can't say 'no' to him. I completely fall apart the moment he touches me," Gabrielle said into the phone. She cleaned the food container she emptied during her lunch break.

"Then don't let him touch you!" Tanya said sternly on the other line.

"But... but I **really** want him to touch-"

"Gabrielle Marie Johansson!"

"Damn... full legal name...?" Gabrielle muttered.

"You need to put an end to this now. There are so many other men you can date. Don't risk everything you worked for... FOR YOUR BOSS!"

Gabrielle sighed heavily, hunching over the table. "You're right. You're right... I... I have to end this before it spins out of control..."

"You can do this. Just don't look him in the eye and keep your distance. If he really cares about you, he'll understand," Tanya advised. Gabrielle hung up the phone and put her head in her hands, tak-

ing a deep breath.

"How is my love life BOTH complicated AND non-existent?!"

~*~

Gabrielle stood at the center of the lab, looking over a few vials. She peered at them with squinted eyes before placing them back in the tray to jot down notes.

"Do you often stay here this late?" Michael asked, stepping into the lab.

"Michael!" she jumped startled. She looked over to see him in a dark, blue suit leaning against the door frame. He looked so damn good. And the way he was staring at her...

"Yes... and no," she said. "I want to get these test results out to a couple of my patients before the end of the week. I don't want to keep them waiting, especially if it's severe."

"We have nurses for that," he said, approaching her.

"They already do so much. I don't want to push them," she said.

"You mean the way you push yourself?" He took her hand and pulled her towards him. She looked up into those beautiful eyes that always made her sweat with desire. His ability to completely disarm her with his gaze always astounded her.

"I...this is what I live for... to help others," she said nervously. Michael smiled at her fervor. It was one of the many things he admired about her.

She looked down suddenly, feeling heavy. "One of the patients may have a life-threatening illness. She's got 4 kids and no husband. Just her elderly mother to help her watch after them. They've gone through so much already with little luck. I just want to be the one good thing for them," she told him.

He held her close in his arms as if trying to take on some of her emotional burden. "You also have to be good to yourself, Gabrielle. You can't take on the weight of the world."

"I don't know how to be good to myself..." she admitted, sourly.

He gently lifted her chin and searched her eyes. A genuine smile crossed his face. "I can be good to you..." he said softly. He pulled her in tighter and kissed her intensely. His tongue eagerly searching out her own. He sat back against the table behind him and pulled her between his legs. His hands impatiently roamed her body, trying to feel every inch of skin and every enticing curve that he missed.

"Michael," she said, extending her hands to push him away. "We can't do this anymore..."

He looked down at her hands, holding him back and then into her eyes that betrayed her words. "Gabrielle... you want me as badly as I want you. I can feel it," he insisted.

"That- that doesn't matter, Michael. You're my superior. If anyone were to find out about us, it could ruin everything," she warned him.

"I would not allow anyone to retaliate against you," he assured her. "I'll protect you."

She gave him a sad smile. She admired his passion to keep her and how relentless he was in having her. She too wanted to pursue what they could possibly have. But she did not want to jeopardize all that she had built.

"Women are not as easily forgiven as men, Michael. Not in general... and certainly not in this field. Please... if you really care about me, then respect my decision."

He groaned, clearly frustrated but nodded in acceptance of her request. He took a step back from her but could not help himself from looking at her with longing in his eyes.

"I-I need to finish up here..." she said meekly. Michael sighed, getting the message. He took a step forward to give her a kiss but caught himself. He nodded and walked out of the lab, leaving her alone.

~*~

"So you fucked your boss?" Angie said, throwing popcorn into her mouth.

Gabrielle threw her hands in the air. "Did you not hear anything that I just said?!" she blurted. She picked up one of Tanya's couch pillows and hurled it at Angie's face.

"Hey!" Angie shouted. She threw a pillow back at Gabrielle, missing and hitting Rhaven.

"We are NOT starting another pillow fight in my house!" Tanya growled. She grabbed a pillow out of Rhaven's hands before she could retaliate. "You did the right thing, Gabby. Relationships with co-workers are messy. Especially with the boss."

"I know. It's just so difficult. I really like him," Gabrielle frowned.

"What about Chris and Charlie?" Angie asked, nonchalantly.

Gabrielle nearly choked on the twizzler she was chewing on. "Excuse me?!"

"Girl, don't play dumb. We all know you got a major lady-boner for those boys," Rhaven said slyly.

"Well, she already tried Chris and we all know how that went," Angie said flatly.

"I CANNOT believe we are having this conversation right now!" Gabrielle said angrily.

"Girl, relax. What you need is some good dick. If it didn't work with Big Daddy Chris and you can't date your Christian Grey of a boss, Mr. Big Dick Bo, maybe Rough Master Flex Charlie is the winning ticket," Rhaven said, sipping her tequila.

“Rhaven, you are doing too much. Charlie is not some random sex gamble! I care about him. He’s my best friend. I could never be romantically involved with him,” Gabrielle argued. There was slight hesitation in her voice.

“I mean you felt the same way about Chris,” Angie teased. “And he still turned that ass out.”

“Alright, let’s talk about something else, shall we?” Tanya said, trying to restore some peace. Gabrielle mumbled under her breath, stuffing more twizzlers into her mouth.

“Ooh! She big mad,” Rhaven chuckled. “Fine. We won’t talk about it anymore. BUT! If Mr. ‘Turn Them Cheeks Out’ Richardson comes knockin’ on your sexually-frustrated door, you better answer that sucka quick or send his fine white ass my way! Ya heard me?”

“You know what-” Gabrielle attacked Rhaven with a pillow, and Angie broke out into hysterical laughter.

“Welp... so much for girls’ night,” Tanya said, shooting back the rest of her tequila.

~*~

15

Stranger Things

~*~

"So, it's agreed then. Our men will continue business in Tokyo, Seoul, Beijing, and now Hong Kong. We will allow your men to ship through New York, San Diego, Seattle, and Boston," Chris said, typing on his laptop.

"Hai, Mr. Richardson. I am pleased with the way these negotiations have turned out. And with such speed. I must admit, I was a bit worried," Mr. Tamayaki said, crossing his legs.

"What can I say. I'm a man of my word," Chris said, looking up with a smile.

"Your reputation precedes you. I'm impressed. And that rarely happens with me. Won't you stay a little longer? My family is hosting a city-wide festival. Very popular and sought after. It'd be a pleasure to host you," the Japanese businessman offered.

"Well... I was anticipating heading back to the States soon thereafter... But I guess one more week couldn't hurt," Chris said, trying to mask his disappointment.

"Excellent," Mr. Tamayaki said, standing to his feet. He walked Chris to the door. "I look forward to celebrating this new partnership with you." Mr. Tamayaki bowed and Chris followed suit.

Chris walked out of the office and exhaled. Taking out his phone, he texted his uncle Eric to let him know the contract had been signed. He walked outside to the car waiting for him out front. The driver opened the door to let him in.

Waiting in the car for him was a beautiful red-haired, buxom woman with skin as white as snow. She pursed her bright red lips that matched the revealing red dress, hugging her tempting curves. A slit ran down her thigh, revealing her long sleek legs. Her arms sprawled out over the seat. She looked at Chris with eyes full of desire.

Chris poured himself a glass of scotch from the mini bar next to him. He took a long sip and raised his eyes to meet her gaze.

"What are you doing here, Jessica?" he said into the glass.

"Isn't it obvious?" Her low, sultry voice hummed as she moved towards him. "Mr. Tamayaki is not an easy man to negotiate with. I would know. He's ruthless. Few of us manage to get on his good side. But you did. I knew you'd seal that deal. You always do. Because you're the best there is. I'm here to help you celebrate, beloved," she smirked.

She glided her hands over his legs, massaging his thighs. Getting on her knees in front of him, she swiftly unbuckled his pants.

Chris looked down at her and continued to sip from his scotch. He watched as she sprung his cock from his pants. She stroked him softly and he closed his eyes. Laying his head back against the seat, he got lost in the sensual feeling. Her hands were slender along his shaft. She had mastered the skill of pleasure. She stroked him, going rhythmically faster.

Chris moaned when she lowered her mouth onto his head, licking vigorously. She ran her tongue along the shaft as her hands gently played with his balls. She bobbed her head, taking all of him into her mouth and down her throat.

Chris gently grabbed her hair, guiding her to take in more of him. And she did. Deeper and faster. Considering how large he was, he was always impressed with how much of him she could handle.

Jessica bobbed her head faster. Chris felt his balls tighten as he reached his climax. He spewed his seed into her mouth and she swallowed it all, licking every last drop. He panted heavily as she buckled his pants back up. Sidling next to him, she rubbed his heaving chest with her slender and expertly polished fingers.

"I missed this... I missed you..." she said, kissing his neck. Chris didn't know how to respond.

The car had just rounded the corner to his hotel when he managed to pull himself together. The driver opened the door to find a flushed Chris and a beaming Jessica. "We're here, sir."

Chris exited the car and gave the driver a large tip. He walked to the hotel door and Jessica followed close behind him. He turned around to face her. "What are you doing?" he asked.

"Is the celebration over so soon?" she said, fake pouting. "There's so much more I want to give you," she said slyly.

"Jessica... no," he sighed, turning around.

"Oh, come on, baby," she whined. She reached around him to rub the front of his pants. "You deserve this. We used to work so well together. In business... and in the bedroom. Don't you miss this? Don't you miss us? Just like old times?"

His breathing hitched a little as she rubbed him, sending his nerve endings on edge. But he removed her hand anyway. "It's best we try to keep our relationship as professional as possible," he said, stepping through the door.

She scoffed, folding her arms in annoyance. "We've already fucked multiple times, Chris."

"Which was a mistake. Have a good night, Jessica." He closed the door as politely as possible and waited for her to walk away.

"Girl problems already, cousin?" Arthur asked. He walked out of the bathroom with a towel around his waist, drying his hair.

"No," Chris said, putting down his things and plopping down on the couch.

"So, I take it you got the deal?" Arthur asked, pouring himself a glass of whiskey.

"Good to go," Chris groaned, rubbing his temples.

"Cheers, mate!" Arthur boasted loudly. He handed Chris the glass. "Tonight we celebrate."

"You're always celebrating," Chris muttered, sipping from the whiskey.

"And you don't celebrate enough. Get some rest and then get ready. I'm taking you out tonight," Arthur ordered. Chris groaned with irritation and fatigue. He fell back on the couch, covering his face with his hand.

~*~

"So, this program of yours. You're really close to pulling it off, aren't you?" Charlie leaned back on the sofa, watching the television screen.

"Just about. It's a lot of work and I feel like there's always something more to do, but... it'll be worth it in the end... I hope," Gabrielle said. She kept her eyes on the screen as her eyebrows scrunched up in concern.,

"I'm sure it will," Charlie said, encouragingly.

"Ha! Knew it! Knew he was gonna die," Gabrielle said, snapping her fingers.

"What a moron. Saw that coming," Charlie said, throwing popcorn into his mouth. Charlie and Gabrielle were sitting on Charlie's couch in his apartment, watching a horror movie. The movie flashed to a scene with a man and woman making out on a couch.

"Oh, great. Here come our next victims," Gabrielle said, munching on a twizzler. "This is like in the top 10 rules of a horror movie. Never make out while a serial killer is on the loose."

Charlie chuckled. "And what are the other 9?"

Gabrielle looked up thoughtfully. "Don't take a shower in your empty house."

"Mm... just have to deal with being funky as shit then," Charlie shrugged.

"Exactly. Better stinky than dead. On that note, don't GO anywhere alone. That's just begging to be killed."

"Gotta have a buddy system."

Gabrielle laughed out loud at Charlie's joke. "Buddy system. So they can die first if you're being chased?"

"Obviously."

Gabrielle rolled her eyes. "Also, don't be black."

Charlie laughed out loud. "Oh, come on."

"You know it's true! Black people don't stand a chance. That's why we don't even show up in horror movies."

Charlie chuckled as he watched the screen. The man took off the woman's shirt exposing her bra. Caressing her chest, he kissed her, eliciting a moan from her.

"You idiots! Don't you know you're both going to die?!" Gabrielle grumbled. She shifted uncomfortably on the couch and began rocking back and forth.

"You okay?" Charlie asked, eyeing her.

"Yup!" she said quickly. She bit her lip and kept her eyes on the screen.

"You look like you have to pee or something, Gabs," he persisted.

"Nope!" she said, shaking her head. Charlie shrugged and continued watching. The man and woman on the screen proceeded to have sex as they went at in on the couch.

"Okay! Maybe we should watch something else!" Gabrielle said suddenly. She hopped off of the couch and turned off the TV. Charlie blinked at her confused.

"What's your deal?" he asked her, surprised.

"Nothing! I just... think we should watch something else," she shrugged.

"Gabs, it took you over half an hour to finally pick a movie and now you want to watch something else," he said, looking up at her.

"Can you just drop it?" she snapped. Charlie shook his head, surprised at her emotional reaction, and put his hands in the air defensively. She sat down on the couch with a loud huff. "I'm just...frustrated," she muttered finally.

Charlie tilted his head in confusion. "Frustrated with what? The movie?"

"No... I'm... ugh... sexually frustrated," she groaned, whispering the last part. Charlie looked at her for a long second before he burst into laughter. "Charlie! It's not funny!" she scowled.

"I'm sorry. I'm sorry," Charlie said, wiping his eye. "That's nothing to be ashamed of, Gabs. We all have needs. You're only human."

"Easy for you to say. You've had girls tripping all over you since high school. You probably get laid like... all the time," she said. She folded her knees to her chest in embarrassment.

"Well... I'm not hard pressed for it," he shrugged. Twirling a twizzler between his fingers, he watched her carefully. "Why don't you just masturbate?"

Gabrielle's eyes nearly bulged out of her head as she looked at him in shock. "Excuse me!"

"What? It's natural. Everybody does it," he said to her.

"Clearly not everybody, Charles! These are the things my mother told me godly girls never do," she sighed in frustration.

Charlie stroked his beard thoughtfully. "Brainwashing tactics. You guys really need to get over that stigma."

She rolled her eyes at him. "Spoken like a man who has never known what it is to be shamed for your sexuality. I was raised to believe masturbation or any sort of sexual gratification was wrong. It seriously messed up my view of sex..."

Charlie frowned at her. "I'm sorry, Gabs. Sometimes I forget how different our upbringing was... it's not fair to you."

She shrugged in defeat. "It doesn't really matter... I've never really tried it before anyway..."

"It's not that hard, Gabs," Charlie smirked at her. "Aren't you a doctor?"

"I know the physiology of the human body, yes, Charlie. But I'm not an expert on how to sexually please myself," she muttered. She put her head on her knees, embarrassed by the whole conversation.

Charlie chuckled at her snark and embarrassment. He held back his laughter so as not to further upset her. They remained silent for a moment. He clenched and released his hands, watching her. He knew he was about to cross a line he promised he'd never take.

"I could... show you," he said calmly. Her head shot up and she looked at him wide-eyed.

"What?" she blurted. "I-I... Charlie, y-you're my best friend. Don't... don't you think that'd be a little weird? I never thought I was your type- I mean-" she stammered. Overwhelmed with anxiety by this revelation, she immediately thought back to her conversation with Rhaven.

"Shit. Calm down, Gabs. I'm not trying to fuck you. Like you said… you're not my type. I'm just trying to help a friend," he shrugged, leaning back.

"Rude," Gabrielle scoffed at him. She bit her lip for a moment, considering his offer. She remembered her conversation with the girls. It's not like she was dating Charlie. This was just a little fun, right? No big deal…

She straightened herself out and turned to face him. He raised a curious brow. "How would you help me," she asked nervously.

Charlie's heart skipped a beat. "Lay down," he instructed her. Furrowing her eyebrows, she bit her lip again. Apprehension was written all over her face. "I'm not going to trick you or anything, Gabs. Just lay down," he insisted.

Gabrielle took a deep breath and lay back on the couch with her knees bent upward. She waited until she felt Charlie's strong hands firmly grasp her hips. His fingers teased the hem of her shorts before tugging them down.

His eyes raked over her long dark brown legs. Licking his lips, he ran a finger over the smooth skin on her thigh. He eyed the detail of her white lace panties complementing her dark skin tone.

"Lace, huh?" He snapped the band of her panties. "Who are you trying to impress," he joked.

"Certainly not you!" she sneered as he laughed. He gently ran his finger over the soft skin of her inner thigh closest to her center. He felt her body immediately tense up at his touch.

"Relax…" he said softly. He moved his finger over her center and her breathing hitched. She felt his finger gently rub over her clit through her panties.

"You like that?" he asked her. She nodded without saying a word. He continued to stroke her and felt her wetness starting to seep through her panties.

"You're teasing me…" she moaned, eliciting a smirk from him.

She waited anxiously as one of his fingers moved the fabric to the side. He placed his finger on her bare clit, rubbing it in tantalizing circles. Gabrielle closed her eyes and exhaled deeply. She bit down hard on her lip and moaned softly, gripping the side of the couch.

Charlie watched with a lulled gaze as Gabrielle sighed deeply. Her hips moved in sync with his hand. He loved the sexy way she bit her bottom lip when she was excited. He licked his lips and felt his pants tighten every time her chest heaved.

Leaning over her, he slowly glided a finger inside her. She moaned loudly, clutching the couch even tighter. He pulled his finger out and glided it in again, agonizingly slow. Bending at the tip, his finger massaged the hood of her pussy. His hand was slicked in her juices.

"Oh god, Charlie..." she moaned loudly, bucking her hips upward.

"Does that feel good, baby?" he asked. He leaned deeper into her, his voice laced with desire. He was rock hard and she looked so delicious beneath him.

"Fuck, yes!" she moaned out. He continued to pump into her, pushing another finger inside her. Her pussy was so wet, it made loud squishy noises every time he entered her. He used his thumb to stroke and rotate her clit, moving his other finger every so often to gently pinch it between his fingers. This sent her into a wild fit, arching her back off the couch.

"Fuck, fuck, fuck!" Gabrielle moaned, clawing at the couch. She felt that rare but familiar feeling start to overwhelm her, as her body reached its climax.

"That's it, baby. Come for me," Charlie growled hungrily. He fingered her faster, rubbing her clit with more fervor. Gabrielle moaned loudly, fully arching her back off of the couch. She clutched Charlie's arm as the feeling washed over her. Her legs trembled and Charlie's grip on her hips tightened.

Charlie watched her slowly come down from her high. He teased her swollen clit once more before slowly removing his fingers from inside her. Her drenched panties snapped back onto her. He instinctively stuck out his tongue to taste her juices on his hand. Her eyes fluttered open to see him licking his fingers, while watching her intently.

"Charlie!" she squealed, blushing.

"What," he smirked at her. "You taste good..."

She struggled to sit up, still feeling woozy. Her legs hardly obeyed her, as she tried to sit upright on the couch. "Why are you so good at this?" she asked, blushing.

"I can't reveal all my secrets, Johansson..." he teased her. "There's your lesson for the day. Make sure you practice at home," he grinned.

"Are you giving me homework, Mr. Richardson?" she said with a sarcastic grin.

Charlie gave her a naughty look and leaned in closer towards her. "That all depends if you're expecting a final exam."

Gabrielle widened her eyes a bit and then playfully punched him in the arm. "Boy, stop playing with me!"

"I've already played with you," he teased her.

"Charlie!" She tackled him and they rolled off of the couch. Charlie laughed, trying to shield himself from her onslaught of pinches.

"Ow! Hey!" he laughed. He grabbed her wrists and rolled on top of her. Pinning her to the ground with both arms above her head, he watched her breathe heavily beneath him.

His eyes lingered on her breasts, tucked inside her tank top, and grazed down to her wet panties. Swallowing hard, he dragged his hand down her chest to squeeze her softness.

She looked up at him, breathing heavily, when a smirk spread across her face. "I thought I wasn't your type," she mocked him.

"You're not..." His fingers trailed down her stomach and sneaked underneath her tank top.

"It sure doesn't seem like it..." she teased him. "You got a taste for chocolate, Charles?"

"I've tasted you, Gabs, and you don't taste like chocolate," he smirked. "Still sweet though..."

Gabrielle felt herself getting feverish again. "Get off you're too heavy," she whined. He smirked and rolled off of her. She sat up on the floor and searched for her shorts which she found lying next to him.

Charlie lay back on the floor with his hands behind his head. His green eyes stared up at her, watching her pull her shorts on. She looked down at him and ran her fingers down his muscled chest, exposed through the black t-shirt clinging to his body.

"I take it the lady is satisfied," he said with a smug grin.

"I am..." she smiled down at him. "Are things going to be awkward between us?" she asked, drawing circles on his chest.

"Only if you make it awkward... Why? You ready for another lesson?" he smirked up at her.

"Don't flatter yourself, Richardson..." she said, rolling her eyes with a grin.

He sat up to face her. He liked this new dynamic forming between the two of them. But it was too risky, and he already told himself not to make the same mistakes as his brother. "I'll be here when you need a... minor release," he said to her.

Gabrielle frowned. "You're my best friend, Charlie. I... I don't want you to think I'm just using you. You're important to me."

Charlie scooted closer to her. "Things have been a little rough for you, Gabs. I see that more than anything. I'm training you on how to defend yourself because it helps you to feel safe, right?" She nodded slowly.

"If I can bring you to euphoria for a couple of seconds as well, I don't see the problem... as long as you're comfortable with it," he assured her.

"And you're okay with that?" she asked him. "Being... friends with benefits?"

"Only if you are. Just don't catch feelings," he smirked teasingly.

"Whatever, Charlie," she said, playfully pushing him.

He chuckled and stood up to stretch. "I gotta take a leak. Why don't you order some pizza and pick out another movie," he said.

Charlie walked into the bathroom and deeply exhaled. Placing his hands on the sink, he looked down at his huge hard-on, protruding from his pants. He had never been this turned on before. Fingering Gabrielle sent him over the edge.

He released himself from his pants and grabbed his shaft to stroke himself. He threw his head back and moaned quietly as he thought about making love to Gabrielle. He thought about her perky dark brown breasts and pert nipples, standing at attention, pleading for him to suck on them.

He thought about taking her from behind as he filled his hands with her perfect round ass. He imagined himself roughly fucking her on his bed until they both climaxed. He felt the buildup and finally came, making a mess in his hands. He breathed heavily, coming down from his high.

There was a sudden knock on the door. "Hey, Charlie! I'm ordering pizza. Do you still like pepperoni and chicken or just-"

"Whatever you want, Gabs," he shouted back, through the door. He listened as she walked back to the living room. He wiped himself up, washed his hands and headed back to see her sitting on the couch. She held up the movie *Pacific Rim.*

"No, duh. He's so fine. But also because it's almost like Transformers without the Michael Bay crap," she chuckled. They turned on the movie and waited for their dinner to arrive.

~*~

Charlie woke up, looking around lazily, to see the sun shining through the window and the TV still on. They had fallen asleep on the couch. There were popcorn and twizzlers sprinkled around them and an empty pizza box on the floor.

He looked down to see Gabrielle cuddling him. Her arm lay delicately across his chest and her face was nestled into his neck. He smiled down at her peaceful face and moved her hair to get a better look at her.

"Oh, Charlie..." she moaned sleepily, hugging him tighter. He raised his brows in surprise. He thought about last night and immediately got rock hard. He quickly reached for a pillow to cover himself and accidentally knocked Gabrielle off the couch. She yelled startled when she landed on the floor.

"Shit," he muttered. He sat up and looked down at her laid out on the floor. "Sorry, Gabs."

"Do you not know how to wake up like a normal person?" she groaned, rubbing her head.
"Something startled me," he said, trying to help her up. She waved him off and pulled herself back onto the couch.

She looked around the messy living room. "Did we fall asleep on the couch?" she asked.

"Yea," he said, standing to his feet. "Hungry?" She nodded and got up to follow him into the kitchen. Charlie pulled out a box of frosted flakes, some milk, and two bowls and spoons.

"I missed hanging out with you," Gabrielle said, taking a bite of her cereal.

"Well, maybe if you visited more often than 10 years," Charlie said, giving her a snarky look.

"Ugh. Please don't start that again," she groaned. "Are we training today?"

"If you're up for it," he said. She smiled and looked down at her cereal.

"So, what were you dreaming about?" he asked her, suddenly.

"What?" she said, looking up at him surprised. "Nothing. Why do you ask?"

"You said my name. Well... more like moaned," he smirked. "What were you dreaming about?"

Gabrielle blushed furiously, giving her darkened cheeks a slight red tint. She looked down at her cereal. "I-I don't remember," she said, biting her lip.

Charlie looked at her curiously and then grinned. "You're lying." He walked towards her and spun her stool around so that she was facing him.

"Charlie!" she said annoyed.

"Come on. Tell me. What were you dreaming about?" he pressed.

Gabrielle sucked her teeth. "It's not like I remember much, Charlie. It was a dream," she huffed. "I mean you were there. That's all I remember."

"Mhm," he grunted. Looking at her intently, he firmly grasped her thigh. "Or were you dreaming about this," he said, rubbing her softly through her shorts.

Gabrielle closed her eyes as he rubbed her gently. She could already feel herself dampening. Then her eyes popped open and she pushed Charlie away from her. "You are not getting me off so early in the morning! Wait... is it morning?" she asked.

"Does it matter?" Charlie shrugged. "And since when does getting off have a time frame?"

"Yes, it does matter, Charlie! I'm a working woman and I have places to be, people to see-"

"People to do," he smirked at her.

She dramatically rolled her eyes. "Shut up, Charlie."

"Hey, you're the one having wet dreams about me," he said, raising his arms in defense.

Gabrielle dropped her mouth open in embarrassment. "I...I was not having wet dreams!"

"Are you wet?" he asked. He folded his arms across his chest and eyed her mockingly.

Gabrielle immediately shut her mouth and turned back to her cereal. "I'm done with this conversation," she said abruptly.

"Babe, you can't possibly be embarrassed after what we did last night," he teased.

"I'm not embarrassed. I just don't want you getting any ideas," she said, not looking at him.

"I already told you, you're not my type," he quipped. He was trying to get under her skin and it was clearly working.

"Whatever! You wouldn't know what to do with all of this anyway, Richardson," she said with a toss of her curls. She gave him a dirty look, but it only turned him on even more.

"Is that so?" he said with a raised brow and an amused grin. "Is that a challenge, Johansson?"

She turned around and leaned back against the table. She folded her arms across her chest defiantly. "You get me off for one night and all of a sudden you think you can handle me?"

The grin on his face widened as he approached her. He placed both hands on the table next to her, entrapping her. She tensed up as he leaned in close bringing his lips to her ear. She could feel his breath on her neck.

"Baby... I **know** I can fucking handle you." He spoke with a low, husky grunt that made her shiver.

She could feel herself getting hot again as he pulled back to look her in the eyes. There was a challenging look in his gaze that said "try me." After 20 years of knowing Charlie, she knew he was extremely competitive. Even more so than Chris. He was also a sex god, or so he was called back in school. She was not at all surprised that **this** would be the thing to excite him. And yet, she gladly walked right into the trap.

With a scoff, she pushed him away and jumped off of the stool. "That remains to be seen..." she taunted him. He smirked knowingly and followed her into the living room.

"I've been in your lair for far too long. I should head back to Eli's. Go shower. I smell like pizza and twizzlers," she said.

"Or... You could shower here," Charlie chimed.

"And be ensnared by you again?" she asked with a raised brow.

He grinned smugly. "I thought you said I couldn't handle you."

"You can't. I thought you said I wasn't your type."

"You're not."

Gabrielle rolled her eyes. "Charlie, you can just admit that I fulfill your wildest dreams."

"Well! Look at all that big game you're talking!" he laughed.

"I'm just saying..." she smirked. "Or do you help **all** your friends get off?"

"Just the ones I like..." he said, with an amused grin.

"Then let's make a bet," she said, putting her hands on her hips. He raised his brow inquisitively.

"You claim I'm not your type of girl, which is a lie. And I'm certain beyond the shadow of a doubt that you couldn't handle me anyway," she said, rolling her neck.

"Which is also a lie," he interjected, with a taunting grin.

She rolled her eyes. "Whoever caves to the other first, wins."

Charlie considered her challenge. He knew it was a set up. Either way it would involve him blowing her back out. And that was something he was trying to avoid at all costs no matter how much he wanted to. But he wasn't one to back away from a challenge...

"Alright, you're on, Johansson." Charlie grabbed his keys and held the door open for her. She gave a satisfied smirk before she gathered her things and followed him out the door.

~*~

Chris woke up feeling the soft skin of the woman lying next to him. Her arm draped over his bare chest. The sheets half covered their naked bodies.

"Gabs?" he called out groggily. He looked down and saw the familiar red hair. He groaned in frustration as he let his head fall back. Gently moving Jessica's hand, he slid out from underneath her. He grabbed a towel on the dresser and headed to the bathroom to shower.

Jessica raised her head in a daze. Her red locks cascaded over her pretty porcelain face. She touched the empty space on the bed, missing Chris's presence. When she heard the water running, she slipped out of bed and strolled to the bathroom. She saw Chris's silhouette behind the curtain and pulled it back slowly. Her eyes hungrily raked over his body, taking in his muscles, his abs, and his manhood that he scrubbed absentmindedly.

"May I join you?" she asked smoothly. When he didn't respond, she stepped into the shower behind him. She greedily rubbed her hands up and down his abs, swirling the soap on his body. She moved in front of him and pushed her large breasts against him, rubbing his manhood against her pelvis.

He looked down at her with those oceanic blue eyes that she fell in love with. As the water ran poetically over them, a pensive look painted his face as if he were in another world.

Thrown a bit off by the way he just stood there staring, Jessica decided to take the lead. She placed his hands on her backside and wrapped her arms around his neck. She kissed his neck and shoulders and pressed herself against him, willing herself to feel more of him.

"Come on, baby. We used to have morning sex all the time... Remember?" she whispered in his ear. "Take me, Chris..."

Chris grabbed her backside, gently pushing his erection into her. She cooed excitedly. He flinched when she leaned forward to kiss the corner of his mouth. He stared at her intently, hoping their sex could help him keep the face of the woman he loved out of his mind. But it was pointless. She haunted him. She consumed his every thought. The more he looked at the beautiful bombshell Jessica, the more he craved the love of his life Gabrielle.

Getting angry with himself, he roughly grabbed Jessica's waist and turned her around. He slammed her up against the shower wall, and she squealed with glee in hopes that her Christopher was back. He entered her from behind, fucking her without mercy.

"Oh, that's the Christopher I missed." She sighed with content as he pounded into her. She moaned her praises for the things he did to her body.

Chris's mind involuntarily soared back to Gabrielle. He fucked

Jessica harder and faster with each thought of Gabrielle that invaded his thoughts. Ever the gentleman, he patiently waited for Jessica to come before he came himself. As she leaned against the shower wall trying to catch her breath, Chris rinsed himself off and stepped out of the shower. Jessica followed suit, accepting a towel that he handed to her.

"I nearly forgot how good your stroke was, Christopher. It's been so long..." she smirked.

"I think you should go now, Jessica," he said, wrapping a towel around his waist.

Jessica pouted. "I thought you were enjoying my company."

"I am! ... I was... I just... I really need to get some work done. I'm sorry," he lied. He knew he really just wanted to be alone.

"That's fair," she sighed. "But you work so hard, Christopher. You're going to end up killing yourself if you don't learn to take a break."

"Yes... of course, you're right," he said impatiently.

They walked back into the bedroom and he handed her one of his shirts and a pair of his pants. "If I remember correctly, you were naked with only a raincoat when you came here last night," he said to her.

She gave him a cheeky grin. Stepping up to him, she ran her red, polished fingernails down his wet chest. "You remember correctly... You used to love when I surprised you like that."

Chris struggled to smile. He remembered quite well when Jessica entered his bedroom, wearing only a raincoat. She dropped it to the floor and pounced on him like a cat. They had a long night of rough, dirty sex where Jessica was proud to show him all he had missed.

"You can have my clothes. I will have my driver take you home," he said to her.

"That's one of the many things I love about you, Christopher. You're such a gentleman."

Chris winced at the word "love." He looked back at her and smiled weakly. "Are you hungry? I'll... make you something to eat while you get ready."

Before waiting for a response, he walked to the penthouse kitchen with a towel still wrapped around his waist. He passed Arthur's room with the door wide open. Arthur was sleeping naked on his bed with two other naked women lying next to him. Chris shook his head and closed the door to give them privacy.

He put some bread in the toaster and poured a glass of orange juice. He cooked eggs in a frying pan and poured them onto a plate for Jessica. She walked into the kitchen wearing his shirt and pants that were quite loose on her, but she made it work. Her hair was tied up into a messy bun.

"Thank you, Christopher. This was really sweet of you," she smiled. She took a seat and proceeded to eat her breakfast, while Chris leaned against the kitchen countertop. He scrolled on his phone, looking at pictures of Gabrielle. After her last bite, Jessica casually looked at Chris and then at the phone he held in his hand.

"You must really love her," Jessica said bitterly. He looked up at her with a sadness in his eyes and then back down at his phone to the object of his affection.

"It doesn't matter. I can never have her," he said, turning off his phone. "Come. The driver is waiting for you downstairs." He escorted Jessica to the car. She placed a gentle kiss on his cheek before he waved her off.

~*~

Charlie had spent hours at his gym training his men. Watching them practice their moves, he walked down the line barking orders. A few of them stopped suddenly and looked towards the door. Charlie followed their gaze to find Vladimir standing with Gabrielle. Wearing black yoga pants, a white tank top, and a pink cardigan, she stood at the door with a large bag over her shoulders. She waved with a huge smile on her face.

Charlie groaned in annoyance and strolled towards them. "Vladimir. You just let her in whenever she wants to now, huh? Just fuck whatever my orders are?"

"I, uh... I just assumed..." Vladimir stuttered.

"Oh, stop it," Gabrielle rolled her eyes at Charlie. "Thank you so much, Vlad. You're my favorite person here and I truly appreciate you," she said to him with a warm smile.

Vladimir blushed with a smile before glancing at Charlie, who was shaking his head in blatant disapproval. "I will go now," Vladimir said nervously, before walking away.

"*Vlad*? You're giving him nicknames now?" Charlie asked.

"I like him! He's my new best friend!" Gabrielle grinned.

Charlie shook his head with a smirk. "You're here kinda early, Gabs."

"I decided to take you up on your offer and leave some of my things at your place. You know... just in case," she smiled.

He raised a surprised brow and the corner of his mouth turned up into a knowing grin. His light, forest green eyes flickered with mischief.

"Besides," she said nervously. "Eli's place is getting boring. You actually have movies I like."

"Uh huh," he grinned amused. "Let me take these to my car then."

He grabbed her bags and turned back to face the men. "Continue as you were," he ordered. He led her outside to his truck and opened the trunk, placing her bags inside.

"So are those men like... your clients or something?" She asked, leaning on the car.

"I'm not Chris. I don't have clients," he said curtly. "They're more like... my team."

"So like your employees?" she guessed.

"I don't run a business, Gabs," Charlie huffed, closing the trunk.

"Well I don't really know all that much about what you do, Charlie," she said annoyed.

He looked at her, amused by her nosiness and turned on by her defiance. "I already told you I run a gym. I train men on how to fight in a variation of styles," he said, leading her back inside.

"Can I sit in? Or just... watch from the back?" she asked.

"That's not really standard protocol," he said, turning to her.

"Come on, please? I'll be really quiet," she begged.

"Don't you have work?"

"Today is my day off and they have me on call," she said, holding up her phone. "If they need me, they'll contact me."

He sighed. "Alright, but in the back. I don't need my men being distracted," he said. They walked inside and the men paused to look at their leader and the woman beside him.

"This is a fellow student. You don't need to know her name," Charlie said firmly. "She will be observing. Don't talk to her or look at her. Disobey at your own risk," he ordered them.

"Jeez, Charlie, that's a little harsh," she muttered.

"I don't tell you how to be a surgeon," he said. He pointed to the back, motioning for her to go. She rolled her eyes and quietly walked to the back to sit on the bench. She watched entranced as the men moved swiftly and effortlessly to execute some of the most complicated moves that Charlie demonstrated. They worked tirelessly, training in pairs, as Charlie watched intently, correcting them on stances, movements, and speed.

"They'll probably be so hungry after this... I wonder if there's a kitchen..." She wandered away from the area and down the hall, until she found a small kitchen.

"Ha! Jackpot! Now, let's see... bread... ham... mayo... I think I can work with this," she said, rummaging through the cabinets and fridge.

She made some sandwiches and a pitcher of lemonade. She carried a tray to the area near the lockers, towards the back of the gym, where they were training. On their break, the men walked by her to unwind and wipe themselves down with their towels.

"Oh! Is this for us?" one of them asked her. He looked at the tray seated on a bench near the lockers. She nodded with a smile.

"Sweet!" another blurted with excitement. They swarmed the bench and devoured the food.

Charlie arrived last and saw the men eating. "What the hell is this?" he asked angrily.

"Just thought you guys might be hungry," she smiled. "Made one for you too." She waved a sandwich at him.

He angrily stalked over to her and grabbed her by the wrist. He pulled her down the hallway, far away from the men, and backed her up against a wall.

"What the hell do you think you're doing?!" he snarled at her.

Gabrielle looked at him confused. "I was just trying to help, Charlie."

"I don't need you making my men soft or getting attached to them with these niceties. This is totally out of line," he snapped. He glared at her with an anger she hadn't seen before.

"I didn't mean to overstep any boundaries," she said. She looked at him worriedly, hoping he would ease up.

"You can't just come waltzing in here acting like you're my woman," he snarled at her. Leaning in, he put his hand next to her head, pinning her further to the wall.

"I-I never said I was, Charlie," she trembled. Her body reacted the closer he got to her.

Charlie felt heated. He looked at her trembling beneath him and noticed her plump lips quivering. Eyes still narrowed in frustration, he leaned in closer, hovering above her. He could feel her short breaths on his lips. They were so close.

Gabrielle felt so confused and worried. She didn't understand how she could have upset Charlie so much just by making sandwiches for his guys. She felt him encroach on her space and couldn't help but feel turned on. But she tried to push those thoughts away as he was clearly upset. She needed to know why.

Still hot and angry, Charlie focused on Gabrielle's lips. The way they trembled pulled him in. And when she bit them, he couldn't control his desire any longer. Before he could stop himself, he kissed her deeply, hungrily, and aggressively. With one hand on the wall next to her head, he wrapped the other tightly around her waist, pulling her flushed against him.

Gabrielle was completely taken off guard when Charlie kissed her. He was so aggressive with his kiss, it felt as if he had been holding it in forever. She felt as if he wanted to devour her. He kissed her like he couldn't get enough. She was so confused as to why, but she didn't want him to stop. His body felt so good flushed against hers and the grip his hand had on her waist made her tingle.

Suddenly, her phone went off, startling Charlie. He immediately released both her lips and her waist and quickly backed away from her.

Gabrielle silenced the phone on her hip and looked back at Charlie, who was breathing heavily. His eyes were still angry but filled with lust and desire.

"You should go," he muttered.

"Wha-? Charlie..." she started.

"Just, go!" he growled. She looked at him hurt and confused before running out of the gym.

~*~

"Hey!" Chris said, answering his phone.

"Hey..." Charlie answered. *"How's it going now that you've sealed the deal? Coming back home yet?"*

"Hopefully," Chris said, tapping his finger on his desk. "I'm just tying up some loose ends over here, and then we should be good to go."

"Good," Charlie sighed relieved.

"How are your men doing? New recruits adjusting?"

"Meh. I need to smack the assholes around a bit. But they're quick learners. And loyal," Charlie said.

"That's most important," Chris noted.

"Mm," Charlie grunted. There was a brief silence.

"There something on your mind, Charlie?" Chris asked.

Charlie hesitated for a moment before speaking. *"I've just been... frustrated,"* he said finally.

"With what?" Chris asked.

"With everything. You not being here. My men being compromised. Knowing the Beaumonts are on our territory. Getting these side gangs under control. Gabs..." Charlie trailed off.

Chris waited a moment for him to finish his thought, but Charlie said nothing else. "Well, I'll be home soon. Don't concern yourself with the Beaumonts. They're not a threat right now," Chris encouraged him.

Charlie scoffed on the other end and remained silent.

"Charl-"

"I fucked up," Charlie blurted.

Chris was silent for a moment. "Fucked up... how?"

"Gabs..."

"Oh," Chris said. He already knew what Charlie meant with such few words.

"Oh?" Charlie repeated.

"What do you want me to say?" Chris asked.

"I don't know. That I'm a hypocrite. That you hate me and I betrayed your trust," Charlie sighed.

"You did nothing of the sort, and I could never hate you. I told you before, Charlie. She doesn't belong to me. We couldn't be together anyway," Chris said, spinning his pen in his hand.

"I don't trust myself around her," Charlie said, rubbing his forehead in frustration. *"I become... a different person."*

"Hmm..." Chris nodded thoughtfully, chewing on his pen. He knew very well what Charlie meant. "I call it the G-Effect."

"The what?"

"The G-Effect. The Gabrielle Effect. She makes you lose all your senses."

"Was it always like this?" Chris heard Charlie sigh on the other end.

"Not this strong..." Chris admitted. Charlie loudly exhaled. "I'm guessing you kissed her," Chris spoke up.

"Mm..." Charlie grunted in acknowledgement. Among other things...

"Did she kiss you back," Chris asked.

"I don't actually know. I was too angry from arguing with her."

"Why were you arguing?"

"She's just so stubborn and frustrating."

"That much is true," Chris chuckled. "Then how did it lead to a kiss?"

"I don't know... I didn't realize what I was doing until after I had done it. We've both been a bit sexually frustrated," Charlie sighed.

"Well her, I get. You, I don't," Chris teased.

"Chris..."

"You've never lacked your fair share of women, Charlie. You have women constantly throwing themselves at you."

"They don't interest me."

"You mean they're not her," Chris corrected him. Chris could hear his brother taking another deep sigh on the other end of the line. "Listen... I get it. You often have better judgement than me," Chris continued.

"Now you're just mocking me."

Chris laughed. "I'm not, Charlie. I'm just saying... be careful. I already fucked up and I'm still paying for it. I don't want to see the same thing happen to you."

"Yea I know..." Charlie said, shutting his eyes. He leaned his head back against the wall. *"I would never forgive myself if anything ever happened to her."*

"Nothing will," Chris assured him. "I've made sure of that."

"I don't know, Chris... something feels... off," Charlie said.

"Like what?" Chris asked.

"I can't really put my finger on it," Charlie said, trying to think. *"It's just a feeling. Just... hurry up and get your ass back home. Alright?"*

"Yea, I'm trying," Chris sighed. "I gotta go. I'll talk to you later."

"Later," Charlie said before hanging up.

Chris put his head in his hands and sighed deeply. He tapped on his phone and scrolled till he reached the name he was looking for. He texted Jessica, asking her to come to his place.

~*~

16

Don't Tempt Me

~*~

"You can wait right over there, Mr. Richardson. She'll be finishing up shortly," the nurse said to Charlie.

"Thank you," he nodded. With his hands in his pockets, he stood in the corner of the waiting area.

Charlie hadn't spoken to Gabrielle for almost 3 days which was too long for them, considering how much time they had been spending together. He thought about that night he yelled at her and then kissed her, replaying the scenario over and over again. Thinking about why he got upset, what went wrong, where the miscommunication was. He came to the conclusion that he ultimately was in the wrong. He never really explained to her why he was upset and just blew up on her. And he knew why.

He felt crazed and not in control when he was around her. His mind was absorbed with all of the ways he imagined worshipping her body. The battle in his mind often manifested itself in his behavior. It was something he needed to actively work on to keep her in his life. He was anxious to apologize. And if he was being completely honest, he missed her. He missed her lips the moment his left hers. He missed touching her in the most intimate of ways. And he ached for more.

Charlie looked up and spotted a well-dressed man standing in one of the narrow corridors, talking to a few doctors. There was something about this man's stance and movement that seemed awfully familiar to Charlie. But he couldn't tell what, as the man's back was to him. He squinted trying to get a better look, but the stranger had already turned the corner.

"Bye, ladies! I'll let you know the status later!" Gabrielle said, walking out of the office. She had a beaming smile on her face that made Charlie melt. But when she laid eyes on him, that smile was quickly replaced with a frown. He immediately stood up to approach her.

"Hey," he said to her.

"Hi..." she said unnerved. She readjusted her bag on her shoulder.

"I noticed Eli's car isn't out front," Charlie said.

"Yea... had to give that thing back eventually," she chuckled nervously. "Public transportation works well too."

Charlie nodded and cocked his head up at her. "Can I… take you home?" he asked.

She hesitated. "Charlie... I...I don't thin-"

"Please," he said, cutting her off. She hunched her shoulders and nodded her head. He turned on his heels and walked her to his car.

"I'm... sorry I was such an asshole the other day. I shouldn't have snapped at you like that," he said to her, as the car pulled off.

"More like yelled," she muttered. "What was that all about?"

Charlie deeply exhaled. "I'm very particular about who talks to my men and who from my personal life they're aware of." Gabrielle nodded her head for him to go on.

"The work I do isn't for the faint of heart, Gabs. Sometimes… many of these men don't come back from what they're sent off to do," he said.

"What kind of work is that?" she asked, slightly horrified.

"I can't talk about that right now."

"Okay... so you just don't want me to be nice to them in case they don't come back ?"

"Something like that. I trust them and they trust me. But if I get attached... it just makes my job so much more difficult," he frowned.

"I understand," she said softly. There was a brief silence before Gabrielle spoke up again. "About that kiss..."

Charlie shifted uncomfortably in his seat. "It was a lapse in judgement," he said quickly.

"A lapse in judgement?"

"I was just really horny," he said, dismissively.

"You get horny when you're angry?" she laughed.

"Just with you, I guess," he smirked.

"I can't tell if that's a good thing or a bad thing," she chuckled.

"Neither. Don't try to purposely make me angry," he warned, giving her a side glance. "You annoy me enough as is."

"Likewise, you ass!" she laughed. "But wait... I thought I wasn't your type."

Charlie smirked, knowing what kind of corner she was trying to back him into. "You don't have to be my type to make me hard," he said flatly.

"Oh!" she scoffed. "That makes no sense, Charlie. Just admit how you really feel about me."

"Let's see," he said, pulling over into the parking lot of an evening bar. "You're annoying. You're stubborn. You aggravate me. You never listen. You're defiant. You're insolent. You're obnoxious."

"You sound like you're describing yourself," she teased.

Charlie gave her a side smirk. "You're not winning this bet, Gabs."

Gabrielle folded her arms across her chest and made a face. "This won't do..."

He glanced at her, trying to gauge her thoughts.

"One of us has to cave soon. I can't live like this," she huffed.

"Well then cave, baby," he teased her.

She scoffed with a roll of her eyes. "I'll think of something..." she murmured.

"You do that. In the meantime, why don't we get a drink," he said getting out of the car.

Gabrielle's eyes widened in shock. "Really? You're letting me drink?"

"Why is that so surprising?"

"Oh, I don't know. Maybe because you turn into my father whenever I drink."

"That's because you're a lightweight, Gabs. I'll make sure to watch you."

"Whatever," she said, rolling her eyes. She got out of the car and followed him into the bar and sat at a corner table. Charlie ordered a beer while Gabrielle ordered a cocktail.

"So, how's work?" he asked her.

"It's... going..."

He gave her an inquisitive look, trying to catch her eye. She looked at him and groaned. "Trying to get this program going is harder than I expected. And my new boss is a tough cookie. All these politics and rich white men pulling all the strings. Nothing is simple. I feel like I'm better off sticking to being a surgeon. I don't know why I feel the need to do more."

"It's because that's who you are, Gabs. You have a passion for helping others. There's nothing wrong with that. I'm sure it will all pay off," Charlie assured her.

She gave him a small smile, her eyes lingering on his lips. From the time he kissed her, she couldn't stop thinking about how strongly her body responded to him. She didn't like that she seemed to crave him. She didn't like having a thing for *both* Richardson brothers.

She heard the sound of pool balls clacking against each other and glanced to the side to see an area with three pool tables. "I got it!" she perked up. Charlie looked at her questioningly. "Billiards!"

Charlie looked backwards to where she was pointing to see a few guys playing pool. He turned back to her shaking his head. "You can't beat me at pool ball, Gabs. Cut it out."

"Excuse me?!" she shrieked. "You must have amnesia, Charlie, cause I kicked your ass several times at pool ball when we were teens."

"I remember that *very* differently," he said with a raised brow.

"You remember it *wrong* is how you remember it," she mocked. "What are you chicken? Afraid I'll beat you and you'll lose this bet," she teased.

A smirk crossed his face as he peered at her with newly excited light, green irises. "Alright... you're on, Johansson."

He followed her to the back, carrying his 2nd beer in his hand while Gabrielle tossed back her 2nd cocktail. She grabbed two pool sticks and handed him one. "Whoever wins the game... wins the bet," she grinned.

"And have we decided what the stakes are yet?" he asked.

"We will when we get that far," she teased. He rolled his eyes, taking another sip of his beer.

"Would you like to break or should I?" she asked.

"Ladies first," he gestured.

Gabrielle plotted how to get him to break. She turned around to adjust her white work blouse, unbuttoning the first two buttons to expose a little cleavage. She took off her blazer and placed it on a chair, before rolling up her sleeves.

"You're playing pool not wrestling me, Gabs," Charlie teased her.

"I'm just trying to get comfortable," she shrugged. She slowly leaned over the table facing him as she angled the pool stick at the cue ball. Charlie watched her carefully, his eyes lingering on her exposed cleavage pushing seductively against the pool table.

She looked up at him to catch his eye and smirked, knowing exactly what he was staring at. She hit the cue ball hard, sending them flying around the table, both solids and stripes.

"Hmm. Solids or stripes. Solids... or... stripes..." She analyzed the table for a few seconds before looking up at Charlie again. He was staring at her so intensely. She moved over to stand in front of him and bent over the table again. Her pencil skirt pulled up just below her round behind, teasing a slither of her light pink panties. Charlie cleared his throat and stepped back. He tried not to stare, but her ass seemed to lure him in.

"Stripes..." She took her shot and sent a striped ball into a hole. Pumping her fist in the air, she glanced at Charlie behind her. He was leaning on the pool stick, his light green eyes now a dark forest green. He stared at her like a ravenous predator.

"Something wrong?" she asked him.

"Just take your shot," he said quickly. She grinned at him and leaned over again, still teasing him. But the ball scratched.

"Shoot, dang it," she pouted.

"My turn," he said walking around. He aimed at a solid and

knocked two in, in one shot.

"I set that one up for you," she teased.

"Sure you did," he smirked at her. As he aimed for another shot, she perched herself on a stool on the other side of the table. He glanced up to see her crossing her legs, giving him another peek at those pink panties that kept taunting him. Her dark brown legs glistened from the light that reflected off of them. He shook his head and tried to focus but ended up shooting in a solid and a stripe.

"Well. thanks for that," she chuckled, hopping off of the stool. After analyzing the table for a few moments, she pouted. "Hm... this is a hard shot," she said, bending over in front of him. "How would you go about this?" She glanced over her shoulder and saw him stroking his beard, his eyes never leaving her body.

"You want me to help you win?" he sneered.

"Just a little friendly advice. Come on. You like good competition," she said sweetly.

He rolled his eyes and approached her, leaning his body over hers. He angled her top hand on the stick, adjusting it slightly. Placing one hand on her hip to steady her, his other hand gently guided her other hand lower on the stick. Gabrielle could feel his warm breath against the nape of her neck, tickling her ears.

His touch lingered on her arms before he slowly backed away. "There," he said, taking a quick breath.

She took her shot and sunk the ball into the hole. It wasn't long before it was Charlie's turn again. As he analyzed the table, he looked up to see her watching him. Leaning on the pool stick, she sensually bit her bottom lip as her eyes became hooded. Not from the alcohol, but something entirely different.

"I know what you're trying to do," he said to her.

She looked at him with surprise. "What am I trying to do?"

“Anything to win this bet, huh?”

“More like trying to prove a point,” she smiled innocently.

Charlie laid his pool stick on the table and approached her. “And what point is that?”

“That you want me,” she smirked at him.

Charlie rolled his eyes. “I already told you-”

“So you’re telling me that kiss meant nothing?”

“I told you it was a lapse in judgement.”

“It didn’t feel like a lapse in judgement,” she grinned smugly. She knew she was starting to annoy him.

Charlie stepped up to her, backing her against the pool table. She leaned back and quickly grabbed the edge to brace herself. He imprisoned her between his arms, gripping the edge on either side of her. She could barely make out his facial features in the dim light.

Leaning forward, he inhaled her sweet perfume. He brushed his lips against her cheek and whispered into her ear.

“Why don’t you just admit you want me to fuck you,” he said huskily.

Gabrielle felt herself dampen at those words as her heart rate quickened. She tried not to give herself away by breathing so heavily. “Don’t flatter yourself, Charlie,” she said with a small voice.

He grunted, turning his face towards her. As much as he wanted to pull away from her, her scent kept luring him back in. He grazed his lips over her earlobe, just barely touching her. He could feel her start to tremble and it brought a satisfactory smile to his face.

He whispered heatedly. “So, what you’re saying is...” He placed his hand between her thighs and lightly grazed the skin on her inner thigh. "...you don't want me to touch you..?"

He teasingly dragged his fingers up her thigh. He could hear her short breaths as her body leaned into him. Gabrielle felt herself getting feverish. Charlie's light touches were driving her crazy, but she didn't want to cave first. Now, she was wondering if any of it was worth it. Her body was crying out for him to take her.

"Tell me, baby... are you wet for me..?" he whispered in her ear and nibbled on her lobe. Before she could answer, his fingers were already up her skirt and grazing against the front of her panties. She felt the reverberation of his body move against hers as he chuckled provocatively. "Of course you are..." he grinned.

Placing his lips against her neck, he kissed her gently. His tongue crept out to taste her skin.

She closed her eyes and exhaled breathlessly. "Charlie..." Just then, he quickly removed his hand from up her skirt and distanced himself from her. She opened her eyes and looked at him with flushed cheeks and frustration aflame in her eyes.

"You're a sadist!" she blurted. He chuckled and grabbed her hand. Pulling her away from the table, he led her towards the door.

"What are you doing?" she asked.

"I'm not fucking you here," he said, glancing back at her.

"Excuse me, Charlie! Who the hell said you were at all?!"

Charlie glanced back at her with a knowing smirk. "Your body did, Gabs..."

She wanted to speak out against him but she knew her body was far more loyal to him than it was to her.

~*~

They were barely through the door when Charlie ripped Gabrielle's blouse off, sending the buttons flying everywhere. His lips locked onto hers as his hands held her body flushed against his. He grabbed her by the hips and pulled her closer, pushing his erect manhood into her.

"Charlie!" she said, tearing her mouth away from his. "This shirt was expensive!"

"I'll buy you a new one," he said quickly, before his mouth was on hers again. He kissed her vigorously, wanting to suck every inch of her body.

Gabrielle felt his hands roam all over her, caressing every curve. He walked her backwards, kissing her from her lips to her neck. Biting and licking without mercy, he elicited coos and moans from her lips. He spun her around and leaned her over the dining room table.

"You've been teasing me all fucking night," he growled. He lifted the hem of her pencil skirt up to her waist, exposing her beautiful round ass. "I've wanted to touch you all night..."

He ripped off her panties, provoking another annoyed reaction from Gabrielle. "I'll buy you a whole fucking set," he said hastily, tossing her ripped panties to the floor.

"Fuck..." He could barely keep himself together. Her perfect plump ass looked back at him inviting him for a nibble, a taste.

Gabrielle gasped loudly when she felt Charlie's fingers invade her center. She braced herself against the table for support as his fingers shamelessly rediscovered her folds. He pinched and rubbed at her nub and she nearly lost her breath. The heat from his hand against her core made her weak. She squealed as he pumped his fingers into her, his hand practically dripping with her juices.

"Ch-Charlie!" she moaned out desperately. He craned his head into her neck and kissed her.

Feeling impatient with her skirt, he tugged the whole thing

down. He lifted her feet out of it and tossed it to the side. He looked her over, nearly fully naked with just a bra on. Roughly grabbing her hips, he spun her around to face him. He wrapped his hands around both her thighs and lifted her up onto the table. Her hands roamed through his long, thick blonde hair, tugging in want. He marveled at the dark-skinned beauty before him. Her black lace bra perfectly cupped her humble breasts.

Gabrielle tugged at his shirt and he obeyed, quickly lifting it over his shoulders. He watched her for a moment as she ran her fingers down his scarred, muscled chest. He tried to give her a moment to appreciate his physique, but the moment he saw her seductively bite her bottom lip, his lips were back on hers again.

Kissing her passionately, his fingers were quick to unhook her bra before he quickly discarded that too. He licked his lips as he watched her beautiful breasts bounce joyously at their newfound freedom. With a moan, he cupped both of her breasts and brought one of her nipples into his mouth. Gabrielle threw her head back moaning loudly. Charlie gently sucked on her pert nipple, licking it and flicking it with his tongue. His lips caressed softly with each suck.

Gabrielle's body was going crazy. This feeling was almost too much for her to bear. She could feel herself coming undone as Charlie did things to her body she had not been prepared for that day. The sensation of his lips on her nipples drove her wild. The way he sucked and licked had her leaking shamelessly on his table.

"Charlie," she panted. He released her nipple with a pop from his wet lips. "Stop... teasing me," she ordered him.

He smirked amused. "You're coming apart in my hands and yet you're still so insolent."

Wrapping his hands underneath both of her thighs, he lifted her onto him as her legs wrapped around his waist. He carried her to his bedroom and laid her down on his bed.

"You were talking so much shit earlier, remember?" he said, turning her over on her stomach. "I'm not done torturing you yet..."

He ran his large palms over her firm cheeks, caressing them softly before roughly grabbing them. He smacked her ass hard, watching it jiggle as she arched off of the bed. He heard her moan into his pillow in ecstasy as he spread her cheeks apart. Lifting her ass in the air for a better angle, he eagerly licked his lips at the delicious view of her wet, dripping pussy.

"Goddamn, baby..." he moaned, as he ran his finger over her puffy, wet lips. He leaned down between her legs, spreading them further apart just enough to get access to her center.

The moment he flicked his tongue over her center, he immediately felt her legs quiver. He held her ass in his hands, spreading her cheeks further apart, and licked her pussy from front to back.

"Charlie!" She stifled her moans into the pillow. He licked her again, wiggling his tongue between her folds and sucking her clit. He could feel her getting wetter as he licked at her juices oozing from her center.

"Baby, you taste so fucking good," he said in-between licks. He continued to lick her, sucking and flicking her clit. He pushed his tongue into her canal and heard her moan loudly. He fucked her slowly than faster with his tongue, frequently taking breaks to tease her clit and lick her from top to bottom and bottom to top.

"Charlie, please!" she begged.

He gently placed her back down on the bed and rolled her onto her back. She was panting heavily with her eyes closed shut, chewing rabidly on her lip. Her pussy dripped relentlessly on his bed sheets.

"Still think I can't handle you, baby?" he asked. He grinned down at her smugly.

"You're such an ass," she groaned.

"Well, I just handled your ass... and I'm not done..." he teased. He ran his finger over her swollen, wet lips still dripping on his bed. "I just wanna hear you say it..."

"I will not!" she said defiantly.

"What was that?" he said. He slipped his finger inside her and rubbed rough, tantalizing circles on her nub with this thumb. Her breathing hitched and she moaned loudly at his intensity. "I didn't hear you, baby..." he said. He inserted another finger and finger-fucked her harder.

"Yes! You can handle me! You win!" she moaned loudly. She bucked her hips towards him and grabbed her breasts trying to contain herself.

"That's what I thought..." he grinned. He got off the bed to remove his pants and discard his boxers. She watched as his muscles flexed with each movement. Her eyes widened when she saw how big he was. Big dicks seemed to run in the family and she was not prepared.

"Jeez, Charlie!" she said, looking at him. He reached for a condom from his dresser and skillfully wrapped it around his manhood.

"Don't worry, baby, I'll go slow... at first..." He leaned over her, with both hands on either side of her. He could feel her tense up beneath him.

"Relax, Gabs," he whispered. "I won't hurt you, I promise. Just... enjoy it..."

She nodded and waited underneath him with great anticipation. She felt his large manhood glide over her wet lips and her stomach tightened. He rubbed himself against her first before slowly entering into her. They both moaned together as they adjusted to each other. His size and her tightness.

Charlie looked down at Gabrielle breathing heavily. "You okay?"

he asked. She nodded with a smile. Charlie made gentle thrusts, trying not to go too fast or too hard for his own sake. He had not expected her to be so tight and it felt amazing. Too amazing as he was afraid he would come right then and there.

With each thrust, Gabrielle tightened around him. "Fuck," Charlie groaned in her ear, trying not to come undone.

"Faster, baby," Gabrielle moaned. She made him melt with anticipation. He grabbed the back of her neck and increased his thrusts as his hips fell into hers over and over. She bit down hard onto his shoulder, trying not to scream from the pleasure he was giving her.

The little squeals that came from Gabrielle with each thrust both amused Charlie and turned him on. He loved the unique sounds she would make whenever he made contact with her body. He lowered his mouth to her lips, kissing her with the same hungry passion as before. He moved down to her neck, sucking on the soft skin and eliciting coos from her.

He pounded her harder and faster as her breathing got shorter, gasping for air. "Oh! Charlie! Fuck, baby!" she screamed into his shoulder. He could feel her body tensing as she prepared to climax. He lifted her leg up to his waist to get a better angle, pounding deeper into her. He growled into her neck, trying to keep his own climax down.

Gabrielle let out a high-pitched moan as she met her release. It vibrated throughout her entire body. Her legs shook, including the one in Charlie's hand. Her back arched significantly, until she could come down from her high.

Charlie came as soon as Gabrielle did, groaning into her neck. He heard her breathing heavily as they both sunk into the bed, tired and exhausted. He eventually pulled out of her and rolled over next to her, trying to catch his breath. They looked at each other, covered in each other's sweat and started laughing.

"You're still an ass," she chuckled, in-between breaths.

"And you're still annoying... though you have a great ass," he smirked. He reached for a handful of her ass and she squealed with laughter.

"I thought I wasn't your type," she pouted at him. Her brown eyes plunged deep into his green ones.

Charlie's lips slowly spread into a smile. "You're my only type, Gabs..." He leaned in and kissed her.

~*~

"This was one of the most pleasant negotiating experiences, Mr. Richardson. Not only have we made an agreement but we're also expanding. My partners and I are overwhelmingly satisfied. That is no easy feat!" Mr. Suku said, shaking Chris's hand.

"I am grateful, Mr. Suku. I look forward to doing further business with you," Chris smiled. He stood from the table and bowed to the men before heading out the door.

His phone immediately rang and he already knew who it was.

"Well?" his uncle Eric's voice came from the other end of the line.

"It's settled. We're expanding further into Southeast Asia reaching Vietnam, South Korea, and now Indonesia."

"Brilliant! I knew I could count on you, Christopher. That's why I've already had your flight booked to bring you and Arthur back home."

"Thank you, Uncle. Though, I'm not so sure Arthur wants to leave just yet," Chris smirked.

"Too bad for him. He's had enough partying for a while. I'll see you when you return," Eric said.

Chris hung up the phone and headed into the car that was waiting for him. When he got to his hotel, who was waiting for him at his door but Jessica.

"I'm guessing you've heard," he said, fiddling with his keys.

"News travels fast in this business, you know that. Congratulations, Mr. Richardson. You officially have the largest international territorial expansion in the industry," she mused with pursed lips.

"You say that like it's something to be proud of," he grimaced.

"Of course it is!" she said surprised. "You've accomplished in 5 years what most of these men have failed to accomplish in 20! You're a legend."

"I beg to differ," he sighed. "But at least now I get to go home." He opened the door and stepped inside.

"Home? So soon? Come on, stay Christopher. Celebrate this great achievement with me. Japan has been so good to you," she said. She grabbed his arm as he pulled off his jacket.

"It has, but I need to get home. I still have a company to run. Things to do and people to see," he said, packing his things.

"You mean *her*," Jessica huffed, folding her arms across her chest. Chris looked at her with a frown. He gently held her by her arms and stared into her emerald green eyes.

"Listen, Jessica. I had a lot of fun with you. But, you and I are not compatible," he said softly.

"That's not what you were saying last night when you were 9 inches deep in me," she sneered at him.

"I mean emotionally, Jessica," he sighed. "We're not a good fit. You know this just as well as I do. We're unstable. Volatile. It has never worked between us and I highly doubt it ever will." He let go of her and continued to pack.

"You used to love our volatile relationship!" she said exasperated. "There was passion! There was excitement! There was intrigue! And the sex was amazing!" She tried to reason.

"There was also stress, depression, anxiety, violence, lies, manipulation..." he said, looking at her sadly. "Our relationship was toxic. We're not good for each other."

"But... I still love you, Christopher. We can still have something together. We can make it work. Don't you love me anymore?" Tears brimmed in her desperate, sad, green eyes as she clung to his arm.

Chris took a deep breath as he slung his backpack over his shoulder. He looked down at her and gently passed his fingers against her tear-stained cheek. "I'll always care about you, Jessica. But my heart has... and always will belong to another... I'm sorry."

He gave her one last remorseful look, before leaving her standing there alone.

~*~

Nestled next to him on his bed, Gabrielle gently touched the skin on Charlie's chest. With her head just underneath his neck, she traced the outline of his scars with her pointer finger.

Charlie looked down at her, watching her pay intimate attention to every detail of his skin. He had one arm wrapped around her and the other rested behind his head.

"When are you going to tell me the story of these scars?" she asked softly.

"You don't need to hear those stories," he said, kissing the top of her head.

She frowned and raised her head to look up at him. "I don't like knowing that someone hurt you," she choked out. He looked upon her with tender eyes, moved by the love and concern he saw in her own.

"It's in the past, Gabs." He stroked her cheek with the pad of his thumb.

"I should have been there," she said, averting her sad eyes away from him. She looked at the scars on his chest again, touching them softly, before lowering her lips to his chest. She delicately caressed the hardened scar tissue. Rubbing her lips against them, she traced the path from his collarbone to his pectoral muscles to his abdomen.

Charlie looked down and watched as Gabrielle pulled the sheet away from his waist, exposing him. She kissed the soft spot between his waist and his thigh, dangerously close to his manhood.

"Ah... there's no scars down there, Gabs..." Charlie said to her hesitantly.

"I know..." she grinned. She looked up at him with a devious smirk that made him want to flip her on her back and take her all over again.

She left soft fleeting kisses on his shaft and poked her tongue out to run it along his length. She could feel the rigidness of his veins as she worked her tongue around him.

Charlie closed his eyes and let his head fall back. He got lost in the feeling of her tongue caressing him. He shivered as he felt her lips enclose the tip of his head, her tongue playing peek-a-boo with him.

"Shit..." he moaned. Being gentle, she sucked softly, making sure to give attention to his jewels underneath. Her tongue danced with his shaft before devouring him entirely into her mouth.

Gabrielle began to pick up speed as she sucked long and hard. Charlie groaned in pleasurable agony. He could feel himself tighten as he neared his release.

Gabrielle quickly removed her mouth from him and looked up at him with a wicked grin. He looked down at her appalled and almost angry. "You fucking tease," he growled.

"Who? Me?" she said innocently. She sat up and straddled him between her legs, looking down at him with authority.

"Don't make me take over," he threatened her. "I will fuck the shit out of you."

"Don't be so impatient, Charlie," she chuckled. She leaned over, pressing her palms against his chest and kissed him softly on his lips. He gripped her hips and felt her maneuver herself above him, slowly sliding down onto him. They moaned in unison as she began to rock against him. She started slowly before moving faster and more aggressively.

Charlie looked up at her face. Her eyes were closed and she seemed to be in another world. Her breasts jumped playfully as she bounced on him with high intensity. Her quick desperate pants made him even more excited. He roughly grabbed her ass with both hands, controlling the speed and force of their thrusts. She whimpered when she felt his hand creep from her ass, up to her abdomen, to take possession of her breast.

"Ch-Char-Charlie! I'm, I'm gonn-"

But before she could finish she was already coming. Charlie held her firmly in his hands as he helped her ride out her high. He roughly grabbed her ass with both hands and pumped into her even harder and faster, making her squeal until he came himself. He groaned and collapsed, breathing heavily on the bed. Gabrielle leaned over to lay on top of him, matching his heavy breathing.

"Shit, Gabs, you wear me out," Charlie chuckled, rubbing his hand against her lower back. She giggled against his chest and raised herself to look into his eyes.

"You havin' a hard time keeping up with me, Richardson?" she said teasingly.

Charlie smirked at her and gave her ass a hard slap, making her squeal. "You already know I can more than keep up with you."

She giggled and pulled herself off of him to check her hair in the mirror. Charlie sat up on the edge of the bed watching her. His eyes roamed her naked body, unable to get enough of her.

"Come here," he said, grabbing her hand. He pulled her towards him. She stood in front of the bed in-between his legs. He looked her up and down, taking in every detail that he missed when he was busy ripping her clothes off the night before.

"You're so fucking beautiful," he said, pulling her closer. He ran his hands up her arms, down her legs, and around her waist. He grabbed her hips and squeezed her ass possessively. She smiled down at him, entangling her fingers in his long, blonde hair. She felt his lips press against her stomach as he massaged her ass with both hands.

"At this rate, we'll never leave your bedroom," she teased him.

"I have no problem with that," he smirked against her stomach.

"Come on, Charlie. I wanna train today," she said, tugging playfully at his ear lobe. He gave her stomach one last kiss and her ass a final squeeze, before he finally pulled himself away.

"Alright, alright. If you insist," he grinned up at her.

~*~

After arriving back in Philly, Chris departed ways with Arthur. He dropped his things at his apartment and called Charlie, but he didn't answer his phone. Next, he called the concierge.

"I believe he's at his gym with a young woman, sir," the man said.

Chris thanked him and hung up the phone. "They must be training." He changed into a fitted sweater, a pair of jeans and headed over to Charlie's gym.

~

"Ah ah! Wrong foot!" Charlie said. He kicked Gabrielle's foot out from under her, causing her to fall to the floor. She landed hard and looked up at him with a snarl on her face. Leaning back, she flipped onto her feet and charged at Charlie. She wrapped her leg around his foot and pushed him back, causing him to fall to the ground.

"Ha!" she grinned, sitting on top of him. In a flash, he flipped her over and slammed her on the ground. He smirked down at her. "Don't get too cocky," he mocked.

She growled at him and swung her legs to jump up. She went to flip him but he pinned her arms behind her back, putting her in a similar deadlock where she couldn't move.

"And here we are again," he teased. She struggled to break free, until she paused to think of a strategy. She elbowed him in the stomach, causing him to release her with a groan. She spun around, grabbing him by the waist and put a foot behind his foot before pushing him to the floor. He landed on his back with a hard thud, knocking the wind out of him.

She sat on top of him with a superior grin on her face. He looked at her wide-eyed and then shook his head smiling. "That's not what I taught you to get out of that lock..."

She ran a finger down his sweaty chest. "I improvised..."

A grin was plastered on his face as he watched her lean down to ensnare his lips in a kiss. "I thought you wanted to train," he smirked. He kissed her deeply, wrapping his arms around her waist and hugging her body to his.

"I do," she whimpered. "You're just so... distracting." She finally pulled her lips away from him. "Every time I see you I just wanna jump your bones," she confessed. "Shoot... that was supposed to be a thought bubble..."

Charlie laughed and pulled her back down on top of him, capturing her lips with his again. She instinctively wrapped her arms around his neck, entangling her fingers in their favorite spot at the nape of his neck. Charlie angled himself upward as he tightly wrapped one strong arm around her waist and the other roughly grabbed a handful of her ass. Gabrielle moaned into his mouth at the sensation of his aggressiveness towards her.

"Umm... hey, guys." Chris cleared his throat to make them aware of his presence.

Charlie immediately released Gabrielle as she scrambled to get off of him. Her eyes widened in shock to see Chris standing at the entrance of the gym.

"C-Chris??" she stammered, completely startled.

Chris leaned against the wall with his hands in his pockets. He watched the two of them scramble to pull themselves together. He didn't know how to interpret seeing his brother groping and kissing the woman he loves.

Charlie jumped out of the ring and Gabrielle cautiously followed after him. He smiled as he walked up to Chris and pulled him into a tight embrace. "I didn't know you were arriving today. You should have told me. I would have picked you up from the airport," Charlie said.

"It's okay. I didn't really want to interrupt your schedule," Chris smiled back. He glanced at Gabrielle who was staring at him nervously. She bit her lip in that cute way she does when she's anxious. He smiled at her and she returned a nervous smile back, though concern still painted on her face.

"Hey, Gabs," Chris said to her.

"H-hey...Chris..." she said, meekly.

"We should get dinner so you can catch us up on your trip to Japan," Charlie said.

"Actually... I think I should go," Gabrielle interrupted. She grabbed her bag and looked between both of them. "I'll... see you guys later..." She hurriedly walked out the door.

~*~

"You should have told me you were coming," Charlie said, driving down the freeway.

"I wanted to surprise you," Chris chuckled.

Charlie shot him a harsh glare. "When have I *ever* liked surprises?"

"I'd like to think I'm the exception."

"You're not."

Chris chuckled to himself and looked out of the window. "So... are you guys like... a thing now?" Chris said, breaking the silence.

"No," Charlie said abruptly. "We're just... having a little bit of fun."

"Dangerous fun," Chris said.

"Is this a guilt trip?"

"It's not. I'm just trying to make sure you're being careful."

"It's not like we're out in public together, Chris. Besides... I didn't mean for this to happen. It just... did. It's hard to resist her," Charlie said, feeling guilty.

"Well, I can't argue with you there..." Chris trailed off, picking at a thread on his shirt.

Charlie furrowed his brows in confusion. "I...I thought that you moved on from her."

Chris looked at him startled. "What gave you that idea?"

"I thought you were back with Jessica," Charlie said.

"Je-Jessica? Why would you think I was with Jes-Arthur..." Chris groaned, covering his eyes.

"He said you guys were with each other all the time and fucking like rabbits. Was he lying?"

Chris groaned. "... No. But I'm not back with her either. It was just sex. She helped me get rid of the urge..." Chris muttered in embarrassment.

"...Shit, Chris!" Charlie said in aggravation.

"What?"

"Now, I feel like a fucking asshole! I should have just asked you instead. I don't know why I took Arthur's word for it," Charlie sucked his teeth.

"It's not your fault, Charlie. It's just... shit. It's all shit," Chris sighed. Suddenly, Chris's phone went off. He saw Arthur's name on the caller ID and picked up.

"Miss me already, Arthur?"

"Chris? Think I've gotten myself into a wee bit of trouble, mate," Arthur said, raggedly on the other end.

"Arthur, we literally just got back to the States. How are you already in trouble?" Chris said. He looked at Charlie who rolled his eyes.

"All I did was stroll into a bar. Ran into something called a Hammerhead, who apparently has beef with the Richardsons because once they heard that name I was attacked," Arthur groaned.

"What?! Where are you?!" Chris shouted. He took down Arthur's location and the two brothers sped off to find their cousin.

~

It was pouring rain when they arrived at the bar Arthur said he was at. The boys rushed inside. While Charlie scoped the area for Arthur, Chris approached the bartender.

"Excuse me. Have you seen a tall British guy? Probably drunk, a bit of a prick?" Chris asked.

"Oh... yea..." the bartender said, cleaning a glass with a towel. "Real ladies man, that one. Got into a bit of a brawl with some other asshole. Had my security drag them out back. They might still be there."

"Thanks," Chris said, motioning to Charlie. They ran out the back of the bar and found Arthur lying on the ground in a huge puddle. He was clutching the side of his stomach, which was bleeding profusely.

"Shit! Arthur!" Chris said, rushing to his side. The boys held him up on each side. They struggled to walk him back to Charlie's car, trying to see through the pouring rain.

"We've gotta take him to a hospital," Charlie said, starting the engine.

"We can't," Chris said, wiping his forehead. "We have to keep him low-key. His presence here isn't supposed to be known. Besides, if he was really shot by a Hammerhead, then they'll have eyes all over the hospital and send someone to finish the job."

"Dammit." Charlie groaned and put his head back on the seat. "Then what do we do?"

Chris thought for a moment and then looked at Charlie. "...Gabs." Charlie looked at his brother like he was crazy. "She's a surgeon. We'll ask her to fix him up," Chris insisted.

"She's gonna ask questions, Chris..."

"Then we won't tell her," Chris said firmly. Charlie groaned and took off towards Eli's house.

~*~

Gabrielle sat on the couch eating a tub of peanut butter and watching Lord of the Rings.

"Don't you lead my girl, Eowyn, on, Aragorn! You can't just come into her life like that and then disappear! And then return like nothing happened! Freakin' men!" she groaned into her tub of peanut butter. She was still reeling from Chris's sudden return.

Suddenly the doorbell rang. She got up and opened the door to a soaking wet Chris and Charlie, holding up a half-conscious Arthur.

"What the hell?!" she squealed at them.

"We need your help," Chris said, stepping into the house.

"What happened to Arthur?" she asked frantically, as they sat Arthur down on the couch.

"He was injured," Charlie said, trying to hold Arthur up.

"No freaking duh! You need to get him to a hospital!" she panicked.

"We can't!" they both said in unison. She looked at them wide-eyed.

"Please, Gabs... We need you to help him," Chris pleaded. Her eyebrows curled with apprehension. She glanced at Arthur who was dimming in and out of consciousness.

"Put him on the dining room table," she said to them finally.

Arthur grunted in pain as they picked him up and followed her into the dining room. When they laid him flat on the table, Gabrielle pushed a towel to his waist. Arthur's eyes bulged as he groaned in agony.

"Push this firmly on his wound. Don't let go," she instructed Chris. "Charlie, there's a first aid kit underneath the sink in the bathroom. I'll be right back," she said running up the stairs.

Charlie returned with the first aid kit and Gabrielle ran down the stairs with a threading kit. "Let me see," she said, moving Chris's hand. She lifted the towel to see Arthur's waist still bleeding. "Shoot. It won't stop bleeding. Press it down again."

Chris held the towel down as Gabrielle put some hot water in a pot and brought it over to the dining room table. She dipped another towel into the water and removed the towel from his stomach. Dabbing away at the blood, she felt at his abdomen.

"There's...there's something still in here," she said, feeling his abdomen. "Guys... you... you really need to take him to the hospital. I don't have the right equipment for this. He needs to be sterilized. He needs-"

"Please, Gabs. A hospital is not an option for us right now. We need YOU," Chris said, looking her intensely in the eyes. She looked back at him with worry and fear completely consuming her face.

"Go grab that thick cloth on the table and bring it back here," she said, rushing to the kitchen. She grabbed a large metal butcher knife and placed it on the burner. Chris handed her the cloth which she rolled up and placed in Arthur's mouth.

"What's that for?" Charlie asked. Gabrielle glanced at him and then looked back at Arthur.

"Arthur... just breathe, okay?" she said, trying to calm him down. She ran her finger over the wound and felt the hard object. When she dug a pair of tweezers into the wound, Arthur screamed out loud, biting hard onto the cloth in his mouth.

"Hold him!" Gabrielle instructed them. "I'm sorry, Arthur, I've almost got it!" She dug the tweezers deeper and pulled out a small round-shaped bullet. More blood gushed from his wound. She ran to get the knife from the burner, and the men looked at her with wide-eyes as she wielded the fiery-red butcher knife.

"I'm going to cauterize the wound. Make sure he doesn't move!" she ordered them. She placed the hot knife on his wound. Arthur's screams drowned out the sizzling sound it made as the smell of his burnt flesh filled the room.

“Breathe, Arthur! Just breathe!” she said, holding the knife down. She counted a few seconds and removed the knife. The bleeding stopped and his skin had been singed together. She inspected the wound and wiped the excess blood.

Charlie and Chris watched her wipe the sweat from Arthur’s forehead with a wet towel as his breathing slowed. “I’m so sorry, Arthur,” she whispered remorsefully.

Chris exhaled, relieved. “Thank you, Gabs.”

Gabrielle glared at both of them. “Are you guys going to tell me what’s going on? Why was this bullet inside of him?” she demanded.

“We-we can’t tell you that,” Charlie said.

“Bullshit! You don’t get to storm in here at 2 in the freaking morning asking me to stitch up your nearly dead cousin and not tell me what happened!” she said angrily.

“Gabs, I know you’re angry. You have every right to be. And we wish we could tell you. But we can’t. It’s for your own safety,” Chris explained, hoping to calm her down.

“I’m not some freaking damsel in distress, Chris! I can protect myself! I want to know what’s going on!” she snapped.

“We know very well you can protect yourself, Gabs. But trust us enough to know that we aren’t telling you for a reason! We’re trying to keep you safe,” Charlie explained.

Gabrielle smacked her forehead and groaned in frustration. She looked at Arthur who was finally breathing regularly. “Arthur could have died,” she glared at them.

“And thanks to you, he didn’t,” Chris said.

She sighed heavily again. They watched her pace the room with her hands on her hips, shaking her head in frustration. She finally stopped and looked at them. "You're both a pain in my ass. 8 years later and I still can't stand either of you," she groaned. "Fine... I'm not going to push it... for now." They both sighed with relief.

"Move him to the couch. He needs to get some rest," she told them.

"We can't. He has to leave with us," Chris said.

"Excuse me? No, the hell he won't!" she snapped.

"Gab-" Charlie started.

"Listen! This is MY patient now. I just dug a bullet out of one of his vital organs and cauterized his freaking gunshot wound! *Without* proper sanitation! I need to make sure your cousin doesn't go into freaking shock or cardiac arrest! You're not taking his ass anywhere! Unless you want his wound to pop back open and watch him bleed out!" she snarled.

The brothers exchanged surprised looks before looking back at her. They decided to back down.

"That's what I thought," she sighed. "Listen... Eli practically lives at Tanya's house. Arthur can stay here and rest. I'll look after him. But he is not leaving this house until I know for sure that he's going to be okay. If you want, you guys can stay here too. You're soaking wet and you look exhausted." Charlie and Chris looked at each other and nodded in confirmation.

"We just gotta talk some things out," Charlie said. He grabbed Chris by the shoulder and pulled him to the side.

"Whatever," she said, rolling her eyes. She turned back to the couch to tend to Arthur.

"I gotta find out why the Hammerheads attacked him. I haven't had issues with them in years. I don't know why they would randomly attack," Charlie whispered. "I have to find out what's going. They may have been the ones to take out my men."

"I really don't want you going out there by yourself. Let me come with you," Chris insisted.

"No. You need to be here when Arthur wakes up. Make sure he doesn't reveal anything to Gabs, and get as much information out of him as possible," Charlie said.

Chris frowned. "Yeah. You're right. Okay, go. And keep me updated. I wanna know where you are and what you're doing at all times. First sign of trouble and I'm coming after you."

Charlie grinned at his brother. "I expect nothing less." Charlie walked over to Gabrielle who was kneeling next to Arthur, wiping away the sweat from his brow.

"I gotta go," he said to her. She looked up at him in confusion and stood to her feet.

"What? Why? It's so late, Charlie. Just stay... please," she begged him.

"I can't, Gabs. I gotta go investigate what happened. But I promise, I'll be back," he smiled at her. He raised a hand to her cheek and caressed it softly. Her eyes closed and she leaned into his touch. Chris watched inconspicuously as she walked Charlie to the door.

"Please be careful," she said with worry in her eyes. Charlie smiled at her lovingly. He wanted so badly to kiss her lips. But out of respect for his brother, he resisted and pecked her on the cheek instead.

"I will," Charlie said. He turned to Chris who was watching them and nodded. Chris nodded back. Charlie left the house, closing the door behind him, and headed out into the night.

~*~

17

All for One

~*~

Gabrielle watched helplessly as Charlie walked out of the house, closing the door behind him. She stood there for a moment, in silence, with a soft prayer on her lips for his safe return.

Turning around, she startled herself when she remembered that Chris was still there. Watching her.

She hesitantly looked at him before speaking. "I-... Eli has some clothes you can borrow. You guys are about the same build, I think," she said to him.

Chris looked at her with softness in his eyes. "I appreciate that..."

He seemed to be analyzing her, and his unwavering gaze made her feel uncomfortable. She habitually chewed on her bottom lip and awkwardly walked past him, making a very obvious effort not to touch him in the process.

"You can stay in this room for the night," she yelled back to him, as she headed down the hallway. She turned into one of the empty rooms and searched the dresser. Rummaging through, she eventually found a pair of sweats and a black t-shirt. She turned around and startled herself again to see Chris standing in the doorway.

"Jeez! What are you a cat!?" she blurted.

"I didn't mean to scare you..." he said softly.

She rubbed her forehead anxiously. "It's fine. Here's a pair of sweats and a shirt," she said, placing the clothes on the bed. "I'll get you a towel."

She started to walk past him when he gently grabbed her wrist, keeping her from exiting the room. She looked down at his hand on her wrist before looking up at him with a suppressed anger bridling in her eyes.

"Can we talk?" he asked with a tinge of vulnerability in his tone.

"What is there to talk about, Christopher?" she said curtly.

"...About us, Gabs..."

Gabrielle scoffed in disbelief. "There is no us, Chris." She yanked her wrist out of his hand. "As far as you're concerned, there never was."

Chris sighed with regret. She had every right to be upset. He knew he couldn't tell her the entire truth about what was going on, but he didn't want her to go on thinking he felt indifferent about her.

"You need to know that my feelings for you, Gabs, are... they're real... they're deep... and they're strong... but they're complicated. My... my love for you is so intense, baby, that sometimes it scares me," he tried to explain.

Gabrielle felt shaken by this declaration, and it angered her. His flip flopping was messing with her head. "Love?! You told me that you didn't love me at all, Chris! That you were just horny, like I was some toy to make your dick wet. You didn't reciprocate how I felt!"

"Baby, I told you... there are some things that I can't open up to you about, because I'm trying to keep you safe. You mean more to me than you can possibly imagine."

"But safe from what?!"

"I can't tell you that, Gabs. Believe me, I really wish I could because it would make things so much easier. But I can't... I honestly can't," he said exasperated.

She slumped her shoulders in defeat. "Well... it's not like it matters anyway because I'm already over you. I've moved on so don't waste your breath." She crossed her arms defiantly.

He peered into her eyes intensely, searching and feeling her out. "I don't believe you," he said finally.

"I don't care what you believe, Christopher Richardson," she scoffed.

"Then... kiss me," he said to her.

Gabrielle's eyes bugged. "Excuse me!" she blurted.

"If you don't have feelings for me anymore... if you truly don't love me, then this kiss will mean nothing. And I'll leave you alone," he bargained.

She rolled her eyes and took another step back. "You're being ridiculous."

"Then prove me wrong, Gabs," he said, his eyes never leaving hers.

She considered his challenge for a moment and bit her lip. "And you'll leave me alone about this?" she asked.

Chris nodded. "I won't bother you about it again," he promised.

Gabrielle shortly exhaled and looked to the side with frustration. "Fine.... One kiss."

She looked up at him nervously and visibly gulped. His purposeful look already made her regret her decision. He took two steps towards her, and she panicked. As she tried to back away, he reached around and grabbed her by her waist, pulling her close to him. He held her body tightly against his. Though she pushed her hands against his chest to give them some distance, he moved her hands out of the way and tilted her chin up so that she was staring directly into his eyes.

Chris searched her eyes knowing... *hoping* in his heart that she still felt for him the way he felt for her. He lowered his lips to hers and kissed her softly. She was slightly resistant as he sensually sucked on her bottom lip. Her body shivered involuntarily against him. He could almost hear the raging battle of emotions in her mind as her hands weakly tried to push him away while her chest heaved against him in want. He pulled her in tighter, waiting for her to fully accept him the way he hoped she would.

But Gabrielle willed herself to push him away. She quickly pulled back, removing her lips from his. "See? Nothing," she said quickly.

Chris was startled by the way she abruptly distanced herself. He looked down to see that her arms were extended in an attempt to keep him at arm's length. "Gabs-" he started.

"There's nothing, Chris!" she whimpered, not even believing herself. "Just... leave it alone!"

Chris could feel his heart ferociously ripping at the seams with these words. He struggled to fight back the tears threatening to escape as he reluctantly released her from his embrace.

"I'm... I'm sorry," he whispered with such sorrow, as his head dropped. Gabrielle felt his heart drop and she could feel her heart dropping with it.

"I'll go- get you that towel," she said, swallowing thickly.

She rushed out of the room and hurried down the hallway before her body slumped against the wall. She tried desperately to catch her breath as her eyes watered and her heart opened up to pour out the anguish. The agonizing mix of pain and want tore at her insides. Who was she kidding? She craved Chris more than she was willing to admit.

She sloppily wiped her wet face when she heard Arthur stir for just a moment before he fell deeper into his slumber.

Chris peeled off his damp clothes with such defeat and dropped them on the bathroom floor with a splat. With a heavy sigh, he stepped into the shower. He tilted his head back and let the warm water run over his face, through his hair, and down his tense body. He was thankful for the water to help disguise the tears cascading from his eyes.

I fucked up, he thought to himself. *I've lost the love of my life...*

Less than a few moments later, he heard the shower curtain pull back. He opened his eyes to see Gabrielle staring at him with bloodshot, watery eyes filled with pain and desire.

She took in his full image, staring him down from head to toe, appreciating his tall, muscular build. She stepped into the shower, allowing the water to soak her shorts and tank top. She met Chris's gaze as his eyes plunged into hers.

His hand throbbed, aching to hold her again. He hesitated to touch her, not willing to risk the mistake he made before. He watched her anxiously, waiting for her to give him permission.

"Show me..." she breathed out. "Show me that you love me."

Chris immediately pulled Gabrielle to him, devouring her with a passionate and possessive kiss. She returned his kiss with equal ferocity, allowing his tongue entrance to explore her mouth. His hands were eager to reacquaint themselves with her body. He firmly grabbed her ass, feeling the soaked shorts and remembering she was still wearing clothes.

Pushing her back against the shower wall, he lifted her tank top over her head and threw the wet material on the bathroom floor with a plop. He admired the way her hair started to curl from the water. Chris watched the droplets trace down her stunning dark brown skin, falling from her shoulders towards her tear-drop smooth breasts.

"You… are so perfect," he smiled at her. Her cheeks puffed up from her smile and his lips instantly crashed into hers again. He palmed her breasts as the water provided the perfect lubrication to massage her plump softness. His mouth descended from her lips to her neck, licking at the water nourishing her skin. Her nipples slipped between his fingers before he took them into his mouth. He suckled it softly and let his tongue swirl around her areola.

His hands strayed to her hips to remove the drenched shorts and panties she was wearing. After discarding her wet clothes, he knelt down in front of her as the water sprayed down her body and over the top of his head and shoulders.

Gabrielle gripped what she could on the wall, only managing to catch the soap ledge as Chris lifted her leg over his shoulder. She felt his lips softly kiss her inner thigh before they landed on her mound. He nuzzled her center affectionately and laid his mouth on her core. She trembled, trying her best to keep steady as his tongue lapped at her heaven like a starving dog who hadn't had nourishment in weeks. Her moans echoed in the bathroom as his tongue sucked and flicked her clit.

Chris slowly dipped his tongue into Gabrielle's center before picking up speed. He could feel one of her hands running eagerly through his hair as she pushed her pelvis further into his face.

"Chris…" she moaned in agony. "Please, baby…" He could feel her getting weak and decided to stop the torture and give her what she really needed.

He planted small kisses along the length of her body as he rose to his feet. His onslaught of kisses finally ceased as he looked into her eyes, holding her gaze with purpose.

"Gabrielle," he said with a serious tone. He leaned forward, grazing his fingers against her pussy. His fingers played with her but he did not allow her to break his gaze.

"Tell me," he said, searching her eyes. She turned her head with a whimper, distracted by his playful fingers. But he used his other hand to redirect her head and hold her gaze once more. "Tell me," he repeated. "Tell me that you still love me."

She looked into his eyes and saw his sincerity. He was very serious. Serious and desperate. She was overwhelmed by the way he looked at her.

"I...I love you, Chris," she said finally. "I never stopped loving you."

She saw a glimmer of excitement play in his eyes before his body completely swallowed her. Cupping her face in his hands, he hungrily kissed her. She could feel the weight of his love and lightness of his relief all at once in that kiss.

"I missed you so much..." he whispered huskily in her ear. His curious hands strayed down her sides and over her hips before caressing her ass.

She pulled back to look at him. "How much?" she said playfully, trying to provoke him.

Giving her a small smirk, he spread her cheeks apart and pressed his manhood against her core. He reached for his shaft and stroked himself before slowly inching his way into her. The volume of her moans increased with each inch that entered her.

Chris couldn't tell if it was because he was standing that made Gabrielle feel extraordinarily tight. He grunted, resting his head on her shoulder for a minute, as he tried to adjust.

"Are you okay," she asked, nuzzling him with her face.

"Yea, babe," he breathed out. "You're just... incredible." He slowly started to move in and out of her. The friction from her pussy around his girth made him work extra hard to keep his climax down. As he picked up his pace, he fondled her breasts and bit gently on her neck.

Her pleading moans and desperate clawing at his back intensified his desire for her. He grabbed her ass, squeezing hard and pushed her deeper onto him, causing her to squeal.

"Sorry, baby, did I hurt you?" he asked as he quickly slowed down.

"No. No, that feels really good. Keep going," she said breathlessly. He possessively held onto her ass and started thrusting deeply inside her. His hands protected her backside from the cold shower wall.

"Damn, this ass," he cursed into her ear. He pounded into her, eliciting more of her praise.

Gabrielle felt her body tingle and her body heat rise as her climax began to build. She buried her head into Chris's neck, listening to him breathe heavily as he fucked her into bliss. She dug her nails into his back as her walls clenched tighter around his manhood.

"Oh! Chris!" she moaned loudly. She reached her climax and came hard, shaking violently between Chris and the wall. Her eyes rolled upward and her toes curled as the erotic sensation of her orgasm washed over her entire body.

Chris watched Gabrielle's face the entire time she climaxed. He loved how hard he could make her come. He took her lips into his mouth and kissed her vigorously. His body heat began to rise as his own climax took over and he came deep inside her. Resting his head on the wall, his hands still gripped her backside as he tried to catch his breath.

He could feel the softness of her lips pecking his nose and cheeks as her hands caressed his face. She moved her head underneath him, causing him to move his head back from the wall. He smiled down at her. He could see that there was something she wanted to say but she was hesitant. So he said it for her.

"I love you, Gabs..." he breathed out. "I love you... *so much.*"

A smile slowly painted her lips. "...I love you too," she said. She took his face between her hands again and kissed him passionately.

"We should probably actually shower," Chris chuckled. He pulled out of her and instantly regretted his removal from his most coveted place of refuge.

"And sleep," she added, playfully pulling on his earlobe. They scrubbed each other down before rinsing and exiting the shower. Chris watched as Gabrielle dried off her body, taking in all of her tempting curves.

"Is it weird that I'm turned on again just by looking at you?" he grinned.

"You better calm your ass down," she teased.

Chris threw on the sweats and t-shirt while Gabrielle went to go check on Arthur. He sat on the bed and checked his phone to see no texts from Charlie. His anxiety escalated.

Gabrielle re-entered the room wearing her panties and a long t-shirt. "He's still sound asleep, thankfully. The more rest he gets, the easier and more effective the healing process."

"He's lucky to have you," Chris said, putting his phone away.

"You *all* are," she grinned. She got up and sat on his lap, straddling him between her thighs.

"Especially me," Chris smiled. He held her by her hips and kissed her chest, nuzzling her breasts through the shirt.

"Chris..." she said softly, running her hands through his hair.

"Yea, babe," he answered. He lifted his head from her chest to look up at her.

"When are you going to tell me what's really going on?" she asked him.

He sighed and lay his head to her chest. "Hopefully never," he groaned.

"Chris," she said annoyed, pulling away from him.

"I told you... I'm trying to protect you, Gabs. The less you know... the better," he said, trying to pull her warmth back to him.

"Shouldn't that be for me to decide?"

"I just don't want you to get hurt..."

"Then tell me what's going on, Chris. I can protect myself."

Chris deeply exhaled and lay back as Gabrielle maneuvered to lie down next to him. Propped on her side, holding her head up with her hand, she looked at him expectantly.

"Soon," he said finally.

"You promise?"

"I promise." He kissed her tenderly and pulled her under the sheets.

~*~

Charlie was back at the bar where they had found Arthur. He asked potential witnesses what took place and what Arthur's attacker looked like. But he received very little information out of anyone. He roamed the alleyway looking for clues, when he looked up and noticed there was a camera on the side of the Starbucks next door.

Walking into the Starbucks, he asked the barista for assistance. The manager greeted him and upon learning he was a Richardson, welcomed him to the security tapes.

The footage eventually showed Arthur and another man being shoved out of the bar by security. Arthur and the man scuffled for a bit, wrestling to the ground. Then the man pulled an object from his coat and shot Arthur in the stomach before running away.

Charlie tried to see which direction the man ran in but only got that he ran down the street. “Can I get a copy of this?” Charlie asked the manager.

“Just take it,” the manager said, with his hands up. Charlie put the tape in his front pocket. He left the building and headed towards his car. Just before he opened the car door, he saw a figure reflected in the car window. He immediately ducked as a bat swung and just nearly missed his head, crashing into the window.

Charlie slipped down to the ground as the man struggled to pull the bat out of the broken window. Charlie grabbed the man’s calves and pulled him down, throwing him to the ground hard as the bat went flying up in the air. Jumping to his feet, Charlie proceeded to attack the man, dealing heavy blows to his face. Suddenly, another man turned the corner with a blunt weapon and charged at Charlie.

Charlie dodged and punched his assailant in the stomach. When his assailant keeled over in pain, Charlie kicked his leg out from underneath him and slammed him to the ground. He glanced up at another sound and saw two other men quickly approaching.

“Cowards... It’s a fucking ambush,” he muttered. He used the edge of the broken car window to propel himself on top of the hood, away from his attackers. They scrambled to pull him from the car as he kicked at them with his feet.

Charlie muttered in aggravation. He had enough of this. He jumped off of the car and took them all head on, knocking each of them out with his calculated movements. Only minutes had passed by the time he had whittled them down. Several men were sprawled out on the street bleeding and heavily injured. Charlie wiped the blood from his mouth and pulled his fist back, ready to punch the last man he held clenched in his fist.

"If you don't want your brother and cousin killed, you'll put him down right now!"

Charlie quickly turned around to see a man in a blue leather jacket approach him with four other men at his side. The man held up his phone which showed the outside of Eli's apartment bordered with several hiding armed combatants.

Charlie growled and forcefully threw the man he was holding to the ground. The man in the blue leather jacket grinned and whistled. In seconds, the four men apprehended Charlie. His green eyes peered angrily at the man approaching him with a nonchalant attitude.

"The famous Blonde Lycan... I've always wanted to meet you..." the man said, looking Charlie over. "Though I thought you'd look scarier... You know... more *feral*..."

"What the fuck do you want?!" Charlie snarled.

"So angry..." the man chuckled. He looked around at the injured men lying unconscious on the ground. "Well, you certainly live up to your reputation..."

"I asked you a fucking question. What do you want? I have no business with the Hammerheads."

The man grinned. "Oh, but the Hammerheads have business with the Blonde Lycan."

"**Stop**... calling me that!" Charlie threatened.

"But why? You earned that name... you should wear it with pride..."

"Stop wasting my fucking time and answer my damn question!" Charlie yelled angrily.

The man sighed with a smirk. He took out a cigarette and looked Charlie's appearance over. "You'll find out soon enough..."

He signaled to one of his armed men. They slammed the butt of their gun against Charlie's head, knocking him out. Charlie was then dragged towards a van and thrown inside.

~*~

Charlie woke up to freezing cold water being thrown on him. He immediately became alert as he thought back to his previous brawl. Looking around, he scoped out his environment. Both of his hands were heavily chained to two cement bricks at the corner where the wall met the floor. He had been forced to his knees like a prisoner. He strained to pull them.

"Don't bother, Blonde Lycan. I've studied you for years. Those chains were built specifically for a man of your... unusual strength."

Charlie looked up and met the gaze of the man who had apprehended him earlier.

"You..." Charlie muttered.

"Me," the man grinned. He crouched down in front of Charlie and mockingly scoffed at him. "You're not so tough when you're chained up like the animal you are."

"Oh, yea? Why don't you grow some fucking balls and release me... you'll find out just how much of an animal I can *really* be..." Charlie threatened.

The man threw his head back laughing. "Damn! You actually are kinda scary! And yet all it took was threatening your brother to get you to submit. I guess everyone has a weakness. Even the Blonde Lycan."

Charlie growled at him with anger aflame in his eyes.

"Speaking of, we should probably get the Blue Kaiser down here, shouldn't we? Make it one big fucking family reunion," the man grinned. He pulled out Charlie's confiscated phone.

~*~

Chris woke up to his phone ringing. He tried to blink the sleep out of his eyes as he adjusted to his surroundings. He noticed the sun peeking through the sliver of the window curtain. He felt a light weight on his chest and soft curly hair covered his neck and shoulders. He looked down to see Gabrielle curled up against him, fast asleep.

Brushing her hair to the side, he gently moved her off of him before leaning over the bed to answer his phone. "Hello?" he whispered.

"Hello, Blue Kaiser."

Chris immediately froze. He hadn't heard that name in years. "Who is this?"

"We have your brother," the voice at the other end said. The chill that ran down Chris's spine contrasted with the heat that was bridling in his chest from the rage he felt.

"Who. Is. This?!" Chris demanded angrily. He tried to keep his voice down so as not to wake Gabrielle.

"I'm at the old orchard building at Longfellow and 5th. You have 1 hour to get here. Come alone or your brother dies."

Chris felt his heart restrict as he clenched his hands in apprehension and anger. Even when the call ended he remained glued to the bed. His mind was racing.

"Shit!" he snarled, finally snapping out of it. He got up, looking for his shoes and picked up his clothes that Gabrielle left to dry. He quickly dialed another number on his phone.

"Chris?" the voice on the other end answered.

"Malcolm! Is Charlie with you?"

"Uh...no. I haven't seen him in 2 days... Why? Is something wrong?"

"Fuck! I was hoping it was another bluff. He's been taken by the Hammerheads."

"What?!"

"They want me to meet them. Only me... We need to launch Code Black."

"Understood... I've turned on his biological tracker... and yours..."

"Good. Then you know what to do."

"Good luck."

Chris hung up the phone to pack his things. While putting on his shoes, he heard the bed stir.

"Where are you going?" came Gabrielle's sleepy voice. He looked back to see her sitting up in bed, rubbing the sleep out of her eyes. Her hair was a fluffy mess of curls on her head that swallowed her adorable face.

"I uh...have to go check up on, Charlie," Chris said to her anxiously. "Go back to bed, babe."

"Wait, I'll come with you," she yawned.

"NO!" Chris blurted abruptly. He sighed heavily when he saw the look of shock and confusion on her face at his startling response. He walked to her side of the bed and knelt down in front of her.

He grabbed her hand and held it to his chest. "I promise I'll be back. I just gotta go help him take care of something, okay?"

Gabrielle nodded hesitantly. Standing to his feet, he wrapped his hand around the back of her neck and pulled her forward to kiss her forehead. Gabrielle watched Chris grab his things before heading out the door.

She waited until she heard the front door close and went to go check up on Arthur.

~*~

The man hung up the phone and looked at Charlie with a taunting smirk. “Your brother should be here soon. So, tell me... is it true? All the stories about your brother...*The Terrible Blue Kaiser*. I heard he once raided the LockJaw gang and took 3/4 of their entire crew out in ONE NIGHT! I mean damn! The fucking LockJaws! **One** man?! What a badass!”

Charlie merely huffed, giving the man his silence.

“Not much of a talker are you? I guess I should expect that from a man like you,” he smirked. “Huh... I get to meet the Blonde Lycan AND the Blue Kaiser all in one day. Liam will be impressed. This is history in the making for me.” He chuckled as he leaned back in a chair opposite Charlie.

“You sound like a fucking fanboy,” Charlie muttered in disgust. He spit blood on the floor.

“You got me!” the man chuckled. “I used to love hearing about you guys. How you conquered territory by territory with a ruthless authoritative hand. You guys are legends. Well... at least you *used* to be. Now you’re both just pathetic. I mean... just look at you... bested by a man who hasn’t even been in the game for more than 3 years.”

“3 years and you talk this much shit?” Charlie chuckled darkly. “Liam hasn’t taught you much then, has he? You’re easy. *Too* easy... You’ll be dead by the end of the night.”

He looked at Charlie coldly with a flicker of fear in his eyes. Then he burst into laughter.

“Sir, the Blue Kaiser is here,” a man called from the door, interrupting his laughter.

“Showtime,” the man smirked as he stood from the chair. “Get him set up,” he ordered the others. Two men approached Charlie. They hit him in the gut with the butt of their guns to disable him long enough to refasten his restraints.

~*~

18

One for All – The Blonde Lycan

~*~

Chris cautiously approached the building. He noted two men drawing near with guns pointed straight at him. He slowly raised his hands as they confronted him. They roughly grabbed him, patting him down to check for any weapons.

"Clear," one of the men said.

They each grabbed one of Chris's arms and escorted him into the building. They led him down a narrow corridor and into a darkly lit room. He immediately noticed Charlie kneeling on the ground with his arms restrained by two chains. His captive brother was surrounded by a group of men pointing their guns at him.

"Charlie..." Chris muttered, as he walked into the room.

"WOW!" Chris heard an excited voice boom from his right. He glanced to the side to see a man in a blue leather jacket approach him.

"The Blue Kaiser! Now **you**... you look exactly how I imagined..." the man beamed.

Chris looked at him with reproach. "...and you are?"

"Izzy," the man said, rushing to shake his hand. "Huge fan!"

Chris looked at the man in confused bewilderment.

"Sorry, I know it's not very professional of me, but I can't help but fan boy over a legend such as yourself." Izzy put his hands on his hips and sized Chris up.

"Nor does it hardly seem appropriate..." Chris said with agitation.

"But of course, you're right. I do have your brother after all," Izzy smirked. He glanced at Charlie, still seething in anger.

"Seems like a bit of overkill," Chris muttered, analyzing Charlie's restraints.

"Hardly," Izzy chuckled. "I know the kind of man, the Blonde Lycan is. We'd be foolish not to have those. I'm actually questioning if they're enough."

Chris quickly scanned Charlie's position before making eye contact with his brother.

"Then where are mine?" Chris said, finally. He turned to Izzy with intimidating anger. "Surely you know how dangerous I am."

"But of course! The Blue Kaiser is the most dangerous of them all!" Izzy was getting excited and it deeply disturbed Chris. Not only did this man know about his past persona, but he was also inspired by it. This guy was a fanatic. And with fanatics... came copy cats...

"I'll never forget when I heard how you disemboweled the leader of the Green Shards with nothing but a pocket knife when you were in Greece. Just for looking at you the wrong way!" Izzy said, practically clapping. Chris flinched as he tried to maintain his cool.

"The speed! The skill! The ruthlessness! You are the definition of a legend! But alas, you're also incredibly smart and entirely rational. Like your brother, you wouldn't risk making a move that would jeopardize his safety."

Charlie's teeth gnashed in anger. This Izzy guy was really ticking him off. He glanced up at his brother who remained calm and collected, though Charlie could tell that Chris was disarmed with the mention of his dark and bloody past.

"I'm assuming you brought us here for something other than fan worship," Chris glared at Izzy, trying to redirect the conversation.

Izzy snickered, running a shaky hand through his hair. "Right, right. Let's get to it," he said. He motioned for his men to bring Chris near Charlie. Izzy clasped his hands together with a smile and looked at both brothers. "There's been a bounty placed on your heads."

They both looked up at him in surprise.

"Well... sort of... See, not only have you been expanding too much, gobbling up too much territory. But you're also physically wiping out all competition in the process."

Chris growled in aggravation. "You pulled this shit over some fucking territory?"

Izzy smirked amused. "Come now, we both know it's more than that, Blue Kaiser. You're not just leaving your mark, you're sending a message. That you're not to be fucked with. And thus, you've become too much of a threat. Perhaps in the old days when you were both more like yourselves and allowed the trade of narcotics, high collateral weapons and sex. You know, the good stuff. But you're not. You're both weak. Your merchandise is weak. Your policies are restricting. And we can't have that. Not when it forces the rest of us to miss out on profitable opportunities. Your operations need to be nipped in the bud before irreversible damage is done. I plan on turning you both over to Liam for a handsome reward," Izzy said, with a satisfied smile.

Chris looked at Izzy like he had escaped from an asylum. He pinched the bridge of his nose and took a deep breath, trying to control his anger. "Listen, kid... I can see that you *think* you've thought this through. That you have it all figured out. But I can assure you, you haven't. I'm going to give you one chance, *just one*, to call this whole thing off. Or I promise you, you'll regret this."

Izzy threw his head back in mocking laughter. "Your reputation may be weakening, but I see your arrogance stays the same!" Izzy taunted. "I know all there is to know about you and your brother. Try anything, anything at all...and..."

Izzy motioned to one of his men. He grabbed a tablet from him and held it up to Chris and Charlie. The screen revealed a live feed showing Gabrielle sitting on the bench swing outside on Eli's porch. Arthur was also lying down on the swing with his head on her lap. She looked to be reading and holding a towel to his forehead while he slept.

"I'll make sure that my men splatter your cousin's brains all over that pretty little porch. See if your bitch can save him from that. Even better, maybe I'll give her as a gift to Liam himself. Courtesy of the Richardson brothers," Izzy threatened with a smirk.

Chris grimaced and felt his stomach hollow. The anger he felt was intense but he felt it radiating even more dangerously from his brother in chains next to him. Izzy was poking a sleeping, ravenous and bad-tempered bear with a stick. It was only a matter of time.

"You have no idea who you're fucking with..." Chris warned Izzy.

"On the contrary, I do. And to be quite frank, I'm a little disappointed. This was far too easy," Izzy shrugged. "Take the Blue Kaiser to the other room while I inform Liam," he ordered the men. "Let's get ready to load them up."

Chris was grabbed by both his arms. He locked eyes with Charlie for just a moment before they dragged him into another room.

~*~

"Okay, try it now," Gabrielle said. She lifted a soup-filled spoon to Arthur's mouth. He looked up from his phone and sipped the soup, swishing it around in his mouth. She waited patiently for his reaction. He looked up thinking before looking at her with a smirk.

"Still needs more salt," he said.

"Oh, come on! There is no way it needs more salt. It tastes fine the way it is!" Gabrielle said, tasting it herself.

"You said you wanted to learn how to make the dish. Who's the Scottish food expert here?" Arthur grinned.

Gabrielle rolled her eyes and turned back to the pot. "Fine, if you want high cholesterol," she muttered.

"The less healthy it is, the better it tastes," Arthur joked, turning back to his phone. Arthur sat barefoot and shirtless in the kitchen, keeping Gabrielle company while she cooked. He lightly patted the bandage wrapped tightly around his abdomen.

"I thought you were trying *not* to send yourself to an early grave," Gabrielle mocked.

"That's why I have you, sweetheart," Arthur smirked.

"Mm, that smells good," Eli said, walking into the kitchen. He was a sweaty mess, wearing a loose basketball jersey and sweats with a football tucked under his arm.

"Taste," Gabrielle said, lifting the spoon to his lips. Her brother leaned down to try it.

"Oh, that's good. Could use more salt though," Eli said, walking to the fridge.

"Told you," Arthur teased. Gabrielle threw her arms in the air in defeat and grabbed the salt.

"Hey man. Pain any better today?" Eli said, guzzling a bottle of water.

"Alright. I'm actually surprised I'm healing so quickly all things considering," Arthur mused.

"Yea, you lucked out with Gabby. Crazy that the hospital wouldn't take you," Eli said. He tossed the empty water bottle into the recycling bin and grabbed a Gatorade.

"Yea, lucky you," Gabrielle said, looking back at Arthur with a hard glare.

Arthur rolled his eyes. "I am forever in your debt, m'lady," he mocked. Gabrielle scoffed and turned back to the pot.

"If you're feeling up to it later, we should go out to one of my hot spots to meet some of the guys from my team. Think they would like you. Plus, you need to get out of the house. You've been cooped up in here for too long," Eli said.

Arthur smiled. "Why not."

"Cool! Just let me know when!" Eli turned to Gabrielle. "You'll be alright, baby sis?"

"Yea, thanks Eli," she said. She kissed him on the cheek before he walked out.

"Your brother's a good guy," Arthur said to her.

"I know." She poured the soup into two bowls and carried them to the table. She placed one in front of Arthur and sat down at the opposite end of the table with her bowl. Gabrielle watched him attentively waiting to see his final reaction on the soup.

Arthur took a sip and smacked his lips. She raised her eyebrows at him, waiting expectantly. He finished sipping and sat back satisfied. "It's perfect," he said.

"Yes!" she cheered. She leaned back in her chair and threw her arms in the air in victory. They sat at the table and chatted while eating.

“That was delicious. Cheers.” Arthur leaned back to rub his full stomach.

She grinned proudly. “Come on. Time to change your bandage,” she said standing from the table. She helped him stand to his feet and walked him to the couch. His arm draped over her shoulder to help keep him balanced while she wrapped her arms around his waist.

She sat him down and grabbed her box of bandages. Arthur watched her appreciatively as she meticulously cut away at the bandage, removing it from his body. She used a damp cloth to clean the scarring.

“It’s healing really well,” she said. She gently ran a finger over the scarred skin and tenderly pushed on the scar tissue surrounding the wound. “Does this hurt?” she asked him. He shook his head. “Good, I think we can start with a smaller bandage from now on.” She took out a smaller bandage and carefully placed it on his wound.

Arthur looked at her intently. “I think I’m in love with you,” he said to her suddenly.

She looked up at him in bewilderment. There was nothing but silence between them as they stared into each other’s eyes. Then the doorbell rang.

“Boy, shut the hell up!” she said playfully slapping him on the shoulder. Arthur burst into laughter at his very effective trolling.

“Was worth a shot,” he joked with a snicker.

Gabrielle opened the door to see Vladimir standing outside. “Vlad?! How did you-? Why are you-?”

“Apologies for the intrusion. I came to see that you and Mr. Richardson are well,” he said cautiously, in his thick Russian accent.

She looked at him bewildered. “Uh, yea, we’re good. Why? Is something wrong? Did Charlie send you? Is he okay?” she panicked.

"Do not fret, Miss. He is fine. I come on his orders. May I?" he motioned for permission to step inside. Gabrielle nodded and moved out of the way for him to enter the house.

"Hey, ya big lug," Arthur smirked.

"Arthur," Vladimir nodded. "Charles wants you to know that Code Black is underway." Arthur gulped as a grave look painted his face. He nodded without saying a word. "Do you need anything else?" Vladimir asked. Arthur shook his head. Vladimir nodded and turned to leave. "Good day, Miss Gabrielle," Vladimir said before leaving.

Gabrielle watched stunned as he walked towards a black van. She saw an Asian guy pushing what looked like 3-4 unconscious men into the van. "What the hell..." she said trying to figure out what she was looking at.

"Close the door, sweetheart, you'll let the cool air out," Arthur said sweetly.

She looked over at him to see the grave expression had been replaced by his signature charming smile again. "What the hell was that all about? What's Code Black?" she asked him.

"Oh, it's just a sports thing. Charlie can be competitive. You know how he is," Arthur said, waving his hand dismissively.

"That doesn't make any sense, Arthur. Charlie and Chris said they were going to check out the men who had attacked you. What's going on? Why haven't we heard from them yet? They won't even answer their phones," she said, impatiently.

"They're probably just heavily into their work. Don't worry about them," Arthur said.

"Arthur! I'm *already* really worried!"

"Ah! Dammit! I think I pulled a stitch!" he said, rubbing his abdomen.

“You don’t have stitches, you idiot!! I cauterized your wound!” she said exasperated.

“Well… I pulled something. Would you stop worrying about those pretty boys and come tend to me? You’re making me jealous,” he pouted with a smirk. She rolled her eyes in frustration and walked over to tend to his injuries.

~*~

“Sir, the van is here,” an armed man said, approaching Izzy.

Izzy grinned. “Perfect. Soon this whole ordeal will be over with and I’ll be sitting pretty with the capture of the Blue Kaiser and the Blonde Lycan on my ledger.”

Izzy heard a low rumble that made him glance out the window, wondering if there was a rapid change in weather. But he realized it was coming from Charlie. A dark chuckle escaped Charlie’s lips.

“What’s so funny?” Izzy asked annoyed. “I’m about to hand you over to your maker.”

Charlie’s chuckle rose to a maniacal laughter as his head flew back, startling Izzy. “You fucking moron,” Charlie said darkly. “Did you really think it would be that easy?”

Suddenly, Izzy could hear shooting coming from outside. “What’s going on?!” Izzy shouted at his men. But they merely looked at him just as confused. “GO FIND OUT!” he yelled. The men hurried outside to see what was happening.

“It’s too late…” Charlie said with a low, menacing tone. He slowly rose to his feet. Izzy looked at him in pure shock that he was actually getting up. He watched in horror as the chains dropped from Charlie’s wrists with a heavy thud.

“What the… how the-?” Izzy stammered.

"I've been shot... stabbed... bludgeoned... burned...and skinned... Dislocating my thumb to get out of chains is a skill I learned years ago..." Charlie said. He effortlessly popped his thumb back into place without flinching.

Charlie looked up at the man before him who was shaking violently. Charlie gave him a terrifying smirk. "Yes... you are correct. I could have gotten out of those chains at any moment. I just needed to make sure the others were safe first."

Izzy heard gunshots and looked outside to see a large Russian man, the Blue Kaiser, and an Asian man taking out his men one by one. "But- how- I don't- what-" Izzy stammered.

"I could tell you, but you won't live long enough for it to matter," Charlie said, rolling out his shoulders.

"St-stop him!" Izzy ordered the men around him. The armed men immediately shot at Charlie but he quickly dodged. He grabbed one of the men by their knee caps and twisted it with a loud crack. The man screamed in pain and fell to the ground before Charlie grabbed the man's head and snapped his neck. Charlie then grabbed the man's gun and shot at the others, riddling them with bullets before they had time to react. In seconds, he had laid every man out on the floor, bleeding and groaning in agony if they weren't already dead.

Horrified, Izzy turned to run. But it was too late. Charlie quickly grabbed him by his throat and lifted him from the ground. Charlie's fingers tightened around Izzy's throat so fiercely that Izzy's eyes started to bulge out of his head . He clawed at Charlie's arms for release, ripping at his skin. But Charlie didn't flinch.

Charlie cocked his head to the side and looked Izzy darkly in the eyes. Izzy saw Charlie's pupils constrict with a subtle flicker of red. His face contorted into a frightening look of cynical amusement and caged rage.

"I told you... you'd be dead by the end of the night..." Charlie snarled. He squeezed tighter, digging his nails into Izzy's flesh. Izzy gurgled as blood started to spurt from his neck.

Charlie pulled him close, still holding him by his neck and whispered darkly in his ear: "You wanted to meet the Blonde Lycan... well here I fucking am..." He crushed Izzy's throat with a loud squish. Blood spurted from his neck and Izzy's body fell to the floor with a lifeless thump. Charlie stood there, still holding a piece of Izzy's flesh in his hands.

"Charlie! Are you o- woooah...." Malcolm said, rushing in. He stopped short when he saw the bloody scene before him. Charlie slowly turned around and looked at Malcolm with dead, emotionless eyes.

"Shit..." Malcolm muttered. Charlie was covered in blood. Malcolm watched Charlie casually drop the last bit of Izzy's fleshy neck on the floor before wiping his hands on his pants.

Charlie strolled towards Malcolm and stopped at the doorway. "Leave none alive..."

Malcolm hesitated. "Charlie..."

Charlie looked Malcolm in the eye and Malcolm immediately swallowed hard. He knew that look in Charlie's eye all too well. It was rare. But it frightened him every single time. It had been years since he'd last seen it... His dear friend Charlie Richardson was gone... That was the look of the Blonde Lycan.

"Right..." Malcolm said, averting his eyes. Charlie exited the room and walked out of the building.

Chris helped Vladimir remove the last guy from the van. "These were all the guys surveying the house?" Chris asked, watching Vladimir toss the body to the ground.

"Yes, sir," Vladimir answered.

"Alright... thank you. I'll have my men come clean this up," Chris said, taking out his phone. He turned his head to see Charlie casually exiting the building with one hand in his pocket and the other holding a lit cigarette. With his face and shirt covered in blood, Carlie looked like something out of the Walking Dead.

"Shit, Charlie..." Chris said, looking at him hesitantly. "Are you-"

"I'm fine." Charlie said curtly. "Let's go."

Chris nodded to Vladimir and Malcolm who watched Charlie and Chris take off in another car.

~*~

Chris sat back on Charlie's couch, typing away on his tablet when his phone went off.

Gabs: *Where are you? I hope everything is okay!*

Chris slowly exhaled, struggling to think of how to respond. He couldn't keep putting off her messages. A shirtless Charlie entered the living room wearing a pair of black sweats and a towel draped around his neck. He had taken a long hot shower to clean the blood and grime off of himself. New scars decorated his bruised skin.

Chris cautiously watched his brother stalk to the window. Charlie ran his fingers through his wet blonde hair. "Are you okay?" Chris asked.

"*Clearly* we need to send another message," Charlie said with a low tone. His voice was a dark and rough rumble that deeply troubled Chris.

"What kind of message?" Chris asked.

"These motherfuckers think just because we've been off the grid for a few years that they can just take us out? I don't fucking think so..."

"Charlie..."

"It's time I pay these bastards a *personal* visit. If they have a grievance, they can say it to my fucking face." Charlie turned to face Chris. His face was cold and hard as stone. His jaw tight with tension.

"I see..." Chris said softly.

"I don't need your help," Charlie said, turning his back on Chris.

"Okay... but I think you're responding out of anger, Charlie. Not with rationale..." Chris said.

"I don't need your fucking patronization either!" Charlie spewed.

Chris sighed heavily and leaned back against the couch. "Put him away..."

"What?!" Charlie sneered.

"Put... the Blonde Lycan.... away..." Chris said more firmly. "You're not him anymore."

Charlie grumbled and clenched his fist in his pockets. "I'm not him now..."

"You sure sound like him."

"You can get the fuck out, Chris!" Charlie said, turning to him angrily. Chris looked at his brother for a moment and stood up. He walked to the door and grabbed the handle. But before he left, he paused briefly and turned back around to face his brother.

"3 years ago... the Blue Kaiser walked into a room of 200 people and killed them all in less than 30 minutes..." Chris said in a low voice. "200 lives... gone... just like that..."

Charlie tensed up, refusing to look at his brother.

"I would have killed 4x that amount in the weeks that followed... if it weren't for you... if it weren't for my brother..." Chris continued. He could see Charlie calming down a bit but he still refused to look in his direction.

"This business... our lives... are fucking shit, Charlie. And you or I could both lose it... lose each other... at any second. And we would deserve it... I... I would deserve it," Chris said, dropping his head. Charlie finally turned around to look at his brother.

"You're the most important person in my life, Charlie," Chris said to him. "No one else could have saved me... could have stopped me. No one, but you. *You* defeated the Blue Kaiser. *You* saved me from myself. And I'll always be here to do the same for you," Chris said, looking him in the eye.

Charlie looked at his brother for a long moment. He could see the sincerity, concern, and deep love in his older brother's gaze. He swallowed hard and averted his eyes with guilt. Dropping his hands from his pockets, he strolled to the couch and plopped down with defeat. Chris walked over to join his brother as Charlie put his head in his hands.

"This life... it makes me forget myself... who I am," Charlie groaned. He shakily ran his hands through his wet hair. "I forget who I am, Chris... and that fucking terrifies me..."

"And I'll always remind you who you are, Charlie," Chris said. He put a comforting hand on Charlie's shoulder and smiled warmly. "You're my brother."

Charlie looked up at him and gave him a weak smile. "I almost lost it there... didn't I?"

"Almost," Chris winked. "But to be fair you never really had it," he teased.

"Asshole," Charlie smirked. His phone went off and he plucked it off the table to see a text from Gabrielle. "Shit..." Charlie groaned, reading over her text.

"We can't keep avoiding her..." Chris said, already knowing.

"I don't want her to see me like this. I don't... I don't want her to see me at all," Charlie said exasperated. He put his head in his hands again. “I can’t hold her… touch her… after what I’ve just done…” Charlie looked at his hands in disgust.

“We need to distance ourselves. The fact that he threatened her. He knew where she was. He was watching her. We can’t allow this to happen again, Chris” Charlie said, looking at him.

Chris nodded in agreement. He knew his brother was right, but his heart was completely torn.

~*~

Sons of the Elite

The Sons of the Elite Series is the first Series in the Marvelous 3 Saga. It centers Gabrielle and her three lovers: Chris, Charlie, and Michael.

Book 1 - Damaged

Book 2 - Stuck In The Middle

Book 3 - Man's Weakness

Book 4 - 4Play

Made in the USA
Middletown, DE
05 November 2022